Praise for De

D0248953

"I've never met a Debbie Mason story that I didn't enjoy."
—KeeperBookshelf.com

"I'm telling you right now, if you haven't yet read a book by Debbie Mason, you don't know what you're missing."
—RomancingtheReaders.blogspot.com

"Mason always makes me smile and touches my heart in the most unexpected and wonderful ways."
—HerdingCats-BurningSoup.com

"Wow, do these books bring the feels. Deep emotion, heart-tugging romance, and a touch of suspense make them hard to put down."
—TheRomanceDish.com

"I always count the days until the next book!"
—TheManyFacesofRomance.blogspot.com

"Debbie Mason writes in a thrilling and entertaining way. Her stories are captivating and filled with controlled chaos, true love, mysteries, amazing characters, eccentricities, plotting and friendship."
—WithLoveForBooks.com

"Debbie Mason never disappoints me."
—FictionFangirls.net

"It's not just romance. It's grief and mourning, guilt and truth, second chances and revelations."
—WrittenLoveReviews.blogspot.com

"Debbie Mason writes romance like none other."
—FreshFiction.com

"Mason takes her romances to a whole new level."
—CarriesBookReviews.com

"The Harmony Harbor series is heartfelt and delightful!"
—RaeAnne Thayne, *New York Times* best-selling author

"Christmas, Colorado, will get you in the spirit for love all year long."—Jill Shalvis, *New York Times* best-selling author

Summer on
Sunshine Bay

ALSO BY DEBBIE MASON

THE HIGHLAND FALLS SERIES

Summer on Honeysuckle Ridge
Christmas on Reindeer Road
Falling in Love on Willow Creek
"A Wedding on Honeysuckle Ridge" (short story)
The Inn on Mirror Lake
At Home on Marigold Lane

THE HARMONY HARBOR SERIES

Mistletoe Cottage
"Christmas with an Angel" (short story)
Starlight Bridge
Primrose Lane
Sugarplum Way
Driftwood Cove
Sandpiper Shore
The Corner of Holly and Ivy
Barefoot Beach
Christmas in Harmony Harbor

THE CHRISTMAS, COLORADO, SERIES

The Trouble with Christmas
Christmas in July
It Happened at Christmas
Wedding Bells in Christmas
Snowbound at Christmas
Kiss Me in Christmas
Happy Ever After in Christmas
"Marry Me at Christmas" (short story)
Miracle at Christmas (novella)
One Night in Christmas (novella)

Summer on Sunshine Bay

DEBBIE MASON

FOREVER

New York Boston

Copyright © 2023 by Debbie Mazzuca

Cover design by Daniela Medina. Cover art by Thomas Hallman. Cover copyright © 2023 by Hachette Book Group, Inc.

Forever
Hachette Book Group
1290 Avenue of the Americas, New York, NY 10104
read-forever.com
twitter.com/readforeverpub

First Edition: May 2023

Forever is an imprint of Grand Central Publishing. The Forever name and logo are trademarks of Hachette Book Group, Inc.

The publisher is not responsible for websites (or their content) that are not owned by the publisher.

The Hachette Speakers Bureau provides a wide range of authors for speaking events. To find out more, go to www.hachettespeakersbureau.com or call (866) 376-6591.

Library of Congress Control Number: 2022057857

ISBNs: 978-1-5387-2531-3 (trade paperback), 978-1-5387-2532-0 (ebook)

Printed in the United States of America

LSC-C

Printing 1, 2023

For my beautiful granddaughters,
Lilianna, Gabriella, and Theadora.
Life is so much sweeter with you in it.

Chapter One

Lila Rosetti Sinclair raised her gaze from her phone to her fiancé. He could pass for Matt Damon if the actor wore thick, black horn-rimmed glasses and had a weakness for argyle sweater vests. But at that moment, it wasn't David's handsome face that captured her attention, it was the black silk blindfold in his hand. "You can't be serious?"

She'd had the same reaction when he brought the blindfold home four months earlier and suggested that it was time to spice up their love life. Only she'd laughed then. She couldn't help it. Wearing a roguish grin while talking about their sex life was completely out of character for David.

They were boringly vanilla in the bedroom and outside it. Something they took pride in. No over-the-top emotions for them. Grand passion was overrated in their minds. They preferred the comfort they derived from their quiet, loving relationship.

Except David hadn't been joking.

Lila had swallowed her disappointment that she wasn't getting her standard Valentine's Day gift of a heart-shaped box of chocolates and went along with David's efforts to spice up their love life. She'd put his role-playing suggestion down to stress. It wasn't as if she could blame it on a midlife crisis. David was thirty. But he had been stressed about the sale of her father's London-based hotel group, where they'd worked together for the past three years—Lila as director of branding and David as director of sales.

Lila supposed her inability to set a wedding date had been responsible for at least some of David's stress. He'd grown impatient with her unwillingness to commit to a date. She had no idea why the thought of marrying him had kept her awake at night. David was everything a woman could want in a husband—smart, ambitious, and dependable— and they shared common values and goals.

It was a moot point now. That silky black blindfold and their uptick in sexy times had taken care of her indecision. They had a baby on the way.

"Come on, honey. Don't be a spoilsport. Put it on." David leaned over, raising the blindfold to her eyes.

Seriously? They didn't do PDA, and now he wanted to get kinky on the commuter plane they'd boarded at Logan International Airport thirty minutes earlier?

She tugged the blindfold from her eyes, lowering her voice so as not to draw the attention of the five other passengers on board. "I'm not a spoilsport."

She was a rule follower, but that didn't mean she wasn't fun. She thought back to the beach parties she'd dragged her cousins away from when things had gotten out of hand, or, more to the point, when Sage and Willow had. Her cousins would probably agree that she was indeed a spoilsport.

But joining the Mile High Club was a horrible idea with high potential for arrest and even higher potential for embarrassment. "You're taking this role-playing a little too far, don't you think? We're not Anastasia and Christian, and this is not your private jet, David." She handed him the blindfold.

He frowned as if he didn't understand what she meant, and then his serious blue eyes widened behind his glasses. "No, that's not why I want you to wear the blindfold." He huffed a self-conscious laugh. "I can't believe you thought..." He shook his head and then whispered, "It has nothing to do with...you know—" He glanced around the plane. "Sex."

Was it any wonder she'd thought he was joking when he brought the blindfold home? He couldn't even say "sex" without blushing. She felt a rush of affection for him. They really were the perfect match. "Then why do you want me to wear it? You've been acting weird ever since you insisted we join your parents for dinner tonight."

David's parents had invited them for a celebratory dinner at their spectacular vacation home in Hyannis Port. Lila knew the Westfields were excited that they'd finally set a wedding date, but she'd tried putting the dinner off until she and David were settled. They'd arrived in Boston the week before, and they needed to find jobs and a place of their own.

"I've been acting weird? You nearly had a panic attack when I mentioned the dinner."

"Because I had to cancel three viewings with the Realtor." The woman hadn't been shy about voicing her displeasure. Lila didn't blame her for being upset. She'd hated canceling at the last minute but David had been adamant they join his parents for dinner. "You know how tight the market is. At this rate we'll be living out of our suitcases at your parents' condo for the foreseeable future."

She was stressed about finding a place to live and a job, but that wasn't the reason for her near panic attack. It was David's parents wanting to celebrate their upcoming wedding at their vacation home. Lila hadn't broken the news to her family, and Hyannis Port felt a little too close to her hometown for comfort. Her family lived on the northern tip of Cape Cod in the small town of Sunshine Bay.

She added "call Sage and Willow" to the next day's to-do list on her phone. She couldn't put it off any longer. She'd need backup when she broke the news to her mother about her upcoming wedding. She was invoking the Cousins Pact, a verbal contract she, Sage, and Willow had agreed to as children. No matter how the others personally felt about whatever news one of them had to break to her mother—and their grandmother—they'd back each other 100 percent.

Except this would be a harder sell than the last time Lila had invoked the Cousins Pact. To say her family didn't believe in marriage was an understatement. And that included her cousins.

"Stop stressing about where we'll live. It's not good for the baby, and I've got a...Just trust me, honey. It's all going to work out," David said as he glanced out the window. He got an *oh crap* look on his face and slammed the blind shut.

"What's going on? Is something wrong with the plane?" She wasn't a nervous flyer. She'd been flying across the pond on her own since she was twelve. But she'd rather know if there was a problem. Her motto was "Be prepared." Even as a little girl, she hadn't liked surprises.

"No, we're landing, and I want it to be a surprise," he

said as he replaced the blindfold and tied it at the back of her head.

She cringed. He knew how she felt about surprises. But wait a minute... "How is us arriving at Hyannis Port a surprise?" They'd visited his parents at their vacation home before, several times in fact. Then a thought hit her, and she groaned. "Please tell me your parents aren't meeting us with balloons and a banner." It was something his mother would do. Jennifer was a sweet woman who looked for any excuse for a celebration. She should've been an event planner.

Even though Lila couldn't see David through the blindfold, she turned to face him and lowered her voice. "You didn't tell them about the baby, did you? You promised—"

He gently rubbed her flat stomach through the beige linen slacks she'd paired with a short-sleeved beige peplum jacket. "Of course not. We agreed to wait until you were twelve weeks," he said. "My mother will be over the moon."

David had been too. No doubt Lila agreeing to set a wedding date the morning after the stick turned blue had added to his excitement. She was still adjusting to the idea that she was carrying a tiny human... and getting married. Of the two, the idea of having a baby was easier to adjust to. She'd been raised by a family of single mothers.

And they'd be just as thrilled that she was expecting. Lila had considered leading with the baby news and keeping quiet about the wedding news. It wasn't as if their wedding would make the society pages. David had agreed, albeit reluctantly, to her request that they get married at the courthouse. But she was avoiding the inevitable. As much as she dreaded breaking the news to her family, she had to tell them.

As David guided her down the aircraft stairs, Lila realized he hadn't confirmed or denied her suspicion that they'd be greeted by his parents carrying a banner and balloons.

"Where are your mom and dad?" She couldn't hear Jennifer excitedly calling their names. All she heard was the quiet conversations of the other passengers, the sound of a car engine idling close by, and the distant cries of seagulls.

"They're, uh, meeting us at the restaurant. No, not yet." He grabbed her hand, stopping her from removing the blindfold.

"David, this is ridiculous. I feel like an idiot."

"You don't look like an idiot. You look beautiful." He pressed a kiss to her knuckles. "Not much longer now."

At the nervous hitch in his voice, she whipped her head in his direction. Something was going on, and she had a feeling it wasn't something she'd like. She lifted her left hand to lower the blindfold but David grabbed that one too, half dragging her after him.

She opened her mouth to give him crap, but then she heard his self-conscious laugh as he explained to someone that he had a special surprise for his bride-to-be, adding under his breath, "Smile, honey. I'm not sure they believe me. They look like they might call the cops."

The last thing Lila wanted was to be the center of attention. Unlike her mother, she preferred to stay in the background. She forced a smile for their invisible audience, saying through clenched teeth, "Then take this blindfold off me."

"Just give me...There's the cab." Picking up his pace, David towed her after him. She heard a car door open and felt a rush of cool air enveloping her—a welcome relief from the heat. His hand still encircling her wrists, David helped her inside the car and then got in beside her.

His grip loosened as he fastened her seat belt, and she pulled her hands free. She managed to get the blindfold off a second before he covered her eyes with his palm.

"David, if you don't remove your hand this—"

"I just need one more minute." He leaned forward, whispering something to the driver. When the car pulled away, David lifted his palm and peered in at her. "If I take my hand away, will you promise you'll let me explain before you yell at me?"

"Why would I—"

"Please," he said, a pleading note in his voice and in his eyes.

"Fine." She prayed she was overreacting. How bad could it be?

He lowered his hand and then turned her to face him. She glanced out the window, and her gaze shot to his. "How could you?"

"I know you're mad, honey. But just give me a chance to explain."

"There's nothing you can say that would explain why we're in Sunshine Bay, David." She turned to the driver. "Can you take me back to the airport, please?"

The man looked from her to David and then glanced in his rearview mirror. "Are you sure about that? The plane just took off, and there aren't any outgoing flights scheduled until tomorrow morning."

"It's okay," David told the driver. "Just take us to—"

"There's nothing about this that's okay, David." Lila was

furious and panicked at the same time. She took several slow, deep breaths in an effort to calm herself and the nausea rising up in her throat before addressing the driver. "Don't take us to La Dolce Vita. Take us to..." She trailed off. Her cousin Willow had recently moved into a new place in Sunshine Bay, and she wasn't sure of her address.

"We're not going to La Dolce Vita, Lila. I wouldn't do that to you. I know you need time to figure out a way to break the news that we're getting married to your family."

She didn't miss the eye roll in David's voice. No matter what he said, he wasn't as understanding about her family's aversion to marriage as he pretended to be. He'd laughed when she'd first told him about the Rosetti curse, and it had become a running joke with him. She hadn't appreciated his making fun of her family's superstition and had told him so. It didn't matter that she didn't believe in the Rosetti curse either. They were her family, and as much as they drove her crazy at times, she adored them.

"If we're not going to the restaurant, where are we going?"

He raised a shoulder, and then, squeezing one eye shut, murmured, "Windemere."

"Are you out of your mind? I'm not going to Windemere." She crossed her arms and shook her head. "No way."

He took her hand in his. "Just let me explain."

She pulled her hand away and turned to face the window. "There's nothing you can say that will change my mind, David."

Familiar sights came into view as the taxi crawled along Main Street behind several people on bikes. The cobblestone sidewalks were crowded with tourists taking in the quaint houses and B and Bs, with their lush and colorful gardens, and the eclectic mix of galleries, shops, cafés, bakeries, and bars that lined the narrow three-mile street that led down to the harbor and Windemere. "It's bad enough that you lied to me about where we were going. But to bring me to Windemere?"

All her family could talk about when she'd surprised her mother for her fiftieth birthday in April—sans David and her engagement ring—was Windemere and their fear that the high-end restaurant and inn would put their restaurant out of business. There were several eateries in Sunshine Bay, but La Dolce Vita had been the only fine dining establishment in town before Windemere's arrival on the scene.

"I'm sorry. I didn't know what else to do. I need you with me, and I knew you wouldn't come if I told you the truth." He tugged on her hand to get her to look at him. "My dad owns controlling interest in Windemere."

"He what?"

"I had no idea. He told me when he invited us for dinner. I think he's going to offer me a job. I'm pretty sure he wants me to run Windemere for him. That would be great, wouldn't it? We wouldn't have to stress about finding jobs or a place to live, and with the baby coming, you'll want to be close to your family."

She searched his face. He was serious. She'd shared her family's worries about Windemere on her return to London. But it wouldn't matter to David. For as long as she'd known him, he'd been vying for his father's attention and respect. If Gavin offered him the job, she had little doubt that he'd jump at the offer. And she wasn't sure that she could come up with a legitimate argument to get him to change his mind.

He rushed on. "I know your family's worried about their restaurant, but they're not seeing the big picture. Windemere will attract a high-end clientele to Sunshine Bay, and that will benefit all the local businesses, including La Dolce Vita," he said as the taxi pulled into the circular driveway in front of the grand historic mansion that housed Windemere.

David paid the driver and got out of the car, holding out his hand. "Please, I need you. I can't do this without you. We're a team."

A team that needed jobs and a place to live, she thought on a sigh. She had no doubt David would eventually bring up the fact that he'd worked for her father and lived in London because of her, so she owed him this. It wasn't an entirely fair argument, but he didn't always play fair.

"I promise, we'll leave as soon as dinner's over. We won't even stay for dessert. I'll rent a car. And you don't have to worry about running into your family," he said as she got out of the cab. "It's not like they're going to patronize the competition."

He made a good point. Her family wouldn't be caught dead at Windemere's grand opening. All Lila had to do was get in and out of the restaurant without being recognized. It shouldn't be hard. She'd left Sunshine Bay for London ten years earlier, and she only made it home for visits twice a year. Something her mother hadn't forgiven Lila's father for. No doubt she'd blame him for Lila's upcoming marriage too. And if Gavin offered David the job, and he accepted...

She pushed the thought away. Her stomach was already queasy with nerves. The maître d' greeted them when they entered the dramatic reception area, smiling broadly when David gave his name. Thankfully, Lila didn't recognize the man. As they followed behind him, she got her first look at the restaurant and sucked in a breath at the view of the shimmering sapphire bay through billowing sheer curtains that separated a white marble dance floor from the patio. The restaurant wasn't only stunning, it was also packed.

"Walk in front of me." She tried to look natural, but it was difficult when she had to bend her knees and duck her head to stay out of sight behind David. "Promise me there are no more surprises," she whispered in his ear.

His shoulders tensed. "There might be, but trust me, you'll be happy about one of them."

Lila was about to stop him and get him to tell her what he meant, but she spotted a man with a familiar head of golden hair and broad shoulders sitting at the table with David's family. It was her father, James Sinclair. Despite having seen him two weeks before, she gave a delighted cry—"Dad!"—and rushed past David to greet her father.

"What are you doing here?" she asked as she hugged him.

"I thought you might need my support. How did your mother take the news?"

"The news?"

"James, don't ruin my surprise." David's mother pouted while standing to greet Lila and David. She hugged them, then gestured at the empty chairs across from her. "Now sit before I burst."

Her stomach gurgling with nerves, Lila greeted David's father and his older brother with a strained smile. While she loved David's mother, she wasn't overly fond of his father and brother. Gavin IV, or Gavin Jr. as she thought of him, was the exact opposite of David in looks and personality. He was a flashy dresser who talked incessantly about himself. Apparently he'd been a big deal in high school and college but hadn't fared as well when he got out in the real world. He changed jobs as often as he did girlfriends. The last Lila had heard, he was working in commercial real estate. She wouldn't be surprised if he'd put the Windemere deal together.

Once they'd taken their seats, Jennifer clapped her hands, her eyes shining. "Okay, are you ready for my surprise?"

Lila's father rubbed his hand up and down the side of his face, something she'd seen him do when he was avoiding breaking unpleasant news. Gavin must've told him he planned to offer David the managerial position. It explained why he'd asked how her mother had taken the news. Lila had talked about Windemere with her father. Unlike David, he understood her family's concerns.

"We're ready for your news, Mom," David said with a covert glance at Lila. He covered her hand with his as if ensuring she wouldn't bolt.

Practically bouncing on her chair, Jennifer made a ta-da motion with her hands. "We're having your wedding here at Windemere! And you don't have to worry about a single thing, Lila. I've taken care of everything. Your wedding will be the talk of the cape. Everyone is so excited. I've already heard back from half the guest list confirming they're coming, and I only sent the invitations out last month. I think it's because it's a weekend-long wedding. They're becoming quite the thing, you know."

"Woman, relax." Gavin shook his head. "Once she gets started about a party, you can't shut her up. But hey, even

I have to admit, I was blown away by the response. Three hundred of the crème de la crème of Boston society coming to Windemere for a weekend? It's just what we need to put this place on the map." He pointed his wineglass at David. "Don't screw it up, son."

Chapter Two

Eva Rosetti willed her body to feel something as the man in her bed nibbled on her neck. She waited for a shiver of desire, a spark of lust, but her body was devoid of anything except frustration. She couldn't say the same about Ryan. The handsome lobsterman was obviously turned on. So much so that he didn't seem to notice that Eva wasn't.

It wasn't his fault. Eva's libido had gone into hibernation the winter before she turned fifty. Up until then, she'd been as passionate about sex as she was about food and wine, and she was desperate to get her groove back.

"Mmm, you like that, don't you, babe," Ryan murmured as he kissed and licked his way from her neck to her chest, his thick head of tawny hair disappearing under the red silk sheet.

Eva supposed she could simply tell him that no, she didn't like it at all. But she couldn't work up the energy for a conversation that would undoubtedly bruise his ego—which she would then have to soothe.

The weeklong heat wave had sapped not only her energy but her patience, which lately had been in short supply on a cool day. Any day, really. By midafternoon Sunshine

Bay had shattered a decades-old record for the hottest day in June.

As perspiration beaded along her hairline, Eva edged up on the mattress to get a look at the air-conditioning unit in the window across the room, wondering if it was on the fritz again. Her bedroom was decorated in dramatic reds and antique golds, the lush velvet drapes keeping out the light but not the heat. Today her bedroom felt more like a sauna than a sanctuary.

"Oh yeah, that's it, babe."

She frowned down at the head moving beneath the sheet. What was he even talking about? All she'd done was . . . bring her breast in direct contact with his mouth. Eva sighed. It wasn't his fault she'd rather be bingeing *Chef's Table* on Netflix or finishing the book on her nightstand than indulging in what was supposed to be some late-afternoon delight.

"Do you like this?" he asked, kneading her breasts with strong, callused fingers.

She bit back an *ow*. She needed to put them both out of their misery. It was too hot for Ryan to work so hard with no reward for his efforts. But just as she was about to fake a foreplay-induced orgasm, a wave of intense heat washed over her, coating her skin in sweat, and not the glowy kind.

Droplets rolled down her face, and beneath the sheet, Ryan froze. Eva was vain enough that she was willing to put up with his groping rather than have him see her with sweat pouring down her face and her hair plastered to her head. She moaned, adding some hip action to distract him.

Apparently her hip action wasn't distracting enough because he shoved his head from under the sheet, his brow furrowing as he patted the mattress along her side. "Babe, did you, uh, wet the bed?"

Eva swallowed a mortified groan. The air conditioner wasn't on the fritz; she was having a hot flash! With as much dignified grace as she could manage with sweat dripping into her eyes, she said, "No. I didn't wet the bed. I'm burning up." She pressed a palm to her forehead. "I have a fever."

He cocked his head. "Are you sure it's not a hot flash? My mother used to have them all the time when she was your—"

She didn't need the reminder that she was old enough to be his mother and cut him off. "It's a fever." Ryan was thirty-two, just four years older than Lila, Eva's daughter.

"Seriously, babe, you have nothing to be embarrassed about." He reached for her as she tugged on the sheet, whipping it off the bed.

"I'm not embarrassed." She stood up and wrapped the sheet around herself.

Then, holding her head high, she started to walk to the bathroom. But her attempt at a dignified exit was ruined when her foot got tangled in the sheet and she tripped. Ryan snagged the sheet, no doubt in an effort to save her from falling on her face. Instead he unraveled her like a burrito.

With a cajoling smile on his face, he reeled her toward him. "Come on, get back in bed," he said while languidly smoothing his other hand over the mattress and the damp outline of her body. It looked like a crime scene. He wasn't quick enough to hide his grimace.

She tugged the sheet from his hand. "Fever, remember? I'm probably contagious."

He came to his feet and closed the distance between

them, tipping her chin up with his knuckle. "You know, the thing I admire most about you, Eva, is that you don't care what people think. You're unashamedly you. No bullshit, no apologies."

And that's why Eva had invited Ryan to her bed. It wasn't just because he was handsome and had a great body; she genuinely liked him. "Fine. I don't have a fever. It's the menopause."

He grinned. "*The* menopause?"

"I was channeling my mother. That's what she calls it."

"Okay, well, at the risk of offending you and never getting invited back in your bed, which I have to tell you was the highlight of my month, maybe my entire year—"

Eva snorted.

"I'm serious. You're gorgeous, and I've been dreaming about being with you since I was sixteen."

Eva was used to men telling her she was the object of their fantasies and usually laughed it off as hyperbole. But she could tell by Ryan's sincere expression that he wasn't exaggerating, and she was relieved she hadn't criticized his performance. If he'd been fantasizing for years about being with her, it was no wonder he'd been trying so hard to please her.

On a rush of affection, she patted his cheek. "You're a sweet bo—man."

"Not exactly what I was going for, but if it means we can do this again, I won't complain." He searched her face. "We're not doing this again, are we?"

"I'm sorry, but no, we're not."

"It's because of the Rosetti curse, isn't it?"

Everyone in town knew the Rosetti women were cursed

when it came to marriage. Eva had never doubted the veracity of the claim. Her mother and sister were proof enough that the curse was real, and if any doubts remained, all she had to do was look up the family history.

The curse had been passed down through generations of Rosetti women. Their fiancés either died in the days leading up to the wedding or left them standing alone at the altar. The few brides who had made it past the wedding cere-mony had found themselves abandoned by their wayward husbands within months of saying, "I do."

For the most part, the curse had little bearing on Eva's life. She had what mattered most to her: her family; their restaurant, La Dolce Vita; good friends; good food; and good wine.

There'd been only one time in Eva's life when she'd wished she wasn't cursed. But in the end, it had worked out for the best. Her love affair with James had ended in heart-break, but she had a wonderful daughter as a result of their brief time together. She smiled. After years of living and working for her father in London, England, Lila had moved to Boston the week before.

"Eva?"

It took a moment for her to remember Ryan's question. "Yes, it's the curse," she said, telling him what she suspected he wanted to hear. "I can't risk falling in love with you."

He smiled, looking pleased that it was a possibility. "We wouldn't have to get married. We—"

This was why she didn't get involved with a man. She was up for a good time, not a long time. Lately, as today had clearly demonstrated, she wasn't even up for a good time. What a depressing thought. She really had enjoyed sex.

"I'm too old for you, Ryan. Fall in love with someone closer to your own age, someone to have babies with, someone to marry," she said, even though she didn't believe in marriage, and it had nothing to do with the Rosetti curse. There was a reason the divorce rate was so high. In her opinion, women would be far happier living the single life, as she and the other members of her family did.

"Is there anything I can say or do to change your mind? I really like you, Eva. I want to be with you."

"I really like you too, which is why you have to trust me when I say it's better this way." She cupped his face between her hands and kissed him. "I have to get to work. Why don't you come for dinner tonight? The special is lobster tagliatelle. On the house." It was the least she could do. It was because of Ryan that they had enough lobster for tonight's special.

When she'd arrived at the market to pick up their orders of fresh seafood earlier today, she'd discovered that the chefs from Windemere had offered above the going rate, leaving the bare minimum for everyone else. Eva had been worried about the impact the recently completed high-end restaurant and inn would have on La Dolce Vita, her family's fine dining establishment. But never in her wildest imaginings had she dreamed they'd be fighting against them not only for customers but also for seafood and produce.

Ryan scooped his board shorts and T-shirt off the hardwood floor. "Can I take a rain check? My sister and her boyfriend are in town, and they're taking the family out to dinner."

Eva noticed the way he avoided meeting her eyes and crossed her arms. "You're going to Windemere like everyone else, aren't you?" Tonight was the grand opening, and it was all anyone in town could talk about.

He winced as he fastened the button on his shorts. "Yeah. But I wouldn't worry about it, Eva. You know how people are. The novelty will wear off."

He didn't look as if he believed that any more than she did.

"We're not worried about it," she said as she walked to the bathroom, turning as she reached the door. "Ryan, what was it you were going to say that you thought would offend me?"

"Just that after my mom started working out and lost fifteen pounds, her hot flashes disappeared." His voice was muffled behind the T-shirt he pulled over his head, so he missed her jaw dropping.

An hour later, Eva stood behind the stove in La Dolce Vita's kitchen. She'd been running the restaurant with her sister Gia and their mother, Carmen, for twenty-five years. Before that, their mother had run the restaurant with their grandmother and great-aunt. The sisters had opened La Dolce Vita in 1936. It was one of the oldest restaurants on the cape.

Not much had changed at La Dolce Vita, Eva thought as she sautéed chopped onion and celery in bacon drippings. But they'd have to make changes if they were going to survive. Now, if only she could convince her mother. Carmen had shut Eva down every time she'd brought up the subject.

Eva added minced garlic to the drippings, looking over as her sister walked into the kitchen and said something to Mimi, their sous-/line chef. She'd been with them for eight years.

Gia joined Eva at the stove. "Sorry. I forgot to make the clam chowder. Probably for the best anyway. Mr. Santos can always tell when I've made it and not you."

For the past ten years, Mr. Santos had been coming in every Friday night for his clam chowder. He said it reminded him of his late wife's. The first time he'd eaten it, he'd gotten tears in his eyes. It was a memory Eva cherished. She loved that food had the power to move people—her food, her family's food.

Eva was usually there to prep for the dinner service, but she'd had a depressing meeting with their accountant earlier in the afternoon. She'd met up with Ryan on her way back to the restaurant.

"It's because you always forget to add the secret ingredient," Eva told her sister as she stirred in the cubed potatoes, chicken broth, and clam juice, adding a pinch of pepper and thyme.

Her sister rolled her eyes. "Love isn't an actual ingredient, you know."

Gia was an excellent cook, but she wasn't passionate about food, not like Eva and their mother. As devoted as Gia was to the restaurant, her first love was her art, even if she wouldn't admit it. In that, she was like her father. He'd been an artist too.

Eva and their baby sister, Camilla, shared a different father. Gia's father had died a week before he and Carmen were to marry. A month later, their mother had discovered she was pregnant. Gia had inherited her father's caramel-streaked brown hair and honey-brown eyes as well as his artistic talent. She must've inherited his temperament too. She was sweet and easygoing, the diplomatic one of the family. Eva, the Madonna help them all, had inherited their mother's temperament. Her ebony hair, green eyes, and tanned skin tone she'd inherited from her father.

He'd left Carmen a month before Eva was born, returning for a two-week reunion with their mother when Eva was three. Camilla had been born nine months later.

"Ma's at the bar. Come join us when you've finished up in here," her sister said.

At the beginning of every dinner service for as long as Eva could remember, the three of them had had a glass of wine together.

Eva nodded and brought the soup to a boil and then lowered the heat. Once it had simmered for twenty minutes, she'd combine the flour with cream and slowly add it to the soup, bringing it back to a boil until it was thick and creamy. Then she'd add the clams and the rest of the cream. She covered the bacon bits with plastic wrap. She'd sprinkle them on Mr. Santos's bowl of clam chowder before serving it to him.

Wiping her hands on the apron she wore over her black wraparound dress, Eva looked around the kitchen. It was unusually quiet for a Friday. The kitchen staff had filled only five orders while she'd been there.

"Keep an eye on the clam chowder for me, Mimi?"

The older woman shooed Eva away from the stove. "I've got it. Your momma needs cheering up. You're good at making her laugh."

"I have a feeling it will take more than a couple of laughs to make her feel better, Mimi, but I'll try." Eva hung up her apron before making her way into the restaurant. Her mother and sister sat at the bar with glasses of wine the size of fishbowls. At the sight of the nearly empty dining room, Eva poured herself an equally large glass of Chianti.

As she did, she racked her brain for something to say that would lift her mother's spirits. Carmen looked as if she were going to a funeral. And not only because of the black wraparound dresses they all wore for work. Her mother's red-painted mouth was clamped tight, and her eyes were too bright. Eva needed something to distract her before Carmen started ranting about their disloyal customers and sent the few diners they had running for the door.

It was a shame Lila had postponed her welcome-home dinner until next weekend. There was no better distraction than having the family together. But Lila wanted to get settled first. Eva imagined her daughter had a long list of things she wanted to accomplish before she allowed herself to relax and have some fun. Lila didn't take after Eva. She was an uptight perfectionist like her father.

Eva used to joke that Lila had come out of the womb in a beige suit with a BlackBerry clenched in her fist. As she got older, Lila would quip that Eva must've come out of the womb in a G-string with a bottle of wine in her hand. Eva smiled. She couldn't wait to see her.

Despite their differences, they had a wonderful relationship. Gia and her daughters, Sage and Willow, had the same kind of close relationship Eva had with Lila. They'd raised their girls together, and it thrilled them to no end that their daughters were as close as sisters.

Carmen pointed her wineglass at Eva, droplets of bold red liquid splashing onto the bar. "Why are you smiling? We've had nine cancellations. We'll be out of business in a month if this keeps up." She nodded at Gia. "This one, she'll be fine. But you and I, Eva, La Dolce Vita is all we've got."

"That's not fair, Ma. I love the restaurant. You know I do. I put in as much time here as you and Eva."

"*Certo*, sure, but it's not the same. You aren't like me and your sister. You have your art, *cara mia*," her mother said, her Italian accent still noticeable despite having been born in Sunshine Bay.

"It's a hobby. I need the money I earn from the restaurant as much as you and Eva do."

"Don't do that, G. You're an incredibly talented artist," Eva protested, as she always did when her sister belittled her talent.

Gia pursed her lips. "Who doesn't make any money from her art."

"Because you don't show it to anyone!"

Carmen, who'd been focused on the nearly empty dining room, patted her chest. "My heart, it's racing. I think I'm having a heart attack. Get me my pills."

Eva held back an eye roll. Carmen had a *heart attack* whenever she was upset or wanted to manipulate her family into doing what she wanted. "Ma, you don't have heart medication. Dr. Alva told you you're as healthy as a forty-year-old, remember?"

Their mother didn't look a day over sixty. It probably helped that there wasn't a single gray strand in her dyed mahogany shoulder-length layered hair. She'd turn seventy-four in December.

Eva had plucked two silver strands from her own head the day before, and one from her chin. Her mother had

pointed out the chin hair in the middle of the previous day's lunch service. She'd spotted it from across the
dining room.

The woman had 20/20 vision since filling the prescrip-
tion that had sat buried in her nightstand drawer for ten
years. Eva doubted she would've filled it if she hadn't
spotted the chic red-framed glasses in the window of the
optical shop.

Carmen took off her glasses and set them on the bar,
pressing her thumbs against the corners of her eyes. "What
does she know? She's a *bambina*."

Dr. Alva was the same age as Eva. They'd gone to school
together.

Bruno, a distinguished-looking bald man in a pristine
white shirt and impeccably pressed black pants, stood at
the hostess stand with a phone pressed to his ear. Bruno
had been working at La Dolce Vita for as long as Eva could
remember. He was a father figure to her and her sisters and
one of their mother's closest confidants. As though sensing
Eva's attention, he turned his back.

Madonna santo. Someone else must've canceled their
reservation.

"So," Eva said, drawing her mother's attention, "you
know how you two keep telling me I'm going through the
menopause? I discovered this afternoon that you're probably right."

She drew out the story, changed it up a bit to protect both
her and Ryan's reputations—portraying him as a talented
lover with no mention of her missing libido—culminating
with Ryan thinking she'd wet the bed.

Her mother and sister stared at her and then started

laughing. The three of them were howling with tears streaming down their faces when Bruno approached the bar.

"Are you going to let me in on the joke?" he asked, but
there was no twinkle in his dark eyes, and his movie-star
smile was missing.

Eva covered her mother's open mouth. No way was she
letting her share Eva's hot-flash story with anyone. She
should've sworn her mother and sister to secrecy before
she'd told them. Their word was their bond.

"Now you have me intrigued. Come on, tell me your joke,"
he cajoled. If Bruno was about to tell them they had another
cancelation, he probably could use a laugh as much as the three
of them. But no way would Eva talk about her sex life with the
man who'd played the role of her father for the past thirty years.

Her mother pulled Eva's hand from her mouth; her eyes
narrowed at Bruno. "What's wrong?"

"Ruth called." He reached for Carmen's glass of wine,
took a large swallow, and then continued. "They had to
cancel their reservation for tonight's birthday dinner. Several
members of the family are ill."

It was bad enough that the reservation had been for a
party of ten. The fact that Ruth Hollingsworth was her
mother's best friend made it ten times worse.

"Give me the phone," Carmen said to Bruno, motioning
with her fingers. Bruno would know better than to argue
when their mother got that look in her eyes.

Eva wasn't so easily put off. She wasn't about to let
her mother say something she'd regret and possibly ruin a
decades-old friendship. "Ma, you can't expect them to come
when members of their party are sick. Let it go."

"Eva's right. We'll store the balloons in the back." Gia

nodded at a pink bouquet of helium-filled balloons at the far end of the bar. It was Ruth's daughter-in-law's birthday. "They'll be fine until next weekend."

Eva could tell by the almost-imperceptible twitch of Bruno's left eye that Ruth hadn't rebooked their reservation. Her sister must've caught it too because she gave Eva an *oh crap* look. Yes, Eva could almost guarantee it was about to hit the fan.

Her mother muttered something in Italian and plucked the phone from Bruno's hand. She brought it to her ear. Ruth answered on the first ring. She was as loud as their mother, and they heard her apologizing for canceling at the last minute. It would've been better if she'd stopped there. Ruth gave herself away when listing the family members who were ill and their particular ailments. She said her daughter-in-law had laryngitis, but they heard her distinct laugh in the background.

The woman was as annoying as her laugh, and Eva wouldn't put it past her to have had Ruth cancel the reservation when she found out her party was being held at La Dolce Vita. She didn't like Eva and Gia and barely tolerated their mother.

Carmen made sympathetic noises. Eva might've believed she was being sincere if not for the sneer on her face.

Her mother disconnected and hopped off the stool. "Come on. We're going to Windemere."

"Why would we go to Windemere?" Eva and Gia asked at the same time.

"Her family's not sick. They're at the grand opening, and no one gets away with playing a Rosetti for a fool."

"*Cara*, what will it look like for people to see you there?"

Bruno asked, his voice soothing while behind their mother's back he motioned for Eva and Gia to help him convince her not to go.

Even Eva knew it was hopeless to reason with her mother now. She saluted Bruno with her wineglass and Gia did the same, and then they sat back to drink their Chianti while Bruno made his case.

"Bah." Her mother waved off what Eva thought were legitimate reasons for Carmen not to go. Their customers were used to seeing them here, and it would look as if they were worried about the competition if they showed up at Windemere, especially if her mother confronted Ruth in the middle of the restaurant. "No one will see us. We'll take the beach and look over the retaining wall."

"*Cara*, the retaining wall is ten feet high."

Their mother shrugged, gesturing for them to follow her. "Come on, girls."

Bruno groaned when Eva and Gia drained their wineglasses and did as their mother said. He should know the Rosetti women stuck together no matter what. They always had, and they always would.

Chapter Three

The white noise rushing through Lila's ears sounded like ocean waves crashing against the shore. It drowned out the conversation about the weekend-long wedding. Lila's wedding. Here, in Sunshine Bay. With three hundred guests.

She'd never fainted before, but she had a feeling that was about to change and snagged the end of the napkin with the tip of her finger, pulling it off the table so that it fell onto the floor. She ducked under the table as if planning to pick it up but instead put her head between her legs.

"Are you all right, honey?" asked a voice close to her ear, David's strained whisper wending its way through the white noise.

She lifted her head above her knees, injecting everything she was feeling into the squinty look she gave David.

With his forefinger, he pushed his glasses up the bridge of his nose and nodded. "I know. I know exactly how you feel, but what was I supposed to do?"

"How about saying, 'No, Mom, Lila doesn't want a big wedding'? Or how about instead of letting me be blindsided, you talked about it with me first? You don't get to make all the decisions, David. This is my life too!" she whisper-shouted.

"I didn't get much say about us getting married at the courthouse, did I? I want our wedding to be special, Lila. I want to celebrate with our families and friends." He searched her face. "Admit it, your family is the only reason you want to get married at the courthouse."

"So what if it is? Don't my feelings matter? Apparently not, since you basically accepted the job to run Windemere without consulting me."

He raised an eyebrow.

"It's not the same. You were thrilled with my dad's job offer, and you loved working for him."

"I did, and I'm equally thrilled about my dad's job offer. Can't you be happy for me, happy for us? We don't have to stress about finding jobs or a place to live now. You'll be close to your family, and it's a great opportunity."

And more important to David was that his dad had offered the job to him and not his brother—even though, with his experience, David was the obvious choice. That wasn't how things typically worked in his family. But David was forgetting one important thing.

"How do you think my family will feel when they find out you're running Windemere?"

He sighed. "Does everything have to be about your family, Lila?"

"Really? Are you trying to tell me that none of this, the wedding, the job, has anything to do with *your family*, David?"

"It's not the same," he said with a mulish expression on his face. He looked a lot like his father at the moment. Far from a comforting thought.

A large, warm hand settled on Lila's back, and then

her dad ducked his head under the table. "Are you okay, sweetheart?"

Her father was protective of her and her half sisters—their knight in shining armor—and he'd move heaven and earth to ensure their happiness. If she told him the truth, he'd whisk her away and back to London. It would be so easy to let him handle everything.

Her mother would be horrified that the thought had even crossed Lila's mind. A Rosetti woman didn't depend on a man to make her troubles go away, even if that man was Lila's father. Lila and her cousins had been raised to be strong, independent women—the architects of their own lives and happiness.

But Lila didn't have only herself to think about. She had a baby on the way. She wouldn't let her child become a pawn, torn between its mother and father. No matter how good and loving her parents were, the continuous battles they'd waged over her while she was growing up had been a nightmare. One she refused to let her child endure.

"Yeah, I'm—" She didn't get the chance to complete the lie. David's mother joined them under the table.

Jennifer worried her bottom lip between her teeth. "Is everything okay? I didn't overstep, did I? You're not mad at me, are you, Lila?"

She'd seen that anxious expression on David's mother's face before—every time Gavin berated his wife for some perceived failing or misstep—and Lila swallowed a sigh. She couldn't do it. She couldn't tell Jennifer how she really felt about the society wedding she had planned, and if Lila couldn't, how could she expect David to?

"Of course not. I just dropped my napkin." Lila held up the white linen cloth.

It was almost worth swallowing her own feelings to see the bright smile light up Jennifer's face. Almost.

"So glad you could all rejoin us," Gavin said when the four of them straightened in their chairs, sharing an eye roll with his eldest son.

David's brother smirked into his wineglass and then held it up. "A toast to the happy couple."

With a forced smile, Lila touched her wineglass to everyone else's and then pretended to take a sip. But when talk immediately returned to the plans for their wedding and how beneficial it would be for Windemere, her stomach rebelled. It was an all-too-familiar feeling. Whenever Lila had gotten anxious as a child, she'd thrown up.

Excusing herself from the table, she pushed back her chair. "Do you know where the restrooms are, Dad?"

"To the right of the piano and down the hall."

"Thanks." At the question in his eyes, she mouthed, *I'm fine*, but she felt his concerned gaze following her as she walked away from the table.

She kept her head down, pressing her fingers to her lips as she breathed deeply through her nose and hurried across the restaurant.

The woman behind the baby grand piano was playing Roxette's "Listen to Your Heart." Even though it was a song from the eighties, Lila knew it well. She should. Her mother had sung it often enough when Lila was growing up.

When Eva was in her early twenties, she'd been a singer in a girl band that covered female artists from the eighties. She'd met Lila's father while doing the European club circuit. According to Lila's grandmother and aunt, Eva could've made it big. Lila had no reason to doubt them. Her mother had an incredible voice.

As a child, Lila had loved when her mother sang to her. She'd been proud of her. But that changed when Lila got older and her mother would agree to sing at some function at the high school or would sing karaoke at a bar Lila had sneaked into with her cousins. She'd been mortified then. Because Eva didn't just sing, she *performed*, ensuring that every male in the audience—some females too—fantasized about taking Eva Rosetti home with them.

Lila quickened her pace and rounded the corner. At the line outside the ladies' restroom, she groaned into her palm. Her eyes went to the stick figure farther down the hall. Of course there wasn't a line outside the men's restroom.

Lila moved to stand behind a thirtysomething woman—thankfully a stranger—but then her stomach heaved, and she knew she'd never make it. She ran the several feet to the men's restroom and pushed open the door. Thankfully, it was empty, but at that point, even if it hadn't been, she wouldn't have been able to leave. She'd barely flipped the lock on the stall and made it onto her knees before she threw up.

Five minutes later, she pulled a handful of toilet paper off the roll and wiped her mouth. She tossed it into the toilet as she came to her feet and flushed. As she watched her lunch and the toilet paper disappear, the temper she was so good at controlling—passionate outbursts reminded her of her dramatic mother—came out, and she turned and kicked the stall door.

She let out a high-pitched sound—a cross between a

shriek and a cry—but it didn't get rid of the anger swirling inside her. The only thing kicking the door had accomplished was hurting her big toe. She had to find a way to release the anger. If she didn't, she was afraid she'd throw up again and she'd never get out of this bathroom. Maybe the key to getting rid of the anger was articulating exactly what she was feeling, words she'd never say to David out loud. Her parents' fraught relationship was evidence of how much damage words said in anger could do.

"You son of a..." Even in the heat of the moment, she couldn't indirectly curse Jennifer. "...of a scoundrel! You knew I wasn't ready to get pregnant, but did you care? No, because you were, and you...you arranged a big wedding behind my back with your mother, and you know I can't hurt her feelings so you get exactly what you want. A baby, a wedding, and a job that, no matter what you say, could put my family out of business. You, you, you..." The word got stuck on repeat as she searched for one that would convey exactly how she was feeling about David at that moment. She couldn't find one and kicked the door instead. "Ouch. Son of a—"

A deep voice cut her off midcurse. "Are you all right in there?"

Her eyes just about popped out of her head, and she covered her face with her hands. What had she been thinking, going off like that in a public place? She wasn't her mother. She didn't do this sort of thing. She cringed, praying the man hadn't heard half of what she'd said.

But if the baby books she'd been reading were right...She placed a hand over her stomach and whispered, "I'm sorry, baby. I'm mad at your daddy, not you. I love you."

"Ma'am, are you okay?"

She squeezed her eyes closed. He was still out there. Forcing a smile that she hoped would convince him he must've imagined the rant he'd overheard, she opened the stall door. The smile froze on her face.

Clearly someone upstairs hated her, or her guardian angel had gone out for a cigarette. Because standing on the other side of the stall door was the last man she'd expected or wanted to see.

Luke Hollingsworth. Her high school boyfriend's older brother. The man who'd seen her half-naked when he'd saved her from giving her virginity to his brother at sixteen.

"Lila?"

She didn't think she'd changed that much. He certainly hadn't. He was still as gorgeous as she remembered. Actually, that wasn't true. He was even better looking at thirty than he'd been at eighteen. She realized she was staring and lifted a hand. "Yep, it's me."

"Yep, it's me"? Really? She'd possibly revealed her deepest, darkest secrets to the tall, dark, and broodingly handsome man leaning against the bathroom stall, and that was all she could come up with?

She glanced at the restroom door, wanting nothing more than to beat a hasty retreat, but she had to find out how much of her rant Luke had overheard. His grandmother and hers were best friends, which meant she had no choice but to address her embarrassing meltdown.

"So, how's your mom and your grandmother?" she asked as she walked to the sink and turned on the tap, carrying on a conversation as if they were in line at the grocery store and not standing in the men's restroom.

His mouth twitched as if he were holding back a smile. He'd never been an easy smiler, but that hadn't stopped Lila from trying to coax one out of him when she was younger. Because when Luke Hollingsworth smiled, it felt as if the sun had come out. At least it had to her. She might have had a crush on him. A small crush, really, really small.

She bent over the sink and cupped her hands under the tap, then rinsed out her mouth with water.

"They're good, thanks. You should stop by the table and say hi."

She met his gaze in the mirror, water dribbling out of the side of her mouth. She looked as if she'd had a stroke. "They're here?"

"Yeah. It's my mom's birthday. She, uh, wanted to have it here." He brought his hand to his ear, rubbing the lobe between his thumb and forefinger. "Gran's pretty upset about it, so do me a favor and don't mention we were here to Carmen."

"Trust me, the last thing I want is for my family to know I'm here." She grabbed a paper towel from the dispenser and wiped her mouth and chin.

He nodded, jerking a thumb at the stall door. "Yeah, I kind of got that."

She winced and then turned to face him, tossing the crumpled paper towel into the wastepaper basket. "How much did you hear?"

"Enough to wonder if I should congratulate you on your upcoming wedding and the baby or if I should offer you a ride out of town."

She could feel the flush working its way up her chest to her face. "I can't believe I did that or that you heard me.

But I guess it's better that it was you than someone else."
She raised her gaze to his. "You won't mention it to anyone,
will you, Luke?"

"Of course not. But you sounded pretty upset. Are you
sure you're okay?"

She considered saying she was fine but ended up telling
him the truth instead. "No. I'm actually a bit of a wreck,
hence the, you know"—she waved her hand at the stall—
"meltdown you overheard. I mean, I'm happy about the
baby. It just came as a shock. It wasn't the best time to get
pregnant. And then I found out, instead of getting married
at the courthouse like we'd planned, David, my fiancé,
and his mother have invited three hundred people to our
wedding, and it's going to be held here, at Windemere. In
a month."

He winced. "You haven't told your family yet, have you?"

"Have you seen my mother running down Main Street
pulling out her hair and screaming bloody murder? Has
my nonna called Father Patrick and made her funeral
arrangements?"

Whenever her grandmother got news she didn't like,
she'd swear she was having a heart attack. Carmen was as
dramatic as Lila's mother. Although, given the news Lila had
to share, she might have an actual heart attack this time.

Luke's lips curved in a crooked smile, a dimple appearing
in his left cheek, and despite feeling as if she might throw
up again, Lila found herself smiling in return. She couldn't
seem to help herself. His smile was endorphin inducing.
Maybe she should bring him with her when she broke the
news to her family.

Their eyes met and held, and Lila couldn't seem to pull

her gaze from his. She blamed it on his eyes. They were the color of storm clouds and framed by eyelashes so thick that they made her envious. But David had nice eyes too, and she didn't get this warm, fluttery feeling in her chest when she held his gaze.

Luke glanced over her shoulder and cleared his throat. "It might take them some time to come around, but in the end, they will. They love you, Lila."

She raised an eyebrow and his dimple deepened. He had to stop smiling at her. "I know they do, but they also believe in the Rosetti curse."

"I take it you don't, since you're getting married."

"No. I don't believe in curses. I just think they're unlucky in love."

"Really, really unlucky," Luke said with a rumble of amusement in his voice. They shared another smile, and then they both looked away.

"And if it's not bad enough that I'm getting married—in their eyes, I mean—the wedding and reception are being held here."

"Why not hold them at La Dolce Vita? You're the bride. Isn't that up to you?"

"You'd think so, but apparently I don't get a say." Feeling disloyal to David, she added, "My fiancé's father owns controlling interest in Windemere, and he's asked David to manage it for him. They're basically using our wedding as a marketing ploy."

"They know your family owns La Dolce Vita, don't they?"

She nodded and told him what David had said about competition.

Luke scoffed, "Easy for him to say."

"I know, right? I don't understand why he can't see it."

"Come on, he has to see it, Lila."

Luke totally understood where she was coming from. She wished David were half as sensitive to her feelings as Luke was. She winced. She wasn't being fair to David. Luke had grown up in Sunshine Bay and knew her family really well. Except David had met her mother and her aunt when they'd come to visit Lila in London late the previous fall, and it wasn't as if she hadn't shared everything there was to know about them with him.

But she hadn't shared her feelings for David with her mother. It would've been easier if she'd told her mother and aunt that he was more than a good friend and colleague, but she hadn't wanted to ruin their visit.

"Apparently he doesn't. But the one thing I do know is I can't put off telling my family any longer."

Luke glanced at the watch on his tanned, muscular forearm. He wore a white button-down with the sleeves rolled up. "Yeah, I better get back to the party."

As they walked to the door, Lila said, "We're waiting until I'm twelve weeks to tell anyone about the baby, so please don't—" She broke off when the door began opening.

Luke reached over and held it shut, gesturing for her to hide behind him. The last thing she wanted was to get caught in the men's room, so she did as he directed.

He glanced at her over his shoulder and then opened the door wide. She slipped behind it. "What the hell, Luke? Why were you holding the door shut?"

"Wasn't me. It must've been stuck."

When the other man disappeared into the restroom and out of view, Luke tugged Lila out from behind the door and gently shoved her into the hall.

As the door closed behind her, Lila heard the man say, "Did you see Lila Rosetti? My sister thought she saw her heading for the restrooms earlier."

"Nope. She must've mistaken someone else for her."

"Didn't you have a thing for Lila back in the day?"

Chapter Four

Stop dawdling, Eva! We have a ten-foot wall to climb, and the tide will be coming in soon," her mother called over her shoulder.

"I'm not dawdling, but unlike you and Gia, my feet aren't as tough as sharkskin." Her mother and sister were jogging down the beach in the hot sand while Eva was "jogging" in the wet sand along the water's edge. Every few minutes, a rogue wave would nearly take her out or she'd step on a seashell.

Eva didn't mind a nice leisurely stroll on the beach, but jogging held as much appeal as a root canal without novocaine.

"We're trying not to be seen, remember? Get over here with us," her mother yelled, waving for Eva to join them.

"If you don't want anyone to notice us, maybe you should stop yelling, Ma!"

Close-set businesses and homes with cedar-shake siding lined the beach all the way to the harbor. Windemere was a short distance from the pier, which at that moment looked about as close as Boston.

Eva picked up her pace, sucking in a pained gasp

moments later. It felt as if someone had grabbed hold of the ligaments in her left side and twisted. She stopped jogging and bent over.

"Eva, are you all right?" her sister called.

"Crab," she gritted out. "A crab bit me." No way was she admitting that she had a stitch in her side. Thankfully, a wave splashed up to her calf, and she shook her leg as if dislodging a crab from her toe. "Go ahead. I'll catch up."

Her sister ran across the sand. Eva found it annoying that, unlike her, Gia was glowy and not sweaty, and she was breathing as if she'd taken a leisurely stroll along the beach. Whereas Eva sounded as if she'd run ten miles.

"How bad is it?" Gia asked.

"Bad. I'm lucky I didn't lose my toe."

Her sister grinned. "A crab didn't bite you. You have a stitch in your side. Here." She took Eva's hand and lifted it gently over her head. "Now stretch slowly to your right and breathe deeply."

Eva grumbled as she did as Gia suggested, surprised when the cramp lessened. She did the stretch twice more and then straightened.

"Good to go?" her sister asked.

"No, but I don't have much choice." She nodded at their mother. "It'll take two of us to convince her not to make a scene."

Gia cupped a hand over her eyes and looked down the beach. The harbor shimmered in a golden haze as the sun lowered in the butterscotch-yellow sky, its reflection glittering on the rolling surf. "How many of our regulars do you think are there?"

"Everyone who canceled their reservations in the past

week," Eva said as they set off toward Carmen, who'd slowed from a jog to a power walk.

Her sister stopped Eva with a hand on her arm. "Tell me the truth. Can we keep the restaurant afloat?"

"Of course," she said with far more confidence than she felt. Gia might be her older sister, but Eva had always felt the need to protect her. "Our food is better, and so are our prices."

Although if the head chef at Windemere kept undercutting them, they'd have to pay a premium for seafood and produce. Either that or adapt their menu. It was something Eva had talked about to Mimi and Bruno after returning from the market. She hadn't mentioned it to her mother.

Carmen motioned for them to hurry up with an impatient wave of her hand. It seemed she'd taken to heart Eva's suggestion to stop yelling. The three of them jogged the rest of the way down the beach. Only Eva's ragged breathing, the sound of the waves rolling onto the shore, and neighbors calling out to one another in their backyards broke the silence.

Fifteen minutes later, they slowed to a walk as the sound of laughter and the smell of woodsmoke from the firepits on Windemere's walled patio reached them.

"Crouch down," Carmen whispered when the half-moon stone wall draped in pink hydrangeas came into view. They duckwalked toward it. Within minutes Eva's thighs cramped and burned, and she fell behind.

When her mother and sister reached the base of the wall, they glanced over their shoulders. Her mother sighed and gestured for Eva to pick up the pace. Eva gave thanks to the Madonna when she finally reached them. She sat on the sand, resting her back against the sun-warmed wall. If she didn't have to move for a week, she'd be happy.

Her sister smirked as if she could read Eva's mind. "You should join my early-morning yoga sessions. I'd have you running the length of the beach in no time," she whispered.

Gia was into yoga, meditation, communing with nature, and hugging trees. Eva was into food, wine, bingeing Netflix, and reading about women who buried their cheating husbands under trees.

Eva mouthed, *Kiss my culo* at her sister. Although they probably didn't have to mouth their words or whisper. Eva doubted anyone would hear them over the laughter and raised voices drifting past them on the humid air. It sounded as if the restaurant was packed.

Gia grinned and then whipped her head around. Their mother was climbing the wall like a monkey. Gia wedged her toes into a crevice between stones and followed after Carmen. Eva closed her eyes, happy to leave them to it as the foamy surf lapped at her hot feet. She blinked open her eyes. The tide was coming in faster than they'd anticipated. Then again, it had taken them almost thirty minutes to get there.

Tipping her head back, she was about to tell Carmen and Gia to move it when she realized how her mother would feel if she discovered the Hollingsworths celebrating at Windemere as Eva fully expected.

She jumped to her feet and tugged on their legs. "Get down and leave it to me. You don't have your glasses, Ma. You won't be able to see anything."

Eva caught her sister's eye, mouthing *Ruth* and *murder*.

As in their mother would murder Ruth on the off chance she was able to see Ruth without her glasses. Not really, but Carmen would defriend Ruth, which would mean they'd have to listen to their mother rant for months to come about the betrayal.

"Eva's right, Ma," Gia whispered, reaching up to pull on the back of Carmen's dress.

It took them five minutes to convince their mother to come down off the wall and for Eva to take their place. She stuck her toes in the same opening between the stones that her sister had used.

Her mother yelped. "Hurry, the tide's coming in!" Placing her hands on Eva's backside, she gave her a boost.

Carmen grunted, putting her shoulder into it. "*Madonna mia.*"

Eva turned her head to eye her mother. "Remember who I inherited my *culo* from."

Admittedly, Eva's figure had grown curvier than her mother's this past year. It was possible Ryan had a point. As today had proved, she was out of shape. But thanks to the hours she spent kneading dough every day, her hands and arms were strong, and she managed to climb the wall without depending too much on her legs, which had yet to recover from jogging in the sand.

Lifting one hand off the wall, she moved the heavy pink hydrangea heads blocking her view. The restaurant was packed and more beautiful than she'd imagined with its acres of white marble and brass finishings.

On a light, humid breeze, smoke from the wood-burning firepits on the patio drifted past her face, and she sneezed. Loudly. Several people turned her way. She ducked behind the flowers as her mother and sister whispered for her to hurry. She looked over her shoulder to see foam-capped waves lapping at their calves.

"Just give me one more second," she hissed. She wanted to see for herself how many of their regulars were here.

Once again, she separated the leafy foliage with her fingers. Only this time, she edged up, her head popping above the tops of the hydrangeas. If it weren't for a cake being carried to a table to the right of the dance floor, the servers singing an off-key rendition of "Happy Birthday," Eva might've missed Ruth and her family—along with several of their other regulars, including Mr. Santos, at adjacent tables clearly enjoying their meals.

"Do you see Ruth and her family? Any of our other regulars?" her mother called up to her.

"No. None of our customers are here." She hoped her mother didn't pick up on the depressed note in Eva's voice. It was hard not to feel disheartened after what she'd seen. She didn't know how they could compete with this. The food smelled wonderful, the customers looked relaxed while they enjoyed their meals, and the restaurant was truly beautiful.

A shadow fell over Eva as she searched for a toehold beneath her right foot. She glanced up. A man had come to stand by the wall. He was close enough that she could smell his cologne. She sniffed, wondering why it smelled familiar. Curious, she moved the hydrangeas aside.

He was looking out over the bay with his hands in the pockets of his black, well-tailored pants. His suit jacket fit his broad-shouldered, slim frame to perfection. The sun glinted off the copper strands in his golden hair and the stubble on his chiseled jaw. He had the stance of a supremely confident man, a man who was used to commanding respect and attention. He'd certainly captured hers, Eva thought at the uptick of her pulse.

He looked down, and piercing blue eyes met hers.

She nearly lost her grip on the wall. "James?"

He blinked. "Eva?"

"What are you doing—?" she began, her train of thought interrupted by a loud splash. She dragged her gaze from his and looked over her shoulder. Her mother and sister were...swimming?

Laughing, they raised their hands. "Come join us. It's the perfect night for a swim," they called out, acting as if this had been their plan all along.

Eva heard people whispering and returned her gaze to James. He was no longer standing at the wall alone, and he was no longer the only one looking at her. They'd drawn a crowd. Eva sighed. There was no help for it. Like her sister and mother, she had to act as if they were out for an evening swim instead of spying on their competition.

She glanced over her shoulder. She wasn't about to fall into the water backward. It wasn't deep enough yet. She had to turn around. Clinging to the hydrangeas, she let go of the wall.

James frowned. "Eva, what are you doing?"

"I'm going swimming, darling. What does it look like?" she said, edging her toes out of the crevices. As she pushed off the wall, James swore, reaching for her as she turned in midair. She heard people gasp just before she hit the water.

It was only a couple of feet deep at the base of the wall,

and she landed on her knees. Better than on her face, she thought, and then she turned onto her back to float out to her sister and mother. Pink hydrangeas bobbed around her, and she imagined it would make a pretty picture. She smiled up at James and waved, even as she had a sinking feeling she knew why her former lover was here. He must own Windemere.

Chapter Five

Lila stood in the hallway staring at the closed door of the men's restroom. Luke Hollingsworth had had a thing for her back in the day? She leaned toward the door, about to press her ear against it to hear Luke's response. She rocked back on her heels. What was she thinking? It didn't matter whether Luke had had a crush on her or not.

When a voice in her head argued that it did so matter, she reminded the teenager she used to be that she was getting married. In a month. At Windemere. With three hundred guests who right now didn't include the five most important women in her world.

She opened her purse and took out her phone, looking for a private place to call her cousins. She couldn't put it off any longer. She noticed a door across from the ladies' restroom, where there was no longer a line. Just her luck. If she'd waited ten minutes longer, she could've avoided embarrassing herself.

But then you wouldn't know that Luke Hollingsworth had a crush on you back in the day, argued her teenage self, who seemed to have taken up permanent residence in her head.

"I'm getting married," Lila said firmly, wondering whom

she was trying to convince. She looked around, praying no one had heard her, because she'd actually said that out loud.

She blamed it on stress. She was stressed and overwrought, and why wouldn't she be after all that she'd learned within the span of fifteen minutes?

You've got cold feet, the voice in her head unhelpfully added.

Lila was pretty sure her feet weren't just cold, they were freezing, but that wouldn't stop her from going through with the wedding—which meant she had to get her cousins on board. The men's restroom door began opening, and she heard Luke and his friend talking. Lila sprinted for the door across from the ladies' restroom, relieved when the knob turned under her hand. She slipped inside. Closing the door quietly behind her, she patted the wall for a light switch and flipped it on. The storage room held shelves of cleaning supplies and toilet paper.

She leaned against the door and brought up WhatsApp on her phone, then pressed the call icon. Her face popped onto the screen. She wrinkled her nose at the streaks of mascara under her eyes, dampening a finger to swipe them away. She was about to pinch color into her pale cheeks when her cousin's face appeared.

Willow stood in front of a green screen wearing a yellow polka-dot bikini. "Hey, babe, I'm on air in ten minutes so make it quick. What's up?"

"You're going on air in *that*? I mean, not that you don't look fantastic, you do." It was true. Willow was drop-dead gorgeous. Her body was toned and tanned, and she wore her sun-kissed blond hair in long, beachy waves.

Willow adjusted her boobs in her bikini top. "The

station put in a new management team. I've been demoted to weather girl."

Willow had worked part-time at the local TV station while completing her master's in television at Boston University. She'd accepted a position on the late-night news desk when she'd completed her degree, with the goal of using it as a stepping stone. She'd been there for five years.

Sage appeared on the screen just as Willow was explaining how her new boss had tried to frame the demotion as a promotion.

"What he's doing is exploiting you," Sage said, wrinkling her nose at her sister. "You can't seriously be going on air in that. It barely covers anything."

Willow leaned off-screen and reappeared with an inflatable duck ring. She fitted it around her waist. The bright-yellow duck, wearing oversize black shades, covered most of her upper body. "Meet Super Duck."

Sage raised an eyebrow. "Super Duck doesn't do a very good job of protecting your *ass*ets, but the employment lawyer at my firm would. So would you please call her? You have her number."

Sage was the Gloria Allred of Boston, which meant that even if she didn't totally buy into the idea of the Rosetti curse, the women she represented in high-profile divorces had ensured that she was a misogamist. Lila hadn't worried about running into her cousin when she and David arrived in Boston. Not only was it a city of over four million people, Sage was a workaholic who basically lived at her office. From the desk and shelves of books behind her, it appeared Sage was there now.

"Zach has me covered. My cameraman," Willow said in response to her sister's pursed lips.

Sage wore her shoulder-length auburn hair scraped from her oval face in an unflattering bun. It was in keeping with the persona her cousin tried to present to the world in an effort to distract from her looks, including by wearing clothes that hid her figure. But she couldn't hide her voluptuous lips, which had earned her the nickname Hot Lips in high school.

"The guy you dated last month?" Sage asked her sister.

Willow was a serial dater. Unlike Lila, and possibly Sage, she believed in the Rosetti curse.

"Yeah, and he's got me covered. Zach won't film below Super Duck." When Sage opened her mouth, no doubt wanting to interrogate Zach and ensure that this was the case, Willow waved her hand. "Enough about me. Lila called. And no offense, babe, but you look like crap. What's going on?"

"I'm, uh, invoking the Cousins Pact. I need you guys, like as soon as you can get here."

"Here where?" Sage asked, bringing the screen closer to her face.

"Sage, how many times have I told you to get your eyes checked? You can't see close-up," Willow said. "And if Lila's invoking the Cousins Pact, she must be in Sunshine Bay." She narrowed her eyes. "Are you hiding in the restaurant's supply closet?"

"Yeah, just not the restaurant you think." Lila swallowed. "I'm at Windemere."

Before her cousins could ask what she was doing at the competition's grand opening, Lila blurted everything out— everything except about the baby and that Luke Hollingsworth had had a crush on her when they were growing up.

They stared at her, and then Willow swore. Her cousin had the face of an angel and the mouth of a longshoreman.

"Lila, you have to get out of there before anyone sees you," Sage said as she got up from her desk. "Willow, calm down and stop swearing."

"Calm down? Is that what you're going to say to Zia, Mom, and Nonna, Sage? Because if it is, I can guarantee they won't hear you above the wailing. Do you remember what happened the last time Lila invoked the Cousins Pact?"

None of them were likely to forget. Lila had invoked the Cousins Pact when she broke the news that she was going to college in London. The difference between then and now was that her cousins had been completely supportive of that plan.

"Of course I do, which is why Lila's leaving Windemere before anyone can see her and hiding out at your place until we can get there and come up with a plan," Sage said while texting.

Willow opened her mouth, and then her section of the screen went dark and the word *pause* appeared. Looking relieved when she reappeared, Willow nodded. "Yeah, okay, that works."

Lila had a sneaking suspicion that Sage had texted Willow. And if the determined expression on Sage's face and the mollified one on Willow's was any indication, her cousins already had a plan—persuade Lila to dump David.

Lila had known she'd have to convince Sage and Willow that she was happy and in love and wanted nothing more than to marry David. She had a list of prompts on her phone for exactly this moment, but things had devolved since she'd made her list, and she had a feeling it would take more time than she had to convince them she was happy. At any moment, someone could discover her in the storage room. There was also another problem.

"Ruth Hollingsworth is here with her family, and I'm pretty sure her grandson saw me."

She couldn't tell them about meeting Luke in the men's restroom. Given that her teenage self couldn't seem to let go of the idea that Luke had once had a crush on her, she'd probably blush, and then, to avoid their probing questions, she'd confess she'd thrown up and had a mini-meltdown.

The last thing she needed was for her cousins to know she was upset and ticked at David . . . except how could they not know after what she'd just told them? It might take more than a few hours to convince Sage and Willow that she and David were a perfect match.

"Pretty sure? The guy knew the second you arrived at a party. He only had eyes for you. And trust me, I'd know this because I wanted those gorgeous eyes on me." Willow fanned herself. "That man is seriously hot."

"I wasn't talking about Adam," Lila said, referring to Luke's younger brother, whom she'd dated in high school. "I was talking about Luke."

Willow frowned. "Yeah, so was I."

"Don't be ridiculous, Willow. Luke Hollingsworth didn't have a thing for me," Lila said, instead of asking her cousin why she'd never told her.

"He totally did, but it doesn't matter if Luke saw you," Sage said. "His grandmother will make sure no one in her family says anything. The last thing Ruth wants is for Nonna to find out she was at Windemere."

"You're right." The tension in Lila's shoulders eased for

the first time since she and David had landed in Boston the week before. Her cousins might not agree with her decision to marry him, but they'd have her back. She'd loved living in London and working for her father, but she'd missed her family.

"I am. At least about the Hollingsworths, but Lila, you have to get out of there without anyone else seeing you. Can you do that?"

Lila nodded. "There's an emergency exit just down the hall from me."

Escaping unseen would be the easy part; figuring out what to text David and her father would be more difficult. Her dad was already worried about her, and her hasty get-away would worry him further. Then again, he'd completely understand why she didn't want to be seen at Windemere. It was only David who didn't seem to get it.

She said goodbye to her cousins and ended the call. It would take Sage a couple of hours to drive from Boston to Sunshine Bay, which was probably a good thing. Lila could work on one cousin at a time. Of the two, Willow would be easier to deal with. She might believe in the Rosetti curse, but she was also a romantic at heart. Sage was a cynical hard-ass.

Lila glanced at a text from Willow, relieved that her cousin's house was in easy walking distance. There was a key under the front mat and wine in the refrigerator. Lila grimaced. The Rosetti women loved their wine. Lila would have to pretend she was drinking. She wasn't a superstitious person, but she didn't want to jinx her pregnancy by sharing the news with her cousins.

Lila shut off the light, texting David as she walked into the empty hallway. As she closed the door behind her, her phone rang. She sighed at the name on the screen and connected the call.

"You can't leave, Lila," David said, his voice muffled. She wondered if he'd ducked under the table again.

"David, I'm not arguing about this. I'm meeting my cousins at Willow's. I can't put off telling my fam—"

"You can't leave. Your father's made a mess of everything. My mother was close to tears! It took me five minutes to calm my parents down, and my brother sat there with a smug grin on his face the entire time."

"I don't understand. Everything was fine when—"

"You ran from the table looking like you were going to throw up?"

"I did throw up!" She blew out a breath. This wasn't helping matters, and the longer she stood in the hall, the more likely it was that someone she knew would see her.

"You sound fine," he said, as if he didn't believe she'd been sick.

"Okay, I'm hanging up now," she said, heading for the emergency exit.

"No, wait. All I'm asking for is five minutes. I just need you to convince your father that you're on board with holding the wedding and reception at Windemere. You're the only one who can get through to James when he's in his lord-of-the-manor mood."

Lila stiffened, offended by the slight to her father. His parents might've been titled members of the British peerage, but there wasn't a high-and-mighty bone in James Sinclair's body. Lila's father treated everyone with kindness and respect. If anyone could be accused of acting high and mighty, it was David's father.

David continued. "My dad was trying to explain why La Dolce Vita wasn't suited to host the wedding festivities. To be honest, I can't believe your father would even suggest it. Anyway, James, in that bloody plummy voice of his, said that as you were the bride and he was paying for the wedding, it would be up to you to decide. And then he tossed his napkin on the table like it was a challenge and strode off."

She didn't like the sound of this at all. She was worried about her father's blood pressure. He'd been diagnosed with high blood pressure the year before. "Where is he?"

"He's on the patio, staring broodingly out to sea."

"Does he look okay? His coloring isn't off, is it?"

"No, he seemed..." He trailed off.

"David, what's going on?"

"I don't know. A bunch of people are crowding around him on the patio."

Lila gasped and disconnected from David, her heart racing as she ran from the hall into the restaurant. She recognized several people on the patio, including Luke and his grandmother. Ruth was wringing her hands, and Luke appeared to be comforting her. Lila searched the throng of people, her heartbeat slowing when she spotted her father. "Excuse me," she said as she made her way to him. She wouldn't be satisfied he was all right until she'd seen it with her own eyes.

She touched his arm, searching his profile. His color seemed a little high. "Dad, what's going on?"

He turned to her and lifted an eyebrow, pointing to the rolling surf. And there they were, the Heartbreakers of Sunshine Bay, her mother, her aunt, and her grandmother, frolicking in the waves, their gorgeous faces lit up with laughter.

"They didn't see you, did they?" Lila asked as she ducked behind him, peeking over his shoulder.

"Afraid so, sweetheart. Your mother was climbing the retaining wall."

Lila heard a hint of disconcerted amusement in his voice. "Why on earth would she...Oh." They'd wanted to check out the competition without being seen.

Several of the other locals in the crowd shook their heads with indulgent smiles on their faces as they shared previous antics of the Heartbreakers. Everyone in town had a story.

"What's going on?" David asked, cupping his hand over his eyes. They widened. "Is that your mother, aunt, and grandmother?"

Lila was too upset with him to respond. This was his fault. Not her mother climbing the wall, of course. But he'd put Lila in this position. There was movement to her left, and she glanced that way. It was Luke. He'd left his grandmother's side to stand at the wall, focusing on the dark, calm strip of water Lila's grandmother was headed toward. Then he yelled the word every swimmer in Sunshine Bay dreaded. "Rip!"

Lila stepped from behind her father, yelling at her mother, aunt, and grandmother with the rest of the crowd, but it was too late. Her grandmother was caught in the strong, narrow current and being pulled out to sea.

Luke kicked off his shoes and removed his white shirt and his chinos. Lila's cheeks warmed, and she averted her gaze from his muscled and golden-tanned physique. Luke Hollingsworth in black boxers was a sight to behold.

Several women gasped as he vaulted over the wall. Lila thought she might've been one of them and avoided meeting David's gaze.

Which is when she noticed that her father, along with a thirtysomething man who looked vaguely familiar, were stripping off their jackets.

Lila stopped her father with a tug on his sleeve. He was an excellent swimmer, but he wasn't used to the waters off the cape, and she worried about his blood pressure. "Look," she said, pointing to her mother and her aunt, who were swimming to her grandmother's rescue with strong, expert strokes.

"Ryan!" someone called to the other man, who was about to jump off the wall. "No need to get wet, lad. Eva and Gia have her."

Now Lila knew why he looked familiar. Ryan had been four years ahead of her and played on the high school football team with Luke.

She returned her attention to the drama in the bay, releasing a relieved sigh. Her mother and aunt—with Lila's grandmother between them—were swimming parallel to the shore and out of the rip. The Heartbreakers didn't need anyone to come to their rescue, especially a man. They took care of their own.

As the three women got closer to shore, they smiled and chatted with Luke, no doubt thanking him for his valiant rescue attempt. Then Lila's mother rose from the surf, her black wraparound dress clinging to her voluptuous curves, her long, dark hair framing a face that belonged on a movie screen. Appreciative gasps came from the men in the crowd, including Lila's father, who caught her raised-eyebrow glance and shrugged. Her mother smiled, well aware of her seductive power, but the smile didn't reach her eyes when her gaze met Lila's.

Her father put his arm around her. "It's okay, sweetheart. I'll go with you. Your mother will understand."

She glanced at her father's face. He didn't believe that any more than she did. She nodded, feeling sick to her stomach.

"Eva!" Lila looked to see Ryan galloping through the surf after her mother, high-fiving Luke as he passed him. Her mother turned, shaking her head with a laugh when Ryan lifted her into the air. He swung her around and kissed her full on the lips.

Lila cringed. Her mother would never change.

Beside her, David made a face. "That guy has to be a decade younger than her."

"And your point is?" she asked David.

"Just that..." He gave her a strained smile. "Nothing." He was about to put his arm around her when he noticed her father's was already there. He let it drop to his side. "It's probably best if I let you talk to your family alone."

"Probably," Lila agreed.

Chapter Six

Handsome boy," Eva's mother murmured as they watched Ryan head back to Windemere.

Eva nodded, unable to come up with a bawdy remark that would make her mother laugh. Her mind was busy replaying the moment she'd seen Lila standing on Windemere's patio at her father's side.

They looked alike with their honey-blond hair shining bright in the setting sun. A golden man and a golden girl. Lila had been more James's daughter than hers since she'd moved away. She imagined their reaction to Ryan twirling her around and kissing her. Lila had never approved of her unconventional lifestyle, and neither had James.

"Are we going to talk about it?" Gia asked, taking Eva's hand in hers. On Eva's other side, Carmen did the same.

Eva glanced at her mother, wondering if they should be doing this now. She'd seen the panic on her mother's face when she realized she was caught in the rip. Fear, an emotion Eva was unfamiliar with when it came to Carmen, had closed a tight fist around her heart. Not because she was afraid her mother would drown—Eva and her sister were accomplished swimmers, well equipped to deal with the currents in Sunshine Bay—but because it was the first time her mother had looked her age, and Eva had realized Carmen wasn't invincible.

Her fingers tightened around her mother's hand. Carmen glanced at her and gave Eva's hand a reassuring squeeze as if she sensed her fears. Gia mustn't have noticed, her voice cutting through a silence as heavy as the humidity. "I know we're all thinking it."

Their mother nodded. "It's James. He owns Windemere, and our Lila works for him."

"Lila and her friend. The one we met in London," her sister said when Eva looked at her blankly. "David. I saw him on the patio, standing next to Lila."

Eva hadn't noticed him. She'd had eyes only for her daughter and James. Then again, Lila's friend hadn't made much of an impression on her when she'd met him.

Gia glanced from Eva to their mother. "You two seem unnaturally calm about it."

Carmen shrugged as the three of them walked hand in hand out of the surf and onto the sand just up from La Dolce Vita. Unlike Windemere, their restaurant was built far enough from the shore to escape the rising tide. The only time the water reached the restaurant's deck was in a storm.

Gia jiggled Eva's hand, nodding at their mother with a look on her face that reflected the fear that had gripped Eva's heart fifteen minutes before. Was that how long it had been? It felt like a lifetime.

At the resigned expression that now came over their mother's face, Eva's temper broke through the shock that had blanketed her emotions. "So what, Ma? We're just supposed to give up now?"

"Our customers have abandoned us. Even my best friend and my granddaughter. People are like rats; they know when a ship is sinking. Maybe it's time we face reality. We can't compete with Windemere."

"We can, and we will," Eva said, furious at Ruth and Lila. Their defection had wounded Carmen deeply, especially Lila's. Her daughter's betrayal was the straw that had broken Carmen's fighting spirit. Family stuck together through thick and thin. It didn't matter that James was Lila's family too. Eva expected better of her daughter, better of James.

"Eva's right, Ma. We're not giving up. We'll figure this out. We're the Rosettis. We're unstoppable."

Their mother let go of their hands as they reached La Dolce Vita's gray, weathered deck, looking to where a couple sat at one of the tables, a candle flickering between them.

Carmen patted Gia's cheek and then Eva's. "*I miei curio*, my hearts. I love you," she said, and then she trudged up the stairs, offering the couple a faint smile and a "*Buon appetito*" as she walked by.

"Oh, Eva, what are we going to do?" her sister asked, her voice thick with emotion.

Eva watched as their mother walked to the far end of the deck and took the set of stairs to her apartment. Eva's and Gia's apartments were on either side of hers. They'd raised their daughters here, sharing meals at a table in the corner of the restaurant's dining room, where later they'd take turns watching through the window as the girls built castles in the sand.

La Dolce Vita was their home, their life, it was who they were. It had been there for them in the good times and the bad times, and Eva would fight for it until her last breath.

"We'll update the menu, match our hours to Windemere, reward our loyal customers, and hold special events." Eva listed the ideas by rote. She'd shared them with her mother when they'd first learned about Windemere, but Carmen had refused to change a single thing. They had no choice now. She hoped her mother understood that.

"I was going to say Ma won't agree to implement any of your ideas—which are excellent, by the way—but she . . ." Gia swiped a finger under her eye. "I'm worried, Eva. I've never seen her like this."

"She'll be okay, G. She had a shock, too many for one day. She'll be herself in the morning."

Gia bumped her shoulder against Eva's as they walked up the stairs to the deck. "What about you? You've had a shock too."

Eva nodded, forcing a smile as they walked past the couple eating the day's special. She'd normally stop and ask if they were enjoying their meal, but her emotions were too close to the surface. Her mother wasn't the only one hurt by Lila's betrayal.

Bruno stepped onto the deck. He took one look at them and opened his arms. Gia stepped into them readily, but Eva held back, afraid she'd break down in his warm, sympathetic embrace.

She cleared her throat. "Who told you?"

"Ruth called. She was beside herself." He held Eva's gaze. "She mentioned that Lila and James were there." He kissed Gia on the top of her wet head and then came to Eva. Taking her face between his big hands, he pressed his forehead to hers.

"There must be an explanation, *cara*. Our Lila loves you and La Dolce Vita. Nothing means more to her than her family."

"James does."

"He's her family too. But he's a good man." He straightened and chucked her under the chin, no doubt in response to the face she was making. Bruno had always liked James. "He wouldn't do anything to jeopardize Lila's relationship with her family or your business."

"He stole her away from us."

Bruno sighed. "No, he gave her an opportunity that she couldn't get here. She's found a career that she loves. She's become the woman you wanted her to be—strong and self-reliant. You let her fly, and now she's come back to you."

"To put us out of business," she muttered, even though what Bruno said held a ring of truth. And maybe that was why it hurt so much to think that her daughter would betray them.

Bruno shook his head with a smile. "You're stubborn like your mother."

"We're worried about her, Bruno," Gia said. "She's not acting like herself. She's gone to her apartment."

His smile faded, and his gaze went to the white-capped waves rolling onto the shore. "She was lucky you two were there. I don't like to think..." He shook his head as if clearing the image from his mind. Despite Carmen's having rejected his marriage proposal years before, Bruno still loved her. Eva believed that their mother loved him too in her own way. "I'll go to her after you both get changed."

"What about Ana? I thought you had a date tonight," Eva said.

Bruno had been dating Ana for more than a year. She

was a nice woman who had the patience of a saint when it came to Bruno's devotion to the Rosetti women. But even a saint ran out of patience, and Eva didn't want Bruno to jeopardize his relationship with Ana because of them.

"We weren't doing anything special. She'll understand. And you"—he pointed a stern finger at Eva—"keep a lid on your temper and give your daughter a chance to explain."

"How do you know she wants to explain anything to me?"

"Because you left your phone on the bar, and I recognize Lila's ringtone. She's been calling you nonstop for the past fifteen minutes. And before you ask, no, I didn't answer. I'm not your mother." He reached in his pants pocket and pulled out her phone, handing it back to her.

She pressed it to her chest. Surely her daughter wouldn't be anxious to reach her if she were involved in Windemere. "Lila loves you too, you know," Eva said to Bruno, leaning in to kiss his cheek. "And so do we."

"We do, and we'd be lost without you," Gia said, taking his hand in hers.

"Then it's a good thing I'm not planning on going anywhere," Bruno said, his voice gruff. "Now go get changed. I'll prepare a tray for your mother."

Eva and her sister picked up the shoes they'd left to the right of the door, and then Eva brought her phone to her ear. As she took the stairs to her apartment, she listened to the message Lila had left her.

"Mom, I'm so sorry. I know how you, Zia, and Nonna must have felt when you saw me. I had no idea I was going to Windemere. You have to believe me. It's the last place I wanted to be. I wouldn't do that to you, to any of you. I'll...I'll explain everything when I see you. I love you."

A small, relieved sob escaped from Eva before she could contain it, and her sister reached for her. "What is it?"

"Lila. She has nothing to do with Windemere. The poor thing feels so bad. You should've heard her."

"Let me." Gia gestured for Eva to replay the message.

Eva did, and she and her sister shared teary-eyed smiles. As much as Lila's suspected betrayal had hurt Carmen and Eva, it would've hurt Gia too. She was a second mother to Lila. Just as Eva was a second mother to her nieces.

"I feel bad for thinking the worst of Lila," Eva murmured. "Bruno was right. I should've known better. Lila loves us and La Dolce Vita too much to have agreed to work for James at Windemere."

"You still think James owns Windemere?" Gia asked as she opened her apartment door. It was the apartment where their mother had raised Eva and her sisters. She'd given it to Gia when she'd moved back home with Sage and Willow more than twenty-five years earlier. Gia had converted the main bedroom to an art studio once the girls moved out.

"Of course. Why else would he be here?"

"You're right. I just . . ." Gia shrugged. "I expected better of him, I guess."

"You're just like Bruno. You always saw the best in James."

"Even you have to admit that he's a wonderful father, Eva. Lila adores him."

And why wouldn't she? James was everything a girl could ask for in a father. When Lila was younger, there'd been times when Eva had wished he weren't so perfect or so rich. He could give their daughter everything, make all her dreams come true, whereas all Eva could offer was her love, hers and her family's.

Except James had offered her that too. His wife had been a lovely woman who'd gone out of her way to make Lila feel like a part of their family, and Lila had two younger half sisters whom she adored. "If he was so wonderful, he would've put his daughter's feelings above his business interests."

"I know, which is why I can't help but wonder if we've got this wrong. As much as you and James have had your difficulties, he wouldn't intentionally set out to hurt Lila or our family. He has to know that's exactly what his involvement in Windemere would do."

"I agree, but I can't think of any other reason for him being at Windemere, and he's the only one who'd be able to convince Lila to attend the grand opening."

Gia nodded as she stepped inside her apartment. "It would explain why her colleague, David, was there."

"We'll have our answers soon enough," Eva said, anxious to see her daughter despite the news she'd share about James and Windemere. Eva would have to be careful how she reacted because no matter how Lila felt about the family and La Dolce Vita, she was extremely protective of her father.

While showering and changing into another black wraparound dress, Eva practiced how she'd react to the news. She still hadn't settled on the best way to respond when she met her sister coming out of their mother's apartment. "Is Ma feeling any better?"

Gia shook her head. Like Eva, she hadn't taken the time to fully dry her hair and wore it pulled back in a ponytail.

"She's in bed. I got a small smile and a nod when I told her about Lila's message, and then she pulled the covers to her chin and turned over."

"Bruno will get through to her, and if he can't, the girls will. Knowing Lila, she's already called Sage and Willow," Eva said as they made their way to the deck.

"The Cousins Pact," Gia said, and they shared a smile.

"It would be nice if my daughter wasn't the only one who's invoked it in the past decade," Eva said, holding the door open for Bruno, who was carrying a tray with several covered dishes and a pot of coffee.

He nodded his thanks. "I've had the staff seat customers at the bar and at the front of the restaurant so you'll have privacy at the family table."

Eva frowned. "Why? When Lila gets here, we'll go up to my apartment."

"She's here, and so is James. I thought you'd prefer meeting in the restaurant, but if—"

"No, you're right." As much as Eva loved her apartment, the lush fabrics and bold colors couldn't hide the signs that the roof and windows leaked or that the floorboards were damaged. The restaurant showed the same signs of wear, and as Eva walked toward the family table in the back corner of the dining room, she couldn't help but compare it to Windemere.

But none of that mattered when she saw her daughter, sitting ashen faced beside her father. And all the carefully worded reactions Eva had practiced while in the shower went out the window.

"How could you?" she practically spit the words at James, who stood as she reached the table.

"Mom, Dad—" Lila began, coming to her feet.

"None of this is your fault, darling," she said, wrapping her arms around her daughter. She pulled back, searching Lila's pale face. Her daughter had been plagued by a nervous stomach since she was a little girl. "Sit. I'll be right back."

Eva cast James another damning glare before heading to the bar. She pulled a basket of breadsticks toward her and filled a glass with ginger ale while scanning the front of the restaurant. There were more waitstaff than customers. She waved over one of their longtime servers, Heather, a young mother with twin boys under five. "After you cash out your table, you can take the rest of the night off. Gia and I can handle it."

An anxious look came over Heather's face, reminding Eva that it wasn't only the Rosettis who needed La Dolce Vita to survive, it was also their staff, who were more like family. Most of them had been with them for years.

"Don't worry, you'll be paid for the hours on the schedule. Take some treats home for the boys." Eva put a hand on Heather's shoulder in response to the question in her eyes, one she no doubt didn't want to ask. Eva imagined the rest of the staff were also wondering if La Dolce Vita could survive the competition. "We'll have a meeting in the morning. I have some ideas on how we can turn things around, and I want to hear what all of you think."

Heather leaned across the bar. "A couple of staff applied at Windemere."

Her mother was right about people abandoning a sinking ship.

Eva nodded. She might be hurt, but she also understood

that their staff had to look out for themselves. "We'd hate to lose you, but if you—"

Heather looked offended. "I'm not going anywhere, and anyone who does is an idiot. No one takes care of their staff the way you do. I'll be at the meeting tomorrow, and I'll let everyone in our group chat know. Ten work for you?"

"Thank you. It does. And let everyone know kids are welcome. We'll set them up at the family table."

Several of their staff were single mothers who relied on babysitters and family members, who often had to cancel on short notice. As a family of single mothers, the Rosettis knew how tough it was, and they had an open-door policy where children were concerned. There were times when Bruno said they might as well open up a day care.

"The boys will be thrilled. They've been trying to get my mom to cancel so they can come to work with me."

"Tell them I'll have their yogurt cake and cookies ready for them."

Heather smiled. "If my mother hears that, she'll come too."

Eva was about to say she was welcome to join them when Willow wheeled her pink scooter into the restaurant. Her niece bringing the scooter inside wasn't a surprise— her last one had been stolen from the restaurant's parking lot. But seeing her wearing a cover-up over a yellow polka-dot bikini and an inflatable duck around her waist was somewhat surprising.

The few customers they had in the restaurant turned in their seats. "What's the forecast for tomorrow, Willow?" one of their regulars called out.

"Eighty in the shade with a light wind from the north,

Tom," Willow said, glancing over her shoulder when three twentysomething men followed her inside.

Heather looked at Eva, her eyes dancing. "I have a suggestion on how we can increase business."

"Don't even," Eva said, returning her niece's air-kiss.

"Bring wine, Zia, and lots of it. We're going to need it," Willow said as she wheeled her scooter to the back of the restaurant.

"Go. I'll bring it," Heather said, and then went to head off the three young men who attempted to follow Willow, offering them seats at the bar.

Willow had parked her scooter against the wall and was greeting her mother and Lila when Eva reached the table. As Eva set the breadsticks and ginger ale in front of her daughter, Willow turned her attention on James.

"Zio James," she said, leaning in to kiss his cheek, hitting him in the face with the duck she'd obviously forgotten she was wearing.

After talking to Heather, Eva felt like hitting him too, only he wouldn't be smiling. It annoyed her that she found his smile as attractive as ever and that her niece still insisted on calling him *Uncle* James. Sage was the same.

Eva had tried to break them of the habit over the years, but it didn't work. Not surprising, she supposed. Whenever James had come to see Lila—their visits had taken place in Sunshine Bay until she was twelve—he'd arrive bearing gifts, and he'd always brought something for Sage and Willow too. He'd spoiled the three of them, especially at Christmas, shipping over boxes of presents. Whenever money was tight—which, to be honest, was most of the time—Eva and Gia would mark half of them as being from Santa.

"Sorry about that." Willow laughed and removed the duck from her waist. She leaned in and hugged James. "It's nice to see you."

"Obviously when Lila invoked the Cousins Pact, she didn't share that her father owns Windemere," Eva said, pulling out the chair between her daughter and Gia.

James frowned. "I what?"

Suddenly weary and deflated, Eva dropped onto the chair. "Oh, please, don't try and deny it, James."

"Eva, I have nothing to do with Windemere."

His deep voice with his sexy British accent had always done it for her, in bed and out. It was annoying that it still had the power to make her toes curl. "I don't bel—"

"Mom, it's true. David's father owns controlling interest in Windemere." Lila ducked her head and took a sip of her ginger ale.

"Your colleague from London?" Eva asked, looking from Lila to James when he slid a protective arm around their daughter.

"David's more than a colleague, Mom." Her daughter's voice dropped, and she mumbled, "He's my fiancé."

"Sorry, I must have misunderstood. I thought you said he's your fiancé." At the looks on her sister's and niece's faces, Eva's laugh sputtered and died in her throat. "Tell me you did not just say you're engaged to that boy, Lila Marie Rosetti."

"Lila Marie Rosetti *Sinclair*," James said, his glacial blue eyes holding Eva's gaze, warning her in his not-so-subtle way to tread carefully.

Her sister did the same—only she lightly pinched Eva's thigh instead of staring her down.

"This is exactly why I put off telling you, Mom. I knew how you'd react. How all of you'd react," she said with a sweeping gesture around the table.

"Don't include me, sweetheart. I'm happy for you. David's a good—"

"Did you expect us to cheer, to be happy for you, Lila?" Eva asked, cutting off James. "We love you, and the last thing we want is for you to be hurt, and that's exactly what will happen if you go through with this. You know our family's history." She reached for her daughter's hand, ignoring the twinge of hurt when Lila pulled it away. "We are—"

"I don't believe in the Rosetti curse, and even if I did, I wouldn't let some silly superstition dictate my choices in life."

Eva turned to her sister. "Do you hear that, G? Your niece believes the curse is nothing more than a silly superstition. Perhaps you want to enlighten her."

"I'm sorry, Zia. I'm not trying to belittle your suffering or Nonna's or any of the Rosetti women's," Lila said, and then she looked at Eva with an obstinate lift of her chin.

Lila might look like her father, but she'd inherited her grandmother's stubbornness.

"But I'm marrying David, and nothing you can say will change my mind. I love you, and I want you to be part of my wedding, but if you can't support me and be happy for me . . . " She trailed off with a shrug as if it didn't matter to her, but Eva saw the shimmer of tears in her eyes.

"Oh, darling, of course we'll support you. There's nothing we want more than your happiness, and if you believe marrying David will make you happy, then who are we to stand in your way?" Eva smiled, and James's eyes narrowed while around the table her daughter, sister, and niece blinked.

They had good reason to doubt her. She wasn't about to let this David and his marriage proposal tear her and Lila apart by objecting to the wedding, but neither was she about to let her daughter make the biggest mistake of her life. Eva just needed time to convince Lila that marrying David would bring her nothing but heartache.

She pushed back from the table and stood up. "This calls for a celebration. I'll get the champagne."

Chapter Seven

Gia looked at Eva as if she'd lost her mind. No doubt her sister had been waiting for Eva to list all the reasons why Lila was making the biggest mistake of her life and then forbid her from going through with the wedding, threatening that if she did, she'd wash her hands of her. It's what their mother had done when Gia told them she was getting married, and it had nearly torn their family apart.

When her sister opened her mouth, Eva told her in rapid-fire Italian—their daughters had never learned the language—that she was just buying time without alienating Lila, but one way or another, they'd stop the wedding.

Her sister's shoulders lowered from around her ears. "That's a good plan." Gia winced, realizing she'd spoken in English, and tried to cover her slip. "Brand. That's a good brand of champagne."

Eva had a feeling that Gia hadn't been quick enough to cover her slip when James stood up. "I'll give you a hand."

Eva waved him off. "Thank you, but it's not necessary."

"I insist," he said, his long-legged stride eating the short distance between them. He leaned in to her as they walked toward the bar. "Whatever you're planning, forget about it."

She shivered in reaction to his warm breath caressing her ear. It was annoying how easily she responded to him. "I have no idea what you're talking about."

He repeated what she'd said to her sister... in Italian.

"I have no idea what you just said. Your accent is atrocious." It wasn't. It was perfect.

His lips lifted at the corner. "I have it on good authority that my accent is flawless."

"How old was she?" The words were out of her mouth before she realized how inappropriate they were, and she briefly closed her eyes. She reached out an apologetic hand and touched his arm. "I'm sorry, James. That was a thoughtless thing to say."

He shrugged off her apology. "I'm used to your sense of humor, Eva."

"I know, but I shouldn't tease you. It hasn't been that long since you lost Grace."

His wife had been an elegant blond beauty, the exact antithesis of Eva. She'd had a soft, cultured voice that Lila swore she never raised. There'd been a time when Eva had resented the woman who was a paragon of virtue in her daughter's eyes, but over the years, her feelings about Grace had changed.

As a mother herself, Grace had been understanding and sympathetic to Eva's worries about Lila living far from home, unlike James, who'd thought she was overreacting and being neurotic. It wasn't long before Eva was corresponding with Grace instead of James, and Eva liked to think they'd become friends.

"It's been over two years," James said, the clipped tone of his voice clearly indicating that he didn't want to talk about it.

The sharpness in his voice didn't hurt or offend her as it had when they were together that long-ago summer. She was older and wiser and understood that his ironclad control over his emotions had more to do with him than with her. James didn't cope well with messy feelings and drama.

He glanced at her. "I know how you and your family feel about marriage, Eva, and I know you're just trying to protect Lila from being hurt. But she's not a little girl anymore. She's a strong, independent woman who knows what she wants."

"And you think she wants to marry this man, this David?" Eva looked over her shoulder at her daughter, who was talking to Gia and Willow. The conversation didn't appear to be a happy one. "She doesn't look like a blushing bride-to-be to me. Does she to you?"

"She was upset you saw her at Windemere, and of course she was nervous about telling you." He looked away, shoving his fingers through his hair.

"What aren't you telling me?"

He lowered his hand and took her by the elbow, steering her toward a table for two where they were out of their daughter's view. "You'll hear about it soon enough, and maybe it's better you hear it from me first." He pulled out the chair for her. "Do you want something to drink?"

"Am I going to need it?" she asked as she lowered herself onto the chair.

He nodded. "Yeah, and I could use one too. I'll get it," he said when she started to get up from the chair.

Heather intercepted him as he turned to leave. She had a bottle of wine tucked under her arm and five glasses in her hands. "Sorry, Eva. I got tied up with the frat boys. They wanted Boston sours, and I had to look it up."

Eva usually worked the bar, but she kept a laminated list of the ingredients for cocktails taped to the counter. One of their servers acted as her backup, and she was on tonight. "Where's Sam?"

"She, uh, left early."

Eva had a feeling Sam was one of the servers who'd applied at Windemere. She was one of Eva's more recent hires. "You should've called me."

"It was fine, really." Heather glanced from Eva to the family table. "Do you want me to leave this with you or bring—" She broke off when Gia hurried over.

"Thanks, Heather." Her sister retrieved the bottle and two wineglasses and set them in front of Eva. "When you have a minute... Never mind, I'll get it myself," Gia said to Heather, and then looked at James, who'd taken the seat across from Eva. "You're going to tell her?" It was more an order than a question.

He nodded.

"Good." Gia gave Eva's shoulder what she must've meant to be a reassuring squeeze but that was anything but, given the expression on her sister's face.

"What is it?"

Her sister smiled, but the look in her eyes said *you're going to lose your mind.* "Lila was sharing her wedding plans with us." Gia glanced at the bottle of wine. "You might need something stronger."

James's broad shoulders rose on a sigh. "I know I will."

Gia nodded and followed Heather back to the bar.

"So you and Lila have already discussed wedding plans without me," Eva said as she poured herself a glass of wine, hurt by the thought, despite knowing it was an irrational reaction.

Of course, given her stance on marriage, they would've gone ahead with the plans without her. She just hoped they weren't too far along in the planning stage. She needed time to change her daughter's mind.

"Okay, don't act like the wounded party. The last thing Lila would expect is that you'd want to help plan her wedding, Eva."

"What mother wouldn't want to be involved in her daughter's wedding, James?"

"You," he said dryly. He glanced at Gia when she plunked a bottle of Jack Daniel's and an old-fashioned glass in front of him.

"Good luck," her sister murmured, and then she headed for the family table with a tray of champagne flutes and a bottle of champagne.

"Look, Eva, Lila didn't want a big wedding. She'd planned to get married at the courthouse."

She caught a whiff of caramel as he poured the whiskey into his glass.

"But David's mother was understandably excited about her son getting married, and, well . . . she got a little carried away."

A simple wedding at the courthouse might've been harder for Eva to interfere with, so she was almost relieved to hear that David's mother had other plans. "Exactly how carried away did she get?"

"She's invited three hundred guests for a weekend-long wedding at . . ." He took a long swallow of his whiskey before continuing, "In Sunshine Bay."

"Funny, I don't remember getting our invitation." Eva drummed her fingers on the table. A weekend-long wedding was ideal—so many opportunities for things to go wrong. But Eva planned to have the wedding called off long before then. "I suppose she was waiting for our guest list. It'll take some time to put it together, but I'm sure there's no rush."

James narrowed his eyes as if suspicious of her mild reaction. "The wedding is a month from now."

"Excuse me?" Her voice went up into screechy territory, which actually seemed to alleviate James's suspicions. But it did little to alleviate her panic. She had only a matter of weeks to change Lila's mind.

James nodded, took another long swallow of his drink, and then cleared his throat. "Don't get upset. I'm working on this, but they're planning on holding the wedding at Windemere."

She was staring at him—stunned—when an all-too-familiar heated flush worked its way from the tips of her toes to the top of her head. This couldn't be happening now. She grabbed the menu off the table, frantically fanning herself to keep the sweat at bay. "Who does this woman"— a droplet rolled down her nose and onto the table. Fan, fan, fan—"think she is?"

Madonna santo, now the sweat was pouring off her, and James was staring at her with an alarmed expression on his face. "Are you having a heart attack?" he asked, rising from his chair as if to call someone over.

She tugged on his sleeve to get him to sit down. "Don't make a scene," she said, and it struck her as funny because the last person to make a scene was Mr. Calm and Coolly Collected. Or it would've struck her as funny if she weren't melting in a puddle of sweat. "I'm not having a heart attack. I'm having a...hot flash."

"You had me worried for a minute," he said, getting up from the table.

At that point Eva was too busy mopping at her brow and chest with a napkin to ask where he was going. He returned with two bar towels and a bucket of ice. He filled one of the towels with ice and then draped it around the back of her neck. Then he dipped the other towel in the bucket of ice and water, wrung it out, took the menu from her hand, gave her the damp towel, and began fanning her himself.

She moaned her appreciation. "How did you know to do that?"

"Grace. She went into early menopause after the surgery."

"Bless her, and I don't mean that in a southern way. Getting older—" She bowed her head. Grace would've given anything to grow older, and here Eva was complaining about it.

"I have high blood pressure," he admitted, graciously letting her remark slide.

"Lila told me. She was worried about you, and so were her sisters."

"They acted like I had one foot in the grave."

After losing Grace, Eva imagined the girls had been terrified they'd lose their father too. "Is that why you sold your company?"

"Yes and no. After Grace died, my priorities changed. I

took a good, long look at my life and didn't like what I saw. I wasn't living my life so much as going through the motions." He angled his glass at her. "I can't believe you thought I bought Windemere."

"It was the only reason I could think of for you being there. You and Lila." She removed the towel. The ice was melting and dripping down her back, and her hot flash had passed.

"Jennifer called and shared their plans. She wanted me here to surprise Lila." At Eva's raised brow, he said, "Yes. I know how much our daughter hates surprises, but I figured she could use the support."

"Because I was going to go off the deep end?"

"You and the rest of your family. And the fact that you're not can mean only one thing, so I'm going to warn you right now, I won't let you ruin this for Lila."

And they'd been having such a nice conversation up until then. She should've known it wouldn't last. "I've just learned that my daughter has been secretly engaged for months and is having an extravagant weekend-long wedding at the resort that is in all likelihood going to put us out of business, so forgive me if I'm not reacting how you expected, James. I'm in shock."

"You're right. Sorry. And I hate to pile it on, but you should know that Gavin, David's father, asked him to manage Windemere, and David accepted. They're using the wedding to boost Windemere's profile."

"And Lila was okay with this? Okay with marrying a man who will be responsible for putting her family out of business?"

"Of course she wasn't," he said, sharing Lila's reaction

to the news with her. "But what was she supposed to do, Eva? David needs a job, and I'm sure he's used the added inducement that they'll be living in Sunshine Bay."

Eva didn't know how she was going to break the news to her mother. "Did they offer Lila a job too?"

"No, and you know she wouldn't take it if they did." He looked around the restaurant. "How big of a hit have you taken?"

"Too big to sustain for long. If we don't turn our numbers around, we'll have to close at the end of the season."

"I told the Westfields that since I'm paying for the wedding, and Lila is the bride, that she should have some say, and at least some of the wedding festivities should be held here. Gavin wasn't impressed, and I'm afraid I hurt Jennifer's feelings. I may have been somewhat abrupt, but in my defense, I'd just watched our daughter run off looking like she was going to throw up."

"My poor baby. I don't know how you can support this wedding after what you've just told me."

He shrugged. "I'm not the one marrying into the family, Lila is. She's smart and cautious. She doesn't jump into anything without thinking it through. The only reason she'd get married is if she wanted to."

He was right. Lila didn't make a decision without going through a long list of pros and cons. And Eva knew from experience that no one could convince her daughter to do something she didn't want to do. But after everything Eva had heard about David and his family and her daughter's reaction to the wedding plans, she was more determined than ever to sabotage the wedding. She'd just have to proceed carefully, especially with James around.

"Thank you for suggesting some of the wedding festivities take place here." She didn't know how her mother would react—dramatically, no doubt—but it was kind of James to think of them.

"It's only fair, but I'm not sure the Westfields are on board." He glanced at the menu. "If you want, I can brainstorm a few ideas with how you might turn things around here. Sometimes it takes an outsider to see what you can't."

She'd be a fool not to take him up on his offer, and Eva Rosetti was no fool. James had run a highly successful and profitable hotel conglomerate for decades and knew the hospitality industry inside out.

"I have some ideas on how we can turn things around, but if you have the time, I'd like to hear your take on things. When do you fly back to London?"

"After the wedding."

"You're staying in Sunshine Bay for a month?" she asked, praying she'd misunderstood him.

"I am. I rented a beach house."

"That's—" She broke off when she spotted Sage striding to the back of the restaurant with a determined look on her face. Eva had no doubt her niece was here to stage an intervention. "Excuse me," Eva said to James, jumping up from the table.

"Sage, darling!" Eva hurried to her niece's side. "I'm so glad you're here. Lila has just shared her happy news with us, and we're going to celebrate!" Eva said loud enough for her daughter to hear.

Sage looked at her as if she was waiting for the punch line, and Eva lowered her voice. "Play along. As soon as Lila leaves, the four of us will come up with a plan to stop the wedding. Smile," she ordered her niece as she backed away, something unyielding blocking her retreat. She turned.

James stood there with his arms crossed and both eyebrows raised.

"Look who's here, Sage. Your zio James." Eva dragged her niece to face James, ensuring that he didn't have a chance to lecture Eva as she hurried to the family table and picked up the bottle of champagne.

"Eva, wait, don't—" her sister began as Eva popped the cork and a plume of champagne sprayed her daughter and niece.

"—open it yet. It fell on the floor," Gia finished with a sigh.

Chapter Eight

Do you really think this is a good idea, honey? Maybe we should put it off for a couple of days." David cast a hopeful glance at Lila as he pulled the candy apple–red Ferrari convertible into the driveway of her father's beach house the next afternoon.

It was a terrible idea, the worst idea ever, but she hadn't had the heart to hurt her mother's feelings when Eva suggested a meet-the-family tea as Lila and her father were leaving La Dolce Vita the night before. Except, other than her mother, Lila's family would be a no-show. She wouldn't have her cousins there for backup. They'd bailed earlier this morning, citing work as an excuse. Lila didn't believe them.

"And why would we put off your parents meeting my mother, David? Shouldn't she get a say in the wedding plans? After all, she is the mother of the *bride*." No matter how many times David had apologized to her in the last eighteen hours, Lila hadn't been able to forgive him for blindsiding her and her family.

Her grandmother had taken to her bed, and as far as Lila knew, she was still there. Lila's mother and aunt were worried about her. So worried they'd yet to share the news about Lila's upcoming wedding and her connection with Windemere. Which was why her aunt and her nonna wouldn't be at this afternoon's meet-the-family tea either.

"Of course my parents are looking forward to meeting your mother. It's just that, with how your family feels about marriage, I didn't think she'd have any interest in our wedding plans."

"Well, she does." Lila wouldn't admit it to David, but she'd been shocked that her mother wanted anything to do with the wedding.

She'd been equally surprised by how easily her mother had acquiesced after her initial reaction. Her aunt and cousins had been the same. Lila should be happy that they'd put their feelings aside to support her, but she was more unsettled by it than anything. Even the news that David had agreed to manage Windemere hadn't shaken her mother's resolve to put a positive spin on everything. She was of course thrilled that Lila was moving home to Sunshine Bay, and thanks to Lila's father, her mother believed that at least half of the wedding festivities would be held at La Dolce Vita. Something Lila should probably work out with David now.

But as she opened her mouth to do just that, her father came around the side of the house wearing a pair of navy shorts and white T-shirt, tugging on a garden hose. He lifted his head and smiled. "Do you need a hand with your bags?"

Lila sighed. Her discussion with David about where the wedding festivities were going to be held would have to wait.

"We're good, thanks," David said, and then he lowered his voice. "I don't like this, Lila. I don't like it at all. You should be staying with me at Windemere. The manager's suite is beautiful."

"You've made it perfectly clear how you feel about it, David. But lately you seem unwilling or unable to see anything from my perspective."

They'd spent the majority of the drive back from Boston arguing about her decision. Her father had loaned them his rental car the night before so they could drive to Boston and pack up their things at the condo. Gavin had insisted David start work right away and had scheduled a meeting with the head chef for later today.

"Maybe because it makes no sense to me. We lived together for a year in London, and we're getting married. We're not living in the Dark Ages."

"You mean in a time when women didn't have any rights and their opinions didn't matter?"

He pushed his glasses up the bridge of his nose with the tip of his forefinger. "Fine, do what you want. But I can't see your mother being any happier than I am that you're staying with James."

David had always been a little jealous of how close she was to her father. He had that in common with her mother. "I'll stay with my dad for two weeks, and then I'll move in with my mom."

At David's dejected expression, she relented. As much as she wanted him to see things from her perspective, it was only fair that she try and see things from his. She knew why taking the job with his father was important to him, just as she knew he needed a job and would do an excellent one managing Windemere. She also knew he wanted their wedding to be special—a big celebration of their love—and even if it was the last thing she wanted, she couldn't fault him for that. It was actually pretty sweet and romantic.

"It might be fun, you know. We've spent every minute of every day together for the past year. We could use a little adventure and romance. We can pretend we're dating."

He nodded slowly, clearly not convinced. "I suppose, but it's not like I can take time off whenever I want."

He'd always been the first one in at the office and the last one to leave. She admired his work ethic. "I wouldn't expect you to, but it's not as if you'll be working twenty-four/seven."

"I might be. With my brother waiting in the wings, I have to prove to my father that his faith in me was justified." He got out of the car and glanced at her father, who was now watering a mass of pink rosebushes that hugged the gray-shingled beach house. "If you'd like, I'm sure I can get you the name of a gardener, James."

"I'm good, thanks. It's time I got some new hobbies."

"You mean hobbies other than work," Lila said as she got out of the car, happy to see her father looking relaxed as he watered the garden. She lifted her phone and took his picture.

He shook his head with a smile. "Photographic evidence for your sisters that your dad's turned into an old fart?"

She laughed. Her father couldn't look like an old fart if he tried. He was in great shape and didn't look a day over thirty-five. "Evidence that you're not surfing tsunami-high waves or swimming with sharks."

"Yet." He waggled his eyebrows. "They're on my list."

Lila wouldn't share that with her sisters. She'd promised she'd keep their father from doing anything overly adventurous. She slipped her phone into the pocket of her white shorts and went to grab the last two pieces of her luggage as David made his way around the side of the beach house with her other bags.

As she hauled them out of the back seat, a car's obnoxiously loud rumble drew her attention, and she glanced over her shoulder. At the sight of her grandmother's mint-green 1967 Ford Mustang coming down the road, she braced herself. Her mother had arrived.

Eva parked alongside the curb and got out of the car. She wore tangerine shorts with a matching short-sleeved shirt tied at her waist. Her brightly colored outfit highlighted her tanned skin and her gold jewelry—big hoop earrings, necklace, and bangles—and showed off her curvy figure.

"Ciao," Eva said with a bright smile, a wicker hamper swinging in her hand as she walked up the driveway in a pair of wedge sandals that showed off her long, golden-brown legs.

"Hey, Mom," Lila said, frowning at the feel of cold water on her feet. She looked down to see her flip-flops drowning in a puddle of muddy water, courtesy of the hose hanging limply from her father's hand as he stared open-mouthed at her mother. "Really, Dad?"

Dragging his glazed gaze from her mother, he followed Lila's pointed stare. "Sorry about that." He tossed the hose onto the lawn and held out his hand to her mother. "Let me take that."

Lila was carrying two heavy bags, and he was offering to take her mother's wicker hamper?

"Thank you," Eva said, looking into Lila's father's eyes with a slow, sexy smile spreading over her gorgeous face.

Eva was the biggest flirt Lila had ever met, so seeing that familiar smile on her face shouldn't have come as a surprise. But her mother did not share flirty smiles with her father, and her father did not look at her mother with a starstruck expression on his face.

Maybe Lila had been wrong in assuming that a fight breaking out between her mother and the Westfields over the wedding was the worst thing that could happen today.

"How did your meeting go?" Lila's father asked her mother.

"Good. The staff shared some of what they've been hearing from customers and offered a few suggestions. I'd like to run them by you and get your opinion whenever you have time."

Say what? Her mother wanted her father's opinion?

"I'd be happy to. Maybe you can stick around after the Westfields leave and—"

"Hold it," Lila said. "Since when do you want Dad's opinion on anything, Mom?"

"Since the restaurant your fiancé will be managing cut our business by fifty-five percent," her mother said at the same time David returned from bringing her bags inside.

Brilliant, Lila. Impeccable timing as always.

But in her defense, whatever was going on between her parents was setting her nerves on edge. Her mother wasn't nicknamed a Heartbreaker for no reason, and the last thing Lila wanted was for her father to have his heart broken again. It was only in the last few months that he'd been more like himself. He wasn't exactly an open book when it came to his feelings, but she knew her stepmother's death had affected him deeply.

David gave her mother a weak smile. "Hi, Eva," he said as he went to take the luggage from Lila's hands.

"'Hi, Eva'? Surely I deserve a hug at least."

David's cheeks flushed, and he lowered the bags to give her mother a perfunctory hug.

Eva stepped back and patted his cheek. "Such a brave, brave boy," she said on a mournful sigh.

"Mom!"

"What? It's true." Her mother placed a hand on her voluptuous chest and widened her stunning green eyes. "Oh no, you didn't tell him about the family curse, did you, darling?"

"Yes, Mom, I did, and David doesn't believe in it any more than I do."

"The arrogance of youth, I suppose. Still, to be on the safe side, I'd make sure your affairs were in order, David. Thirty percent of Rosetti women's fiancés die before they make it to the altar."

"Why don't we go inside?" her father suggested, placing a firm hand at the small of her mother's back.

"What happened to the other seventy percent?" David asked as he took the bags from Lila and they followed her mother and father down the garden path to the side door.

Lila nudged him. The last thing her mother needed was encouragement. If she sensed the slightest hesitation in David, she'd pounce on it.

Eva glanced over her shoulder as she stepped around the bags David had left in the entryway. "Fifty percent of their fiancés left them standing at the altar."

David put down the two bags and smiled at Lila. "That's not something Lila has to worry about."

"I'm very glad to hear that, David." Eva stopped Lila's father with a hand on his arm as he began walking into the living room. "My daughter is precious to me, and the last thing I want is to see her hurt, which is why Sage drew up these." She lifted the lid on the hamper and took out two manila envelopes, handing one to David and one to Lila.

David frowned, looking from his envelope to Eva. "What's this?"

"The other twenty percent of Rosetti women who actually got past the *I do*s were left heartbroken, penniless, and pregnant within the first year of their marriages. And this"—she tapped the envelope in David's hand—"will ensure it doesn't happen to my daughter. It's a prenup."

"We already have one," Lila said. Just because she didn't believe in the Rosetti curse didn't mean she'd ignored her family's life lessons entirely. Her father had also insisted that she protect herself financially. "I mean, I do. Dad's attorney drew one up for me."

Lila's mother smiled at James, who Lila was relieved to see was now looking at Eva with a suspicious glint in his eyes instead of a spellbound one. "I'm sure you have an excellent attorney, James, but this is what Sage does for a living, and she's very, very good at her job."

David pushed his glasses up the bridge of his nose with his forefinger. "You never mentioned anything about a prenup to me, Lila. I just assumed that—"

"We'll talk about it later," Lila said, well aware that her mother was watching them.

"That's an excellent idea, and I have the perfect person for you to talk to. Or I should say Willow does." Her mother reached into the hamper and withdrew a business card, handing it to Lila.

Lila glanced at the card and raised an eyebrow at her mother. "Really, Mom? This is a marriage counselor."

"A marriage counselor who does premarriage counseling. Willow says several of her friends went to her, and she's excellent."

"What friends exactly? As far as I know, none of Willow's friends are married."

Her mother gave her a beatific smile, and Lila's father shook his head. "I don't know about anyone else, but I could use a drink." He gave her mother a pointed look. "Unless you have something else in that hamper you want to share with us, Eva."

Her mother looped her arm through his. "Just some fabulous desserts that I thought would work for the dessert table at the reception."

David opened his mouth, and Lila said under her breath, "Let it go. We'll talk about it later."

"David, can you do me a favor and bring Lila's luggage upstairs? Second room on the right," her father called over his shoulder as he walked through the living room to the kitchen.

"Lila's not staying with you, James. She's staying with me. David, be a darling and just move the luggage out of the way. You can put it in my trunk when Lila and I leave."

David gave Lila an *I told you so* look, and she glared at him. A little sympathetic understanding would be nice. He knew how difficult it was for her to be caught between her parents.

Her stomach gurgled with nerves. "Uh, Mom, I'm staying with Dad for the first two weeks, and then I'll move in with you."

"But darling, your father has had you all to himself for years. Besides, we have so much to do to plan for your wedding. It would be easier if you just stay with me. Your aunt and grandmother will love having you there, and Sage and Willow will come whenever they have a chance." She glanced at David and grudgingly added, "You're welcome to visit too."

"Eva, you're making a big deal over nothing. It's not like Lila won't see you every day. We're a couple of miles away. Honestly, she should just stay here. There's more room for her here than at—"

"Her home, James. It was her home for eighteen years, and she was perfectly happy there until you stole her away from us!"

The doorbell rang, and Lila's father said, "We'll talk about it later."

Her mother tossed her head and stormed off in the direction of the kitchen. As David moved to open the door, they heard the slamming of cupboards.

"I'd better get in there before she starts breaking things." Her father gave Lila's shoulder a reassuring squeeze. "Don't worry, sweetheart. It'll be fine." At the stream of rapid-fire Italian coming from the kitchen, her father got a look on his face that no doubt reflected the one on Lila's.

It was at times like this that Lila missed her stepmother's calming presence. There hadn't been a social situation that Grace couldn't handle. She would've known exactly what to say to soothe Eva's temper and ensure that the tea went off smoothly, without drama. She'd charm David's parents with her poise and good manners.

"I wish Grace was here," Lila murmured.

"Me too, sweetheart. Me too."

Chapter Nine

Eva slammed another cupboard, swearing in Italian. She couldn't believe Lila had chosen to stay with James over her. She'd been excited about having her daughter back home for more than a quick visit, envisioning late-night chats, picking a new series to binge-watch together on Netflix, family dinners on the deck, early-morning walks along the beach...She sniffed and swiped a tear from under her bottom lashes, annoyed that she was getting emotional.

Not the getting-emotional part per se—she was a passionate woman, so strong emotions were part of her personality—but she could count on two hands the number of times she'd truly cried in her lifetime. Ninety percent of them were due to James and Lila. However, since the day she'd turned fifty, happy stories her customers shared, sappy commercials, even a particularly beautiful sunset, made her cry. She'd even found herself watching rom-coms, and she was the least romantic woman she knew.

She bent down and opened a bottom cupboard in search of a serving tray, nearly banging her head on the counter when, from behind her, James said, "Would you mind not slamming the cupboards? The Westfields might get the wrong impression."

She straightened and turned to him. "I need a serving tray, and this kitchen has everything but." It was a gorgeous kitchen, a chef's dream with its top-of-the-line appliances, huge white granite island with a cooktop, and fabulous natural lighting.

He frowned as he moved past her and opened a drawer in the island, then handed her a silver tray. "Are you crying?"

"No," she scoffed, angling the tray so she could see herself in the reflection. It was hard to tell, but she thought a bit of mascara had run down her cheek.

He held up his finger. "Do you mind?" he asked as he moved closer. He was near enough that she could feel the heat from his body. He smelled like ocean breezes and fresh laundry.

She shook her head, not trusting her voice.

He held her gaze as he gently smoothed his finger over her cheek. "I suggested Lila stay here because I thought it would be easier on everyone, Eva. I didn't do it to hurt you."

The muscles low in her stomach quivered in response to his touch, to the feel of him standing so close. It reminded her of that summer in London when they were young and in love. Her skin warmed, and her pulse quickened as the memories washed over her. They couldn't get enough of each other back then. They'd said things, made promises that neither of them could keep.

"Mom, Dad, what's going on?"

Their daughter's voice broke the spell, and they jumped apart. Eva turned. "I had a lash in my eye."

Lila eyed them warily, and then her gaze dropped to the pastry box in her hands. She put it on the island. "David's mom brought some desserts."

"From Windemere?" Eva asked, flicking open the lid with her tangerine-painted fingernail. "How nice."

"Lila, why don't you show the Westfields around while your mother and I prepare the tea?"

"It's okay, you can show them around, Dad. I'll help Mom."

"I need to talk to your mother for a minute, sweetheart."

Lila looked from her father to Eva. "You're not going to fight, are you?"

"Why are you looking at me? If anyone is going to start a fight, it's your father."

James snorted. "Yeah, right. Don't worry, Lila. We'll be fine."

Their daughter placed a hand on her stomach. "Okay, but don't be long. David and his father have a meeting at three."

"I thought she would've outgrown her nervous stomach by now," Eva murmured as Lila left the kitchen.

"She's anxious about introducing you to David's parents."

"Oh, so this is on me?" She shook her head. "Typical. Why don't you take the Westfields on a tour of the house? I can make the tea."

"I don't trust that you won't put salt on the desserts Jennifer brought."

Eva's defensive response stalled in the back of her throat at the teasing smile on his face. "*Pft.* As if I'd need to stoop so low. Those fancy French pastries can't hold a candle to my biscotti, cannoli, and anginetti," she said, and began removing her pastries and cookies from the hamper, arranging them on the tray.

She glanced at James as he filled a kettle with water. "So what did you want to talk to me about? Or was that just an excuse because you don't trust Lila and me to make the tea?" The British were so particular about their tea.

"You both have a habit of not warming the teapot, and you let the tea steep too long, but no, I wanted to run something by you. There was another reason besides more room that I wanted Lila to stay here."

"My apartment isn't that small, James. And Lila was perfectly happy growing up there. We—" The latter was true, the former not so much.

"Can we not do this, please?" He plugged in the kettle and turned to her. "I'm thinking about buying the beach house for Lila as a wedding gift, and I wanted her to spend some time here to see if she likes it."

Eva tamped down the tiny flicker of resentment she felt because she couldn't afford to give their daughter such an extravagant gift. Over the years she'd come to terms with the fact that she'd never be able to do for their daughter what James could. "How could she not love it? It's gorgeous. Although it's very white."

His lips twitched. "I'm sure Lila will let you help decorate."

She raised an eyebrow. "You know perfectly well she won't let me near this place with a paintbrush."

He smiled as he warmed the teapot with hot water from the tap. "So you don't have a problem with me buying it for her?"

She appreciated his asking. "Are you putting it in her name only?"

He nodded. "Don't get me wrong. David loves Lila very much, and he's a good man. He's stable and responsible."

She rolled her eyes. "He's a stuffed shirt with absolutely no personality."

"You barely know him. Give him a chance."

"So why put the beach house in Lila's name only?"

He emptied the teapot, then unplugged the whistling kettle and poured the boiling water into it. "As much as you think I spoil her, I really don't. And that's mostly because she won't let me. Lila's independent and wants to make it on her own. I admire and respect that about her."

Eva smiled, pleased that all the hard-earned life lessons she and her mother and sister had drilled into her daughter had stuck. Sage and Willow were the same way. But Eva had to give credit where it was due. James's parents had been wealthy, but he'd also insisted on making it on his own merit.

"And as much as I like David and think he and Lila will be happy together," James continued as he reached into a cupboard for teacups and dessert plates, "I don't ever want her to feel trapped in an unhappy marriage."

Eva picked up the tray of pastries. "You're a good father. Lila's lucky to have you."

James's head came up, and his gaze roamed her face as if he were waiting for the punch line. Then he gave her a tentative smile. "Thank you. I appreciate that, Eva. More than you know."

The words, as much as the quiet way he stated them, bothered her. Did he really not know how wonderful a father he was? She remembered some of their fights over the years and wondered if she bore some responsibility for that. And then she responded as she always did when she got uncomfortable or emotional and made a gimme gesture with her hand. "*My* turn now."

He shook his head and laughed, picking up the tray with the teapot, teacups, dessert plates, and napkins. "You'll never change."

"Admit it, you wouldn't want me to."

"Surprisingly, I think you're right."

Their eyes met and held for a moment too long. "Let's go meet the parents," she said, sounding breathy and flustered, which was exactly how she felt at that moment.

"For Lila's sake, please don't bring up the Rosetti curse or tell Westfield what you think of him owning Windemere."

There was no sign of that breathy, flustered voice when she said, "I am who I am, and I don't change for anyone, James. Some people actually think it's one of my best qualities. And if you, our daughter, or the Westfields have a problem with that, you'll all have to deal with it, because it's not my problem. It's yours."

"Eva, don't—"

She flipped him off and walked into the living room. Lila and David and his parents were just coming in from touring the two-tier deck. David's mother wore a pretty pink floral sundress with delicate pink sandals, while his father wore a powder-blue button-down with white pants and white dock shoes without socks. Eva rolled her eyes at his outfit as she placed the tray on the rattan-and-glass coffee table, and then she straightened and smiled.

David's mother came forward with an outstretched hand and a frozen smile. She was a beautiful woman with dark shoulder-length hair and warm dark eyes, who had perhaps gotten a little too much Botox—the frozen smile and shiny forehead were dead giveaways. Her husband obviously went to the same plastic surgeon. But whereas his wife's eyes were warm, his were cool and condescending.

"I'm David's mother, Jennifer, and you must be Lila's cousin," the woman said, taking Eva's hand in hers.

Eva smiled. "I'm Lila's mother, Eva, and I can tell you and I are going to be fast friends, Jennifer," she said, clasping the woman's hand between both of hers.

"Gavin Westfield the Third," David's father said, nudging his wife out of the way to shake Eva's hand.

Unable to resist, she said, "Eva Rosetti the Fourth." The man was a pompous prig.

Beside her, James choked on a laugh, which he covered with a cough.

"It's not possible. Only men use the suffix," Gavin said.

"Actually, that's not true, but even if it was, it wouldn't stop me from using it."

"Why don't we all sit down?" James said, and took a seat on the white leather couch opposite the matching love seat where Jennifer and Gavin now sat.

Eva moved to sit on the white leather club chair closest to Jennifer, but David got there first. Lila glanced at her father and Eva before sitting in the club chair beside David. James raised an eyebrow at Eva and patted the place beside him.

Instead of joining him, Eva picked up the tray of pastries in one hand and the dessert plates and napkins in the other and offered them to Gavin and Jennifer.

Gavin waved his hand. "None for me, thanks."

"They look delicious, Eva," Jennifer said, reaching for a cannoli.

Gavin stopped her with a hand on her arm. "You had carbs at lunch, remember?" He smiled. "We want to look good for the wedding photos."

"I'll have one, Mom," Lila said, no doubt in an effort to draw Eva's narrow-eyed attention from Gavin.

It didn't work. "You don't want to offend me, do you, Gavin? I made these especially for you and Jennifer." Eva put down the tray, piled several desserts on a plate, and handed it and a napkin to David's mother. "You're the last person who has to worry about their weight, Jennifer. You're gorgeous."

Jennifer hesitated, glancing at her husband before taking the plate. She offered Eva a sweet smile. "Thank you."

"Sit down, Mom. I'll get ours," Lila said as she got up from the chair. She chose a pastry from Windemere and a biscotto each for herself and David.

"Anyone want tea?" James asked.

"Yes, please," Jennifer said.

"I'll take mine black, Eva," Gavin said.

"I don't do tea. That's James's specialty. He's very fussy about his tea." Eva smiled at James. "Milk and two sugars for me, darling."

"Obviously you don't worry about your weight, Eva," Gavin said with a jocular laugh that faded when he glanced at James, who'd stopped pouring the milk into Eva's teacup to stare at him.

"Life's too short to worry about something so ridiculously superficial," Eva said, patting James's knee before reaching for a wedding cookie. She changed course and took a pastry from Windemere instead.

"They're amazing, aren't they?" Gavin asked after she'd taken a bite.

Eva nodded. "They are, but you might want to suggest to your pastry chef that his choux could use a touch more butter."

"He graduated from Le Cordon Bleu in Paris, so no offense, but I don't think he needs your advice."

Eva shrugged. "None taken." She smiled at Jennifer. "How was your cannoli?"

"Divine, and these iced cookies are delicious too."

"I'm glad you like them. They're Italian wedding cookies," she said, accepting the cup of tea from James.

Gavin took a cannoli from the tray. "Not bad," he said after swallowing the last bite. "Where did you get your culinary degree?"

"From my nonna and my mother."

Eva had a feeling he wanted to roll his eyes but didn't dare with James there. Instead he said, "That's right. You own an Italian restaurant in Sunshine Bay."

"We do. It's been in my family for three generations."

"Best Italian food outside of Italy," James said.

"I love Italian food," Jennifer said.

"Good, because I planned to invite you all to dinner tomorrow. I thought we could choose the wedding menu then."

"We have the wedding menu sorted," Gavin said. Then, after glancing in James's direction, he added, "But we can come to dinner tomorrow."

Jennifer reached for a leather-bound book propped up against the love seat. She leaned forward, offering it to Eva with an apologetic smile. "I'm afraid I got a little carried away and started planning the wedding. Lila was so busy with the move, I thought I could take some pressure off her." She cast another apologetic smile in Lila's direction. "But I'm afraid I may have overstepped."

"You didn't," Lila said, smiling at David's mother. "Your ideas are amazing."

Eva paged through the book. Overstepped? Jennifer had everything planned right down to the smallest detail. Eva glanced at her daughter, who was chewing on her nail while Jennifer looked equally nervous. "I think you missed your calling. You should have been a wedding planner, Jennifer. Lila's right, this is amazing."

"Really? You're not mad?"

"Of course not. Why would I be?"

"You're the mother of the bride."

"*Pft.*" She waved her hand. "As Lila will tell you, I'm not...I'm clueless when it comes to weddings."

"I'd be happy to help you. We still have so much to do."

"We do?" Eva and Lila asked at the same time.

"Oh yes, we have to shop for the wedding dress, pick the color scheme, and flower arrangements." She came over to kneel beside Eva. "These were just ideas I had. I thought this would be the perfect style of dress for Lila. And I thought this cantaloupe color would show beautifully against the sand and water."

"We should probably talk about what the plans for the weekend are and which events will be held at Windemere and which will be held at La Dolce Vita," James said.

Eva didn't know what came over her, but she had a sudden urge to lean over and kiss him.

"There's nothing to talk about. We're holding everything at Windemere," David's father said.

"Gavin," Jennifer gasped.

"What? Windemere is a wedding venue. Can you say the same about La Dolce Vita, Eva? From what I've heard—"

"It's our daughter's wedding, and if she wants the entire weekend held at La Dolce Vita, then that's where it will be held," James said in a voice that offered no compromise. He was clearly in his CEO mode.

As the two fathers argued, their voices rising, Eva struggled not to laugh. And James had been worried about her making a scene. Eva glanced at Lila and David, who were sinking lower in their chairs, and sighed.

"Be quiet, both of you. Lila and David are the ones getting married. They'll decide where the events for their wedding will take place without any interference from us."

"Thanks, Mom," Lila said with a grateful smile. "David and I will talk about it, but I'd like to hold a couple of the events at La Dolce Vita."

"Lila, I don't think—" David began, looking from his father to his bride-to-be.

Lila crossed her arms. "You don't think what, David?"

Eva ducked her head, hiding her smile. It looked as if the wedding might be off without any help from her. She reached for a cannoli. Life was sweet indeed.

Chapter Ten

"Come on, live a little, Lila. Vanilla ice cream is boring," Willow said as they placed their orders at Sunshine Bay Creamery the next day. "Take a taste of mine."

Lila made a face at her cousin's offer of her bubble gum ice cream cone. "Vanilla is not boring. It's a classic," Lila said, thanking the teenager behind the counter when she handed her the cone.

"Boring," Sage said. "I'll have three scoops of Boston cream pie, thanks."

Willow and Lila shared a glance. Sage was a one-scoop woman. She must've caught their silent exchange because she said, "Don't ask," and took the cone from the server, paying for their order.

"So how did meet-the-parents go?" Willow asked, acknowledging several customers in line with a smile as they walked out of the creamery.

They took a seat at one of the tables on the patio, a sherbet-colored striped umbrella shielding them from the sun. Thankfully, the heat wave had broken, and it was seventy-two degrees, the sweet smell of the yellow flowering bushes that bordered the patio and the sidewalk on Main Street wafting past them on a gorgeous ocean breeze.

"Yeah, give us the scoop. Did Zia Eva behave herself?" Sage asked.

"Mom was amazing. David's mother adored her. She was all Jennifer could talk about when I joined them for dinner at Windemere last night. It was Dad who was the problem."

"Zio James? No way. I don't believe you," Willow said, and Sage agreed. Lila's cousins thought her father walked on water.

"I'm serious. If it wasn't for Mom, I swear Dad and David's father would've gotten into a fistfight. Honestly, though, at one point, I wanted to punch Gavin myself. He was a jerk to Mom. I still can't believe she let it go." It was why Lila hadn't said anything to David's father. She'd been sure her mother would eviscerate him with her sharp wit and her even sharper tongue.

Sage stopped eating her ice cream cone. "What did he do?" she asked in a voice Lila was familiar with. It was the same voice she'd used whenever Lila or Willow told her someone had been mean to them at school.

Lila told them about Gavin intimating that her mother was overweight.

"No wonder she didn't react," Sage said. "She has an amazing body, and she knows it. I'd give anything to have her boobs and her butt."

Willow nodded. "Me too, but it was still a jerky thing to say."

"Yeah, I thought Dad was going to lose it on him then. He gave him the look. You know the one I mean." Lila did an impression of her father staring Gavin down.

Willow laughed. "Yeah, I remember when I got 'the look.'"

"When? I don't remember," Lila said.

"Seriously? You don't remember when he came to visit that summer before you started spending your vacations with him in London? You must've been eleven. He rented the presidential suite at the Ritz-Carlton in Boston, and Sage and I begged him to let us come too."

They wouldn't have had to beg too hard. Her father was a pushover where her cousins were concerned. "Okay, now I remember. And can you blame him? You cleaned out half the minibar and were sick as a dog."

Willow made a face. "I still can't look at hard liquor without feeling like I'm going to puke."

"What about the time we all got 'the look'?" Sage asked, shaking her head when they stared at her blankly. "The back-to-school beach party at Paradise Cove? We were past our curfew, and your dad came looking for us."

Willow and Lila covered their eyes, groaning at the memory.

"We also got the lecture about boys, which was way worse than 'the look,'" Lila said.

Sage laughed. "I think he was as embarrassed giving us that lecture as we were receiving it. His face turned scarlet."

"He was ahead of his time, talking to us about consent, respecting our bodies, and figuring out our boundaries." Willow sighed. "I love Zio James."

This was not news to Lila. Both her cousins did. When they were in grade school and Father's Day rolled around, Sage and Willow had made cards and crafts for Lila's dad. It hadn't bothered her. She loved sharing her father with her cousins.

"So what did your dad and David's father nearly come to blows over, if not Zia?" Sage asked, biting into her cone.

Just watching her gave Lila brain freeze. "Where the events for our wedding will be held. Dad's insisting that they should be equally divided between La Dolce Vita and Windemere, and David's dad is insisting they be held exclusively at Windemere."

"What do you and David want? It's your wedding," Sage said, looking as if she had brain freeze when she asked the question. All Rosetti women got that look on their faces when they talked about weddings. All of them except her, Lila supposed.

"I think it's only fair that we host some of the events at La Dolce Vita, and let's face it, the restaurant could use the exposure."

"Yeah, even Mom, who you know is all about thoughts becoming things and putting out positive vibes, admitted she was worried," Sage said.

"Nonna called Father Patrick," Willow shared. "He was just getting there when Sage and I left to meet you."

Lila lifted a hand to her throat. "For the last rites?"

"What?" Willow laughed. "No, to bless the restaurant."

"Oh, good. Mom invited the Westfields for dinner at La Dolce Vita tonight, and she said she was going to tell Nonna about the wedding and David managing Windemere this morning."

"Maybe she was waiting for Father Patrick to get there, because I can guarantee Nonna didn't know when we left," Sage said.

"You're not going to work at Windemere, are you, Lila? Because that might send Nonna over the edge," Willow said.

"No, I couldn't. I wouldn't." She'd been waiting for David to bring it up, but he hadn't mentioned it.

She had a feeling Windemere didn't have the budget. She was almost afraid to ask David about his salary. They'd made excellent money working for her father's company, but it was a large chain of luxury hotels. She didn't think Windemere could afford to pay nearly as well.

"I could put out feelers for you in Boston," Sage said. "I'm sure one of the hotel chains would offer you a job in a heartbeat. Your dad must have tons of connections."

"He does, and he offered to talk to a couple of people on my behalf, but that was before David agreed to take on the management position at Windemere. I've actually been giving some thought to setting up a consultancy business on my own."

With a baby on the way, it was the perfect solution. She could work from home and do virtual meetings, or line up face-to-face meetings that required a commute only once a week.

Sage smiled. "Knowing you, if you're admitting you're thinking about it, you've weighed the pros and cons and already have a business plan."

Lila laughed. Her cousins knew her so well. Too well sometimes.

"That's a great idea, babe. No bosses, and you get to work from home," Willow said, tapping her almost-finished ice cream cone against Lila's.

"It is a great idea, and one you should start thinking about too, Willow. Maybe it's time you freelance instead of just giving the idea lip service." Sage glanced at Lila. "What does David think?"

"With everything going on, I haven't had a chance to mention it. I also haven't found a place for us to live, and I have to get on that." She didn't mention that David had been hoping they'd live at Windemere. She had a feeling he hadn't given up on the idea. She glanced at her phone. He also hadn't responded to her message from this morning. She'd invited him to join her and her cousins for ice cream.

"Are you looking to buy or rent?" Sage asked. "If you're looking to rent, you'll have more luck at the end of summer. But you should talk to Megan. She's into real estate now and doing really well."

"I'll do that. And if we can afford to, I'd like to buy. But I haven't had a chance to look at what's available. Willow—" Something had caught her cousin's attention, and she'd tuned out of their conversation.

"Hot guy alert," Willow said. "That man is so fine."

Her cousin was as big a flirt as Lila's mother. Lila glanced over her shoulder with a laugh. "Who are you...Oh." Her laughter dried up at the sight of Luke Hollingsworth walking their way. Luke who might've had a thing for her back in the day. Luke who wore khaki board shorts, a white T-shirt, and a smile. A really great smile.

"Watch out, Sunshine Bay, the Rosetti cousins are back together again," Luke said as he approached their table. "You ladies enjoying your day?"

"We are." Willow pushed out the empty chair with her foot. "Why don't you join us?"

He glanced at his watch. "Sure. I've got a few minutes. I'll just grab a cone. Anyone up for seconds?"

They declined and watched him walk into the creamery,

holding open the door for two older women. "How is that man still single?" Willow asked.

"Is he?" Lila asked, her curiosity getting the better of her.

"According to the members of my book club, he is. He's a regular topic of conversation," Willow confided.

"Do you actually discuss the books you read, or do you just drink wine and gossip?" Sage asked.

"It depends on the book." Willow laughed and then said to Lila, "You should totally join. You know some of the women in the group. They're a fun bunch." She leaned over and hugged Lila. "I'm so glad you're moving back home, even if you had to get married to do it."

"I don't *have* to get married, Willow," Lila said defensively. "I want to marry David."

"Right, of course you do," she said, sharing a telling glance with Sage.

Lila didn't get a chance to call them on it because Luke had rejoined them at the table.

Willow eyed Luke's ice cream cone. "That looks so good. What kind is it?"

"Salted caramel brownie."

"You see, Lila. Luke's not boring," Willow said, adding for his benefit, "She only ever orders plain vanilla."

Luke was definitely not boring, Lila thought as she watched him lick his cone.

"You don't know what you're missing. You want to give it a try?" He offered her his cone.

"You want me to lick your cone?" Lila asked, and then held back a groan. That just sounded wrong.

"When you say it like that..." He smiled and handed her his cone.

She made the mistake of looking at him as she licked the ice cream, and their gazes met and held for what felt like a long time. "It's really, really good," she said, hoping the warm flush rushing through her hadn't translated into bright-red cheeks or, if it had, that no one noticed.

Her cousins shared another one of their annoying glances.

"So next time you'll order salted caramel brownie?" Sage asked, but Lila had a feeling she wasn't talking about ice cream.

"No, I think I'll stick with vanilla." Vanilla was safe. She needed to stick with vanilla.

"You're hopeless," Willow said, and then turned to Luke. "I thought you'd be out on the boat. No charters today?"

"Yeah, we're booked solid. But I've got a good crew this summer, and I take off Sundays and Mondays to get caught up at the shop."

"Luke builds handcrafted paddleboards and kayaks," Willow explained. "You should see them, Lila. They're incredible."

"You started that in high school, didn't you?" Lila asked. "I remember you talking about it."

He smiled. "I've improved since then, at least I like to think I have."

"You're being modest," Willow said. "The station featured him in May, and he was on the cover of *Paddling* magazine."

"Luke, that's amazing."

Sage's narrowed gaze moved from Luke to Lila. "You two are a match made in heaven, and you don't even know it."

"Sage!" Lila had no doubt her cheeks were cherry red and noticeable to anyone who bothered to look, which Luke was doing. He seemed as shocked by her cousin's declaration as she was.

Sage rolled her eyes. "I wasn't talking about a romantic match. I was talking about a business match. Lila's opening a consulting business," she told Luke. "And if you're serious about building your business into more than a hobby, you need her. She was director of branding for her dad's company, and he said she was the best there is."

"He's my father, Sage. He has to say that."

"Don't listen to her, Luke," Willow said. "She didn't get her job because of nepotism. She got it on merit."

"I don't doubt that Lila's good at her job," Luke said. "In high school she was voted Most Likely to Succeed."

She'd forgotten about that and wondered how Luke knew, then remembered that his brother, Adam, had graduated with her. He'd probably shown his family his yearbook.

"What exactly would you do for someone like me, I mean my company?" Luke asked, and then he gave her a self-conscious smile. "I'm not sure it even qualifies as a company. It's just me and two part-time employees, but it's definitely not a hobby anymore."

"I could tailor a plan specific to your goals for your business, but essentially, I'd focus on developing your brand's profit-and-loss performance and image and positioning compared to your competitors. Do you have a social media presence?"

"We do for the charter business, and I'll post on there once in a while. Does that count?"

She smiled. "No. But if you'd like, we can set up a time to talk, and I'd be happy to give you some suggestions."

"Do you have time now? You could come take a look at the shop."

"Yes!" Willow cheered. "We're business matchmakers."

"It was my suggestion, Willow. Not yours," Sage said.

Lila hesitated, thinking this might not be the best idea. She hadn't even talked to David about starting a consultancy business on her own, and she didn't completely trust that her cousins weren't attempting to use Luke to drive a wedge between her and David. But her worries were over-ridden by her interest in Luke's business and the potential to take on her first client.

"Sure. You guys will be at the dinner tonight, right?" Lila asked her cousins as she got up from her chair.

"Wouldn't miss it," Sage and Willow said at almost the same time, and the way they said it made Lila wonder if she'd regret that they were there.

"If this isn't a good time for you, Lila, we can do it another day," Luke said as she joined him on the sidewalk.

"The dinner isn't until seven, and I don't have anything else going on. But Luke, you don't have to hire me. Sage and Willow put you on the spot."

"Not at all. I think they're right. This could be a good opportunity for both of us. I haven't put enough energy into building the business, either one of them, and it's mostly because I don't have the time or the expertise. And it'd be easier for you to attract more clients if you already had a couple lined up, especially outside of the hotel industry, wouldn't it?"

"Absolutely," she said, her pulse quickening at the thought that she was really going to do this. It was the first time she'd felt excited about work since she and David had packed up their life in London.

"This way," Luke said, turning down Church Street.

"How's everything going with the wedding and your family?" He smiled when she hesitated. "Feel free to tell me to mind my own business."

She might have if he hadn't seen and heard her at her worst. Not to mind his own business, of course, but that everything was wonderful and that she was fine. Instead she shared what the past two days had been like. Ten minutes later, as they turned down Forest Ridge Road, she groaned. "I'm sorry for talking your ear off. I totally overshared, didn't I?"

He lifted a broad shoulder. "Doesn't bother me if it doesn't bother you. But it sounds like you've got a lot going on. Are you sure this is a good time for you to be taking on a client?"

"It's probably the best time. I need a distraction from all the wedding drama."

"Okay, but if it gets to be too much for you, just say the word." He nodded at a large building with traditional cedar-shake siding. A sign above the closed rolling door read *SUP Sunshine*, and to the left, above a regular door, another sign said *Office*. "Here we are."

She smiled. "I like the name."

Luke rubbed the back of his head. "My grandmother's contribution to the business."

SUP was the acronym for *stand-up paddleboarding*. "It works, but you mentioned you make kayaks too?"

"My main business is paddleboards, but I've had a couple requests for custom sea kayaks." He shrugged and rolled up the door. "Money was too good to pass up."

The warm, earthy smell of sawdust greeted her as they walked into the shop. Luke hit the lights, and they flickered to life, revealing kayaks hanging from the rafters and paddleboards and paddles leaning against the walls.

"Luke, these are incredible," she said, finding it hard to believe he'd made them. She walked across the concrete floor to a worktable and ran her fingers over a board. The wood with its glass-like finish and varying shades of chestnut, carmine, and dark ginger was stunning, but it was the leafy golden tree etched into the board that elevated it to a work of art. "Does anyone ever buy these to hang on their wall?"

"A few, and I've just completed a couple of countertops for Surfside, the bar on Main Street."

She gestured to the boards on the wall and kayaks hanging from the rafters. "You haven't sold all of these, have you?"

"I keep a few on hand for someone who doesn't want to wait, and we rent out the ones over there"—he pointed to a wall of boards and kayaks at the far end of the shop—"but the rest are sold. They'll go out for delivery or pickup tomorrow."

"And this one?" she asked, her fingers tracing the delicate golden-brown leaves.

"That's a custom. I'm delivering it today."

"Do you mind me asking how much you sold it for?"

"Five thousand." And then, as if embarrassed at the price, he went on to explain the work involved in making one.

"Tell me more."

"You sure?"

"Yes, absolutely."

He walked her around the shop, showing her the equipment he used to cut out the patterns, explaining how he'd had to source parts to adapt it to his specific requirements. How his boards contained almost no plastic, and how he had managed to eliminate most of the foam, making them ecofriendly.

His watch beeped, and he glanced at the time. "I can't believe I talked that long. You should've told me to shut up."

"No way. It's fascinating."

"I could go on for hours, but I have to deliver this board. And you have a dinner to go to, don't you?"

She groaned. "Don't remind me. What time is it anyway?"

"Four. I can give you a ride if you want."

"Sure, as long as it isn't out of your way. I'm staying with my dad on Ocean View."

"Lila, nothing is out of the way in Sunshine Bay."

They talked about setting up another meeting as he locked up the shop and loaded the board he'd wrapped in a protective covering into the back of an old-model silver pickup truck.

"Don't mind the mess," he said, holding the passenger-side door open for her and reaching in to toss a jacket and clipboard into the back.

"You forgot something," she teased, lifting her hip to retrieve a granola bar wrapper.

"You're lucky it wasn't a half-eaten burger."

As they drove through town, they talked about people they both knew and what they were up to now. Lila didn't want to ask, but she thought it would seem odd if she didn't. "So, uh, how's Adam?"

Luke glanced at her, lifting a hand off the steering wheel to rub his earlobe between his thumb and forefinger. "Yeah,

I guess we should talk about what happened that night at Paradise Cove. We never did."

She huffed a self-conscious laugh. "And I'm perfectly happy to keep it that way. It ranks as one of the most embarrassing moments of my life."

He winced. "Sorry about that. I probably shouldn't have hauled my brother off you. But you'd had quite a bit to drink, and I wasn't sure you wanted to... well, you know."

"You don't have to apologize. I'm glad you stopped us. You were right. I'd had too much to drink, and I wasn't ready to have sex. I actually didn't want to, but..." His face got hard and a little bit scary, and she held up her hand. "Adam didn't force me, Luke. He didn't do anything wrong. I just didn't know how to say no." It had more to do with her friends than with Adam. They'd all started having sex, and she'd felt like the odd one out. She'd also been sad she was leaving for London the next week and, thanks to those same friends, worried that Adam would hook up with someone else over the summer.

"Don't make excuses for him, Lila. Adam was a jerk back then."

"Maybe a little bit of one," she agreed. Three days after that night at Paradise Cove, Adam had wanted to pick up where they'd left off. When Lila said no, he'd broken up with her. "But who wasn't, right?" Luke wasn't. He'd never been a jerk.

"I can think of a few people who weren't," Luke said. "But to answer your earlier question, Adam's good. He's married with two little girls who are going to give him gray hair before he's thirty-five."

"Does he run the charter company with you?"

"No. He moved to the West Coast two years ago so his wife could be closer to her family."

Luke didn't give much away, but she sensed he'd been disappointed when Adam left town. He'd left Luke with the responsibility of running the charter business and dealing with their family on his own, which didn't leave him a lot of time to devote to SUP Sunshine. And it was obvious that was where his passion lay.

"I really enjoyed myself today," Lila said as they turned onto Ocean View Drive. "I'm looking forward to working with—" She broke off at the sight of her mother leaning against her grandmother's car, talking to Lila's father.

"What's wrong?" Luke asked.

"Nothing. It's just that I didn't expect to see my mother here."

Her parents walked over as Luke pulled the truck into the driveway.

"I think they want to say hi. Do you mind?" Lila asked. She felt as if she'd been out on a first date and her parents were waiting to interrogate her.

"Not at all. I should probably apologize to your mom that we were at Windemere's grand opening anyway."

"You attempted to save my grandmother's life. I'd say that earns you a pass."

He didn't get a chance to respond before Lila's mother opened the passenger-side door. "Is everything okay?"

Honestly, it felt as if she were sixteen again. "I was hitchhiking, and Luke picked me up."

"Lila Marie Rosetti, what have I told you—?"

"She's teasing you, Eva," Luke said. "Lila was with me."

"And what was my darling daughter doing with you,

Luke? Something fun, I hope." Clearly, from her mother's tone of voice, she hoped it was something fun and scandalous. Lila doubted she would have said the same thing to David. It was obvious her mother liked Luke a lot more than she did Lila's fiancé. Then again, she'd known Luke forever.

"We were talking about Luke's business, Mom," Lila said as they got out of the pickup.

Luke rounded the truck and joined her, introducing himself to Lila's father. "Lila's agreed to take me on as a client."

It wasn't exactly how she'd wanted her parents to find out she was starting a consulting business, but at least she knew they'd be happy about it. David was another story.

Her parents weren't happy, they were thrilled. After they'd hugged her and her mother had hugged Luke, congratulating them both, her father wanted to know all about SUP Sunshine.

Luke told him some of what he'd told her, Lila interrupting when he downplayed his talent, and then showed James the custom-ordered board in the back of the pickup.

Her father reacted as Lila had, trailing his fingers over the detailed etching. "This is a stunning piece of work. Any chance you'd have time to make me one?"

"Absolutely. You can drop by my shop, and we can talk about a design." Luke glanced at his watch. "Sorry to cut this short, but I promised I'd have the board to my customer before five. It's an anniversary present for his wife."

"Don't let us keep you," her father said, helping Luke cover the board in the protective wrap. "Let me know when you have time to talk."

"You can talk to Luke tonight, James," Eva said.

"He can?" Lila and Luke asked at almost the same time.

Her mother nodded. "Ruth made reservations for your family at seven. Didn't she tell you?"

Luke glanced at Lila and rubbed his earlobe between his thumb and forefinger. "No, I guess she forgot to mention it."

As they watched Luke drive away, Eva cast a sidelong glance at Lila. "He's such a handsome boy, isn't he?"

Lila responded with what she thought was a noncommittal "Umm." But it must've sounded more like a committed "Yum" because her mother grinned.

Lila felt a headache coming on and wondered if she could use it as an excuse to get out of tonight's dinner.

Chapter Eleven

I'd better go," Eva said, kissing her daughter's cheek and smiling at James, who she prayed wouldn't delay her. She had to talk to Ruth before Luke did, and James had that look in his eyes. The one that said he thought she was up to something, which of course she was.

The previous day's meet-the-parents fiasco hadn't resulted in the wedding being called off as she'd hoped, but it had created a noticeable rift between Lila and David, and Eva would do whatever she could to exploit it. She had to be careful, though. She couldn't give her daughter or James any reason to suspect what she was up to.

"Hang on a sec, Eva. I forgot to give you something," James said, and then he jogged to the beach house. The man was in amazing shape, as Eva had discovered earlier. He'd just come back from a run on the beach, shirtless and sweaty, and Eva's libido had stretched and opened one eye.

"What were you doing here, Mom?" Lila asked with a suspicious glint in her eyes, one strikingly similar to her father's, which didn't make sense.

Lila had no clue what Eva was up to. Her performance as the supportive mother of the bride the day before had been award winning if she said so herself; even James had bought it. So maybe Eva was seeing something that wasn't there.

"I dropped off a box of photo albums. I thought you could use some of the photos for the slideshow at the wedding reception." They'd also remind Lila of the important part La Dolce Vita had played in her life and that her fiancé and his father were putting it at risk.

"Thanks, Mom." Lila hugged her. "That was so thoughtful of you. I really appreciate how supportive you're being."

"You know I'd do anything to ensure your happiness, darling." She patted her daughter's cheek. Even though it was true, and she believed with her whole heart that what she was doing was in her daughter's best interest, Lila's gratitude made her feel a little guilty.

"How did Nonna take the news?"

"She was upset at first." She'd totally lost it. "But she came around when I pointed out that David managing Windemere meant that you were moving home to Sunshine Bay and the benefits of your wedding being held at La Dolce Vita."

They might've been selling points if Eva had used them, but she hadn't needed to. All she'd had to do to get Carmen on board was share her plan to stop the wedding. It had been a relief to see enthusiastic fire in her mother's eyes instead of defeated acceptance.

Lila wasn't quick enough to hide her wince, and Eva inwardly cheered. Obviously her daughter and David were still at odds over where the wedding and reception would be held.

And to ensure they remained that way, Eva said, "I didn't want to say anything yesterday, but your father was right.

You're the bride, and I think it's only fair that we host your entire wedding weekend at La Dolce Vita."

Lila audibly swallowed, and Eva hugged her, feeling bad for her distress. But that was David and Gavin's fault, not hers. "We'll understand if you have to bow to David's wishes to keep the peace. No hard feelings, darling. I promise."

"Everything okay?" James asked as he rejoined them.

"Everything's wonderful, and why wouldn't it be? Lila's moving home and opening her own consultancy business. I'm so proud of you, darling."

Lila and James had no idea just how thrilled Eva was. She'd been worried that when the wedding was called off, Lila wouldn't have a reason to stay in Sunshine Bay and might decide to move back to London with James. But with her opening a business here and already signing on a client—an extremely handsome and talented client, who'd brought color to her daughter's cheeks and a sparkle to her eyes—Eva was over the moon.

"Your mother's right. It's great news. We'll celebrate tonight," he said, handing a file to Eva.

"What's this?" she asked.

"I took a look at the numbers you sent me last night and expanded on some of your ideas."

"Thank you," she said, touched that he'd gone to the trouble. She leaned toward him, catching herself before she planted a grateful kiss on his mouth.

"No problem." He turned to Lila, who had that suspicious look in her eyes again. "You should take a look at your mother's plans for the restaurant, sweetheart. They'd benefit from your expertise, and it wouldn't hurt to have more than one client on your list before you approach other potential clients."

"Mom and Nonna aren't as receptive to my ideas as they seem to be to yours, Dad."

Eva had yet to share James's suggestions, and her own, with Carmen. After delivering the news about Lila and David and Windemere, she'd been afraid to rock the boat. "We'd love to have your input, darling. And I'd sing your praises in my letter of recommendation." She frowned. "Do they do that anymore, or do they just share on your social media?"

James smiled. "I know that look, Lila. You already have an idea, don't you?"

Lila chewed the inside of her bottom lip, nodding. "I do, and I actually think it might be a winner. Mom, do you still sing when you cook?"

"Do fish swim, darling?" Eva asked, and then she smiled and belted out the chorus from "Con te partirò," a song Andrea Bocelli had made famous, one that she, her mother, and her sister often sang together while cooking, and one Lila was familiar with.

Her daughter grinned. "Oh yeah, this is totally going to work. Prepare to go viral, Mom."

Eva laughed. "I'll see you tonight."

It didn't escape her notice that unlike Lila, James wasn't smiling. He'd shoved his hands in his pockets, watching Eva with a pensive expression on his handsome face.

She wondered if he was remembering the day he'd ruined her singing career.

Eva pushed the thought aside. It was in the past, and she'd forgiven him, something she hadn't thought she'd be able to do. She wondered if she'd ever told him. She wasn't sure that she had.

Eva called Ruth as soon as she got into the car. She put the phone on the passenger seat and pressed the speaker icon, then launched into the plan for Ruth to win back her best friend as soon as the older woman picked up. It wasn't Eva's actual plan; it was just how she sold it to Ruth. By the time Eva had parked in the lot beside La Dolce Vita, she'd convinced her mother's oldest friend that Carmen wouldn't poison her food in retaliation for her betrayal and gotten her to agree to a family dinner at La Dolce Vita tonight. Now she just had to convince her mother to go along with the plan.

"Where have you been?" her sister asked as soon as Eva walked into the empty restaurant.

They were typically closed on Sundays and Mondays, but in an effort to compete with Windemere, Eva had decided to open for dinner service both days. As James had shared with her the night before, he disagreed with this decision, and she imagined she'd find a cost analysis to back up his argument in the file folder. But she'd already changed the hours online and on the outdoor sign, and she wanted to give it a chance.

"I told you, I was dropping off the box of albums at the beach house. Why? What's up?"

"Ana's mother died, and Bruno doesn't feel comfortable leaving her alone, so he won't be coming in. Needless to say, Ma is not happy, and she was already in a mood because you forgot to tell her we were opening tonight."

"You think Ma could be a little more compassionate. The woman's mother just died. Of course Bruno would want to comfort her." Eva walked behind the bar to pour herself a glass of wine. She lifted the bottle, and Gia nodded. "As to me not mentioning we were opening tonight, I had to tell her about Lila and David and Windemere. The least you could've done was break the schedule change news."

"I was working my way up to it, but she took the call from two of the servers. They gave their notice effective immediately and won't be in tonight. I called everyone else to see if they were available to fill in, but they already had plans. Heather said she'd work the shift but she'd have to bring the twins with her. She can't get anyone to babysit at short notice."

James had been concerned they wouldn't have the staff to fill the extra hours, but Eva had argued that they were overstaffed the rest of the week trying to give everyone the hours they needed and that opening Sunday and Monday would give her the ability to do so.

"So that just leaves you, me, Ma, Sage, and Willow, and I want all of us to have some time with David and his family. Do we have many reservations?"

"Three tables of four at six and four tables of two at seven."

"Okay, we don't have a choice. We'll have to bring Heather in. I don't want her to work a full shift, though. The twins can't stay up that late. If she can give us an hour and a half, it'll give you and Ma some time to spend with the Westfields. And we have an additional table of six at seven."

"We do?" Her sister frowned, and then she must've picked up on something in Eva's expression because she groaned. "What did you do?"

"I called Ruth. She and her family are coming. Don't worry," she said when Gia stared at her with her mouth hanging open. "Ma will understand once—"

"What will I understand?" Carmen asked, taking a seat at the bar.

Eva poured her a glass of wine without asking and slid it toward her, only to pull it back, thinking it might be best to wait until after she'd shared the news about Ruth. "Your best friend, a woman who has stuck by you through thick and thin, is devastated that going along with her daughter-in-law's wishes to celebrate her birthday at Windemere has cost her your friendship. She's beside herself, Ma, completely torn up about it." Okay, so maybe Eva was being a tad dramatic, but she had to get her mother on board.

Carmen reached for the glass of wine.

Eva moved it farther away. "To make it up to you, they're going to celebrate her daughter-in-law's birthday here. Tonight. They're coming at seven."

Carmen smiled. "*Certo.* Sure."

Eva knew better than to trust that particular smile. "I'll be cooking their meals, and you're not getting near them." She didn't trust her mother not to add a laxative.

"Then they can't come."

"Okay, Ma, I have an ulterior motive for wanting them here. But just to be clear, it shouldn't matter. Ruth has always been a good friend to you, and it wasn't her fault her daughter-in-law wanted to go to Windemere for her birthday dinner."

Her sister's eyes narrowed. "What exactly are you up to?"

Eva told them about Lila opening a consultancy business with Luke as her first client, how she was almost positive that David had no idea about it, and that once he met Luke, he might not be as supportive as Lila had hoped. "I might be wrong, but I don't think I am, and if I'm right, this will drive them further apart. And the only way to get Luke here without raising anyone's suspicions, including his, was to have his family come to dinner."

"Why didn't you just say that in the first place?" her mother said, gesturing for Eva to give her the glass of wine. Eva did, and Carmen raised her glass. "To breaking up our Lila's engagement." They touched their glasses together. "We like the mom, this Jennifer, but we don't like the father, this Gavin. He's a *culo*, right?"

"He is, but Ma, no playing around with his food. We want Lila to be proud of us, proud of La Dolce Vita. We're just setting the plan in motion." Eva picked up her wineglass and walked around the bar. "I have to change." She leaned in to her sister and whispered, "Don't let Ma near the kitchen."

Twenty minutes later, Eva was standing in the restaurant's kitchen when a familiar wave of intense heat washed over her.

Her sister walked in, took a look at her, and plucked the glass of wine from her hand. "No more wine for you. You've had your quota for the day."

"G, give me my—"

Her sister tossed the sauvignon blanc back in a single gulp.

"I can't believe you just did that."

"I'm not the one having hot flashes, and everything I've read said wine makes them worse. You'll thank me when you get through the dinner without sweating through another dress." Her sister reached in the fridge, pulled out a bottle of sparkling water, and handed it to Eva. "By the way, Ruth called. Her daughter-in-law won't be joining them, so they're now a table for five."

Eva nodded, fanning herself with her apron. "It's probably better she's not coming anyway."

It took a few minutes for Eva's hot flash to subside. Once it had, they went over the menu with Mimi. She'd take care of the appetizers: prosciutto-and-arugula crostini, fried calamari, and fried zucchini blossoms.

Eva had already made the lobster-stuffed ravioli and the brandy and plum tomato sauce with piccoli gamberetti for the pasta course. She had the entree, pollo Piemonte—breaded chicken breast stuffed with broccoli and goat and mozzarella cheeses with a roasted red pepper cream sauce—prepared and ready to go into the oven. It would be served with potatoes, diagonally sliced carrots, and zucchini. Gia and Carmen had made tiramisu and panna cotta for dessert.

They chatted with Mimi about the latest gossip in Sunshine Bay while Eva and her sister stuffed homemade cannelloni with a three-cheese filling and Mimi prepared the sausage and ground beef for the lasagna La Dolce Vita was famous for.

Eva felt the weight of someone's gaze and looked over to see James watching her, his hands in the pockets of his black slacks.

"Please tell me the Westfields aren't here already," she said, flustered. Which wasn't like her. She'd grown up in this kitchen. Her passion for food and her love of cooking ensured that everything that left the kitchen looked and tasted as good as anything from a Michelin-starred restaurant. She'd never doubted her abilities, but for some reason, she was on edge tonight. Most likely the nerves came from wanting to impress the Westfields for Lila's sake.

"No. I'm early. David and his parents are picking up Lila. I was hoping to talk to you."

"Go, we're good," her sister said, smiling at James, before introducing him to Mimi.

"Is everything okay?" Eva asked as she followed him out of the kitchen, ignoring their sous-chef, who was waggling her eyebrows. She didn't need Mimi to tell her that James was an exceptionally fine-looking man. "You seem...subdued."

He looked around the dining room. Eva's mother was seating a table of four while chatting up a threesome at another table. "Do you mind if we go on the deck and talk?"

"Not at all. Are the girls all right?" she asked as he held the door open and she walked outside.

"They're good, thanks."

There was a light breeze, and it felt wonderful against her skin after the heat of the kitchen. She was sure it, not the wine, was to blame for her hot flash, information she planned to share with her sister later. Eva leaned on the rail, and James joined her, looking out at the waves rolling onto the shore before glancing at her.

"You have an incredible voice, Eva. I'd forgotten just how powerful and moving it was until today."

"James, I—"

"No, let me finish. I thought I was doing the right thing when I threatened to file for custody of Lila. My only excuse was I was young and arrogant."

"I think I said rich and entitled."

"You did, and you were probably right."

"I blamed you for ruining my career, for ruining my chance to make it big, to make something of myself, James. It took several years—I blame my stubbornness on my mother—before I realized that you were right. We were never going to make it big."

"Don't say that. Your voice is—"

"I know I can sing, but that's not enough. We were just a cover band. None of us wrote music or played instruments. You acted out of love for Lila. You were worried about her well-being. But I was young and arrogant too. I couldn't see past my dreams for my career that being on the road was no way to raise my...our daughter."

"It wasn't your fault that she fell. I shouldn't have blamed you. It could've happened to anyone."

"But it happened to Lila." Lila had been three when she fell off the stage while Eva was rehearsing with the band. She'd broken her arm and gotten a concussion. They'd been playing in a pub outside London, and in her panic Eva had called James.

"I could've offered to pay for a nanny while you were on the road. I could've offered—"

She shook her head. "In the end it turned out for the best for Lila, for me, for my family. I was needed here. Lila had a good life here, far better than she would've had on the road. We had, have, a good life, James. I'm happy. I don't regret anything. I forgave you a long time ago. I should've told you that."

"I should've talked to you about it years ago. I should've told you how sorry I am for the way I acted, for the things that I said."

"You're forgiven." She leaned in to kiss his cheek, but he turned his head and her lips landed on his mouth instead. She closed her eyes on a rush of emotion, at the familiar feel of his mouth beneath hers.

His lips were warm and firm, and then they softened. He deepened the kiss, his fingers sifting through her hair. She went up on her toes, unable to resist the taste of him, the feel of him. It had been so long.

He groaned deep in his throat and pulled back from her. "I'm sorry. I shouldn't—"

"Don't be silly. It was an accident." She smiled and patted his cheek as if he hadn't just rocked her world. "I'd better go help my mother."

Chapter Twelve

Sorry we're late," David said when Lila opened the door to the beach house. "We were trying to lock in a convention for next September, and the meeting went longer than expected." He smiled. "You look beautiful."

She wore a white sweater over a white eyelet sundress and had taken more time with her hair and makeup than she usually did, but she didn't smile or thank him for his compliment. She was upset that he'd ghosted her for the entire day.

"I've been trying to reach you for the last three hours. I told you we needed to talk." She had to tell him about taking on Luke as a client before her mother or father did. She had no doubt her parents would mention it, especially with Luke and his family at the restaurant. "You never even responded to my invitation to meet my cousins and me at the creamery."

"I thought you were joking. I told you last night that I had a full day of meetings ahead of me, Lila."

He had, but he'd also been unhappy she was staying with her dad and even unhappier with how the meeting between their parents had gone, especially when Lila had shared her opinion of his father's unacceptable behavior. Which had resulted in an argument over which of their fathers was at fault. So she'd taken David's failure to respond as a sign that he was sulking, but maybe she was being unfair.

"I understand that this is a busy time for you," she said as she locked the door, "but surely you could've taken five minutes during lunch to get back to me."

He sighed. "I'm here now."

A car horn blasted, and they both glanced at his father sitting behind the wheel of a white Lexus, motioning for them to hurry up.

"I wanted to talk to you in private, David."

"Why? What's wrong?"

She sighed. "Other than there's a fifty-fifty chance a fight will break out between our fathers tonight?" Toss the wild card that was her family into the mix, and Lila held out basically no hope the evening would be uneventful.

"I've talked to my father, and so has my mother," David said out of the side of his mouth as they walked toward the car in the driveway. "He's promised to be on his best behavior tonight. I assume you've warned your father to do the same."

She nodded. She hadn't. She didn't think it was necessary. Gavin had clearly been the one at fault.

She glanced at the Lexus. They were less than six feet away. The timing wasn't great, but she had to tell David. "What I wanted to tell you has nothing to do with the wedding or our parents. I've decided to open my own consultancy business, and I already have a client lined up. Two if you count La Dolce Vita." She smiled.

David didn't return her smile. He simply stared at her. "You what?"

"Hurry up, you two!" his father shouted out the open driver-side window. "We're already late thanks to your mother."

"You heard me, David. And while you don't seem happy for me, I am."

"You should've talked to me about this, Lila."

"Like you talked to me about our wedding and managing Windemere?" She shook her head. She had to let that go, or their marriage was doomed before it began. "I talked about going out on my own when we decided to move back to the States. You know that."

"But I took the job at Windemere for us. I'm thinking about our future."

"So am I."

"You and I are a team. I assumed you'd be working for...with me at Windemere. My father does too. He thinks of us as a package deal."

"This is the first time you've said anything to me." Probably because he knew she wouldn't take the job. "But you had to know I—"

The passenger-side window lowered, and Jennifer called out, "Is everything okay?"

"Fine, Mom," David said, and then he whispered to Lila, "We'll talk about this later."

Lila supposed she could tell her mother and father not to say anything, but they'd want to know why. After their conversation this afternoon, they wouldn't believe she was having second thoughts about going into business on her own, so she'd have to tell them the truth, which wouldn't win David any brownie points with either of her parents, especially her mother. Plus, Sage and Willow would be there, and asking them to keep quiet about it would trigger controlling-fiancé red flags in her cousins' minds.

"I was just telling David the good news," Lila said as she slid into the back seat, and she shared with them about her business, ignoring David staring at her as if he didn't know who she was.

Jennifer reached back and gave her hand a congratulatory squeeze. "Lila, that's wonderful."

"Thank you. I'm excited about it."

"David and I assumed you'd be working for us at Windemere, Lila," Gavin said as he backed out of the driveway.

"Neither of you mentioned that to me, Gavin. But to be honest, I wouldn't have accepted if you had."

"And why's that?" Gavin asked.

"I'd think that would be obvious." She glanced at David, expecting him to come to her defense, but he sat beside her in stony silence.

"Of course it is, dear," Jennifer said. "I told you it would be unfair to ask Lila to work on Windemere's marketing campaign, Gavin. She has her family to think about."

Lila offered Jennifer a grateful smile. She really did love David's mother.

"David's her family. He deserves her loyalty." Gavin glanced in the rearview mirror and held Lila's gaze. "Something you should consider. Yours and David's future depends on Windemere's success."

"David's extremely good at his job. I have complete faith that Windemere will be a success under his management," Lila said.

David linked his fingers with hers. "And I know if I ask Lila for her feedback on my marketing and branding plans, she'll give it to me, Dad. The same as I'd offer my advice on her consultancy business if she asks for it." He leaned in and kissed her cheek, whispering, "I'm sorry for how I reacted. I was just surprised. I'm happy for you."

Her shoulders relaxed, and she returned his smile. "Thank you."

"Looks like we'll have the restaurant to ourselves," David's father said as he pulled into La Dolce Vita's parking lot.

And just like that, Lila's tension was back. "The restaurant's usually closed Sundays and Mondays. It will take a while for customers to be aware of the new hours," she said defensively.

"You can't judge whether a restaurant is busy or not based on the number of cars in the parking lot here, Dad. Pretty much everyone walks everywhere in Sunshine Bay."

Lila appreciated David coming to La Dolce Vita's defense. She just hoped he was right because it would be embarrassing if they were the only ones there. But as they walked into the dimly lit restaurant, it wasn't the lack of customers that bothered her, it was seeing the restaurant through the Westfields' eyes.

It fit perfectly with people's preconceived notions of what an Italian restaurant looked like: red-and-white checkerboard tablecloths, plastic grapevines decorating the shelves on the gold-veined mirrored wall behind the dark wood bar, a statue of Venus to the right of the hostess stand sitting in a small gurgling fountain filled with coins tossed in by people making wishes.

Lila and her cousins used to love tossing coins into the fountain and making wishes, which had inevitably led to one of their mothers or their grandmother pointing out that

Lila and her cousins, and no one else, were responsible for making their dreams come true.

But even Lila didn't believe a wish was going to help turn around La Dolce Vita's fortunes, and neither would a successful social media campaign. She hadn't read her father's notes yet, but she couldn't see him not mentioning that the restaurant needed a face-lift, even to spare her family's feelings. Getting her grandmother on board would be another story.

David's mother inhaled deeply and then hummed. "There's nothing like the smell of garlic, basil, and tomato sauce, is there? Can you tell how much I'm looking forward to this meal?"

Lila smiled. "I promise you won't be disappointed." It was a promise she had no qualms making. No one cooked like her family.

"Really, Jennifer? We stole Jean Guy from a Michelin-rated restaurant, and our sous- and pastry chefs trained at La Cordon Bleu in Paris." Gavin was too busy scowling at his wife to notice Lila's grandmother walking toward them.

"*Cara*, you're home." Carmen Rosetti brushed past David's father to enfold Lila in a welcoming hug.

Tears welled in Lila's eyes at the warmth of her grand-mother's greeting. She'd been worried about Carmen and hated to think that it was because of her that her grand-mother had taken to her bed. She'd been afraid Carmen wouldn't want her around when she learned about the wedding and Windemere, and Lila hadn't known how she'd deal with that.

It was fine to say she didn't believe in the curse and wouldn't let her family dictate how she lived her life—they didn't let anyone dictate how they lived theirs—but it was another thing to face the fact that it might tear them apart. She didn't think she could live with that, whether it was unfair of them or not.

"You look good, Nonna. I was worried about you," Lila said when her grandmother released her.

"It was my heart, but I'm good now." She smiled and patted Lila's cheek, the eyes behind her red-framed glasses as sharp as ever. "But you, you're peaked. Are you feeling okay, *cara*?"

"I'm good, Nonna."

"Good. That's good." She turned to David. "And you must be the fiancé." She lifted her hands and pinched his cheeks. "I can see why my granddaughter likes you. You're a handsome boy." David winced, whether because Carmen had pinched his cheeks too hard or because of the *like*-not-*love* comment Lila didn't know. But she had a feeling both had been intentional on her grandmother's part. Lila was just relieved she hadn't told him he was a brave boy, as her mother had.

"And you, you're the mother. Jennifer. I can see where your son gets his good looks." She took David's mother's hands in hers. "But you could use some fattening up, if you don't mind me saying."

Her grandmother wouldn't care if Jennifer minded or not; she always spoke her mind, just as Lila's mother did. They were bluntly honest and authentic, true to who they were, traits Lila admired, even when it wasn't always fun to be on the receiving end of their home truths.

Unlike her grandmother and her mother, Lila thought things through, weighing the consequences before speaking her mind. She cared about how her words affected the recipient. She worried about their feelings. But there were times when she wished she were more like her mother and grandmother.

It was obvious from Carmen's remark that Eva had filled in her grandmother, and no doubt Lila's aunt, on everything that had transpired at the previous day's family meeting. Lila wasn't surprised. The three of them shared everything. There were no secrets among them. Which meant that Lila was holding her breath when her grandmother released Jennifer's hands and turned to David's father.

"And you must be the father. Gavin. You—"

Whatever she'd been about to say was cut off by Willow, who joined them. Lila's cousin wore a pink flirty dress and sneakers. "Hi, Westfields. I'm Lila's favorite cousin, Willow."

The Westfields introduced themselves.

"My sister, Sage, sends her regrets. She's a divorce attorney and has a big case to prepare for. If you ever need her services, I'm sure she'd give you the family discount. It's wasted on us. The Rosettis never marry." Willow grinned. "Until Lila, that is."

Her grandmother chuckled, appreciating her cousin's humor. Lila not so much.

"And your aunt Camilla. The actress. She's been married three times, hasn't she?" David asked. Then he looked from her grandmother to Lila. "Did I say something wrong?"

Lila stared at him. She'd told him they didn't talk about her other aunt. The only reason Lila had told David about Camilla was that her aunt had been in London the year before for the premiere of one of her movies, and he'd commented on her resemblance to Lila's family.

Lila and her cousins had no idea why their aunt was estranged from their family. They just knew not to talk about her. Something Lila had shared with David. She wondered if he'd mentioned her aunt to get back at Willow for her underhanded jab, or was he simply pointing out the fact that obviously one Rosetti woman had needed a good divorce attorney? Either way, it was unacceptable and unkind. She expected better of David.

"What are you all doing standing...?" Lila's mother began as she walked toward them with a smile that faded as soon as she saw Carmen's face. "Ma, what's wrong?"

Lila's grandmother waved her hand in David's direction, obviously relaying to Lila's mother in Italian what he'd said. Eva blanched, replied to her mother in Italian, and then guided Carmen toward the bar.

"I'll take you to our table," Willow said, looking contrite for the part she'd inadvertently played in upsetting their grandmother.

"I can't believe you did that," Lila whispered to David, following Willow and his parents to the back of the restaurant, where his brother sat at the family table with Lila's father. "I told you they're estranged."

"I'm sorry. I reacted to your cousin's shot without thinking. But they all act as if no one in your family has ever been happily married when it's obviously not true. Your aunt proves that the Rosetti curse is bogus."

"No, David, in their minds her marriages prove the exact opposite. None of them have lasted more than a year, and there was always some kind of a scandal attached to them."

"Not the last one," he said.

"Have you been cyberstalking my aunt?"

He shrugged. "She's kind of famous, and I like her movies. I thought it might be nice to have her at our wedding."

She was about to threaten him with bodily harm if he so much as dared contact her aunt when two little boys in pajamas ran by with a harried redhead chasing after them. "Sorry," she said as she brushed past them.

"Heather?"

"Hey, Lila. It's been a while." There was a crash, and she cringed. "I'd better get them before they wreck the restaurant."

Lila took in her white shirt and black slacks. "Are you working?"

She nodded. "We're short-staffed. A couple servers handed in their notice today, and I volunteered to come in, but I couldn't get anyone to look after the boys."

"You go do what you need to. I'll look after the boys."

"But it's your dinner with the family. I don't want to impose."

"She's right, Lila. I'm sure someone else—"

"Go. We'll be fine," she said to Heather, cutting off David.

Heather glanced from David to Lila and then smiled, handing Lila a blue quilted bag. "This should keep them busy. Thanks, I really appreciate it."

"This is ridiculous," David said when Heather rushed off and Lila hurried to the back of the restaurant, following the boys' giggles.

"No, David, this is what my family does. And right now, I'd suggest you don't argue with me since you and your family's business are obviously the reason we're short-staffed."

"You can't seriously be blaming me that their staff chose to leave here for Windemere?"

She turned to face him. "What do you mean by that?"

"Come on, Lila. Look around," he said, gesturing at the empty tables. "The restaurant is—"

She raised her hand, cutting him off before he said anything else. Before the words swirling around in her brain shot out of her mouth. She was seconds away from calling off the wedding, but she knew better than to react when she was emotional. She had the baby to think of.

"Join your family, David. I'll be there in a minute." She continued walking, following the sound of Heather's twins. She stopped short at the sight of Luke, sitting at the table across from theirs with his family, Heather's boys on his lap.

Behind her, David huffed an irritated breath. "I nearly walked into you. What are you— Oh, good, you don't need to look after the boys. They look happy enough with that guy."

Luke was entertaining them with the salt and pepper shakers. "That guy is my client," she said, and headed for his table. David hesitated and then turned and walked away. Lila said hi to the five members of the Hollingsworth family and crouched in front of Luke.

"Thanks for rounding them up." She smiled at the boys. They had their mother's curly red hair, their adorable faces sprinkled with freckles. "I can take them off your hands now. Let you get back to your dinner with your family."

"Don't worry about it. Go and enjoy your dinner with

yours." He nodded at the table at the back of the restaurant, where her father was now talking to David and his father and brother. James looked as if he needed rescuing, but at that moment, Lila didn't trust herself not to make a scene.

"Besides, we're having fun, aren't we, guys?" Luke said.

"Yep." The boys nodded with impish grins as they poured salt and pepper in Luke's water glass.

"Don't worry about my grandson, Lila. I'm sure he prefers the boys' conversation to ours," Ruth said with a twinkle in her eyes.

"Maybe if my granny and aunties would quit trying to manage my love life, I'd enjoy their conversation more."

"Do you hear that? The poor boy thinks his dating life counts as a love life," Ruth said to her sisters and sisters-in-law.

The four of them laughed, clearly enjoying themselves at Luke's expense. And it was just as clear that they adored him. Which Lila knew from her experience with her own family didn't make their interference any easier to deal with.

"We need some seashells, Captain Luke," one of the boys said, stirring half the contents of the pepper shaker into the glass.

"Good idea. Let's go look for some." Luke stood with the boys in his arms and moved away from the table. "Order me a steak, Gran, and if Heather comes by, let her know I've taken the boys to the beach."

"Oh, we will, dear boy," his grandmother said before sharing with the other women in an overloud whisper that she thought Heather and Luke would make a lovely couple.

Lila didn't know what was wrong with her, but she had the oddest reaction to the thought of Luke with Heather.

Before she could think too long and too hard on the sudden spike in her heart rate and the heavy weight in her stomach, she heard raised voices coming from her family's table. Lila groaned and lifted her eyes to Luke's. "How bad is it?"

"You know how sharks act in a feeding frenzy? It looks a little like that." He smiled, the dimple deepening in his cheek. "You're welcome to join us."

He had no idea how much she wanted to, but after her confusing reaction to his grandmother's comment about him and Heather, Lila knew it would be a very bad idea. She could almost hear her mother's voice telling her to go for it, to take the risk, to play with fire. You don't always get burned. Sometimes it was the only way to find out who you truly are and what you really want.

But Lila wasn't her mother. "Trust me, I'd love to, but I think I'd better go rescue my father." She looped the quilted bag over Luke's neck. "Have fun," Lila said, turning to wade into the shark-fest.

Chapter Thirteen

Y ou're quiet. Are you thinking about Camilla?" Eva asked her sister as she turned the car onto Main Street.

She hadn't had five minutes alone with Gia since Sunday's dinner with the Westfields. After closing that night, Willow had stuck around to dissect the family dinner, and Sage had joined via Facetime. They'd all agreed that the odds of the wedding taking place were about the same as those of snow falling in Sunshine Bay in July.

But in case they were wrong, Willow and Sage had decided to throw Lila a bridal shower the following weekend, and for the past four days, they'd been preoccupied with getting everything organized. Now that Eva finally had her sister alone, she wasn't about to let it go. Gia hadn't been acting like herself, and Eva was worried about her.

Gia shook her head. "No, and I'd rather not talk about her, if you don't mind. It just makes me mad and nervous and scared when I do, so I don't. Besides, we haven't heard from her in years. It's a waste of energy to worry about something that probably won't happen. As long as Ma is good with it, so am I. Although you might want to talk to Lila and make sure David and his father don't try and take advantage of our connection to her. We have enough to worry about. Did you see Ma's face when she found out Bruno was going to Puerto Rico for Ana's mother's funeral?"

Carmen had gotten the call from Bruno at closing the night before.

"I didn't have to see her face. She broke three glasses in the kitchen."

"She was taking her anger out on the bread dough this morning. It's too bad she didn't want to come with us today. It might've been the distraction she needed."

They were on their way to Wedding Bells to shop for Lila's dress.

Eva didn't completely buy that her sister wasn't thinking about Camilla or worrying about the fallout that would ensue if she returned to Sunshine Bay. She had a feeling Gia was using their mother's reaction to Bruno's trip as a distraction.

"We'll talk to Ma when we get back to the restaurant. Between us, we can usually tease her out of her mood. But for now, put it out of your head." Eva glanced at her sister as she started to turn down the narrow alley between Wedding Bells and Sunshine Flowers. Noting the way Gia's mouth pulled down at the corners, Eva chanted, "Om," the word vibrating in the back of her throat.

At the very least, she thought it might draw a smile from her sister, but instead Gia's eyes widened. "Eva, the car won't—"

At the screech of brick scraping against metal, Eva's shoulders went up around her ears. "*Madonna santo!* This car is like my *culo*. I always think it's smaller than it is."

Gia looked at her and started to laugh.

"It's not funny, G. Ma is going to kill me," Eva said, looking over her shoulder as she put the car in reverse—only it didn't move. She revved the engine and tried again.

"It's stuck," Gia said, her voice gurgling with laughter.

"I know!" Eva said, and tried opening her door. She'd be lucky to get her foot out. "We're stuck too, G. What are we going to do?"

Her sister was laughing so hard she couldn't talk, and that set Eva off. She was howling with laughter when her cell phone rang. She wiped the tears from her eyes and looked at the screen. "It's Lila."

She shushed her sister before answering and cleared the laughter from her throat. "Hi, darling. Yes, I know. No, we're not trying to get out of it. There's nothing I want more than to help you pick out your wedding dress. Yes, five minutes. I promise," she said, making big eyes at her sister while trying to figure a way out of the car. She couldn't disappoint Lila.

"Grab your purse and roll down your window," Eva told her sister after disconnecting, and followed her own directions.

"Eva, we're not going to fit. The walls are too close to the windows."

"You're right. We can get out through the back doors," she said, sliding over the seat and into the back, her legs still in the front seat from her knees down.

"Nice underwear," her sister said. "Is it new?"

Eva pushed her sundress down. "Ma always told us to wear nice underwear in case we were in an accident."

"I have a feeling even Ma didn't envision you getting us stuck in the alley."

Eva snorted. "Duck so I don't hit you when I bring my legs over." She rolled onto her back and swung her legs over the headrest.

"Okay, hug the door," Gia said, and then gracefully slid into the back seat. She gave Eva a smug grin. "I'm telling you, you have to start coming to my yoga classes."

Three minutes later, they discovered the back doors wouldn't open but there was enough room to get out the back windows. At least for Gia there was. Eva's legs and butt were hanging out the window. Struggling to keep her dress from riding up with one hand while pushing herself the rest of the way out of the window with the other hand, she muttered at her sister, who'd gotten out of the window as easily as she'd gotten into the back seat. "G, what are you doing? I could use a hand here."

Her sister's head popped up in the open window on the other side of the car. "I dropped my purse, and my change fell out. Just give me a sec."

"Leave it! I think we've drawn a crowd, and I can't get out of the window."

At that moment, large, warm hands that definitely didn't belong to her sister settled on either side of Eva's waist and a deep voice with a British accent said, "Mind your head."

When Eva's feet landed firmly on the ground, she leaned against James's hard body and tilted her head back. "My hero."

The corner of his mouth twitched, taking her back to Sunday night and their accidental kiss. She'd spent an inordinate amount of time during the dinner thinking about that kiss. It had thrown her off her breakup game as much as David bringing up Camilla had.

Eva needn't have worried, though. David and Gavin had done a bang-up job without any help from her. And inviting Luke and his family had been an inspired idea. She hadn't missed the way Lila's gaze kept going to the table across from them, and neither had David.

"You do know that you just flashed half of Sunshine Bay and that several people had their phones out?"

She turned in his arms. "Good thing I was wearing nice underwear." Over his shoulder, Eva spotted Johnny Wright, a guy she'd gone to school with and the owner of Surfside, glancing at his phone with a grin on his face. "Johnny, you better not put that up on the bar's Instagram account."

Johnny crossed his heart. "No way, babe. This is for my own personal use."

She was pretty sure he was joking. "You need to start dating, Johnny. You really do."

"You keep turning me down," he said with a wink as he walked back into the bar.

"That really doesn't bother you?" James asked.

She shrugged. "Why should it? My underwear covers more of me than half the women's bathing suit bottoms do."

"Half the women don't look like you," he muttered.

"Was that a compliment, James?"

He held her gaze, and she felt as she had the first time her mother left her in charge of the dinner service—flustered, afraid she wouldn't get it right and it would end up a disaster.

She cleared the nerves from her throat and dragged her gaze from his, turning her head to get a look at the car. "My mother really is going to kill me."

"I'll take care of the car. You go deal with our daughter."

"What's wrong?"

"I think she has cold feet."

Eva couldn't help it. She smiled.

"On second thought, you take care of the car, and I'll take care of Lila."

"Don't be silly. It's the mother of the bride's job to shop for the wedding dress, not the father of the bride's."

"If the mother of the bride wasn't trying to sabotage the wedding, I'd agree with you."

She pressed her palm to her chest. "How can you say such a thing? I've been nothing but supportive, James."

He leaned in to her, almost bringing them nose to nose, his spearmint-scented breath warming her cheek. "You can fool some people, but you can't fool me, Eva."

She'd thought she had. This was a complication she didn't need. If Lila really did have cold feet, this would be the perfect opportunity for a come-to-Jesus moment with her daughter.

Excellent timing, she thought when her sister joined them. She looped her arm through Gia's. "James is going to take care of the car for us so we can enjoy our day with Lila without worrying Tim is going to gouge us."

"I don't think Tim would take advantage of us, Eva. He's been trying to date you—" Eva pinched the underside of her sister's forearm. "Ow. I mean oh. You're right. She's right," Gia said to James. "The last time we brought the car in for bodywork, it took us months to pay off the bill."

This was true, but not because Tim had overcharged them. He'd given them an excellent deal. It was just that they didn't have money to spare.

"Come on, G." Eva tugged on her sister's arm and headed

for the door, calling over her shoulder, "Thanks again, James. And don't worry about Lila. I'll find her the perfect wedding dress." One that wouldn't arrive in time for the wedding.

"What's going on with you and James?" her sister whispered in Italian as Eva reached for the door.

"He thinks I'm trying to sabotage the wedding."

"You are."

"I know that, and you know that, but I thought I'd done an excellent job playing the part of doting mother of the bride."

"Because you are a doting mother of the bride."

"I mean acting like I'm excited and fully supportive of the wedding."

"That's the thing—you're *acting* excited and supportive, but even you can't be on your game the entire time. If James watched you long enough, he'd know you were faking it. And trust me, all that man did at the dinner with the Westfields was look at you. Which brings me back to my original question: What is going on with you two?"

Eva told her sister what had happened on the deck.

Gia's eyes went wide. "You kiss—"

"There's nothing to talk about. It was an accident. A one-time thing. It won't happen again," Eva said, and opened the door.

Lila stood on a raised dais, looking seconds from bursting into tears. "Mom, where have you been?"

Jennifer and Willow, who were sitting on an antique-white sofa in front of the dais, turned to Eva with *thank God you're here* looks in their eyes.

"I don't care if we want to ruin the wedding, she is

not wearing that dress," Gia said under her breath. "She looks like her head is sticking out of a four-tiered wedding cake."

Eva pressed her lips together to keep from laughing at her sister's apt description. "We had a little issue with the car, but I'm here now, darling. I'll take care of everything." Eva blew kisses to Jennifer and Willow as she walked past the sofa to the dais. She held out the layers of lace, lowering her voice in case Jennifer or Paloma, the owner of Wedding Bells, had picked out the dress. "This isn't you. Go to the changing room and relax, and I'll find you the perfect dress."

Lila chewed the inside of her bottom lip, her eyes filling with tears. "I don't want..." The words came out on a shuddered sob.

Eva held her breath. *Just say it, darling.* She'd seen the doubt on Lila's face at the dinner with the Westfields. *Just say it, and I'll take you home and feed you, and everything will be all right.*

Lila sniffed back tears and straightened her shoulders. "...a big wedding or a fancy dress. I just want to get married."

Eva's shoulders sagged, and she managed a smile. "I know. It's been a lot. We can come back another day. You don't have to do this now."

Lila shook her head. "We can't put it off. Paloma said we'll be lucky to get the dress on time as it is."

Eva helped Lila off the dais. "You let me worry about it. Go and relax. I'll have Paloma make you a cup of tea."

"Thanks, Mom." Lila hugged her. "I'm glad you're here."

"I wouldn't be anywhere else, darling."

Lila gave her a watery grin. "Even though you hate weddings as much as I do?"

"Yes, even though I think they're an atrocious waste of money." She patted her daughter's cheek. "I'm happy to spend your father's."

As Lila hiked up the dress and headed to the back of the shop, Eva caught Willow's eye and lifted her chin in Lila's direction. Willow shook her head.

Gia sighed and pulled her daughter off the couch. "Lila needs us."

"Don't say I didn't warn you when she bites your head off," Willow said.

"Paloma," Eva called to the attractive dark-haired woman helping another customer at the cash register. "When you have a minute, could you get my daughter a cup of tea and some cookies while I find her a dress? I can get it if you're busy."

"Eva Rosetti, I'll get your daughter whatever she wants as long as I can take a picture of you and Gia in my shop. Any chance you can get Carmen here?"

"Kiss my *culo*," Eva said with a laugh as she walked to the racks of dresses along the wall, rolling her eyes when Paloma started telling her other customer about the Rosetti curse.

"I'm so glad you got here when you did, Eva. I was afraid Lila was going to call off the wedding." Jennifer glanced in the direction of the changing rooms and then said in a conspiratorial whisper, "I don't blame her, you know. I don't know what's gotten into my son. David has always been the sweetest, most considerate boy, and I know he adores Lila, but lately he's been acting like"—she made a face— "his father."

"I don't know David well, but it seems to me he's trying very hard to please Gavin."

As much as Eva wasn't happy her daughter was marrying David, she knew he must have some wonderful attributes, otherwise Lila wouldn't have been attracted to him or said yes when he proposed. And there'd been a couple of times during the dinner the other night when Eva had had to restrain herself from coming to David's defense when Gavin made fun of his ideas to attract two large conventions to Windemere. In the end Eva hadn't had to. James had.

"He is, and I wish Gavin could see it. He does the same thing to our boys that his father did to Gavin and his brother. But whenever I bring it up, he just sloughs me off."

"He seems to do that to you a lot, Jennifer," Eva said as she flicked through the dresses. "I thought your ideas for hosting weekend events targeted at women were wonderful. David seemed to think so too." Until Gavin had shot them down, making both mother and son feel foolish.

"Thank you, but I shouldn't have mentioned them last night. That was thoughtless of me." She touched Eva's arm. "I'm sorry that you're struggling because of us. I'd like to help if you'd let me."

Eva stiffened. As much as she liked Jennifer, she didn't want anyone's pity or charity. "We'll be fine, thank you."

"I offended you. I'm sorry. It's just that James mentioned you were planning to update the restaurant, and I thought I might be able to help."

At the family dinner Sunday night, James had mentioned the restaurant getting a face-lift while they were discussing which parts of Lila and David's wedding would be held at

La Dolce Vita—none if Gavin got his way. David's father hadn't been very subtle in his opinion of their restaurant's decor. Eva would be the first to admit it needed to be updated, but Gavin's remarks had been tactless and cutting and would've earned him her glass of wine on his head if not for James covering her hand and intervening.

"I love decorating," Jennifer said as she flipped through the dresses with Eva. "It's the one thing Gavin let me do at Windemere."

"You decorated Windemere?"

She nodded. "It was the happiest I've been in years," she admitted, then shrugged as if she'd given too much away.

"I accept your offer," Eva said. "I can't pay you, but I will feed you."

Jennifer's face lit up with a smile, and she held out her hand. "It's a deal."

"And I think I just found the perfect dress for Lila," Eva said, working it from among the other dresses on the rack. She held it up. The dress was a simple but elegant sleeveless A-line gown in brushed white satin with a jewel neckline.

"Simple but gorgeous. Lila will look absolutely stunning in it," Jennifer declared.

Ten minutes later, Lila stood on the dais modeling the dress with a happy smile. "This is it. It's perfect."

Eva dabbed at her eyes, sniffing back tears. She hadn't expected to feel so emotional, and it had nothing to do with the possibility that Lila might actually go through with the wedding. Seeing her like this, it felt as if her daughter had grown up in the blink of an eye.

As Lila stood there looking breathtakingly beautiful,

every special moment in her daughter's life flashed before Eva's eyes—the night she'd given birth to her, her first smile, the day she'd first said Mama, her first step, the morning she'd lost her first tooth, her first day at school, the days she'd learned to swim and ride her bike without falling, her first crush, her high school graduation, and the day she'd left Sunshine Bay to go to college in London. So many moments of sheer joy, bitter frustration, sweet laughter, and utter heartbreak had all morphed into this moment.

Her sister leaned in to her and whispered in Italian, "*Brava.* You're a better actress than I gave you credit for."

"You look beautiful, sweetheart."

Eva glanced over her shoulder to see James standing with his hands in his pockets, looking at Lila with love and pride shining in his damp eyes. His gaze moved to Eva, and he smiled. "Good job, Mom." His voice was husky, no doubt filled with the same emotions that had overcome Eva just moments before.

Gia snorted and muttered under her breath, "Accident, my *culo.*"

Chapter Fourteen

Feeling better, sweetheart?" Lila's father asked as they drove back to the beach house.

She tipped her head back, enjoying the feel of the wind whipping through her hair. "Yeah, sorry about the meltdown at Wedding Bells. I was feeling a little overwhelmed."

"Understandable. It's not the wedding you'd envisioned." He glanced at her. "Are you sure you want to go through with it, Lila?"

"With the marriage?" She was surprised he'd ask. It was a question she would have expected from her mother, not her father.

"I meant the big wedding, but if you're having doubts..."

Her doubts had morphed into a near panic attack as she'd stood on the dais. She'd been seconds away from pulling a *Runaway Bride* when her mother had arrived. It was weird that her mother had been the one who'd calmed her down. Not so weird, she supposed; she'd always been able to talk to her mom about anything. Eva would kiss her hurts when she was little and make her feel better, and as Lila got older, she'd help her make sense of things. Unless it had to do with her father.

"I'm not having doubts, Dad. Not about getting married." For all that David was acting like a jerk lately, she knew that underneath all the raging insecurity and his need to please his father was the man who'd been her best friend for the past three years. A kind, loyal, dependable man who, like Lila, would do anything to ensure his child's happiness.

"But you are having doubts about the wedding?"

"Too many to count." She closed her eyes, letting the sun shine on her face. "There's just so much to do. Not to mention all the family drama. I wish I could blink my eyes, and I'd be standing on the beach saying, 'I do.' Then it would all be over, and we could get on with our lives."

"We got the family dinner out of the way, so that should cut down on the drama for a few weeks at least."

"You're forgetting the family dinner at Windemere next Sunday." Gavin had insisted that they sample the wedding menu and check out the space where the dinner and reception would be held.

Her mother had graciously conceded the dinner and reception should be held at Windemere—no doubt because their family restaurant didn't have the space to hold the now four hundred guests who were apparently attending the weekend-long wedding—while Gavin had *un*graciously conceded that they could host the lunch for the guests arriving Friday afternoon and the rehearsal dinner Friday evening at La Dolce Vita, as long as the restaurant's face-lift was completed by then.

The prewedding lunch on Saturday, and Sunday's morning-after brunch, had been a bone of contention until her father had suggested they leave it up to the wedding guests to decide where they wanted to eat, and Gavin—

his wife and his son elbowing him from either side—had agreed to place menus from La Dolce Vita in the wedding guests' rooms.

"Right, but now that we've got the meals mostly ironed out, the family drama should be minimal."

Lila snorted. "Did you forget that Mom will be there?"

He laughed. "You have to admit that your mother has been uncharacteristically sweet and gracious."

"I know. It boggles the mind, doesn't it?" She glanced at her father. "You and Mom have been getting along, which is equally mind-boggling." And worrying. She hadn't missed their sidelong glances at the dinner with the Westfields.

Her dad shrugged. "We're older and wiser, and you're an adult. We both want the same thing, for you to be happy."

If only they'd gotten along this well when she was younger. But she couldn't shake the feeling there was more going on between them. "You're not interested in Mom, like in a romantic way, are you?"

"No," he said slowly, "but would it bother you if I was?"

He so did want to date her! And while the past week had been one disaster after another, combined they'd barely rank as a Category 1 hurricane. Her parents getting together? Easily a Category 5.

"Ah, yeah, you know what Mom is like, Dad. There's a reason she's known as the Heartbreaker of Sunshine Bay. She doesn't do relationships. And you're vulnerable. You're just getting over losing Grace."

"Look, your mom and I are adults. We've known each other a long time. You don't have to worry about me." He glanced at her. "I thought you'd be glad we're friends."

As long as they stayed just friends and not friends with benefits, she supposed she could deal with it. Although that wasn't something she'd say to her father. "Of course I am. I don't think I could handle it if you guys were fighting too."

"You and David still on the outs?" her father asked as he pulled the Ferrari into the driveway.

"That's one way of putting it."

"Would it be easier if you stayed at Windemere?"

"Are you kicking me out of the beach house?"

"No, I love having you stay with me. It's just that you and David aren't getting any time on your own."

"I know, but to be honest, I have a feeling me staying at Windemere would make things worse, not better. I'm pretty sure Gavin hasn't given up on me being part of Team Windemere. And David hasn't given up on us living in the manager's suite." She undid her seat belt. "It doesn't help that I haven't had time to start looking for a place to live."

Her father tapped his fingers on the steering wheel. "I was planning to wait until your wedding day, but it might alleviate some of your stress if I give you your present now."

"No way, Dad. You're not giving us a wedding gift. You're paying for the wedding," she said as she got out of the car.

"Just like I'll be paying for your sisters' weddings when and if they decide to get married, and they'll also be getting a wedding present." He joined her on the driveway. "I want to do this for you." He took her hand, placing a key in her palm.

She stared at the key and then looked up at him. "You're giving us the Ferrari? I thought it was a rental."

He laughed. "I'm not giving you the Ferrari. I'm giving you the beach house. I signed the papers yesterday."

"The beach house? You're giving us the beach house?" she repeated, positive she must've misunderstood him.

"Yeah, but if it doesn't work for you, we can—"

"Are you kidding me? I love this place. I never dreamed of living in..." Overcome with emotion, she trailed off. "It's too much, Dad, way too much. And I know I should say no, but I can't." She swiped at her eyes. "I love it, and I love you. Thank you." Half laughing, half sobbing, she threw her arms around him.

"I love you too, sweetheart." He patted her back while she got her happy tears under control. "But there's something I need you to do before I sign the house over."

She stepped away from him, unable to take her eyes off the beach house. She still couldn't believe she'd be living here for real. "What's that?"

"I'm putting the house in your name only. I've talked to your mother about it, and we both agree. It has nothing to do with me not trusting or liking David. I just want you protected."

She had a feeling David wouldn't see it the way her father did, but Lila had to admit there was a certain level of comfort in knowing the house would be in her name. "Did your lawyer draft a revised prenup?"

"It wasn't necessary. There's a clause that covers the beach house. You and David haven't looked it over yet, have you?"

"No, but I promise we'll do that this weekend." She made a face. "Just one more thing to add to my list."

He slung his arm around her shoulders. "How about we make a spreadsheet of everything you have left to do, and we'll divvy things up between me, your mom, and Jennifer? You're on your own with the prenup, although I'm sure your mother would be happy to mediate."

She shuddered. "Can you imagine? I'd be better off making an appointment with Willow's friend for premarital counseling."

"It's not a bad idea."

"It's probably a good idea, but with just over three weeks until the wedding, there's no way we can fit it in with everything else we have going on." And there was a tiny part of Lila that was afraid the therapist would tell her she was making a mistake.

"Let's see what the spreadsheet has to say about that."

Apparently the spreadsheet, along with her father, thought she had time to schedule a premarital counseling session with Willow's therapist friend. Lila promised she would if she and David couldn't come to terms on the prenup.

She texted David that her father had given them their wedding present early and that she wanted him to come to dinner at the beach house so they could celebrate. She didn't mention he'd given them—technically her—the beach house. She wanted to surprise him, and she figured it would be as good a time as any to get the prenup out of the way.

Her dad had left for La Dolce Vita five minutes before. Jennifer was meeting him and her mom there, and the three of them were going to have dinner together and go over their list of wedding duties while coming up with a plan for updating the restaurant as inexpensively and as quickly as possible.

Lila wished her mother enjoyed David's company as much as she did Jennifer's. She also wished her father hadn't looked quite so happy at the prospect of spending the evening with her mother. At least Jennifer would be there to chaperone.

Lila pushed her worries about her parents' relationship out of her head and opened the refrigerator. She hadn't inherited her mother's talents in the kitchen, but she was competent enough to put a simple meal together. She pulled out two steaks and seasoned them with salt and pepper, leaving them on a platter on the counter. David would be there in an hour, which she knew from her mother was enough time to bring the steaks to room temperature.

There were two twice-baked potatoes in the fridge that would work well for a side, and she found a package of mushrooms behind the romaine lettuce. It took less than fifteen minutes to make garlic butter mushrooms, and she moved the pan off the burner, turning off the element. She'd reheat them just before serving the meal. She put a tomato salad together, careful not to touch her eyes after adding the minced garlic and slivers of jalapeno, and glanced at her phone on the counter. Ten minutes until David arrived.

She grabbed a bottle of water and brought up the summer playlist she'd made years before, syncing it with the speaker. Aerosmith's "Livin' on the Edge" filled the main floor, and she hummed along as she opened the patio doors. She hadn't realized how loud the music was until she stepped onto the deck. She'd forgotten there were speakers out there too.

She leaned on the railing of the upper deck and lowered

the volume, taking in the reflection of the sun glittering on the turquoise water. There were two sailboats in the distance, skimming across the calm, glassy surface.

Her cell phone rang, and she glanced at the screen. "Hey, where are you?" she asked as soon as the call connected.

"I've got good news and bad news," David said. "Remember the guy from the dentist convention I told you about? He's agreed to meet with me. He's joining me for dinner."

"That's great news. You must be stoked," she said, and then she realized what his bad news was. "He's joining you for dinner at Windemere tonight, isn't he?"

"He is. I'm sorry, honey. I couldn't risk putting him off. You understand, don't you?"

"Sure. It's not a big deal. We can do dinner tomorrow."

"Actually, I'm meeting with one of our suppliers for dinner tomorrow. How about lunch here? I can fit you in between one and two."

"Really? Between one and two?"

"Come on, Lila. Don't be like that. If you stayed with me here, this wouldn't be an issue. It's something we need to talk about."

"You're right, we do. We also need to talk about the prenup. It has to be signed this weekend."

"I don't understand why this is suddenly an issue. Your mother's making a big deal about it, isn't she?"

"No, she's not. I told you I was the one who had my father's lawyer draw it up, and now—"

"I have to go. Drop off the paperwork tomorrow, and my dad and I will take a look at it."

She stared at the phone. He'd disconnected without

saying goodbye. Lila lost her appetite and walked into the house. She wrapped the steaks and put them back in the fridge, then transferred the mushrooms into a bowl. She snapped on the lid and shoved them beside the steaks, deciding to walk to La Dolce Vita and hang out with her parents and Jennifer. She shelved the idea almost as quickly as it had come to her.

As supportive as her mother had been, it wasn't a good idea for Lila to be around her tonight. She was too perceptive, and Lila had a feeling she wouldn't be able to hide that she was royally ticked at David. Instead she turned off the music, shut the patio door, and took the stairs down to the beach.

Her bare feet sank in the cool sand, and she wiggled her toes, looking up at the house. She still couldn't believe it was hers. If David wasn't happy about the prenup, she imagined her father's wedding present to her wasn't going to improve his mood. It should, though. They'd be living in a gorgeous house on the beach that they never would've been able to afford on their own.

She walked down to the shoreline, lifting her maxi sundress to her knees to let the foam-capped waves roll over her feet. The water was chilly, but she enjoyed the feel of it lapping at her calves. Her anger at David dissipated with the rhythmic shushing of the waves and the warm salt-scented breeze lifting her hair.

"Admiral, no!" a familiar deep voice called out.

Lila turned in time to see what looked like a black bear hurtling across the sand toward her. She lifted her hands to ward him off, but he jumped up, placing his gigantic paws on her shoulders. His weight pushed her backward and into the water, and she fell on her butt. The animal licked her face and then galloped through the waves with its tongue hanging out as if it was off on a great adventure.

Somewhat dazed, she watched as it swam out to sea.

"Lila, are you okay?" Luke helped her to her feet with a worried expression on his face.

"What was that?" she asked.

"My dog." He put his hands on her shoulders. "Are you okay? He didn't hurt you, did he?"

Luke's reaction to her falling on her butt seemed a little over the top until she remembered that he knew about the baby. "I'm fine, honestly. But is he okay? He's pretty far out."

"He's in his glory. He's a Newfie. They love the water." He put his fingers between his lips and whistled. "Admiral, get back here!"

Lila laughed. "He looks like he just flipped you off."

"I wouldn't be surprised," he said with a smile. Then he glanced at his watch. "Hey, doofus," he called to the dog again, "if you don't get in here in the next fifteen minutes, you'll be shark bait, and I'm not swimming out there to save you."

The locals knew not to swim at dawn or dusk. The sharks were more active then. "You would totally swim out to save him."

"I totally would, but he doesn't know that." He glanced at a couple of laughing boys running down the beach with their brightly colored kites flying behind them. "He'll come in now. The only thing he likes better than the water is kids."

Sure enough, Admiral was swimming back to shore. "You might want to warn them."

"I plan on grabbing him before he gets his paws in the sand. You might want to stand back," Luke advised as he waded into the water up to his muscular calves. He wore board shorts and a T-shirt and had a beach towel around his neck.

As if he knew what his owner was up to, Admiral made a beeline for the shore several yards from where Luke was standing. But Luke was faster, probably because the dog's waterlogged coat slowed him down. He clipped the leash to the dog's collar before Admiral got his paws out of the water and onto the sand.

"I'm impressed," Lila said, walking toward them, which she instantly regretted when Admiral did a full-body shake, spraying water everywhere.

Luke looked up from rubbing down the dog with the towel. "Don't say I didn't warn you."

"It's fine. I was already wet." She reached out to pet the dog. "Is it okay?"

"He'd be disappointed if you didn't."

"He's a gorgeous dog. At first I thought he was a bear."

"Yeah, sorry about that. Ruth let him out when she saw me coming up the walkway to pick him up, and he decided he wanted to go to the beach without me."

"He stays with your grandmother?"

"When I'm working at the shop, he does. He either stays with Grams or one of the aunts. They fight over who gets to look after him."

"He goes out on the boat with you?"

He nodded as he dried Admiral's webbed feet. "Newfies

were bred as a fisherman's working dog. He's trained in water rescue. He's much better behaved at sea than he is on land. Aren't you, doofus?" he said, rubbing the dog's head.

Her stomach gurgled nosily, and she placed a hand over it. Luke smiled. "Someone's hungry."

"David canceled our dinner date." Now why had she said that? "He's busy with potential clients." Oh my gosh, she just couldn't seem to help herself. "Have you eaten?" Her blood sugar must've bottomed out—either that or being around Luke was causing her to act like a flustered teenager.

"Is that an invitation?"

"If you want it to be, it is. Admiral's welcome too."

"You sure about that?" Luke asked, looking up at the beach house. "From what I can see, that place looks like a show home."

"It is, but it's my show home, and I want you both to come."

"Seriously? You own the beach house? I thought your dad was renting it."

"He bought it for me. I just found out today."

"You're one lucky lady. And you've got yourself a dinner date with a dog who promises to be on his best behavior. Don't you, boy?"

Woof.

As soon as Lila opened the patio doors, the dog barreled through them like a tenpin bowling ball, heading straight for the white love seat.

"Admiral, get back here," Luke yelled as he gently moved Lila out of the way and headed for the couch. The dog took off and led Luke on a merry chase. He got a tour of the entire house whether he wanted one or not. Lila tried to help corral Admiral at the bottom of the stairs, but he was surprisingly agile and fast for a giant dog. Luke managed to snag his collar as Admiral tried to scoot past Lila.

"You're making a liar out of me, doofus," Luke said, half dragging, half lifting Admiral out of the house.

"Do you have a carrot?" Luke asked as he wrangled Admiral to the far end of the upper deck.

"He's a vegetarian?"

Luke laughed. "No, but he does like carrots."

"I have carrots and an extra steak." Lila walked back into the house, smiling as Luke cajoled the dog into doing what he wanted with the promise of a juicy steak.

He had him settled and tied to one of the posts when Lila returned, balancing a plate of raw cut-up steak and a carrot on top of a bowl of water. She handed them to Luke. "Will he be okay if we eat out here?"

He glanced from Admiral to the BBQ and table at the other end of the deck and nodded. "It's far enough away, and he'll probably zone out once he's eaten."

"Great. I'll go get the food." She was reheating the mushrooms when Luke joined her in the kitchen.

"Smells good," he said as he placed the empty plate in the sink, turning on the tap to rinse it. Then he washed his hands.

Lila smiled. "It won't be up to La Dolce Vita standards, but it will be edible."

He reached over her shoulder and filched a mushroom. "Don't sell yourself short. These are awesome. I fired up the grill." He nodded at the platter of steaks and foil-wrapped potatoes on the counter. "I can get these started if you want."

"That'd be great, thanks."

"Medium well for you, right?" he asked as he picked up the platter.

"Yeah, how did you know?" Because she was pregnant, any meat she ate had to be well cooked, but she didn't think that was common knowledge for most single guys.

He shrugged and said, "A friend," but she didn't miss the shadow that darkened his eyes.

The sweet, woodsy aroma of hickory-flavored wood chips greeted her as she carried out another platter loaded down with plates, cutlery, tomato salad, mushrooms, and the semmel rolls her mother had sent home with her the other day.

"Do you want something to drink? I've got sparkling water, wine, beer, or soda," Lila said as she unloaded the contents of her tray onto the glass-topped table.

"Do you mind if I have a beer?"

"Not at all. I'll drink vicariously through you." She glanced at Admiral as she opened the patio doors. His head rested on his paws, and he appeared to be sleeping. "Should I bring more water for Admiral?"

"He's good, thanks. With any luck, he'll stay that way while we eat."

Lila glanced at the speaker as she carried Luke's beer and her water back to the patio, wondering if it would feel too much like a date if she put on music. She decided she was overthinking it and resynced her playlist to the speakers, turning down the volume so as not to wake Admiral.

Luke shook his head as he plated their steaks and potatoes

and took the seat opposite her. "We could've had a hell of a party here when we were kids."

"I have a feeling, once Willow knows I own this place, she'll start planning one."

Luke smiled. "She hasn't changed much." He gestured at the house with his fork. "Your fiancé must be thrilled."

"He doesn't know," Lila admitted. "I was going to surprise him at dinner tonight."

"That's some surprise. He's a lucky guy," Luke murmured, lowering his gaze from her to his steak.

"I'm not sure he'll feel that way when I tell him the house is in my name only." She told Luke about the prenup. "I didn't think it would be a big deal, but David was offended. He's putting the blame on my mother, acting like she's somehow the bad guy in this."

"Prenups are pretty commonplace, aren't they?"

"They are, but he seems to think that the only reason someone wants one is because they believe their marriage is going to fail."

"Not that my opinion matters, but I agree with your mom and dad, and obviously you. You need to protect yourself, Lila, and not to be crass, but your father is a wealthy man."

"So are David's parents."

"There you go. They probably feel the same way as yours do, and it won't be an issue."

"I hope so. We don't need to add another *issue* to the ever-growing pile."

"Weddings don't always bring out the best in people, do they?"

Poor Luke, he'd had no idea that his simple—and most

likely rhetorical—question would result in her sharing how unreasonable David was being and what a disaster the past week had been.

"You want my advice?" he asked after she'd spilled her guts for ten minutes.

She didn't know why she found him so easy to talk to, and it threw her a little to realize she'd shared more with him than with anyone else. Maybe it was because he'd seen her at her most vulnerable and had kept her secrets to himself. She trusted him.

"Please."

He shook his head with a laugh. "You sound like you think I have the answers to your and David's problems."

"You don't?" she asked, only half teasing.

He smiled. "My advice, for what it's worth, is to kick back and relax. We've just enjoyed a great meal, we've got amazing music playing in the background and a truly spectacular sunset to enjoy." He lifted his beer bottle. "To the good life."

She smiled and lifted her water bottle. "La Dolce Vita." And to her handsome dinner date, she thought as the tension seeped from her body. *Companion*, Lila corrected herself in her head, and then she corrected herself again: *friend*.

Chapter Fifteen

Eva stood in her bare feet on La Dolce Vita's deck, wearing a man's white T-shirt and a pair of black leggings, wondering how much wine she'd actually consumed the night before. She was positive it had been only two glasses, and small ones at that because her sister was monitoring her wine consumption in an effort to eradicate Eva's hot flashes. But she must've sneaked a few when Gia wasn't looking. It was the only explanation for how her sister and Jennifer had talked her into joining Gia's early-morning yoga class.

Eva glanced at the cluster of people standing in the sand several yards from the restaurant. There were at least twenty of them in varying states of undress. The majority of them were women who wore brightly colored yoga pants with sports bras or tank tops, along with a couple of men who wore spandex shorts with T-shirts. One brave soul wore a Speedo.

Her sister and Jennifer stood at the front of the class. Apparently they had coordinated their outfits. They were wearing neon-green yoga shorts and matching sports bras, which showed off their firm and lean bodies. They clearly spent a lot of time with their yoga mats.

Eva turned to head back to her apartment. With the number of people in the class, she doubted her sister and Jennifer would even notice she wasn't there. She'd tell them she'd sneaked in late for the class and left early.

"Eva!" Jennifer called, waving a blue mat. "I found an extra one for you."

The woman was annoyingly chipper this morning considering she'd nearly polished off an entire bottle of wine on her own the night before. She'd been vivacious and funny, open and at ease, while they discussed how to update La Dolce Vita and how to take the pressure off Lila.

Eva didn't believe the full-bodied cabernet sauvignon she'd paired with bacon-wrapped Gorgonzola-stuffed dates and a savory mushroom tart was responsible for Jennifer letting her hair down. It was more likely due to her getting out from under her husband's thumb. Eva had told her she should do it more often while ignoring James's warning glance. She'd also tucked Sage's business card into Jennifer's purse when he wasn't looking, before loading her into a cab.

At Jennifer's greeting, Gia looked up, seemingly surprised that Eva had honored her promise. Eva didn't know why. She'd never broken a promise to her sister before. Still, she was considering offering an excuse—Carmen needed her in the kitchen—until Gia's gorgeous face split into a wide grin that held a hint of a challenge.

Eva sighed as she stomped down the stairs to the beach. She never backed down from a challenge, something her sister knew only too well.

It was a gorgeous morning with cotton candy clouds sailing across the cerulean sky on a light breeze, ensuring that the sand was cool between Eva's toes. She smelled coconut sunscreen as she made her way around the other participants, who were getting situated on their mats.

"Thanks," she said to the smiling Jennifer, and took the proffered mat.

Jennifer patted the sand. "I saved you a place."

"I think I'll pass. I'm about as flexible as a fork. I'll be more comfortable at the back of the class. You can join me if you want to."

"Do you mind if I stay here?"

"Not at all," she said, secretly relieved. Unlike her, she imagined Jennifer was as flexible as a wet noodle. She also seemed like the type of woman who'd sat at the front of the class in school, waving her hand for the teacher to call on her. The last thing Eva wanted was Jennifer drawing attention her way.

Gia, who'd been talking to Speedo Guy, smiled and pointed to the spot Eva was scoping out for herself. Instead he plopped his mat at her sister's feet. She gave Eva big eyes, nodding at the place beside him—no doubt thinking Eva would keep him in line.

Instead Eva said, "Have fun," and walked to the very back of the class, adding a couple of extra feet for good measure.

A shadow fell over her, and a mat landed two feet on her right. She turned her head to warn the person away with the Rosetti stare. It had no effect on this particular man. James had grown immune to it over the years.

He smiled. "Good morning to you too."

"What are you doing here?" she asked him while half listening to her sister, who was telling the class to inhale the joy and light and to welcome the day into their bodies.

"I was invited, remember?" he said as he sat on his mat. He wore shorts and a T-shirt that hugged his broad shoulders and impressive pecs. Of course he worked out.

"You forgot to shave," she said with a tinge of annoyance. He looked altogether too handsome with that sexy scruff on his face.

He stroked his chin between his thumb and forefinger. "I'm thinking of growing a beard."

"You really are bored, aren't you?"

"You have no idea," he said.

She was pretty sure that she did. Lila was the same way. The two of them didn't know how to relax. They always had to have a project on the go. Their fingers in fifteen pies at a time.

"What's your excuse?" he asked.

"I'm being a supportive sister."

"Try again," he said, glancing at the people in front of them.

"I may have had one glass of wine too many."

"Admit it, you're hoping the exercise helps with your hot flashes."

"Among other things," she said, trying to copy what he was doing. His large hands were flat on the mat, supported by arms with impressive biceps, his exceptionally fine butt in the air, and his long, muscular legs stretched out with his feet flat on the mat.

"Like what?"

Instead of mentioning the night sweats, mood swings, and weight gain, she said, "According to my mother, I could grow a beard faster than you. She gave me a gift card for electrolysis on my birthday."

His mouth twitched at the corner. "I didn't want to say anything, but your toes are a little hairy."

She laughed. It sounded more like the noise an excited seal makes. Possibly because she was trying to force her butt to stay in the air while stretching her legs out. Just as she was about to make a witty comeback, she farted. A wave of embarrassment flushed her face. From under her arm, she peeked at James, praying that, at fifty, his hearing was starting to go.

He'd turned his face away from her, his shoulders shaking. The *culo* was laughing. She stretched out her foot and swiped his out from under him. He landed on his mat with a heavy thud and barked out a laugh.

"You're so juvenile," she muttered. "It was my mat." She rubbed her sweaty palm on the blue rubber. She glanced at him to see if he bought it.

He'd rolled onto his back, the sun shining down on his tanned and handsome face, killing himself laughing.

"Eva Rosetti, stop disrupting the class," her sister said.

"It's not me. It's him. Don't you dare," she warned James when he turned his head, a mischievous glint in his blue eyes.

He waggled his eyebrows and then rolled into the next position, all that muscular strength contained in one graceful, easy movement.

Eva's movements were anything but graceful as she stretched out her legs, bending forward over her knees to try to wrap her hands around her heels. She'd be lucky if she could clasp her ankles. By the time she'd managed to get her fingers an inch from her ankles, the class was moving into the next position, the hero pose. Eva sat back on her heels, resting her hands—palms up—on her knees. She decided she'd remain in that pose for the rest of the class, but then she started losing feeling in her feet.

The warrior pose wasn't bad, though, Eva decided, and she was beginning to think she might like yoga, after all. As her sister walked among the participants, positioning arms and legs, she glanced at her. Eva gave her a *look at me nailing this* smile.

Gia shook her head as she walked over. "You can't just stand there with your arms out," she said, and then she positioned Eva's legs, one bent at the knee, the other stretched straight out. "Now focus on your breathing."

"This better take care of my hot flashes," she muttered as her sister walked away.

At the snort of amusement beside her, Eva glanced at James. "What are you laughing at?"

"You can't honestly think that your hot flashes are going to vanish with a couple of yoga sessions."

"A couple? I was hoping they'd be gone today. I've cut back on my wine too."

"Is this about you going live on Instagram today? Are you worried you're going to have a hot flash?"

Lila had booked their first Instagram Live for *La Dolce Vita* this afternoon. They were filming in the kitchen at the beach house. Lila wanted a cozy, coastal vibe, which the restaurant's industrial kitchen couldn't provide.

"Of course I am. You've seen how bad they are."

"I'll jack up the air conditioner while you're filming, and that should help. But look, if it does happen, just be honest about it. I'm sure a lot of women can relate."

"Yes, but apparently Lila has a script. Knowing our

daughter, she has every second accounted for. The last thing she'll want is me throwing off her schedule to take a hot flash break."

"She's not as anal as you seem to think she is," James said while contorting his body into the next position. He made it look so easy.

"She's a perfectionist and a control freak just like you are," Eva said as she rolled onto her back, ready to take a nap. She turned her head to admire his precise, controlled movements. "And speaking of your mini-me, where is she? She's supposed to be bringing over the script so we can do a dry run." Eva had been hoping she'd be here by now and give her an excuse to escape the yoga class with at least some of her dignity intact.

"I dropped her off at Windemere on my way here. She was, uh, leaving the prenup with David."

At the slight hesitation in James's voice, Eva rolled onto her stomach so she could see his face. The movement had the added benefit of making it look as if she were following along with the class. "Why didn't she give it to him when he came for dinner last night?"

"He had to cancel at the last minute. He had a meeting with the organizer of the dental convention," he said, acting as if that were a good enough reason for David to cancel the date.

"Why didn't she join us last night? Was she too upset?"

He gave her a look. "You'd like that, wouldn't you?"

Of course she would. It wasn't even about the Rosetti curse anymore; it was about the man her daughter was marrying. Lila was stressed and unhappy, and Eva blamed David. She supposed that was hypocritical of her since she believed you were responsible for your own happiness. But the situation with Lila and David was different.

"Of course I wouldn't. The last thing I want is for Lila to be hurt." Which was why the wedding had to be canceled sooner rather than later. "And I don't know how you can continue taking David's side. He's barely spent any time with her, and they've been here for more than a week."

"I'm not taking his side. It's just that I understand the work that's required to make an inn a success, and so does Lila. This isn't easy for David, you know. He's used to having Lila's support. They worked together as a team for years, and now he's basically doing it on his own. Not to mention the pressure he's under from his father."

It didn't matter that Eva knew James was right. "Even so, he could've taken an hour to have dinner with Lila."

"You sound more upset about it than she did."

"As if she'd tell you."

"She would, which is why I know she had a nice night with Luke. She ran into him on the beach, and they had dinner together."

"Well, why didn't you just tell me that in the first place?" she asked while trying to keep a *this is the best news ever* look off her face. "I'm so glad she didn't have to spend her Friday night alone."

"That look right there is why I didn't want to tell you." He pointed at her face with a scowl on his. "It was a business meeting."

"Of course it was." She smiled.

"Eva, I'm warning—"

A shadow fell over them, and they looked up to see her sister standing in front of them with her hands on her hips.

"Okay, you two. You've disrupted my class long enough. Pack up your mats and go."

"But I was just getting the hang of it," Eva protested as she practically leaped to her feet and began rolling up her mat.

"I'm sure Gia would let us stay if we promised to be quiet. I mean, it's only taken her three years to get you—"

Eva cut him off before her sister relented. "You can stay. I have to prepare the food for this afternoon."

"Nah," James said, coming to his feet. "It wouldn't be nearly as fun without you. Nothing against your class, Gia. It was great."

"Um," her sister said, her narrowed gaze moving from James to Eva. Eva had a feeling her sister wasn't about to let this go as easily as she had James and Eva's accidental kiss.

⌐

Eva hadn't shed a single drop of sweat, and they were two minutes away from wrapping up the live cooking session on Instagram. Probably because the beach house was a shiver-inducing sixty degrees and they'd precooked the summer pizzas and toppings earlier in the day.

Singing a rousing rendition of "That's Amore" with her mother and sister while she tossed and twirled the pizza dough in the air with dramatic flair had helped keep the shivers at bay. As had the heat from the cooktop when she demonstrated how to char slices of tender chicken, juicy peach, and smoky red onion on a grill pan before transferring them onto the creamy ricotta cheese she'd spread onto the thin-crust pizza with its golden-brown edges.

Her mother had demonstrated how to make a perfect béchamel sauce for a white pizza with toasted garlic and provolone, mozzarella, and cheddar cheeses, while Gia had mixed Boston lettuce and microgreens with a red vinegar salad dressing, placing it on the pizza crust before garnishing it with a layer of sliced red onions, pepperoncini, and mozzarella balls.

They'd worked as seamlessly together as they had for decades in La Dolce Vita's kitchen, laughing and joking, at times forgetting they had an audience. A quiet throat clearing from Lila or a low laugh from James would remind them that it wasn't just the three of them.

As the segment drew to a close, Eva removed the cooked pizzas they'd prepared earlier from the oven, displaying them for the viewers. Then she sat with her mother and sister at the small kitchen table, pouring each of them a glass of wine. "Refreshing and tart with notes of green apples and lime, a sauvignon blanc is the perfect pairing for Gia's salad pizza. And for Carmen's white pizza, I recommend a pinot noir. Its earthy notes complement the flavors without overpowering them. And if you're a fan of sweet and salty, I'd recommend pairing my grilled peach, chicken, and ricotta pizza with a semi-dry Riesling."

"Because everything is better with wine," her mother ad-libbed, and Gia and Eva nodded, laughing.

The three of them lifted their glasses, smiling for Lila behind the camera. "Mama, Gia, and I look forward to seeing you at La Dolce Vita this summer," Eva said. "And remember, the most important ingredient in any meal you make is love."

She and her mother and sister clinked their glasses together. "To the good life."

Chapter Sixteen

Lila had expected this afternoon's bridal shower to be the most stressful part of her day until David had arrived at the beach house with a bouquet of lilacs, a box of pastries, and a bone to pick with her mother.

"I'm sure she didn't mean anything by it," Lila said, burying her face in the purple flowers. She took a moment to inhale their sweet, heady fragrance while praying for patience. "Thank you, they're gorgeous."

David nodded without returning her smile, apparently unwilling to let this go as she'd hoped. "She put your cousin's business card in my mother's purse, Lila."

"From what I heard, they had quite the party at La Dolce Vita Friday night. I'm sure it was just a joke." Knowing her mother, Lila was 100 percent positive it wasn't. "Your mom must've thought so too, or she wouldn't have mentioned it to you." Lila was actually surprised that Jennifer had, but she didn't plan on admitting that to David.

"She didn't tell me. The card fell out of her purse at breakfast this morning."

Admittedly, Lila was on the same page with her mother. There'd been several times over the past few years that she'd been tempted to tell Jennifer that she should divorce Gavin. But there was enough drama between their families without her mother stirring the pot, which she planned to tell her this afternoon. "How did your father react?"

"He was on his phone and didn't notice, thank goodness."

Lila's father came around the corner, jiggling his keys in his hand and whistling a happy tune. "What are you two doing standing in the foyer?" He smiled. "Nice flowers. Pastries smell great. Save me some," he said.

"Where are you going?" Lila asked, catching a whiff of his cologne as he moved around them to the door. He looked dressed for a date in a pair of chinos and a crisp white button-down with the sleeves rolled up, and that didn't bode well.

She'd heard all about her father and mother doing yoga on the beach the day before. At first she'd thought they were joking, and then she'd wished that they were. They'd spent the entire time while they prepared the kitchen for Instagram Live laughing and teasing each other. Her grandmother and aunt had noticed too, but unlike Lila, they wouldn't care if her mother and father had a summer fling. They knew her mother and wouldn't worry that it would become something more. They didn't know her father like Lila did. At heart he was a romantic who still believed in happy ever afters, despite losing his wife to cancer.

"I'm heading to La Dolce Vita. Your mother and cousins have a few things they want me to pick up for the shower. Do you have any plans for this afternoon, David? Luke is taking me paddleboarding, and you're welcome to join us."

The muscle in David's smooth jaw bunched. "I appreciate the offer, but I have a meeting to prepare for."

On one hand, Lila was disappointed that David had turned down the invitation. She liked him spending time with her dad and thought it would be good for him. Her father would be only too happy to share his expertise, and David could unburden himself without worrying that James would judge him.

But on the other hand, the idea of David spending an afternoon with Luke made her as nervous as her parents spending time together. She'd told him about Luke having dinner with her Friday night, and to say he hadn't been happy about it would be an understatement.

Her father opened his mouth and then shut it. Unlike her mother, he didn't stick his nose in Lila's personal life. He trusted that she could and would deal on her own with whatever issues she and David were having. She appreciated his faith in her, but she was beginning to doubt her ability to handle all of her issues with David by herself. It didn't help that she couldn't confide in her cousins. They were her go-to sounding boards, and without them she felt alone. Except she hadn't felt alone Friday night.

"I didn't realize James liked paddleboarding," David said after the door closed behind her father.

"It's his first time, but I'm sure he'll enjoy it." She decided a subject change was in order. "Do you have time for coffee and pastries? It's a beautiful morning. We could sit on the deck."

"Yeah, there are a few things we need to discuss," he said, and followed her into the kitchen.

She put the flowers on the counter and reached for the mugs. "That sounds ominous."

"My dad's not happy that my mother's redecorating La

Dolce Vita." He pushed his glasses up his nose with his forefinger. "He thinks your mother is a bad influence."

She looked up from pouring the coffee into the mug. "You can't be serious."

"Lila, the coffee!"

She jerked, and the hot liquid splashed onto her hand holding the mug and onto the counter. "Instead of yelling at me, you could've grabbed the coffeepot," she said, shoving it back on the burner. She snatched a cloth off the counter, and he took it from her hand.

"Let me." He dampened it with cold water before giving it to her. "Put it on your hand and go sit on the deck. I'll take care of this."

She nodded, afraid of what would come out of her mouth if she opened it. She wondered if David knew she was seconds away from having a meltdown, from saying things she couldn't take back. She was so tired of this. They couldn't go a day, an hour, without something putting them at odds.

This wasn't them, she thought as she took a seat on the patio. They'd never fought in London. David had been her best friend, and she'd been his. Maybe they weren't... She squashed the thought before it sprouted roots so deep that she couldn't get it out of her head. Best friends married all the time. Their marriages were based on things that really mattered, like respect, loyalty, and honesty.

The over-the-top kind of love that they write about in romance novels doesn't last. It was the kind of love her parents had once shared, and look how that had turned out. Her dad and Grace had been best friends since grade school. They'd had a wonderful marriage, a happy marriage. They'd never fought.

David pulled out the chair beside hers. "I'm sorry," he said, taking her hand in his and pressing a gentle kiss on the red mark left by the coffee.

"I can't do this anymore, David. It's not healthy. It's not good for the baby."

"I know it's not. I'm sorry—"

"*Sorry* doesn't cut it anymore. It doesn't mean anything unless you actually plan to stop doing what you're apologizing for."

"That's not fair. This is not all on me, Lila. I'm not the one who decided they preferred to live with their father or the one who decided they needed a prenup because they don't have faith that we can make our marriage work or the one who was having dinner with another man when—"

"Really, David? I was having dinner with a client. I didn't say anything when you stood me up to have dinner with a client, did I?"

"That was different."

"How was it different?"

"Come on, Lila. I'm talking about a weeklong convention with a hundred and fifty dentists. And this guy owns what, a little paddleboat shop?"

She shook her head and went to stand up. "I'm done. We had this same argument yesterday. Just like we had the same argument about the prenup and me living with my dad."

"I'm... You're right. I'm being a jealous ass. Your mom, and your dad apparently, like the guy, and I guess I'm feeling a little insecure." He reached for her hand. "Please, sit down. Have a pastry with me?" He opened the box and, with a familiar, sweet smile, offered her one.

She sighed. "My mom hasn't gotten a chance to know

you, not the real you. Because, I have to be honest, David, you've been a bit of a jerk with her."

"Me? What about . . ." He held up his hand. "You're right. Maybe the four of us could spend some time together."

"That's a good idea," she said, taking a bite of a pastry. She swallowed, wiping the powdered sugar from her mouth. "This is really good."

"Better than your mother's?" he asked with a teasing grin.

She relaxed in the chair. "Close, but don't tell her I said so."

He sat back and stretched out his legs as he looked around. "This place is incredible."

"You didn't seem to think so when I told you yesterday morning that my dad had given it to us as a wedding present."

He raised an eyebrow, and she winced. "You're right. No more wedding talk, and no more rehashing our arguments."

"But to be fair," he said, "you have a point. In my defense, I'd just had an argument with my dad about my mom helping yours with the renos at La Dolce Vita. It didn't help that my brother was there and egging him on."

"You should've told me."

"It didn't go so well when I did," he said, and nodded at the red mark on her hand.

"What's happened to us? We never fought. We were always on the same page."

"Do you ever wish we'd stayed in London? We could've kept our same jobs. Nothing would've changed."

He was right. They would've had the same life, albeit with a baby. But as bad as the last week had been, she could honestly say she hadn't thought about moving back to London. "We could probably catch the red-eye if you're interested."

"Probably," he said with a smile. "But as difficult as dealing with my father has been, I'm really enjoying the job, and there's something about Sunshine Bay that's growing on me." He gestured at the sailboats skimming over the water. "I mean, look at this view. It's incredible. And this place—never in a million years could we afford something like this. And yes, before you ask, I'm signing the prenup. I just have to wait for my dad's lawyer to go over it."

She leaned in and kissed the corner of his mouth. "Thank you."

He turned his head and gave her a sweet, gentle kiss. "I've missed you. I've missed us."

She rested her head on his shoulder and looped her arm through his. "You can stay here, you know. It's your house too."

"I appreciate the offer, but right now, I think it's better that I stay at Windemere. I don't trust my brother not to undermine me with my father."

"Is it really that bad?"

"You have no idea," he said. "But let's not talk about that. Mom mentioned she was checking out floral arrangements for the tables with your mom and aunt tomorrow, and she wanted my opinion. Do you have any preferences? Tall, short?"

"Could we maybe not talk about the wedding? I trust your mother's taste completely. My aunt's too. I'm sure, between the two of them, they can get my mom to go along with whatever they choose. Because her taste I totally don't trust."

It wasn't long before they ran out of things to talk about,

which surprised her a little. They'd never had that problem in London. Then again, a lot of their conversations had revolved around work. Which she supposed was how they'd ended up talking about both their jobs.

"I got a chance to check out your Instagram Live last night before I turned in, by the way. It was fantastic."

"It turned out pretty great, didn't it? The feedback has been phenomenal. They're being inundated with marriage proposals."

David laughed. "You're not letting them respond, are you?"

"No. They don't actually go on and read the comments. But I'm sure they'll hear about them soon enough." She'd caught her father scrolling through them earlier this morning with a frown on his face.

"Your grandmother and aunt did great, but your mom's a natural. And her voice, wow. I didn't know she could sing like that."

"If you think that was great, you should hear her when she's not hamming it up."

"Do you think she'd sing at our—" He made a face. "I forgot, no more wedding talk."

"It's fine, and I'm sure she would, just as long as it was only one or two songs. I want her to enjoy our wedding too. But you have to admit this has been nice."

"It has. We need to do this more often. Just you and me." His phone dinged, and he pulled it from his pocket, scanning the text. "Duty calls. Any chance you want to have dinner with me tonight?"

They'd just gotten back on track, and the last thing she wanted was to have dinner with his father and brother.

"In my room, just the two of us," he clarified, obviously sensing her hesitation.

"I'd love to."

He hugged her and kissed her forehead. "Oh, I almost forgot. Your cousin sent me questions for the he-said, she-said quiz. Do you want to go over our answers?"

"No." She laughed and swatted his chest. "It's just a silly shower game."

"I know, but what if we blow it? Your family will take it as proof that you shouldn't marry me."

She sighed. "David—"

He held up his hands. "I know. No more wedding talk. Can I at least tell you to have fun at the shower?"

"Yes. Thank you," she said, even though she highly doubted she'd have fun.

⌣

Lila hated to be right. She swore her cousins' prerequisite for an invitation to her bridal shower had been either a nightmare breakup or a nightmare divorce. At least the food was as fantastic as she'd known it would be. She stood at the buffet table, filling her plate with tomato pesto tarts, passing over the blue cheese, pear, and honey crostini, and reaching for the strawberry balsamic bruschetta, melon prosciutto skewers, and chicken avocado roll-ups as she half listened to Megan Blake's rant about her cheating ex.

"At least you have your family to support you when your marriage goes to hell," Megan said.

Lila caught herself midnod as she clued in to what Megan had just said to her. "Sorry?"

Megan continued as if she hadn't heard her. "With your family's history, I thought you'd be smarter than the rest of us, Lila." Megan shrugged and took a sip of her chardonnay slushie. "Great shower, though. Thanks for inviting me. It's always fun to catch up with old friends and your family. They saved me when jerkface cheated on me, you know. Your mom, Gia, and Carmen are the best. I don't know where I'd be without them."

"I'm glad they were there for you, Megan. Willow tells me you've done really well for yourself." Megan was a successful Realtor on the cape and one of her cousin's best friends.

"Top seller for the second year in a row," she said, raising her glass. "Did Willow tell you we're going into business together?"

"She's becoming a Realtor too?" she asked, catching a glimpse of her cousin behind the bar.

She was making more chardonnay slushies and peach-basil sangrias with Lila's mother, which Carmen was enjoying with Ruth and her sisters at the family table, where they'd been holding court all afternoon. No doubt handing out advice to the lovelorn.

Megan laughed and waved her glass. "No, we're going to flip houses. I'm putting up the capital, and Willow will take care of everything else. She has Gia's artistic eye, and she knows all the skilled laborers in town. I think she's dated half of them."

Megan was probably right, but this seemed like a big leap for Willow. The only building her cousin had ever done, that Lila was aware of, was making houses for their Barbies when they were young. Granted, Willow had done amazing things with cardboard boxes, scraps of fabric, and a glue gun. "She's quitting her job?"

"I wish. But no, she'll do it on the side. And it's not like she'll be doing the actual labor. I love her, but that woman is a klutz." She turned her head at the sound of laughter.

A group of women, including Lila's aunt and David's mother, were laughing at something Sage had just said. No doubt another divorce horror story.

"Your mother-in-law-to-be seems nice. I met her at Windemere," Megan explained. "I take my assistant for lunch every Friday." She made a face.

Lila assumed it was because she was embarrassed that she was taking her assistant to lunch at Windemere instead of La Dolce Vita. *Apparently not*, she thought, when Megan continued. "I can't say I'm a fan of your father-in-law-to-be. It's probably a good thing your fiancé is the face of the restaurant. The waitresses certainly seem to love him. You might want to keep an eye on that."

"My David?" Lila laughed at the thought and then realized how that must've sounded. "I mean, obviously, I know he's handsome and sweet, but he's not a flirt."

"Trust me, it's the quiet ones you have to watch," Megan said, and walked off, calling to one of her friends.

"All right, ladies. It's time for the games," Willow announced as she walked over to hand Lila a peach-basil sangria. "Take a seat."

"Smells amazing," Lila said, wishing she could actually have a drink. She had a feeling she was going to need it. She didn't like shower games, but she supposed they were better than stories about cheating exes and warnings that her fiancé might become one of them.

"Tastes even better. Drink up," Willow said as she guided her toward a chair in the center of a circle of tables.

The chair had a tulle skirt with a big bow at the back and a gold bride-to-be banner. The vases of red roses on each of the tables had been decorated with tulle to look like wedding dresses. According to Jennifer, red and white wasn't the color scheme for Lila's wedding, but they were the only colors that worked in the restaurant.

"Hey, Megan just told me your big news. How come I'm the last to know?" she asked as a means of distracting her cousin from the fact that Lila wasn't drinking her sangria. Plus, she wanted to know if it was true.

"She didn't..." Willow scowled and yelled at her friend, "Megan Blake, I said keep it on the down-low, not give everyone the lowdown!"

"So you're not really going to flip houses with her?" Lila asked so only Willow could hear.

"Yeah, but it's not something I want everyone to know, not that you're everyone. My paychecks aren't much, but until we actually make some money from this, I need them. And my new boss is looking for any excuse to get rid of me."

"Oh, I didn't—" Lila began, but she was cut off by her mother.

"Here you go, darling," Eva said, pulling a small table in front of her. She took the plate and glass from Lila's hand and placed them on the table and then added a bowl of sour candy rings beside them, along with a wooden skewer.

"Are they dessert?" Lila asked.

Her mother didn't answer. She'd stolen a chicken avocado roll-up from Lila's plate and was eating it as if she were starving.

Willow laughed. "You better not let Mom catch you,

Zia. She's put her on a low-carb vegetarian diet to help with her symptoms," her cousin explained at Lila's questioning look.

"What symptoms? Mom, are you okay?" Lila's heart thumped a worried beat at the thought that something was wrong with her mother.

"She's fine. It's just a change-of-life thing," Willow explained for Eva, who'd turned her back as she scarfed down another roll-up. "And these are for the game. We're playing put a ring on it."

Eva pulled up a chair beside Lila and patted her cheek, sharing about her hot flashes, mood swings, and weight gain as she sneaked a tomato-pesto tart off Lila's plate. She was raising it to her lips when Lila's aunt yelled, "Eva Rosetti, you put that down right now."

"What are you talking about? It was for Lila," her mother said, and shoved the tart in Lila's mouth.

Willow snorted. "Aren't you glad you moved back home, Cuz?"

Actually, she was. Over the past week, she'd come to realize just how much she'd missed her crazy, loving family.

Forty-five minutes later, she was having second thoughts. Her mother had won the first game by sliding ten sour candy rings onto the wooden skewer with her hands behind her back. She'd also won put a knot in it—the objective of the game was tying a cherry stem into a knot with just your tongue—which had resulted in ribald tales of her mother's sexual prowess with said tongue. Which Lila didn't need or want to hear. But it was her family's reactions to Lila's incorrect answers during the he-said, she-said game that had resulted in her now less-than-loving thoughts about her family.

"Okay, this is an easy one," Willow said. "Who made the first move?"

Lila's shoulders lowered from her ears. "David."

"Right! Who is more romantic?"

Lila smiled. "David."

"The bride-to-be is on a roll! Who said I love you first?"

"David."

"Right again," Willow said with a little less enthusiasm. "Who wanted to get married the most?"

"David!" Lila gave her cousin a smug smile. Did she know her man or what? It had to be obvious to everyone now that they were the perfect match.

Willow nodded. "Who loves the other the most?"

"David!" Lila looked around when no one cheered. She wasn't sure why until she got a look at her mother's face and thought back to the questions and her answers. Lila pressed a hand to her stomach and got up from the chair. "Too much sangria," she said with a fake smile, and hurried to the ladies' restroom.

Lila had barely gotten the stall door shut and locked before she was on her knees, throwing up. As she ripped off a piece of toilet paper to wipe her mouth a few minutes later, she heard whispering behind the door.

"I don't want to talk to either of you," she said, knowing full well who it was.

"Too bad. We're not going anywhere until you do," Sage said in her lawyerly voice.

"Please talk to us. We didn't mean to upset you. We love you," Willow said through the door.

Lila flushed the toilet, then glared at both when she opened the stall door. "People who love you don't try to sabotage you at your bridal shower. Don't give me the innocent eyes. I know exactly what you're up to. Did you have to pay everyone to tell me their divorce horror stories? Is everyone in on it?"

"No, and it's not our fault that most of our friends have horror stories to share. If you think those are bad, you should come to work with me," Sage said as Lila moved past them to get to the sink.

"That's not why you threw up, Lila. You were fine up until the he-said, she-said game. Okay, not so fine with tales of Zia and her magic tongue, and trust me, I could've done without those myself."

Lila met her cousins' eyes in the mirror. "So what? I got a few questions wrong. It doesn't prove anything."

"This isn't about the questions you got wrong. It's about the ones you got right," Sage said, her voice unnaturally soft.

"David loves you, babe. That much is obvious. But do you really love him?" Willow asked, holding Lila's hair back as she rinsed her mouth.

The tight rein she'd been keeping on her emotions for the past week snapped, and the truth came out. "I'm pregnant. I'm having David's baby."

Her cousins stared at her and then pulled her in for a hug. Willow jumped up and down squealing, and Sage held Lila tight. "We're going to be aunties," Sage said, sounding a little emotional. For all that she was a hard-ass, Sage had a tender heart.

And while technically they'd be cousins, Lila knew what Sage meant. The three of them had been raised more as sisters; it was how they'd always felt. She just wished they were as happy about her getting married as they were about the baby.

Sage drew back. "But you don't have to marry David because you're having his baby. The only reason you should be marrying him is because you can't live without him."

Willow looked at her sister as if Sage had been possessed by someone who actually believed in love and happy ever afters. Then she shook her head and put her hands on Lila's shoulders. "You were raised by three single mothers, babe. We all were, and we turned out all right."

"You don't understand. You can't. You didn't go through what I did. You didn't spend your childhood always worried that you'd upset one of your parents if they knew you were missing the other, pretending you were happy when you were missing your mom and her family or your dad and his. Feeling like you were being ripped in two, blaming yourself for their fights, for making your mom cry and your dad angry."

She swiped at her damp cheeks. "Every summer I had to leave my mom and you guys and my friends, and I hated it. And then I'd hate it just as much when I had to leave my dad and Grace and my little sisters in September. I won't put my baby through that. I won't. David's a wonderful man. He's sweet, he's kind, and he's loyal. He'll make an amazing father, and our baby will have two parents under the same roof." She finished on a shuddered sob.

Chapter Seventeen

Eva stumbled back from the ladies' restroom door. It felt as if a chef's knife had been plunged into her chest. Lila's every word, every sob, had cut off a chunk of Eva's heart until she could've sworn she was bleeding out on the hallway's threadbare carpet. Except it wasn't blood, it was tears.

"Eva, what's going on? Is Lila all right?" her sister asked, walking toward her.

For once Eva was glad of the dim lighting in the hall. She leaned against the wall with her back to Gia, smoothing her palms over her cheeks, brushing away her tears. "She feels like Sage and Willow sabotaged the shower. She's upset with them."

It took everything Eva had not to confide in her sister. They didn't keep secrets from each other. But she couldn't share this with Gia. Eva couldn't tell her that Lila had hated her life. That she'd grown up unhappy and sad, torn between Eva's family and James's. Her sister was like Lila's second mother. She didn't want Gia to feel even half the devastation Eva was feeling right now.

"I did warn them, but Eva, maybe it needed to happen. You heard Lila. It was almost like she didn't realize until she

played he said, she said that she's not in love with David."
Gia glanced into the dining room. "Jennifer's upset. You
need to talk to her."

"I can't. I have to...I have to go to the grocery store."
It was the first thing that came to mind. She needed time
to figure out what to do, what to say to her daughter. She
needed time to get her emotions under control.

"You can't leave now." Gia reached for her arm, turning
Eva to face her. Her sister gasped. "What's wrong?"

The lighting obviously wasn't dim enough to cover the
ravages of her tears, and saying nothing was wrong wasn't
an option. Gia wouldn't let it go. "We're running low
on appetizers, and I was making bacon-wrapped jalapeno
poppers. I was rushing and touched my eyes." Eva shook off
her sister's hand. "I won't be long. Serve the desserts."

"But you should be here when Lila opens her gifts."

Despite Lila's having asked people to give money to their
favorite charities in lieu of buying gifts, some guests had
brought them anyway. "I will be," she promised, but it might
be one promise she couldn't keep. She didn't know how she
could sit there pretending her heart wasn't broken.

"Let me get someone to drive you."

"I can drive myself, G," she said from between clenched
teeth, tears burning the backs of her eyes, threatening to
overflow at any moment.

"Eva, the car is still in the shop."

She hadn't thought of that. "It's okay. I'll walk fast. Get
Ma and Jennifer to help you." She needed them distracted.
She didn't have to worry about Lila. Sage and Willow would
take care of her. They'd protect her, which was more than
Eva could say for herself.

She'd never meant to hurt her daughter. All she'd ever done was try to give her a happy life. She'd loved her with every fiber of her being.

As Eva hurried to the door with her head bowed, frantic to get away before anyone stopped her, she caught a glimpse of Willow's electric scooter. With tears dripping off Eva's nose and her chin, she grabbed the scooter and ran out the door. Willow had let her try out the scooter when she'd first bought it. Eva hoped she remembered what to do.

She kicked the stand up and then slipped off her heels, leaving them behind the rosebush by the restaurant door. She rolled the scooter to the street, put one foot on the deck, and then kicked off. As she brought her other foot in front of it, she pressed and held the Start button. The engine kicked in.

People called out to her as she whizzed down the road. She smiled and waved through her tears. Her friends and neighbors didn't seem to notice. Either they thought they were from the sun in her eyes or the light breeze was drying them up as fast as they fell. It was as if the scooter knew where she needed to go before she did. She was headed in the direction of the beach house. To James. To the one person who would understand how Eva felt. He'd be devastated too.

She'd fallen in love with him that long-ago summer in London. He'd introduced her to fine wines, art, and literature. She'd introduced him to picnics in the park, swimming naked in a pond, and making love under the stars.

They'd had three magical weeks together before their worlds collided. James had taken her home to his family's country estate for his parents' thirty-fifth wedding anniversary. His parents and his friends were excruciatingly polite, but it had been obvious they thought her too loud, too brash, too uncouth for their adored son and friend.

Eva's bandmates had been equally unimpressed with James when they reunited after their break to prepare for the second half of their tour. They'd understood why she'd fallen for him, of course—he was gorgeous and wealthy. But they held those same attributes against him—he was too handsome, too rich, arrogant and entitled. Men like James didn't marry girls like her, like them. They married women who were equally gorgeous and wealthy and whose family were members of the British aristocracy. That was how it was in England, how it would always be. Their warnings didn't bother Eva. She had no intention of ever marrying.

She and James had managed to make their long-distance romance work for five more weeks. James came to their show in Ireland, one in Paris, and one in Italy. They'd been sitting under an ancient olive tree in a vineyard in Tuscany having a picnic when he'd asked Eva to marry him. If not for the Rosetti curse, she might've said yes. He had been then, and was now, the only man she'd ever loved.

James hadn't taken her rejection well. He'd vowed to win her over, to fight for them. Eva had always wondered if things would've turned out differently if he hadn't received the phone call that had changed his life within an hour of his proposal. She was far from her family's influence and young and naive enough to think their love was special, that they'd be able to overcome not only the curse but all the other obstacles that stood in their way.

But James didn't have time to fight for her, for them. That phone call had turned his world upside down. His parents had eventually succumbed to the injuries they'd sustained in the motor vehicle accident they'd been involved in. She'd tried to be there for him, to provide solace and comfort, but he'd been buried under his responsibilities and grief. She'd sat by herself at the funeral, completely out of her depth. He'd been surrounded by his extended family and friends, who knew far better than she how to support him. She'd left the day after the funeral. She had to honor her commitment to her bandmates. She wasn't sure James had even noticed she was gone.

Two months later, the tour had ended, and Eva was back in Sunshine Bay praying for a recording deal that never materialized. It was then that she discovered she was pregnant with Lila. She didn't tell James right away—her mother had advised against it.

Looking back, Eva supposed she'd been hoping he'd call her, but he hadn't. Despite her mother's warning, Eva knew she couldn't live with herself if she kept James's child's existence from him. She'd convinced herself she didn't expect or want anything from him, but there'd been a tiny kernel of hope buried deep inside her that this child, who'd been created from their love, would bring them back together.

Eva had waited until she'd safely delivered her beautiful and healthy daughter before making the call. James had taken the red-eye from London that very night. He'd fallen in love with Lila the moment he held her, but it seemed his love for Eva wasn't as constant as hers. He'd married a month after she'd returned to Sunshine Bay, and he and his wife were expecting a child of their own. Eva had met Grace, his wife, at his parents' anniversary party and at their funeral. The beautiful, willowy blonde had grown up on the estate adjacent to the Sinclairs'. She was everything Eva wasn't. Eva had blamed her tears on baby blues. She didn't know if James had believed her.

He visited Lila in Sunshine Bay three times that year. He'd wanted to come more often, but his company was growing, and he had a baby of his own. For Eva, three visits a year was more than enough. It was hard to see him and pretend indifference. It was hard to watch him walk away with Lila, strolling her down the road in the baby carriage he'd had shipped from England.

She'd wanted her daughter all to herself. Lila had filled the hole James had left in Eva's heart. She was the greatest gift he could've given her. Then he'd spent the next eighteen years trying to take her daughter from her, and she'd grown to resent him as much as she'd once loved him.

And that resentment, Eva's actions in the past, were the reason Lila was marrying a man she didn't love. Eva's fights with James, the tears and the rants, all came back to her, and she cringed in shame and regret. A horn blasted her out of the past. She was driving the scooter down the middle of the road. She raised a hand in apology and steered toward the side, only she oversteered and hit a grate, the tire jumping the curb. The scooter wobbled, dumping her onto the neighbor's driveway of crushed shells, and then continued on its way, right into the candy apple–red Ferrari.

Eva pushed herself to her feet and dusted herself off. She was lucky she'd made it to the beach house with nothing more than a scraped knee. James's rental car hadn't fared as well as she had. The scooter had gouged a foot-long scrape in the passenger-side door. Eva knew she should try to buff out the scratch, check that her niece's scooter had survived unscathed, but she was desperate to see James and ran past the car and the scooter and down the side of the house. She opened the door, relieved that it was unlocked, calling out for James as she rushed into the house.

"James!" He didn't respond. Her pulse quickened as she searched the main floor, running to the patio doors. He wasn't on either of the decks or down by the water. "Please don't be on a run," she cried, growing increasingly frantic by the minute. She heard a sound coming from the second floor and ran up the stairs, searching the rooms as she called his name.

"Eva?" He came out of the main bedroom, rubbing his wet hair with a white towel that matched the one wrapped around his waist.

"James!" She ran to him, throwing her arms around his neck.

"What is it? What's wrong?"

"Lila," she cried, sobbing into his neck. He was warm and damp and smelled like soap and safety.

His fingers closed around her biceps, and he held her away from him, looking as frantic as she'd felt before she was in his arms. "She's not hurt, not physically."

"Thank God." He blew out a breath. "You scared the hell out of me." Then he looked her over and frowned. "You've been crying. Why? What's going on?"

Through her sobs, she told him what she'd overheard. "It's because of us she's marrying him, James. She doesn't want her baby to grow up like she did."

"Don't cry. It's going to be okay," his said, his voice gentle and soothing. He wrapped an arm around her and walked her into his bedroom, guiding her to his bed. "Sit down."

He left her sitting on the edge of the mattress and walked into the bathroom, returning seconds later with a box of tissues, a cold cloth, and a glass of water.

"Thank you." She sniffed, taking a tissue and wiping her nose.

"You've got blood on your leg. What happened?" He crouched in front of her and wrapped his hand around her calf, lifting her foot to rest it on his knee.

"I had to get out of there. I didn't want Lila to see me like this. I needed you."

He looked up from cleaning her knee, the damp cloth stilling in his hand.

"I mean, I needed to talk to you," she said, flustered by the sight of him crouched in front of her. His bare, golden-tanned chest made it difficult to get the words out without stammering. "You...you're the only one who would under-stand. I told Gia I had to go to the grocery store, but I forgot the car was in the shop, so I took Willow's scooter."

His lips twitched. "You rode the scooter here?"

She nodded. "And I may have accidently driven it into your car."

"You drove it into my car?"

"It actually drove itself into your car after it dumped me into your neighbor's driveway. I'll pay for the damage."

He laughed and shook his head. "Don't worry about it," he said, leaning in, his lips almost touching her sensitive skin.

She was no longer worried about his car. She was worried about the heat building inside her at the feel of his warm breath caressing her knee as he blew on the scrape.

On what felt like one of the worst days of her life,

her libido had decided to come out of hibernation. She supposed she shouldn't be surprised. It was James, after all. A man who'd once turned her on with a glance, a smile, or a brush of his fingers against hers.

She felt the heavy weight of his gaze, watching her as he pressed a soft kiss on her knee. She shivered, desire spiraling out of control inside her.

"James," her voice came out on a breathy exhalation. She sounded breathless and needy. "We have to—"

"Did you mean what you said, Eva?" His voice was a rough rasp. "Did you need me?"

"No," she said, because she didn't need anyone. And then he pressed a kiss on the inside of her leg just above her knee. "Yes."

"Good, because I've wanted to kiss you since the night at La Dolce Vita." His hands skimmed the outsides of her thighs as he rose up on his knees. "Can I kiss you?"

"Yes. Please."

He took her face between his hands. "I don't remember you being so polite," he said, then whispered what she'd asked him, begged him to do to her one long-ago summer night. When she'd loved him, and he'd loved her, and they couldn't get enough of each other.

He kissed her then, and it was the same as it used to be. His towel hit the floor, and her clothes soon followed. They explored every inch of each other with their hands and mouths until Eva didn't think she would last another second. "James, please," she begged.

He reached out a hand toward the nightstand without removing his mouth from hers, and then he groaned. "I don't have condoms."

"I haven't been with anyone for more than a year." It was closer to two but she was loath to admit it. "And I've always been careful. It's also highly unlikely I can get pregnant."

"The odds of you getting pregnant by me are next to impossible." He smiled. "I've had a vasectomy, and I haven't been with anyone for more than three years."

She caressed the side of his face. He hadn't been with anyone since Grace, and some of her desire ebbed away at the reminder.

He turned his face and nipped her palm. "So, are we good?" he asked, then rested his forehead against hers. "Please say we're good, baby."

She nodded. "We're good." And they were very, very good. In fact, they were exceptional.

Afterward, she lay boneless beside James, resting her cheek on his chest, stroking his rock-solid abs with the tips of her fingers. Their bodies had changed—hers more than his—but making love with James had felt the same as it had that summer in London. They couldn't get enough of each other, then or now. Their chemistry, their passion, was off the charts. She hadn't had sex this incredible before or after him. Maybe it was because she'd never been in love with her romantic partners. James was the only man who'd gotten past the wall she'd built around her heart.

But she was older and wiser. She couldn't, wouldn't, let him sneak past her defenses again.

"What are we going to do now?" she asked, tipping back her head to look at him.

He smiled, trailing his fingers down her side. "As much as I want to make love to you again, and I really, really do, it might take a while. I'm not twenty-three."

She snorted. "I wasn't talking about sex." It hadn't been sex. It had been as close to an out-of-body experience as she'd ever had.

"Well, that's a little disappointing. It mustn't have been as mind blowing for you as it was for me because doing it again is all I can think about."

"Trust me, that's not something you have to worry about. You were always an incredible lover, and that hasn't changed. If anything, you've improved with age." She noted the tiny frown line at the corner of his brow and raised herself up to kiss it away. Something she'd said must've bothered him. Then again, maybe not, she thought when he took her face between his hands and brought her mouth to his, kissing her with an intensity that said he wanted nothing more than to prove her right. But as much as she wanted to make love with him again, she wasn't sure if she should take the risk. Besides that, they had to talk about Lila and David.

Eva was breathless by the time she finally managed to drag her mouth from his. As important as talking about Lila was, she'd found herself unable to stop kissing him. It was as if her body had decided, now that it had gotten him back, it didn't want to let him go. The thought was almost as terrifying as that of her daughter going through with a wedding to a man she didn't love.

She leaned back, pushing her damp hair from her face. "We need to talk about Lila."

"No, we don't," James said, drawing her against him. He kissed her neck just below her earlobe and then made his way slowly down to just above her collarbone.

She shivered. "Yes, we do." She groaned when he nuzzled

her neck. "James, you weren't there. You didn't hear her. We have to talk about our daughter." She was desperate to make him stop and just as desperate not to.

He nipped her shoulder and then rolled onto his back, tucking his muscled arm behind his head. "Okay, talk."

She stared at him, shocked. "Why did you say it like that?"

"Like what?"

"Like you're not as upset about this as I am."

"You were and are an amazing mother, and I like to think I was and am a pretty great dad. We both love Lila, and we never gave her any reason to doubt our love. Did we screw up sometimes? Of course we did. It wasn't easy for either of us not having her with us full-time. But life isn't always easy or perfect. We did the best we could under the circumstances."

"I don't think Lila feels that way. And as much as I appreciate you not blaming me for this, I know it's mostly my fault. I didn't do a very good job hiding my feelings when Lila would leave for her summers with you."

"Or when she decided to go to school in London and then work for me full-time? I think you accused me of stealing her from you," he said with what sounded like amusement.

She leaned back to look at him. "Are you laughing at me?"

His mouth kicked up at the corner. "Maybe a little, but trust me, there were times when I wanted to throttle you."

"Is that right?"

"Yeah, it is."

"So I guess you missed the part about Lila trying to protect your feelings too. She felt torn between the two of us, James. You played a role in this too."

He sighed. "There's nothing we can do to change things, Eva. We can talk to Lila about it, apologize, but we can't change how she feels. All we can do is tell her how much we love her and assure her that we'll support her no matter what decision she makes."

"James! We can't let her marry David now. She doesn't love him!"

He scrubbed a hand over his face. "Did she say she didn't love him?"

"No, but I know that she doesn't. She said he's her best friend and that he'll make a wonderful father."

"I'm sure he will."

She threw up her hands in exasperation. "How are you not upset about our daughter marrying a man she doesn't love just because she's having his baby?"

He lifted a shoulder. "Grace was my best friend, and we had a great marriage."

She twisted her fingers in the sheet, holding it closer to her chest, shifting away from him. "Yes, but Grace wasn't only your best friend, you loved her."

He looked away, his chest expanding on a long, inhaled breath before he said, "Grace was in love with Seamus, my parents' driver. She discovered the day before the funeral that she was pregnant."

Eva stared at him, stunned. Everything she'd believed about his marriage wasn't true. She hadn't known the man's name at the time, but she'd been aware that the Sinclairs' driver had also died in the accident. Thinking back, it better explained how Grace had acted at the funeral. At times she'd been almost zombielike, clearly in shock, but then she'd rouse herself for James. He'd been solicitous of her, protective. Eva remembered seeing them sitting together in the front pew, James's arm around her, their golden heads bent together.

As she sat alone, several pews from the back, a twinge of jealousy had twisted in Eva's chest. It was why she hadn't been completely shocked when James had told her he'd married Grace. "Sheena?" Eva asked past the wedge of emotion stuck in her throat.

He nodded. "She isn't my biological daughter. No one knows but you. There was no reason for us to tell anyone."

"Is that why you married Grace?"

"We were both grieving, and we were there for each other. We'd always been close. Losing Seamus and my parents at the same time brought us that much closer." He glanced at her, holding her gaze. "I loved you, but you either didn't want or couldn't make a commitment. I wanted more from you than you were willing or able to give, and I understood that. It didn't mean it wasn't hard knowing that, by marrying Grace, I was closing the door on us. One of the hardest things I've ever done was walk into the hospital room that night, seeing you with Lila, knowing what might've been."

"I'm sorry."

"There's no need to be sorry." He smoothed his thumb over her cheek, wiping away a tear. "Grace and I were happy. We had a good marriage. And you got the life you wanted. You've been happy too, haven't you?"

She nodded, not trusting her voice. She was caught up in the memories and was afraid she'd reveal things that were better left unsaid. She'd never let herself think too long or too hard on what might've been. The family curse had been her saving grace.

"What are we going to do about Lila?"

"We just talked about this, Eva. She'll either marry David or she won't. She's a smart woman who knows her own mind. She just needs to know that we'll support her whatever she decides. And Eva, I'm almost one hundred percent certain she'll go through with the wedding. And if she does, you will support her, right?"

"No." She shook her head. "I can't, not knowing what I do now. You and Grace had a good marriage, James, but David isn't like you. And Lila has a baby to think about."

"And she wants to marry the baby's father."

"Which is a stupid reason to get married. And for a smart man, you obviously aren't thinking straight if you can't see that."

"It's hard to think straight with you naked in my bed." He scooped her into his arms, rolling her on top of him. "I'd rather make out with you than talk about our daughter." He kissed her, murmuring against her lips, "And this will be a first for me. I've never made out with a hot grandma before."

Eva's eyes jerked to his. "We're going to be grandparents."

James laughed, and then he kissed her, obliterating thoughts of anyone but him, them, on a flood of sensation and passion.

Chapter Eighteen

What was it with her and bathrooms? Lila wondered as she leaned toward the mirror, wiping mascara from under her bloodshot eyes with a wet paper towel. She'd had another meltdown. Only this time, instead of sharing her deepest, darkest secret with Luke—a man she trusted— she'd told her cousins, the sisters of her heart, and she didn't trust them as far as she could throw them. Not when it came to this.

She glanced at Sage and Willow in the bathroom mirror. Now that they'd stopped celebrating her baby news, they were having a whispered conversation behind her. And Lila knew exactly what they were whispering about.

"I'd marry David whether I was pregnant or not, so if you think this changes anything, you're wrong." Lila lowered her eyes from Sage's penetrating stare and squeezed the water from the paper towel.

She didn't trust her cousin not to see through the lie. If Lila hadn't been pregnant, she wasn't sure she would've agreed to marry David. At least not right now. There'd been a reason she'd been putting off setting a wedding date. She hadn't been ready to get married, and it had nothing to do with David. That wasn't exactly true either. She hadn't wanted to hurt him, which was a ridiculous reason to accept his proposal. But they'd been together for almost three years, and he'd made a persuasive argument for why getting married was a good idea. An excellent one, actually.

They weren't getting any younger, and they both wanted children one day. They'd invested three years in their relationship. They trusted each other. They were compatible. They wanted the same things in life. They knew each other really . . .

She tossed the paper towel in the wastebasket. At least she'd thought they knew each other until she'd played that stupid shower game.

"This is a first," she said, turning to face her cousins. "Do you have nothing else to say?"

"Trust me, I have plenty to—"

Willow elbowed her sister. "We're here to support you. If you say you're happy and over-the-moon in love with David, we believe you."

Lila narrowed her eyes at Willow, wondering what her cousin was up to. She'd never said she was over-the-moon in love with David. Lila wouldn't ask her, though. She didn't think Willow would tell her the truth. But if she did, Lila wasn't sure she was ready to hear it. They had a restaurant full of women waiting for them.

"Thank you. We'd better get out there." Lila brushed past her cousins as she walked to the door. "Please don't say anything about the baby. David and I are waiting until I'm twelve weeks." Which was next week. After how her cousins had reacted to the news—positive the baby was the only reason she was marrying David—Lila decided it would be better if they waited until she was sixteen weeks.

"And when are you twelve weeks exactly?" Sage asked, glancing at Lila's still-flat stomach.

"The week after the wedding, actually," Lila said smoothly. She made a mental note to tell David they were postponing the baby reveal, sighing when she realized that he'd want to know why. If she told him the truth, he might start questioning her motives too.

"Convenient," Sage murmured.

Her hand on the door, Lila turned to her cousin, but she didn't get a chance to say anything. Her grandmother and aunt nearly took Lila out when they burst into the restroom.

"What did you say to your mother?" her grandmother demanded.

"Ma, you don't know that Lila said anything. Eva said she was going to the—"

"Bah." Her grandmother waved her hand. "You said she looked like she'd been crying, and she's not at the grocery store. I called."

"You said she was crying, Ma! I told you she'd been chopping jalapenos and touched her eyes."

"My Eva wouldn't—"

"Stop! Please stop," Lila said, pressing a hand to her racing heart, afraid that her mother had somehow overheard her. "Where was Mom when you saw her, Zia?"

Willow swore under her breath, no doubt thinking the same thing as Lila.

"Here." She pointed to the door. "She was standing outside the restroom." Her aunt's gaze moved from Lila to her daughters. "What's going on? What did my sister hear that upset her?"

Lila pressed a hand to her mouth, afraid she was going to be sick again. Everything she'd said to her cousins was true, but the last thing she wanted was for her mother to have heard her. She would never hurt her like that. It's why she'd never said anything to either her mother or her father when she was younger.

It was a lose-lose situation. They'd have blamed each other, and it would've made everything worse. She loved them, and she'd never, not once, doubted their love for her. They had been the best parents a kid could ask for. They'd just sucked at sharing her.

Her cousins moved closer to Lila, while her grandmother and her aunt—their mouths tight, their expressions fierce—stared at her, waiting for her to answer.

As much as Lila had never doubted that her grandmother and her aunt loved her, she also knew that their loyalty lay with her mother. The three of them were closer than anyone Lila knew. They'd lived and worked together for decades. There wasn't anything they wouldn't do for each other. It was a beautiful thing to witness. Unless they suspected you'd hurt your mother, and then they were downright scary.

"Stop looking at her like that," Sage said, stepping in front of Lila and crossing her arms. "We were having a private conversation. Zia shouldn't have been listening at the door."

"Lila's having a baby," Willow blurted, no doubt in an effort to protect Lila, but that didn't mean Lila was happy about it.

"You never could keep a secret," Sage muttered, stumbling back when their grandmother and their mother rushed forward.

"A bambino!" her grandmother cried, grabbing Lila's face between her hands and kissing her cheeks. "We're going to have a bambino."

"Lila, that's the best news," her aunt said, blinking back tears. "I'm so happy for you. For us." She nudged Carmen out of the way to hug Lila.

Then her grandmother and her aunt looked at each other and started to laugh. "Can you hear Eva telling her boy toys that she's not only fifty, she's a nonna too?" Carmen said, her voice gurgling with laughter.

"She doesn't tell them she's fifty. She tells them she's forty," Gia said, and the two of them hooted with laughter. Tears streamed down their faces as they continued sharing how Lila's baby news would affect her mother's sex life.

Lila sighed. She really didn't want to hear this. She was tempted to put her hands over her ears and start humming, but then her grandmother and aunt stopped laughing and started frowning. This couldn't be good.

Her grandmother lifted her red-framed glasses to wipe the tears from her eyes. "Something isn't right. As much as Eva hates getting old, she'd be happy about the bambino."

"You're right, Ma. She'd be over the moon, and she wasn't."

Her aunt and grandmother turned to look at Lila, and she caved. They were going to find out anyway. Maybe it was better coming from her. She told them what she'd said and how much she regretted her mother overhearing her.

Her grandmother nodded as if she wasn't surprised by Lila's confession, and her aunt patted her shoulder. "We knew it was hard on you. It was hard on all of us."

Lila let out the breath she'd been holding, relieved that

they didn't question her further. Though she had a feeling she wasn't off the hook yet.

"We have to find Eva," her grandmother said. "There's no telling what she'll do when she's upset."

"She'll go to Surfside," her aunt said, and then she and Carmen started arguing about which bar she'd go to.

"We have a restaurant full of guests. We can't just leave," Sage pointed out.

If it weren't for her cousins, Lila didn't know how she would've gotten through the next forty-five minutes. They ran interference for her while Gia and Carmen fulfilled their hostess duties as if nothing were wrong. Clearly the Rosettis were accomplished actresses.

"Are you sure you're all right?" David's mother asked as Lila walked her to the door. "I didn't realize you were allergic to canola oil. I'll have to let the chef know. Tell Eva goodbye for me. I hope she's okay. She seemed really upset."

"Honestly, I'm more concerned about Mr. Balderson, the owner of the market." Especially because everyone at the shower now believed his oil was mislabeled. Her grandmother should've thought about that before she'd come up with her excuse for Lila's blotchy face and her mother's disappearance.

"You could've died, Lila. Your mother has every right to be upset with him. Can you imagine how she would've felt if something had happened to you? She really should consider suing the man."

Lila held back a groan. Once her grandmother had gotten going, her story had become more dramatic with each telling.

"I didn't want to say anything in front of my grandmother,

but you know, it's possible my mother grabbed the wrong bottle." Lila didn't want the chefs at Windemere to boycott the market.

"Do you really think so?"

"I do." Lila nodded, then smiled. "I'll probably see you at Windemere tonight. David and I are having dinner together."

"Oh, good," Jennifer said, looking relieved. "I was a little worried after, you know, the game."

Lila waved her hand. "I knew the answers. I was just winding up my cousins."

"I thought she was never going to leave," Sage said when the door closed behind Jennifer. "Willow, hurry up!"

"I called every bar in town, and they said they haven't seen her," Willow shared when she joined them.

"It doesn't mean she's not there. They've been covering Eva's *culo* since she started sneaking into bars at seventeen," her aunt said, hiking her purse over her shoulder.

"You're coming too?" Sage asked her mother as she pushed open the door.

"We both are," Carmen said, joining them outside the restaurant. She locked the door.

They'd gone back to closing on Sundays and Mondays. In part because her father's arguments against changing their days of operation after decades were sound, but also because they needed at least two days a week to work on the restaurant's face-lift, which was scheduled to begin the next morning.

Thinking of her father made Lila queasy. She had to tell him what she'd said, what her mother had overheard. She imagined he'd be just as upset as Eva to learn the impact their tug-of-war had had on Lila. But even if her father guessed that the baby had played a role in Lila's decision to marry David, she knew he wouldn't try to convince her she was making a mistake.

He'd support and stand by her no matter what. He was the same way with her sisters. Even if he knew they were setting themselves up for failure—like her sister Sheena in her latest business venture—he wouldn't try to talk them out of it, but he was always there to pick them up and give them a pep talk when things didn't work out.

Lila piled into Sage's car with her family. Willow called shotgun before her, so she was stuck in the back seat between her grandmother and aunt. She was worried they'd ask what had precipitated her rant, but Sage turned on the radio. It was set to a golden-oldies station, which wasn't her cousin's taste in music at all. When Carmen started singing along with Otis Redding's "(Sittin' on) The Dock of the Bay," Lila met Sage's eyes in the rearview mirror and mouthed her thanks.

Her cousin smiled and started singing along with Carmen, and the rest of them joined in. The windows were down, a warm ocean breeze blowing through their hair, music blasting as they cruised the back roads of Sunshine Bay. It brought back fond memories. They'd had an old station wagon when Lila was growing up. All six of them would pile into the car on Sundays and go for a drive.

Sage parked on a side street. Between pubs, cocktail bars, restaurant bars, and patios, there were at least twenty places her mother could be. They split up. Lila went with her cousins, and her aunt and grandmother went together. They'd call if they found Eva, and Lila would do the same.

If they didn't find her mother on Main Street, they'd pile back in the car and hit restaurants and bars on the outskirts of town. But it made sense she'd be on Main Street. It was in easy walking distance of La Dolce Vita. Then again, her mother knew practically everyone in town and could easily find someone to drive her wherever she wanted to go.

Forty-five minutes later, they'd hit nine bars on their list. Willow looked back longingly at the patio they'd just left. "Aw, come on. It's almost dinnertime, and those sliders looked amazing."

Sage snorted. "It's four, and it wasn't the sliders you were drooling over."

Willow grinned. "What can I say? I have a thing for a man in uniform."

Lila's phone pinged, and she glanced at the screen. "Nonna and Zia haven't had any luck. They're meeting us back at the car."

They walked into Surfside, the last bar on their list and one of her mother's favorite hangouts. Her mother wasn't at the bar, but Lila's fiancé was. He was sitting at a table near the back with ten people, and he seemed to be having a really good time.

"Someone's having fun," Willow murmured.

Sage leaned forward, squinting as she removed her sunglasses. "Isn't that Sam?" she asked Willow.

"Who's Sam?" Lila asked as they made their way to the back of the bar.

"The brunette with the big boobs whispering in your fiancé's ear. She used to work at La Dolce Vita. She left to take a job at Windemere," Willow said, sharing a glance with her sister.

Lila rolled her eyes. She wasn't a jealous person, and it didn't bother her that an attractive woman was whispering in David's ear. The bar was loud, so it made sense she'd have to lean in to talk to him. But what did bother Lila was that David looked happy and relaxed. Happier and more relaxed than she'd seen him in a while. He threw back his head and laughed, and Lila's jaw practically hit the floor. She couldn't remember the last time she'd heard him laugh like that.

Sam nudged him, nodding in Lila's direction. His laughter dried up, and he pushed back his chair, awkwardly coming to his feet.

"Hey, honey, what are you doing here?" He leaned in to kiss her cheek.

"Looking for my mother. It's a long story," she said when he frowned. "I'll tell you about it later. You haven't seen her, have you?"

"No, and we've been here about an hour."

"What are you doing here, David?" Sage asked.

He gave them a sheepish smile, gesturing to the people sitting around the table, who were mostly women. "The staff decided to throw me a shower."

There were a gift basket, wrapping paper, and what looked like a couple of gag gifts on the table.

David introduced them around the table. They all offered Lila their congratulations, although a couple of women wore self-conscious smiles. Lila imagined they were the ones who'd worked at Windemere. Sam didn't seem self-conscious about it at all.

"How are you ladies enjoying working at Windemere?" Willow asked.

Sam lifted her chin. "It's great. David's a wonderful boss." Three other women murmured that they liked it.

Afraid of what else might come out of her cousin's mouth, Lila said, "We should get going." She leaned in and kissed David's cheek. "I'll let you know if I'm going to make dinner tonight. I have to talk to my mom."

"Don't worry about it. We've just ordered, so I probably won't be hungry anyway."

"Oh, okay, so I shouldn't drop by tonight, then?" she asked, a little embarrassed that he had brushed her off so easily in front of his staff.

"Of course I want you to come. I just meant you don't have to rush on my account. You obviously have things you need to talk about with Eva."

"You know what, you're right. You just stay and party here all night. I'll catch you tomorrow." She cast a smile around the table, gave David a friendly pat on the arm, and then walked away. "Don't say one word," she warned her cousins.

"Okay, don't bite my head off," Sage said as they left the bar. "But that was nice what they did. David doesn't have any friends in Sunshine Bay, and he probably could use a break from Windemere. And you were a little harsh, Willow. Mom and Zia haven't been able to give the servers as many hours as they need, and some of those women are single moms."

"I sounded pretty harsh too, and just for the record, it's not because I'm jealous," Lila said.

"You're right. Mom and Zia would be the first to tell them to apply at Windemere. It's just that they're short-staffed, and they already work so hard. I'll take on some hours," Willow said, before adding, "Hang on a minute," and heading back into Surfside.

"I can take on some hours too," Lila said as she texted David. She apologized for how she'd acted, explained what had happened, and then told him to have fun.

Willow came out of the bar, linking arms with them. "I bought them a round from us."

Sage's cell phone rang. She glanced at the number. "I have to take this," she said, unhooking her arm from Willow's and bringing her phone to her ear. She walked ahead of them, putting her finger in her other ear as she talked to whoever was on the other end.

"That doesn't sound like a work call to me," Willow said, glancing at Lila, who was looking at her own phone. "It's pretty loud in the bar. I'm sure David doesn't know you texted him."

"Yeah, he hasn't read it."

Sage waited for them to catch up. "I have to head back to Boston. Any other ideas where Zia might be?"

Willow and Lila didn't have any idea, but when they got to the car, her aunt did. "She might've gone to the beach house."

"I don't think so, Zia. Mom wouldn't..." Lila trailed off. Her aunt was right. Her mother had probably gone straight to the beach house. She wouldn't take any of the blame on herself. She'd blame everything on Lila's father, just like she always did.

"I'll call Dad." Lila braced herself. She didn't want to do this over the phone and was privately relieved when the call went straight to voice mail.

The five of them got back in the car and headed to the

beach house anyway. Everyone was subdued on the drive over. Lila because she was afraid she was walking into a fight between her parents, and her aunt and grandmother because Willow had mentioned seeing their former servers at Surfside.

They all jumped when Willow shrieked from the front seat, "She stole my scooter!"

Lila leaned forward. "And drove it into my dad's car." This was going to be bad. She pressed a hand to her churning stomach as Sage pulled into the driveway.

Willow jumped out of the car and ran to her scooter. She cradled it to her chest like it was a baby.

Lila got out of the car. "Is it okay?" She hoped it was in better shape than her dad's rental, which had a foot-long gouge along one door.

"I think so." Willow glanced at their grandmother and her mother, who'd gotten out of the car. "Nonna, Mom, Sage has to get back to Boston, and Lila's got this."

"Thanks," Lila murmured when her grandmother and aunt got back in the car. She didn't need an audience when everything came out.

Sage leaned toward the open passenger-side window. "Call me if you need me."

"Call me. I'm closer," Willow said, and gave her a hug.

Lila waved goodbye to her family and then walked toward the house, listening for sounds of her mother yelling or of breaking glass. Instead she heard music and laughter and splashing coming from the deck.

She recognized her parents' voices as she walked down the path, stumbling when she heard what sounded like a couple making out. They couldn't be. She walked down the side of the house until she reached the lower deck and pulled herself up on the ledge. She got a look at the couple in the hot tub and squeezed her eyes closed. They were definitely making out.

She spun around and ran back to the house, grabbed the keys to the Ferrari off the console table in the hall, and took off. She got into the car and revved the engine. She didn't know where she was going as she backed out of the driveway. She just knew she couldn't be here.

If she stayed, she'd say things to her mother that she couldn't take back. She didn't want Eva with her father. There was no doubt in Lila's mind that she'd break his heart. Her father deserved someone who would fall head over heels in love with him, and her mother didn't do love. He needed someone who believed in commitment and happy ever afters, and her mother didn't believe in either.

It was as if the car knew where Lila wanted to go before she did. She was headed to SUP Sunshine.

Chapter Nineteen

Lila had a moment of hesitation, a twinge of guilt because it was Luke she wanted to see and not her fiancé. But David was partying with his new friends, and the last place she wanted to talk about her mother and father and what she'd just witnessed was in a bar. David wouldn't understand, but Luke would. He knew her mother. And Lila didn't have to pretend with him or watch what she said. He wouldn't use her fears or concerns like a weapon against her mother. He'd keep her secrets.

Luke's pickup wasn't parked outside his workshop, and the level of her disappointment took her aback. If her reaction to his not being here was this strong, it was probably for the best he wasn't.

She was about to pull away when a man walked out of the shop, wiping his hands on a rag. He smiled. "Can I help you?"

"I was looking for Luke."

"He took off about an hour ago. You can probably catch him at his place." He cocked his head. "You don't know where he lives, do you?"

"No I don't, but it's okay. I just had some ideas I wanted to run by him. I'm Lila, by the way."

"Bodhi. Luke mentioned you," he said as he walked to the car. "I'd shake your hand, but you'd end up smelling like turpentine." He held up the rag. Then, without her asking, he gave her directions to Luke's house. It was around the corner at the end of the road. "He's pumped about you taking him on as a client. We all are. Luke figures, with you on board, he'll need us full-time, which would be great. I've got a little one on the way." He grinned. "No pressure, though."

Maybe she should go see Luke. As with her family's business, there were a lot of people depending on him to be successful, and not just with SUP Sunshine. She'd taken a look at his profit-and-loss statements for the charter business and found several areas that needed improvement. She had some ideas about how he could make those improvements and planned to bring them up when she met with him the next night.

"I work best under pressure," she said. "I just hope I can live up to his expectations."

"Trust me, you have no worries there. The guy thinks you're the bomb."

"I think he's pretty great too," she said without thinking, probably because she did.

"Best guy I know." His gaze went to her hand on the steering wheel, the sparkling diamond ring on her finger. "He's gone through a lot these past few years, wouldn't want to see him hurt again." He smiled as if he hadn't just delivered a not-so-subtle warning. "Better get back to work. When you see Luke, tell him the guy he took out this afternoon placed an order for four more boards."

"James Sinclair?"

"Yeah, you know him?"

"He's my dad."

Bodhi whistled. "Lucky lady. I hope I haven't just ruined your surprise because I'm pretty sure one of the boards is for you."

Lila was pretty sure it was too, and just as sure two were for her sisters. And she was afraid she knew whom the fourth board was for. "It's okay. I hate surprises anyway."

He laughed, and they said their goodbyes. As Lila backed out of the driveway, Bodhi's warning about Luke sat heavy on her mind but probably not for the reason it should. She wanted to know who'd hurt him. She wondered if it had to do with the shadow she'd seen in his eyes when he talked about his friend's baby.

She drove slowly along the road. Apart from Luke's work-shop, it was a residential street that backed onto the woods. Growing up, she'd had a friend who'd lived one street over. They'd played hide-and-seek in Whispering Woods, the locals' name for the nature preserve. She remembered there was a pond nearby and wondered if Luke's house was anywhere near it.

It looked as if she was about to find out. But as she approached the pretty marine-blue house with a covered porch, she noticed a car parked beside Luke's pickup and didn't want to intrude. The door opened just as she'd pulled into his driveway to turn the car around, and two little boys raced down the stairs with Admiral barreling after them. Then he spotted Lila and headed her way.

"No," Lila cried, not sure if it was because of the dog bounding toward her or Heather kissing Luke on the cheek on the front porch. *The dog, definitely the dog*, Lila told herself when Admiral placed his big paws on the car and leaned in to lick her face.

Luke smiled and shook his head, coming down the stairs with an arm slung over Heather's shoulders. "It's official," he said. "My dog's in love with you."

She managed a smile for Heather and Luke, which Admiral must've thought was for him, because he seemed to be smiling at her with his tongue lolling from his mouth as he backed away from the car.

"Admiral, no!" Luke yelled at the same time the dog took a running leap and tried to jump into the car with her. "Idiot dog," he said as he half lifted, half dragged Admiral off the car, cringing at what sounded like nails on a chalkboard.

"Idiot dog!" the twins yelled through their laughter, running over to hug Admiral. "Oh, oh," one of them said, pointing at the side of the car. "Idiot dog is in trouble now."

Luke cursed under his breath and then pointed a finger at the twins. "Don't repeat that." He glanced over his shoulder at Heather, who'd walked over. "Sorry about that."

Heather laughed. "You've heard my mother, aka Trucker Mouth, haven't you? Don't worry about it. Hey, Lila, how was the shower?"

"Great, really great," she said with forced enthusiasm.

Luke looked at her and frowned. Then he turned to Heather, giving her a one-armed hug as he kept a firm grip on Admiral with his other arm. "Thanks again for the photos. You did an amazing job."

"Photos?" Lila asked, looking from Luke to Heather.

"I do photography on the side. I got some great shots

of Luke the other day, and I thought he might want to use them on his new website. That was a good idea, by the way," she said to Lila. "This one doesn't do enough to promote his talent."

"Pot, kettle. You should see her photos, Lila. They're incredible."

"I'd love to. Can I see them?"

"Sure." Heather held her camera out to Lila. "Do me a favor and don't mention it to your mom. I don't want her to worry I'm going to leave them in a lurch. It's just a hobby."

Lila scrolled through the photos, stopping at several of Luke on his paddleboard on the water with the sun setting behind him, one with Luke on the board with Admiral, his head tipped back laughing, and a couple of him with Heather's boys on the board. "These are incredible. Don't sell yourself short, Heather. You should be doing this for more than a hobby."

Luke nudged her, and Heather shook her head, nudging him back. "I had great subject matter."

She really did. "You also have a great eye. The lighting and composition are perfect." She scrolled through the photos again. "A couple of these would work for the ad campaign I'm putting together for Luke as well as the website. But I'd also like some shots for the charter business and of inside the shop. Maybe we could set up a time to talk?"

"Sure, that'd be great." She glanced at her boys, who were tackling Admiral on the lawn. "I'd better get these two home. Thanks for watching them, Luke."

"Anytime." He scooped up the protesting twins, tossing each of them over a shoulder. He walked them to Heather's

car and buckled them into their car seats. "Be good for
your mom." Lila couldn't hear what they said, but Luke
responded with, "Yeah, if you are, I'll take you on the boat
next week."

"That should buy Heather a few hours' peace," he said,
his fingers latched around Admiral's collar as he returned
the twins' salutes.

"I didn't know you two were dating."

"We're not. We're just good friends. I help out with the
boys every once in a while, and Heather takes photos for
me. She took the ones on the charter boat's website."

"She really is an excellent photographer."

"She is." He crouched down by her door, trying to buff
out the scratches with the hem of his T-shirt. "So the
shower, how did it really go?"

"It was a disaster."

"So is this door. I'll need more than my T-shirt to buff
the scratches out." He lifted his chin at the house. "Do you
want to come inside?"

"Are you sure you're not busy? I don't want to keep you
from whatever you're doing."

"I wouldn't invite you in if I was. I was just going to
grab something to eat before I head back to the shop." He
stepped back as she opened the car door. "Behave, doofus,
or you'll scare Lila away."

She closed the car door, patting Admiral's big head as she
followed Luke to the house. "I stopped by the shop. I met
Bodhi. He seems like a nice guy."

"He is. Talented too. I'm afraid I might lose him if I
can't give him more hours," Luke said, holding the front
door open for her.

"He mentioned he has a baby on the way," she said as she stepped into the house and looked around. "Wow, this place is great, Luke." It wasn't a showplace like the beach house or a tricked-out bachelor pad. It was all warm woods and big, comfortable-looking furniture in shades of blue, a little messy, but that only added to the charm.

He snorted. "I've seen your house. This place would fit in your main floor." He snagged a couple of magazines off the scuffed hardwood and tossed them onto a coffee table. "Ignore the mess. I'd like to blame it on the twins and doofus, but I can't."

"Okay, if you tell my dad I said this, I'll deny it. But I'd rather live in a house like this. It's warm and cozy. I can see myself curling up on that chair by the fire with a book or out on your deck, which is amazing. Did you build it?"

"Thanks. I did." He walked to the kitchen and opened the refrigerator. "What can I get you to drink?"

"I'd have a soda if you have any." She could use a sugar rush. She hadn't realized how tired she was until she'd walked into Luke's house. She supposed it was no wonder with the drama of the past week, but she had a feeling it had more to do with her pregnancy. Which reminded her, she had to call the health center and set up an appointment for this week.

She walked to the patio door. "Great view." The woods butted up to the back of Luke's property. "How long have you owned this place?"

He came to stand beside her, handing her a glass of soda. "A couple of years."

"Thank you." She glanced at him. His jaw was tight, a muscle flexing in his cheek. She had a feeling he hadn't bought the home for himself. It was a home you bought when you were starting a family. She was tempted to ask him what had happened. Who'd hurt him and put the shadow in his eyes. But she didn't think he'd appreciate her asking.

"You want to sit inside or out?"

"Inside, if you don't mind. It's a little muggy out."

"Yeah. There's a storm coming in tonight." He gestured to the couch. "Admiral's called dibs on the chair, and I can tell you, from past experience, he won't give it up, but you're welcome to try."

"I wouldn't want to disturb him," she said, taking a seat on the couch. "Are you sure about the storm? According to Willow, there's no rain in the forecast."

He laughed and joined her on the couch, seeming more like himself. "She needs to look up at the sky once in a while. You can tell by the clouds. When they start moving fast, the weather's going to change." He pointed out the window. "You see how thin they are? We'll get rain in a few hours."

"I bet this place is even cozier in the rain."

"You really do like it," he said, shaking his head as if he couldn't understand why.

"I love it. As soon as I walked in, I felt like I'd come home." Her cheeks heated. "That didn't come out right." Except it was exactly how she'd felt. "Don't mind me. I've had a crappy day. And when I walked into your house, the tension seemed to ebb away."

"What happened?" he asked, his arm resting along the back of the couch.

"Let's just say I'm never going into another restaurant's restroom for the rest of my life."

"That's all you're going to give me?"

"Please, you have to be sick of listening to me complain. It's all I ever do when I'm with you."

"It's not all you do when you're with me. You fed me and my dog the other night, and doofus just scratched the hell out of your father's car. Who, by the way, is a great guy. I enjoyed my afternoon with him."

"He must've enjoyed his day with you too. Bodhi told me to tell you he ordered four boards."

"Really? Wow, that's fantastic. That in itself earned you at least an hour of ranting time." He motioned with his hand. "Don't hold back."

"I thought you had to work."

"You're right, I do. How do you feel about an omelet?" he asked, getting up from the couch. "I'll cook and you can talk."

"Okay, but don't say I didn't warn you." She followed him to the kitchen and took a seat on a barstool at the island. As he got eggs, cheese, cream, and ham out of the fridge, she told him about the he-said, she-said shower game and how she had totally bombed, and how not only had she failed miserably, but her last few answers had made it sound as if David was in love with her, but she wasn't in love with him.

Luke turned with a yellow ceramic bowl in his hand, whisking together the eggs and cream. "It's just a shower game. Anyone can have an off day."

"I know, right?" She dragged her gaze from his biceps. The man had incredible arms. She cleared her throat. "They were ridiculous questions. Like what's your favorite color and your favorite flavor of ice cream. What does that have to do with anything?"

"Lila, even I know your favorite color is purple and your favorite flavor of ice cream is vanilla."

"How did you know purple's my favorite color?"

"Because you said so the other night when we were watching the sun set." He turned away and placed the bowl by the stove, then bent over to pull out a frying pan from the cupboard. "Is that it?"

She shouldn't be surprised he knew. Luke paid attention, and he was also a great listener. And it definitely shouldn't be giving her the warm fuzzies that he did. Although the warm fuzzies might be because she was at that moment admiring the way he filled out his jeans.

"Lila?" He placed two plates and utensils on the island.

She looked up and met his gaze. "Sorry, I was just admiring your...stove."

He rubbed his earlobe between his thumb and forefinger. Then he turned back to the stove, melting a large glob of butter in the pan. "So, was that it?"

"I wish. But no, it got worse. I knew what my family was thinking, and I got nervous about what was to come, and when I get nervous, I get sick to my stomach."

"Okay, I see where this is going. You had another melt-down, and now your family knows you're expecting."

She nodded. "Pretty much."

"That's not a bad thing. The stress isn't good for you or the baby. Maybe now everyone will back off. You don't need this."

She wished David were here right now listening to Luke. He could learn a thing or two. "There's one problem. I didn't stop there. Sage and Willow were trying to talk me out of marrying David because of that stupid quiz, so I told them I was pregnant, and when they still didn't seem to get why I was marrying him, I told them what it had been like for me growing up."

He turned with the pan in his hand, cutting the golden omelet down the middle with a spatula. It smelled incredible.

She held up her hand. "That looks and smells amazing, but I won't be able to eat half. I ate a lot at the shower."

He didn't try to talk her into eating more, sliding a third onto her plate. She glanced over her shoulder. "Admiral's nose is twitching."

Luke smiled as he plated his part of the omelet. "Don't worry, he won't steal yours. The twins wore him out, and they also fed him half his treats when I had my back turned."

He put the pan, bowl, and spatula in the sink and then came around the island, taking a seat on the barstool beside her. "What was it like for you growing up?"

She told him everything she'd said to her cousins. "The worst part was finding out my mother was listening at the door and heard everything."

He winced. "That must've been hard for her to hear. You never said anything to your parents when you were growing up?"

"No, I didn't want to hurt them."

"I get that." He nodded. "But in the end, it's probably better that it came out. How did your mom and dad handle it?"

"They didn't seem fazed by it at all, from what I saw. They were making out in the hot tub."

Luke choked on his omelet, and Lila patted his back. "Yeah, that's pretty much how I felt too."

"Thanks, I'm good." He cleared his throat. "I take it you're not happy your parents were, uh, together."

"No, no way," she said, and told him why. "Now I just have to find a way to ensure this doesn't go any further."

"You're not thinking of breaking them up, are you?"

"If this lasts more than a day, of course I am. My dad's vulnerable."

"Maybe Eva is too, Lila. Have you ever thought that the reason she's only interested in short-term relationships is because she's protecting herself? It makes sense that she would, given your family's romantic history. Maybe she's afraid of getting her heart broken."

"My mom? No way. She doesn't believe in commitment or long-term relationships. And if my dad falls in love with her again—and trust me, I understand why he would; my mother is not only gorgeous, she's funny, and kind, and cooks and sings like a dream—she'll break his heart."

"I don't know. Your father seems like a guy who knows his own mind. Just my opinion," he said, getting up to take their plates, "but I'd think twice about trying to break them up. It might end up being your relationship with your parents that gets damaged."

"No offense, but you spent an afternoon with my dad, Luke. You weren't there when he lost Grace. It was horrible. He's only just beginning to act like himself."

"You're right. I shouldn't have said anything."

"No. I'm sorry. You were sweet enough to listen to me and make me something to eat, and I bit your head off."

"You didn't bite my head off, Lila. You simply told me why you disagreed with me."

"I know, but I want you to tell me what you think. I like hearing your opinion on things."

"Yeah, well, I can almost guarantee you won't like my

opinion of you getting married because you're having the guy's baby."

She sucked in a shocked gasp and got up from the barstool. "I should probably leave now."

Luke came around the island and put his hands on her shoulders, ducking his head to hold her gaze. "I didn't mean to hurt you. But come on, Lila, you have to know that marrying David because of the baby isn't fair to any of you. You'll end up resenting him, and he'll end up resenting you, and the baby will feel that."

She blinked back tears and wrapped her arms around her waist. "I love David. He's my best friend."

"I'm glad to hear it. It's just that, when you were telling me what you said to your cousins, you left that part out. And the thing is, I know you, Lila. I know that you're sweet, and kind, and so damn loyal that you'd stick with someone even when you should kick them to the curb."

"What do you mean?"

He raised an eyebrow. "My brother?"

"Okay, but I was sixteen. I'd like to think I'm smarter than that now."

"Wouldn't we all," he said, then glanced at his watch. "I have to go, but you're welcome to stay if you want to put off talking to your parents. Admiral would enjoy the company."

"You're sure you don't mind?" She wasn't ready to talk to her parents just yet.

"Not at all." He glanced at Admiral. "He'll probably be out until I come back." He reached in his pocket and pulled out a key. "If you want something else to drink or eat, help yourself. Just lock up when you leave."

After she'd put up the windows and roof on the Ferrari, she stood at the door watching Luke jog down the road, everything he'd said running through her head. She shut the door, glancing at her phone on the coffee table. David hadn't responded to her text. She stretched out on the couch, and her eyes drifted closed. She was so tired and confused.

She opened her eyes to misty morning sunlight filling the living room and jerked upright, reaching for her phone. It was five thirty in the morning, and she had twenty-two missed calls and just as many missed texts.

Chapter Twenty

Eva woke up to the early-morning sunshine bathing the room and the man beside her in a golden light. The white sheers framing the open window fluttered on a warm ocean breeze, the sound of waves lapping against the shore peaceful and familiar. The panic rising inside her was familiar too, and she breathed through the growing tightness in her chest.

She shouldn't have stayed the night with James. She didn't let men spend the night with her. James was the only man she'd ever woken up with in the morning. The only man she'd ever wanted to spend her days and nights with.

It had been a mistake then. It was a mistake now.

Slowly, carefully, she lifted the sheet and slid off the bed, glancing at James as she did. He didn't move. He'd always been a sound sleeper. He looked younger in his sleep, the lines that fanned from the corners of his eyes and bracketed his full mouth smoothed out. She preferred his lines, this new face that life with all its joys, sorrows, losses, and victories had left behind. He was more beautiful now than he'd been in his twenties.

Unable to resist, she placed a knee on the bed, leaning

over to softly kiss the corner of his mouth. His lips twitched, and he smiled in his sleep, tempting her to kiss him again, to tease him awake. But she was afraid that if he woke up, she wouldn't have the strength to leave.

She walked around the bed and picked up her clothes, dressing quietly and quickly before she changed her mind. As she left the room, she glanced over her shoulder one last time.

They called it the walk of shame when a woman left a man's home wearing her clothes from the day before. Eva had always thought it a ridiculous phrase, probably made up by some man to shame a woman. She'd never felt shame before, and she didn't feel it now. What she felt was fear. She was afraid that her love for James had never died, that like her libido it had gone into hibernation only to be awakened by his touches, his kisses, his smiles, and his laughter.

She crept down the stairs, tiptoeing around the corner to the front door, letting out a startled scream when she walked into her daughter. "Lila!" Eva pressed a hand to her chest. "You nearly gave me a heart attack. What are you doing?"

"Me? What am I doing, Mom? I'm not the one sneaking out of dad's bed at five forty-five in the morning!" Lila made a face and then threw up her hands, her shoes clutched in her fingers.

"Shh, you'll wake your father."

"Her father's awake," James said, coming down the stairs, wearing nothing but his boxers. "What's going on?"

"Dad! Put some clothes on!"

James's brow furrowed, and he glanced down at himself.

He looked so sweetly befuddled that Eva smiled and patted his cheek. "I'll make coffee."

She couldn't leave him on his own to deal with Lila in the state she was in, and then Eva remembered why her daughter was upset, what she'd overheard from the other side of the ladies' restroom door. The reason she'd come to James. They hadn't talked about it, not really. They'd spent the day and night getting reacquainted with each other's bodies.

James covered her hand with his, turning his face to plant a kiss on her palm. There was more than just gratitude in his sea-blue eyes, there was a question too, and Eva had a feeling it had more to do with her sneaking out than with their daughter's state of mind.

"I don't believe you two," Lila huffed, and stormed past them.

"Lila, you're not going anywhere until we talk," James said in a voice that brooked no argument.

James rarely raised his voice at his daughter, and it was clear from Lila's startled expression that it surprised her. And it was for that reason alone, Eva surmised, that their daughter acquiesced. Not gracefully or without attitude; she was Eva's daughter, after all. James shook his head as Lila stomped past them, then flung herself onto the love seat like a teenager having a tantrum.

Eva almost wished they were going to lecture her about boys and breaking curfew, the dangers of drinking too much or experimenting with drugs. Those lectures had seemed like such a big deal back then, but they were nothing compared to the conversation they were about to have with her. Their beloved daughter who'd been so deeply traumatized by Eva and James fighting over her that she was willing to marry a man she didn't love.

As if he knew what Eva was thinking, and no doubt feeling the same way, James hooked his arm around her neck. Drawing her close, he whispered in her ear, "It'll be okay, sweetheart. We're in this together."

She felt a little emotional at his words and nodded. "Go get dressed." As she watched him jog up the stairs, she felt the weight of her daughter's stare and turned.

"You should be ashamed of yourself, Mom. He's not one of your boy toys. How could you do this to him? He's just getting over Grace." Her daughter's face hardened, a touch of fire in her eyes. "If you hurt him, I swear I'll never forgive you."

Eva didn't think she could feel worse than she had the day before standing outside the ladies' restroom, but Lila had just proved her wrong. She drew on an inner strength that had served her well in the past. She was who she was, and she wouldn't let anyone, not even her daughter, shame her for how she chose to live her life. "I understand you're hurting right now, but I suggest you remember who you're speaking to, Lila Marie Rosetti. I am your mother, and not only do I not deserve to be spoken to the way you just did, I won't allow it."

"I'm sorry, Momma," her daughter said, a shimmer of tears in her eyes, eyes the same sea blue as her father's. "It's just that—"

Eva raised her hand. "Don't," she warned, and walked into the kitchen. She made the coffee, her fingers digging into the edge of the counter as she watched it drip into the pot, listening to Lila's and James's muffled voices in the living room.

"Hey," he said, coming up behind her. He wrapped his arms around her waist, dipping his head to nuzzle her neck. "Lila's upset. She says she hurt your feelings. Take whatever she said with a grain of salt. She's not herself right now."

Eva nodded. "I know."

He turned her around, frowning as he raised his hands, smoothing away her tears with his thumbs. "What did she say?"

She doesn't want me with you. She thinks I'll break your heart. She doesn't realize that you could just as easily break mine, like you did the last time I fell in love with you. "Nothing. It's not important." She waved him away. "Go talk to her. I'll bring the coffee in."

⌒

Three hours later, after a draining and, as far as Eva was concerned, unproductive conversation with their daughter, James drove Eva back to La Dolce Vita.

He glanced at her. "So, are you going to tell me why you were sneaking out of the beach house?"

She lifted a shoulder. "I'm an early riser. I didn't want to wake you."

"I wish you would have," he said, waggling his eyebrows.

She snorted. "That would've gone over well with Lila."

"What? Just because we're in our fifties we're not supposed to have sex? We're consenting adults."

"We're her parents."

"Okay, you've got a point. No kid wants to think that their parents have sex. I know I sure as hell didn't." He pulled into the restaurant's parking lot and turned off the engine. "So how do you think it went?"

"With Lila?"

He nodded. "I felt like all we were doing was going around in circles."

"It would've helped if you backed me about her not marrying David simply because she's having his baby."

"I did, but she was adamant that she loves him and would marry him even if she wasn't pregnant."

"You didn't find it interesting that it was Luke she went to and not David?"

"She explained why she did, three times. You weren't very subtle, you know."

"Have you ever heard the phrase 'The lady doth protest too much, methinks'?"

He laughed. "I should. I was the one who took you to see *Hamlet*, and I'm pretty sure I said the same thing to you."

Eva was about to respond when she spotted Bruno getting out of his car at the back of La Dolce Vita's parking lot. "Thank the Madonna, he's back. He's the only one who will be able to convince my mother that taking down the wallpaper is a good idea."

"I could get a health inspector to convince her. That stuff is so old, it probably has fungus growing on it."

"James!" She swatted his chest. "Don't tell me that."

"It's true." He laughed, grabbing her hand and kissing her fingers. "Any chance we can sneak off to your apartment later?"

"You have a one-track mind," she said, trying to ignore the butterflies in her stomach. They were easy to ignore when Bruno walked around the side of his car and opened the door for a gorgeous Latina woman.

"When it comes to you, I do." He frowned. "What's wrong?"

"Bruno's brought Ana with him. What was he thinking?"

"Who's Ana?"

"His girlfriend. I have to get in there before they do and warn my mother," she said as she got out of the car. "Go stall him."

"How am I supposed to do that?"

"Turn on the charm, Sinclair. You're very good at distracting people when you want to."

"You think I'm charming, do you, Rosetti?" he called after her as she ran to the restaurant, waving and shouting hello to Bruno and Ana. "Eva, you don't have any shoes on!"

Obviously he hadn't been looking at her feet when they'd left the beach house. She scooped them up from behind the rosebush where she'd left them the day before and held them up. James didn't notice because he'd walked over to shake Bruno's hand.

Eva's sister was blocking off the back of the dining room from the front with tape. "Couldn't you find something other than yellow tape? It looks like a crime scene," Eva said.

Her sister dropped the tape and ran over and hugged her. "Ma and I were so worried about you." She held Eva away from her. "Did you stay with James last night?"

She nodded, praying her face didn't give anything away. "We had to talk to Lila."

"We couldn't reach her either. You two need to keep your cell phones on. Ma was beside herself."

"I'm sorry. I will from now on. But we have bigger things to worry about. Bruno's here, and he brought Ana."

Her sister raised her hands to her face and shook her head. "Don't tell me that. Ma's already on a tear. She's making noises—really loud ones—about us removing the wallpaper, and she says she hates the color Jennifer picked for the walls. She's gone to the hardware store to get a color deck."

Eva hadn't been thrilled with the warm butter color Jennifer had chosen, but she trusted her vision for the restaurant. The woman had impeccable taste. "Okay, I'll phone the hardware store and get them to stall her. Where's Jennifer?"

"She's not coming."

"What do you mean she's not coming?"

"Don't yell at me!"

"Sorry, it's been a morning. But she has to come. She promised she would." Jennifer had been excited about it. But Eva knew someone who wouldn't be. "How did she sound?"

"Not as ticked off as you. What are you thinking?"

"I'm thinking that her *culo* of a husband wouldn't let her come," she said as she slipped on her high heels.

"Eva, what are you going to do?" her sister asked with a nervous hitch in her voice.

"I'm going to get her, and just let her husband try and stop me." She turned to head for the door and nearly ran into James.

"Where are you going?"

"Yes, Eva, tell him where you're going," her sister said. "Hopefully, you can talk some sense into her, James."

Eva arched an eyebrow at her sister. "Really, G?"

"Hey, since when do I rate just a wave and a hello?" Bruno asked, walking over to join them. Despite the jocular tone of voice, Eva thought he might've been a little hurt.

She hugged him and kissed his cheek, and her sister did the same. "We missed you," Eva said, smiling at the woman at his side. "Hi, Ana. We were very sorry to hear about your mother."

"Thank you." She looped her arm through Bruno's. "It would've been much more difficult if I didn't have this wonderful man with me. He took such great care of me."

"I'm sure he did," Eva said, glancing at her sister, wondering if she was also getting the impression that Ana was making a point.

Ana smiled up at Bruno. "Are you going to tell the girls our news, or shall I?"

Bruno stuck his finger under the collar of his buttoned-up chambray shirt as if it were cutting off his airway. "Ana and I are getting married."

Gia recovered faster than Eva. "That's wonderful," she said, and hugged Bruno and then Ana.

Eva's sister turned to her and made big eyes. "Isn't that wonderful, Eva?"

"Yes, yes, of course it is," she said, and hugged them both.

"But you didn't hear the best part," Ana said, and Eva stiffened, hearing something in the other woman's voice she didn't like. "Bruno."

Eyes downcast, he murmured, "We're moving to Puerto Rico."

"No, Bruno, say it isn't so," Eva pleaded. "You can't leave us."

"That's rather selfish of you, don't you think, Eva? Bruno has devoted his life to you people, and what does he get in return? Your mother—"

Bruno attempted to cut her off. "Ana, not now."

But Ana ignored him. "—fired him. A man who—"

"Our mother did what?" Eva looked at Bruno. "Tell me she didn't."

He lifted a shoulder and gave her a sad smile.

Eva held out her hand. "James, I need your keys."

"Where are you going, Eva?" he asked, reaching into the pocket of his jeans.

"I'm going to kick some *culo*."

He bit back a smile. "Exactly whose ass are you going to kick?"

"My mother and Jennifer's husband. He won't let her come help us."

"Eva, you don't know that," her sister said.

"Oh yes I do." She made a gimme gesture with her fingers to James.

"*Cara*, don't have a fight with your mother over me. Please," Bruno said.

Eva tugged on Bruno's arm, moving him out of Ana's reach and earshot. "Tell me you're happy. Tell me this is what you want, and I'll back off."

"Sometimes we can't have what we want. Sometimes we have to settle for what makes us content." He dipped his head to meet her eyes. "You know that as well as I do, *cara*," he said, casting a pointed glance at James.

She pretended she didn't know what he meant and gave a decisive nod instead. "Okay. That's all I needed to hear."

James joined them and placed his keys in her hand, curling her fingers around them. "Just do me a favor and don't get any more dents or scratches on the car. It's going to cost me more in repair work than it would to buy it," he said, and then took her chin between his fingers and gave her a hard, fast kiss. "Don't do anything to get yourself arrested."

She laughed, grateful that he didn't try to stop her. "I went to school with the chief of police, and she likes me." Most of the time she did.

Lila walked in as Eva was walking out. "Mom, where are you going?"

"Ask your father," she said, and then decided her relationship with her daughter was on shaky ground as it was. "Jennifer isn't coming, and I'm almost positive that your father-in-law-to-be is behind it. If he is, I'm bringing her back with me, and if he tries to stop me—"

"You're going to kick his *culo*." Lila nodded. "Good. It's about time someone did."

"Good," she said, and walked to the Ferrari without smiling or patting her daughter's cheek. Lila had hurt her badly.

"I love you, Mom," Lila called to Eva as she got into the Ferrari.

"I love you too, darling." She smiled as she drove away. It was a start, but Eva's hurt went deep.

She spotted her mother coming out of the hardware store on Main Street, flirting with the owner, who was twenty years her junior. Carmen wore a cute red top, white shorts, and red heels.

Eva rolled to a stop. "Hey, old lady, get your *culo* over here before I come and get you and throw you in the car."

Carmen gaped at her before hurrying over. "What's wrong with you, calling me 'old lady'?" she asked as she got in the car, smiling at the hardware store owner and giving him a flirty wave.

In her mother Eva saw herself twenty years from now, and it was no longer a comforting thought. She glanced at the road and then the car. She didn't have time to waste, but neither did she want to ding up the Ferrari by taking a shortcut through an alley. "Hold on," she told her mother, and pulled a U-turn into oncoming traffic, wincing at the sounds of tires screeching and horns blaring.

"What has gotten into you?"

"What has gotten into me? You fired a man who's devoted his life to you, to us, and to La Dolce Vita. A man who has loved you for decades, and a man who you love too. A man who has just announced he's marrying Ana and moving with her to Puerto Rico."

"He's what?" her mother whispered.

"Yeah, he's getting married and moving away because he's finally realized you're never going to give your relationship a shot."

Her mother's chin trembled. "The curse."

"F the curse."

"Eva Maria!"

"Maybe we're the curse, Ma. Maybe it's our stubbornness and pride. Maybe it's fear of getting hurt that keeps us from letting the right person in. Or maybe the Rosettis just have really crappy luck and crappy taste in men. I don't know if the curse is real or not, but I do know that if you don't fight for Bruno, you'll regret it for the rest of your life." She pulled in front of the restaurant. "And Ma, I don't know if I'll be able to forgive you if you let him go."

Her mother nodded. "I shouldn't have fired him. I'll give him his job back," she said, and got out of the car.

"He doesn't want his job, Ma. He wants you," Eva said.

She started to drive away and then called after her mother, "Hey, old lady, Bruno and Ana are in there now." She got a look at her mother's face in the rearview mirror and smiled. "Go kick some *culo*, Carmen."

Upon arriving at Windemere, Eva walked through the reception area. She saw David leaning on the bar, talking to Sam. Eva had always liked the young woman, who reminded her a little of herself. She was carefree and passionate, a little wild and a lot flirtatious. She was flirting with David, and he seemed to be enjoying it. Eva hadn't seen him smile or heard him laugh like that before. When he did, she could see what had first attracted her daughter.

"Hello, David," Eva said, arching an eyebrow at Sam. The girl had the good grace to blush. "Sam, long time no see. You look like you're enjoying your job here."

Sam glanced from David to Eva, giving her a tentative smile. "I am."

"Good. I'm glad." Eva looped her arm through David's and patted his hand. "I heard you threw my future son-in-law a shower. That was very nice of you. My daughter tells me you were enjoying yourself, David. She was glad you've made friends. Although, darling, you should respond to her texts in a more timely fashion. She's expecting your baby, after all. Congratulations, by the way. We're all very excited to welcome a new baby to the family."

So she didn't know David and Lila were expecting, Eva thought, as Sam's startled gaze went to David. Eva didn't believe their relationship went any further than some innocent flirtation. She was a good judge of a man's character and trusted that David wouldn't cheat on her daughter. But she also didn't believe that Lila and David would be happy together. They were too much alike. And she could also understand why David would need a little distraction. Working under his father's thumb wasn't easy for him.

"Thank you." His cheeks flushed, David glanced at Sam, who'd moved away to serve a customer. "Nothing happened, Eva. I love Lila. I'd never cheat on her. We were just having a little fun." He lifted a shoulder. "It hasn't been easy, and I needed to blow off some steam. I didn't see Lila's text until I got back to Windemere. I texted her right away, called her too, but she didn't answer until this morning. She sounded okay. Nothing's wrong, is it?" The panic in his voice sounded genuine. Yes, Eva thought, David loved her daughter. There was no denying it.

"She's fine. You should drop by the restaurant. She's helping us with the reno."

"Do you think that's a good idea? With the paint fumes and all?"

"You know her father. He bought her a gas mask," she said, rolling her eyes.

David smiled. "He's a bit over the top when it comes to protecting his daughters."

"He is, and I have a feeling you'll be the same with your baby whether it's a boy or a girl." She looked around. "I'm glad I ran into you and we got a chance to have a little chat, but I'm here to see your mother. She was supposed to help us with the reno, and I wanted to make sure she was all right."

He pushed his glasses up his nose with his forefinger. "About that, my, uh, father wasn't on board with it. He thinks it's some kind of conflict of interest."

"And what do you think? Or, more to the point, what does your mother think?"

David sighed. "I was fine with it, and my mother was

excited about it. She's really talented, but my father's old school. He doesn't want her to work."

"Or does he just like keeping her under his thumb?" she murmured, and then turned to the man who might very well become her son-in-law and the father of her grandchild. "David, I've heard some of your ideas and your mother's for Windemere. They were wonderful, and I hope the two of you will follow through with them. I think you and your mother would work beautifully together."

"Thanks, Eva, I do too. It's just that my father has other ideas."

"Then perhaps he should buy himself another inn and run it himself. He hired you as his manager for a reason. Don't let him undermine your confidence. I have it on good authority that you're excellent at your job. Lila and James both say so. And take my advice as someone who's dealt with her fair share of bullies, you have to stand up to them and set your boundaries. And if your father continues crossing them and making you feel small, then you tell him what he can do with his job and walk away."

"But I really like my job, and I'm good at it. I know I can make something of this place."

"I believe you, and if you stand up for yourself, your father will believe you can too." She patted his cheek. "Now, where is your mother?"

"Out on the patio," David said with a resigned sigh.

Behind the bar, Sam was grinning and gave Eva a thumbs-up. Eva winked and walked out to the patio. "I knew I'd find you here," she said to Jennifer. The woman looked miserable. "Come on, princess. You have a job to do."

"My wife has more important things to do than play decorator for you people."

"Gavin!" Jennifer turned to Eva, her eyes pleading. "I'm sorry. I can't come today."

Eva cocked her head. "But you were looking forward to it, and so were we. What changed your mind?"

"I did," Gavin said, wiping eggs Benedict from his mouth. "My wife isn't your hired help."

"No, she's not. She's my friend, who just happens to be an incredibly talented decorator."

Gavin snorted and shook his head.

Jennifer looked at him and then pushed back her chair. "You're right, I am. And La Dolce Vita needs all the help it can get," she said, smiling at Eva.

"Jennifer, where do you think you're going?"

"To do the job I was hired to do," she said, and looped her arm through Eva's. "Don't wait up for me, Gavin."

"You know we can't afford to pay you, right?" Eva whispered as they walked away.

"He doesn't know that. Besides, I don't need the money, Eva." She sighed. "I should've just gone to La Dolce Vita, but I didn't have the energy to fight with him."

"You can tell me to mind my own business, and I won't be offended, but why do you stay with him?"

"For my boys." She smiled at David as they walked by, and his jaw just about fell to his chest.

"Again, you can tell me to mind my own business, but I don't think you're doing your sons any favors. Gavin's doing to them what he does to you, Jennifer. They're patterning their behavior after yours."

"I'm beginning to see that. I never really noticed until I bought Windemere."

Eva pulled her to a stop. "Excuse me. *You* bought Windemere?"

She nodded. "We've been living off my trust fund since we got married. The way Gavin spends money, there'll be nothing left when we reach our golden years. I thought Windemere would be a good investment and a good opportunity for David and Lila."

"*Cara*, I'm making you an appointment with my niece as soon as we get to the restaurant."

Jennifer smiled. "I already made one. I met with her last night."

Chapter Twenty-One

Lila had arrived for her appointment at Sunshine Bay Health Center forty-five minutes ago. So far David was a no-show.

"We can reschedule the ultrasound if you want," Dr. Alva said, her smile as warm as Lila remembered. Dr. Alva was a former classmate and a friend of Lila's mother. She'd been their primary care physician for the past twenty years.

Lila had been excited about seeing her baby for the first time. She'd thought David was too. But Dr. Alva had a waiting room full of patients, and Lila didn't want to take up any more of her time.

"That would be—" Lila began, a knock on the door cutting her off.

Dr. Alva's nurse poked her head inside. "We have a waiting room full of Rosettis who want to come in, including the nonna-to-be. Just thought I'd mention that in case you were planning on saying no, Lexi," the nurse said, holding back a grin.

Dr. Alva snorted. "I've been waiting for Eva to show up. But it's entirely up to you, Lila."

Unlike Dr. Alva, Lila was surprised her mother and, from

the sounds of it, her whole family were here. She hadn't mentioned that she'd made an appointment with Dr. Alva for this very reason. She'd wanted their first prenatal visit to be special, a private time for her and David to share. She got a little teary eyed that he hadn't bothered showing up. If she couldn't share the first look at their baby with David, at least she could share it with her family, who were obviously more excited about it than the daddy-to-be.

There was a commotion in the hall, and the nurse glanced behind her. "Eva, I told you to wait—" The nurse sighed as Lila's mother, her aunt, and her cousins attempted to get into the room.

Dr. Alva raised an eyebrow at Lila. "I can take her, you know. I won every one of our fights in grade school."

Eva hesitated, holding the rest of the family back with her arm.

Lila smiled. "If it's okay with you, I'd like them to stay, Dr. Alva. And if you have time, I'd like to go ahead with the ultrasound."

Eva beamed, rolling her eyes at Dr. Alva as she hurried to Lila's side. "The only reason you won is because you fought dirty, Lexi."

"Of course I did. I have four older brothers," Dr. Alva said, swiveling on her stool to pick up a tube of gel and the handheld transducer.

"How did you guys know I was here?" Lila asked.

"Ruth saw you, and she called to ask if you were okay. You are, aren't you? You and the baby are fine?" her mother asked, taking Lila's hand in hers as she glanced at Dr. Alva.

Dr. Alva sighed. "You know I can't say anything, Eva."

"It's okay, Dr. Alva. You can tell them what you told me."

Her mother looked as if she was going to throw up. Lila gave her hand a reassuring squeeze. "Mom, I'm fine, and Dr. Alva said the baby's heartbeat is strong." Lila smiled at the memory of hearing the baby's heartbeat for the first time.

"You are, but as I said, I'd like you to gain some weight and keep your stress levels to a minimum, Lila." Dr. Alva gave Eva a pointed look.

Eva opened her mouth, then closed it and nodded.

Dr. Alva lifted Lila's blouse, squirting the cold gel on her stomach. "Now let's have a look at the baby." She motioned for Lila's aunt and cousins to come closer.

The three of them crowded around Lila, jostling for position. Sage frowned, pointing at the screen. "What is that?"

"It's the baby," Dr. Alva said.

"Really? It looks like an ali—" Sage clamped her mouth shut when Lila, Willow, Gia, and Eva turned their heads to glare at her.

Dr. Alva pointed out the hands and feet as she took measurements. Lila stared at her baby on the screen and blinked back tears. She glanced back at her aunt and Willow, who were sniffling and wiping at their eyes, while Sage stared at the screen with her brow pleated.

Lila's mother squeezed her hand, giving her a tender smile. "She's beautiful, darling. Just like you."

"Thanks, Mom. But you can't tell if it's a boy or a girl."

"Of course it's a girl. Rosetti women only have girls."

"Okay, but the Westfields have boys."

"Bah, our genes are stronger," her mother said, sounding like Carmen.

Dr. Alva looked as if she was struggling not to laugh, and then she asked Lila, "Are you sure you still want to know the baby's gender?"

Lila nodded. It was something she and David had discussed before she'd made the appointment.

Dr. Alva smiled. "Your mother's right. You're having a girl, and she's developing beautifully."

She printed off two copies of the sonogram and handed them to Lila, who promptly burst into tears. Her baby was healthy. She hadn't realized how worried she'd been about the baby until that moment. Willow and Sage stared at her. "Sorry. I don't know why I'm crying. I'm happy."

"We know you are, darling," her mother said, giving her a hug. "We've all been through it. It's just hormones."

"Your mother's right. Your hormones will level out in the next couple of weeks." Dr. Alva handed Lila a tissue to wipe her stomach. "And speaking of hormones, how are yours, Eva?"

Her aunt got in on the conversation, and while the three women talked, Lila glanced at Sage. "What are you doing in Sunshine Bay?"

"Jennifer told Gavin she wants a divorce. She wanted me there for support."

Lila felt bad that she'd been angry at David for missing the appointment. She just wished he'd let her know. She could've been there to support him. "How did it go?" Lila asked as she got off the examination table and tossed the tissue in the wastepaper basket.

"Not great. Gavin apparently had no idea this was coming."

Lila felt sorry for David. It wouldn't be easy for him

being caught between his parents. She hugged her cousins. "Thanks for being here with me, even if you think my baby looks like an alien," she teased Sage.

"I wasn't going to say she looked like an alien." Sage glanced at the picture in Lila's hand. "I was going to say she's adorable."

Lila laughed at her cousin's attempt to hide her grimace. "Sure you were."

Sage grinned. "When she grows into her head, I'm sure she will be."

"Well, I think she's adorable. Look at that cute nose," Willow said, then glanced at her cell phone. "I have to go. Let's celebrate this weekend, and we can talk about decorating the baby's room. This is so exciting," she squealed, hugging Lila again. "We're having a girl! We're going to have so much fun."

"We are, and I should go too. I want to check on David."

"I'm not sure that's a good idea, Lila. Especially if Gavin or Junior are there," Sage said.

"They're blaming Mom, aren't they?"

"Yeah, the Rosettis are pretty much persona non grata at Windemere."

Lila was sure that didn't apply to her. After all, she was marrying Gavin's son and having his grandchild.

Her mother and aunt joined them. Sage and Willow said a quick goodbye and then left.

Dr. Alva looked up from her iPad. "I'll see you in a month, Lila, and I'll see you in September, Eva. If your symptoms haven't improved by then, we'll talk about hormone replacement. Yes, Gia, I know menopause is as natural as childbirth, but it doesn't mean women have to suffer."

They followed Dr. Alva from the room, and Lila thanked her for everything.

Eva's mother offered Lila a ride as they walked out of the health center. "Thanks, Mom, but I think I'll walk. I want to check on David." She hugged her mother and aunt and then handed Eva a copy of the sonogram.

Her mother stared at the picture with a soft smile on her face. "She's so beautiful. Look at her little hands and feet. Isn't she beautiful, G?"

Lila's aunt smiled, nodding her agreement before wagging a stern finger at Lila. "And you are going to take better care of yourself."

"Gia's right. You need to eat more and rest more. And remember what Lexi said about stress." Eva glanced down the road. "Do you think you should be going to Windemere today? Sage told you how Gavin reacted to Jennifer's announcement, didn't she?"

"She mentioned it. But I want to show David the sonogram and tell him about the appointment."

It took several minutes for Lila to convince her mother and aunt that it would be fine, but as Lila walked through the doors of Windemere ten minutes later, she wondered if maybe she should've listened to her family.

Gavin had just come out of the office when he spotted her. He slammed the office door and strode toward her. "This is your family's fault. Your mother and your cousin have torn my family apart, and for what? To get rid of the competition? Is that their plan?"

David must've heard his father because he opened the office door and hurried to her side. "Dad, keep your voice down." He put his arm around her. "This has nothing to do with Lila."

"Are you sure about that? Maybe she's in on the plan."

"I understand you're upset, Gavin. But my family—"

"Upset? You think I'm upset? My wife of thirty-three years just asked me for a divorce. My wife who was perfectly happy in our marriage until she started hanging out with your mother!" he bellowed, then stormed off.

"This might not be the best time for you to be here, Lila," David said, and began walking her toward the door.

"You want me to leave?"

"Yeah. I'll drop by the beach house tonight... Actually, I'd better stick around here. I'll call you later." He gave her a perfunctory peck on the cheek and started to walk away.

"David, I've just come from our appointment with the doctor."

He turned, rubbing a distracted hand over his head. "Was that today?"

She nodded. "I texted you, but you didn't respond. I went ahead and had the ultrasound." She took the sonogram from her purse and held it out to him.

"What's that?" He pointed at the picture.

"Our daughter," she said, striving to remain calm despite the hurt and anger bubbling up inside her. She knew he'd had a horrible couple of hours, but couldn't he work up a little enthusiasm?

"Really?" He leaned in to look more closely. "I was sure we were having a boy."

"Well, we're not. But in case you were wondering, she's fine, and so am I." She put the sonogram back in her purse.

"I'm sorry, honey. I'm happy. Honestly, I am. It's just been a crappy few hours. I'll make it up to you, okay?

We'll celebrate once everything settles down here." A door slammed, and he winced. "I'd better go."

Lila walked down to the beach and slipped off her shoes, disappointed and hurt by David's reaction. She thought about going to La Dolce Vita but didn't want to face her mother. She'd know something was wrong.

"Lila!" She turned. Her dad waved. He and Luke were walking behind a group of people on the pier. Her dad must've gone out on the *Captain Joe*, Luke's boat. It was named after his father. The charter company was also named Captain Joe.

Lila's dad jogged over and hugged her. "Eva sent me a photo of the sonogram." His eyes got shiny, and he hugged her again. "A baby girl. That's the best news, sweetheart." He held her out from him and searched her face. "Your mom says the doctor wants you to eat more and rest. No more stress."

"I'm fine, Dad." Her cell phone rang. It was David. "Sorry, I have to take this."

"No problem, sweetheart. I'll see you later, and we'll celebrate." He kissed her cheek and then went over to talk to Luke, who was at *Captain Joe*'s ticket booth talking to his mother while keeping a firm grip on Admiral's collar.

"I'm sorry, honey," David said as soon as Lila answered. "I was just so mad at how my dad treated you, I wasn't thinking straight. Can you send me a photo of the sonogram? I want to show my mom."

"Sure." She removed the sonogram from her purse, took a photo, and then sent it. "How is your mom?"

"Sad, angry, and maybe a little relieved too. I don't know. It's a mess, and somehow I have to keep it from impacting

Windemere. Both of them refuse to leave, and I'm stuck in the middle trying to mediate while my brother stirs the pot."

"I'm sorry, David. That sucks. Why don't you stay at the beach house with me? At least you'll get a break for a few hours."

"Trust me, there's nothing I'd rather do, but I can't leave them on their own."

"Okay. Let me know if there's anything I can do."

"Thanks, honey. I will. I'll call you later, okay?"

She disconnected just in time to avoid getting bowled over by Admiral.

"Sorry. I got distracted, and he got away from me," Luke said, reaching out to clip a leash on Admiral, which earned him an unhappy woof. "It's either the leash or doggie jail, doofus. He took out Sergeant Mills on the beach yesterday."

Lila made a face. "I remember Sergeant Mills. He used to break up our parties at Paradise Cove, didn't he?"

"He did, and he's gotten crankier with age." Luke smiled. "So, a baby girl? Your dad's over the moon."

"He is," she said, scratching Admiral behind the ears.

"And both you and the baby are healthy?" His gray gaze was intent as he searched her face.

She angled her head. "We are." Then she sighed, realizing what was behind the concern she saw in his eyes. "Don't listen to my dad. Both he and my mom are overreacting. Dr. Alva just wants me to eat more."

"And rest more and avoid stress," he said, raising an eyebrow.

"Yes, just like every other expectant mother in the world.

So," she said, anxious to change the subject, "my dad went out on the boat with you?"

"He did, and I should warn you, he's got it bad. I think he loves being out on the water as much as me and doofus. He was talking about—" He broke off when a sixtysomething woman approached him. "Hi, Rhonda. How's it going?"

"Good, thanks." She smiled at Lila, and Luke introduced them. After they'd said hello to each other, Rhonda cast an uncomfortable glance at Luke. "I hate to bother you, but I haven't heard back from you, and I was wondering if you had a chance to look at my résumé?"

"I'm kind of at a loss here, Rhonda. What about a résumé?"

"Your mom didn't talk to you about it?"

"Nope, she didn't."

"Oh, okay. I actually feel better now. It's not like you to blow anyone off."

As they learned, Rhonda, who was a marine biologist, had left a résumé for Luke with his mother at the ticket booth the week before. She ran a program for children during the school year but was looking to fill her time in July and August.

"Sorry about that, Rhonda. We're changing booking systems, and my mom is a bit overwhelmed. Resend me your résumé, and I'll get back to you before the end of the week." Luke gave Rhonda his personal email, and she put it into her phone.

"Thanks, Luke. Nice to meet you, Lila."

Lila could barely contain her excitement as Rhonda walked away. "Luke, you have to hire her. She's exactly what you need to compete with the other charters."

"Lila," he said in a deep growly voice, the one he used whenever she suggested something that would cost him either money or time.

"Luke." She mimicked his voice.

He laughed and shook his head. "Don't you have to go celebrate with your parents or something?"

"No. They'd expect me to be celebrating with David or to bring him to celebrate with them, and that's not going to happen today."

"How come?"

She explained about the divorce and the state David was in and then shrugged. "It's not a big deal. We can celebrate another time."

"It is a big deal. Come on." He took her hand.

"Where are we going?" she asked, trying to ignore the way his big, work-roughened hand felt wrapped around hers.

"We're going to celebrate. But first, we're dropping doofus at my grandmother's."

Thirty minutes later, they were sitting on a patio on Main Street, eating lobster rolls. "This was a great idea, Luke," she said, licking the sauce off her fingers. "I can't remember the last time I had a lobster roll here."

"You want another one?"

"You're kidding, right? I couldn't eat another bite."

"You better have room for dessert. I ordered it especially for you." He nodded at their waitress. He must've ordered dessert when Lila was in the restroom.

Moments later, the waitress returned with two pink-iced cupcakes decorated with purple flowers. Luke thanked her and smiled at Lila. "Congratulations. You're going to be a wonderful mom."

"Luke!" She waved her hands in front of her face in an effort to ward off the tears filling her eyes.

"What's wrong? You don't like cupcakes?"

"No! I love cupcakes." She covered her face with her hands.

He reached over, peeling her hands from her face. "Are you crying?"

She sniffed and nodded. "Hormones."

"Ah, okay." Once again he waved over the waitress, then paid for the meal and asked if they could have the cupcakes to go. He came around the table and helped Lila from her chair, thanking the waitress who'd returned with the boxed cupcakes. Taking Lila by the hand, he led her onto the sidewalk. "How about we have dessert at my place?"

"I'd like that." And she did—she liked it a lot.

They sat on Luke's back deck, watching as the sky darkened, streaked with shades of orange, pink, and purple, listening to the crickets and bullfrogs down by the pond. Lila couldn't think of a nicer way to celebrate the baby girl growing inside her. Except she wasn't celebrating with her baby's daddy, she was celebrating with a man who had taken her to dinner and bought her pink cupcakes. A man whose smile made her heart hurt.

Chapter Twenty-Two

Eva stood at the counter in the restaurant's kitchen, using both hands to crack the shell of the last lobster tail for tonight's featured soup. "Your heart is as hard as these shells, Ma."

"Eva, let it go," her sister said under her breath as she sautéed onion, carrot, and celery for the soup's base.

Eva pulled back the sides of the tail and extracted the meat, then tossed the shell into the pot of steaming water that they'd cooked the lobster tails in to make a rich, fragrant stock. "Let it go? She accepted Bruno's resignation letter without batting an eye. He's leaving in September, G." Unless they found a replacement for him before then. Eva knew they wouldn't. Bruno was irreplaceable.

"It's almost two months away. We've got time to change his mind," her sister said.

"There's only one person who can change his mind, and she won't do it." Eva looked to where her mother stood at the sink, washing dishes. "Will you, Ma?"

Her mother shrugged. "What do you want me to do? I offered him a raise and another week off with pay."

"None of that matters to him, and you know it," Eva said, taking her frustration and anger out on the lobster meat.

Her mother craned her neck. "You're cutting the pieces too small. The meat looks mushy. How long did you parcook the lobster?"

"I've been making lobster bisque since I was fourteen, Ma. I think I know what I'm doing." She looked down. The pieces were more pea size than bite size.

Her mother said something under her breath in Italian.

"Ignore her. She's just trying to distract you," Gia whispered.

Eva didn't take her sister's advice, which resulted in a shouting match between Eva and her mother as they critiqued each other's cooking techniques.

Someone clearing their throat brought their heads around. James stood at the entrance of the kitchen. "You might want to take it down a notch, ladies. I could hear you when I walked into the restaurant."

Her mother shrugged. "We have a warning on the menu."

This was true. There was a note at the top of the menu advising customers that real Italian cooking was going on in the kitchen, which at any time could result in shouting, arguing, yelling, and cursing, but to just sit back and relax and enjoy the meal. Bruno had suggested they add the warning after a customer called the cops, positive someone was being murdered in the kitchen.

"Don't look at me," Eva said to James, jerking a thumb at her mother. "She started it. And do you know why she—"

Her sister cut her off. "Impeccable timing as always, James. Eva was just saying how excited she was about your date."

"What are you talking about? We don't have a date." Eva turned to James. "I never said that. She's just trying to get me out of the kitchen."

"We kind of did have a date. You told me to come by the restaurant to celebrate when you sent me Lila's sonogram."

"You're right, I did. I'm sorry. I got—"

"It's the menopause," her mother said. "She forgets the simplest things, including how to make lobster bisque the way I taught her."

"You know exactly why I forgot I'd made plans with James, Ma. And it has nothing to do with the menopause. It's because, not fifteen minutes after I'd texted James, I found out Bruno gave you his resignation letter, and you accepted it!"

"Keep your nose out of my business." Her mother wagged a soapy wooden spoon at her. "You have your own business to take care of, and from what I can see, you're not any closer to breaking up our Lila's wedding than you..." She trailed off, her shoulders moving up to her ears. She cast Eva an apologetic glance and then turned back to the sink.

"Off you two go," Gia said with a wide and slightly panicked smile as she pushed Eva toward James. "Have fun!"

As they walked out of the kitchen, Eva reached back to untie her apron and glanced at James. He met her gaze with an *I don't believe you* look in his eyes.

"Don't listen to my mother. She's more upset about Bruno than she's letting on, and she's not thinking straight."

She sighed when her sister started yelling at their mother in Italian, forgetting once again how far their voices carried and that James also spoke the language. Between the two of them, they basically laid out every plan Eva had made to break up Lila's wedding and how badly each one had failed.

"Is that the best you can do?" James asked dryly.

"I didn't have a lot of time to come up with a plan. If I had more than a month to work with——"

"Eva, I was talking about your excuse for Carmen busting you." He held open the door to the empty deck. "I thought we agreed to stay out of it and support our daughter no matter what she decided."

"That's what you decided, not me." She tossed her apron on a chair and leaned on the rail. James joined her, and she took in the hard set of his strong, stubbled jaw. "Don't worry. It's a moot point now. Even if I think our daughter is making a mistake, which I do, I'm going to back off. I won't try and break them up."

"How come?"

"Can't you just accept what I say at face value?"

"No, because I've heard it before. What's different this time?"

"Lexi, Dr. Alva, talking about Lila's stress levels. She looked right at me when she said it."

James put his arm around her. "Come on, you're not to blame for Lila being stressed."

Eva raised an eyebrow, and he laughed. "Okay, not entirely to blame. But as far as I can tell, Lila has no idea you've been trying to sabotage her wedding. She's commented a couple of times about how supportive you've been."

"Lila must've said something for Lexi to look at me as if I was to blame."

"I'm sure Lila did tell the doctor she's stressed, and maybe Lexi just assumed it had something to do with you because of your stance on marriage. But Lila's got a lot on her plate with starting her own business, and she——"

"As much as I appreciate you defending me, James, Lila is just like you. She's excited about her consulting business. For her it's more energizing than stressful."

"True, and while I'm loath to admit it to you, it's probably the wedding that's stressing her out."

"I don't know how it can be. There's nothing for her to do. Jennifer has everything under control." Eva moved her head back and forth, thinking. "You're right, it's not me. It's David and Windemere. It's caused a lot of tension between them."

"Agreed, and it doesn't help that Lila's worried about La Dolce Vita."

"Or that we are." Eva sighed. "I told you I'm to blame."

"No, it's not all on you." He tweaked her ponytail. "That said, I'm holding you to your promise. No more trying to sabotage the wedding."

"I won't, just don't tell my mother. Gia felt the same as I did after the appointment. I didn't talk about it with Sage and Willow, but I'm sure they don't want to do anything to upset Lila either."

James ducked his head to look her in the eyes. "Our daughter isn't the only one who's stressed, is she?"

Feeling a little emotional, Eva wrapped her arms around his waist and rested her cheek against his chest. "It's bad enough that we're struggling to keep La Dolce Vita afloat, but when you add Lila getting married—to the man who's managing Windemere, no less—and then finding out how she felt growing up, it's been a lot. And now Bruno leaving?"

James leaned back. "You need a break. You need to get away from the restaurant and forget about everything else for a while. You need to have some fun, Rosetti."

"Do you have something in mind, Sinclair?"

"I do. I thought we'd go clamming at Blueberry Beach and then back to my place to eat."

"What about Lila?" After the night Eva had shared with James, the idea of spending more time alone with him made her nervous. She couldn't risk falling in love with him, and she was already worried she was halfway there.

"I saw her at the pier before I headed to the bait and tackle shop for clamming gear. David called her, and I'm pretty sure they'll want to celebrate on their own. We can do something with them this week." He glanced at his watch. "Tide goes out in a couple hours, so if there's anything you need me to pick up, I can go get it while you get changed. Fried clams and chips or linguine and clams?"

He'd obviously given their night a lot of thought, and she didn't want to disappoint him. Besides, he was right. She could use a break, and she hadn't been clamming in ages.

"Who's cooking, you or me?" she teased.

He waggled his eyebrows. "We're cooking together."

The last time they'd cooked together, they'd ended up naked and making love on the kitchen table, counter, and floor.

"If we leave in the next fifteen minutes, we can pick blueberries for dessert. Unless you have something else in mind," he said, drawing her back into his arms and kissing her soft and slow.

"You obviously have something else in mind," she murmured against his lips.

"I do, but we can start with blueberries and go from there." He nipped her earlobe. "I'll get the whipped cream."

⌒

James looked over from where he was picking blueberries and showed Eva his basket. "Is this enough?"

They'd been picking for almost an hour, and he had only a cupful to show for his efforts. "Yes, because unlike you, I don't eat seventy percent of the blueberries I pick." She showed him her basket. She'd nearly filled it.

"Show-off," he said, and smiled.

She laughed. "Your pearly whites are blue."

"It turns you on, doesn't it?" He came over and dumped his berries into her basket and then leaned in and kissed her. "Tide's out."

She was about to open the cooler to put the basket of blueberries in when she noticed the reflector tape on the cooler's lid. She shook her head and laughed. "Is there anything you didn't think of?"

"I doubt it. You know I like to be prepared."

"I do, and your daughter is exactly like you."

"Perfect. I know."

"Careful, or we won't be able to fit the lamp on your big head," she said, putting on her headlamp.

The moon was bright and almost full, shimmering on the water and the sand. But James had insisted they wear the lamps, as clamming at night could be dangerous. He was right, and Eva hadn't teased him. Although she had teased him when she caught him putting fluorescent tape on the handles of the clamming rake and shovel.

They weren't the only ones out clamming tonight. There were three other couples and a Marine and Environmental Sciences officer on the beach. "You did get a shellfishing license, didn't you?" Her family renewed theirs every year, even though it had been at least two years since they'd gone clamming. "And you brought a gauge?" she whispered. If he didn't have both, they'd get kicked off the beach.

He gave her a look and handed her gardening gloves.

"I'm sorry for doubting you, Mr. Perfect," she said, fighting a smile as she attached the mesh clamming bag to her shorts. Everyone else had pails or buckets, but James had bought them bags. They made it easier to maneuver, so she wasn't about to tease him or complain.

In less than thirty minutes, they'd filled their bags with the allotted take for the night. It was more than they'd use.

"Take whatever we don't need for tomorrow's special. You can make linguine and clams." They'd decided to have fried clams and chips, as James called fries.

"Sounds good," she said, bending down to take the basket of berries out of the cooler.

James emptied both their bags of clams into the cooler and then filled it with water. They'd leave them there for at least twenty minutes before preparing them for dinner.

Clamming was a dirty business, and they used the outdoor shower, which delayed dinner by more than an hour. They had a little too much fun cooking together and didn't end up eating out on the deck by candlelight until ten o'clock. They decided to leave the blueberry crumble for another night and instead danced under the stars.

It was almost midnight when James drove her home and walked her to her door. She couldn't remember a night she'd enjoyed more than this one. Unless she counted the nights she'd spent with him in London. It was exactly what she'd needed, and she didn't want their night together to end.

She opened the door and tugged him inside. "Stay with me."

"I thought you'd never ask." He closed the door with his foot, picked her up, and carried her to her room.

She ignored the uptick in her pulse. It would be okay. They'd enjoy a few weeks of each other's company, and then James would go back to his life in London, and she'd go back to her life here. They'd pick up where they'd left off whenever he came back to visit Lila. It was the perfect relationship, really. Kind of like having your cake and eating it too.

Chapter Twenty-Three

Lila opened the door to the bridge and joined Luke in the relatively small, confined space. He glanced at her. "You should've brought a jacket. Grab mine."

"I always forget that it's ten degrees cooler on the water." She slipped the fleece-lined windbreaker off the back of his captain's chair. Lila and her parents and about seventy other passengers were whale watching on the *Captain Joe*.

"Where's your boyfriend? I thought he'd be keeping you warm."

"He threw me over for a cute blonde."

Luke smiled, nodding at the bow of the boat. "I wouldn't feel bad. It looks like he threw the cute blonde over for your mother."

Lila moved in beside him and leaned forward. "Who but my mother would sing 'My Heart Will Go On' when we're on the ocean?" It was the theme song from *Titanic*, of all things.

Luke laughed. "I think it's okay. I can guarantee I'm not going to run into an iceberg. But is it just me, or does she sound exactly like Celine Dion?"

"She does, and the passengers seem to love it."

"Admiral too. He's singing with her."

The dog had his head thrown back, howling. "Okay, that's just too cute not to film." And post on Captain Joe's, La Dolce Vita's, and SUP Sunshine's Instagram accounts. She managed all three. Admiral was as big a draw on Luke's accounts as her mother was on the Rosettis'.

"Your dad has you covered."

"Of course he does." Lila sighed. Eva was never far from his sight. It had been a week since her sonogram, and her parents had been attached at the hip ever since. They didn't have sleepovers at the beach house, but there'd been several nights when her father hadn't come home. She was also pretty sure her mother showed up at the beach house the moment Lila left.

Meanwhile she'd been spending a lot of time with Luke, working on his business plans. They had fun together, so it never really felt like work. They talked over the plans for his businesses while walking to the sand dunes with Admiral, kayaking in the pond near his house, or biking the trails. Luke had lent her a bike and a helmet that Lila was almost positive had belonged to someone important to him, maybe his friend with the baby. She hadn't worked up the nerve to ask about her. He'd gotten distant when he'd offered Lila the bike and the pink helmet.

"So I take it your plan to break up your parents isn't going that well." His lips twitched as if he was fighting back a laugh.

"Ha-ha, easy for you to laugh. You don't have to be around them."

"At least they get along."

"Are you kidding me? They fight all the time. Okay, maybe 'fight' is a little strong. My dad will do stuff to tick my mother off, and I swear he does it just to wind her up. He actually seems to think she's hilarious when she loses it on him, which of course just encourages her, because she likes nothing better than to make him laugh. Yesterday she was making a marinade for the steaks, and he kept tasting it and saying it needed more garlic or more salt. She believed him, and then she tasted it and started swearing at him in Italian, which he speaks fluently, by the way, and he threw her in the pool."

He winced. "How did that go over?"

"With her laughing and my dad jumping in the pool and the two of them making out."

"Sounds like they have fun together."

"They do, and it sucks because they're happy, especially my dad. I haven't seen him this way in... To be honest, I've never seen him like this."

"Maybe this time they'll get it right."

"I wish I believed that, but my mom is just like my grandmother. Carmen's been in love with Bruno for years, and it's obvious to anyone who sees him with my grandmother he's in love with her too. But he's marrying Ana and moving away. You'd think that would be the wake-up call my grandmother needed, but it wasn't. Bruno's agreed to stay on until the fall or until they find someone to replace him. My mother's furious with Carmen. All they do is fight, and my poor aunt's stuck in the middle trying to play peacemaker."

"Life has a way of working out the way it's meant to. In the end, Carmen might surprise all of you."

"Do you really believe that, about life working out the way it's supposed to?" she asked, putting her hands in the pockets of his jacket.

"Yeah, I do, don't you?" Before she could answer, he leaned forward and reached for his binoculars, swearing under his breath at whatever it was he saw. He blasted the horn several times and then told the passengers to take a seat and brace. Hooking an arm around Lila's waist, he pulled her onto his lap.

"What's wrong?" she asked, struggling to free her hands from the jacket's pockets, but it was like she was in a strait-jacket. The jacket had pulled tight at the back, sealing the pockets shut.

"Fishing boat headed directly into our path. It's too far away to see if there's anyone on board." He gritted his teeth. "Lila, stop moving." Then he blasted his horn again and began turning the boat.

"Sorry, it's just that my hands are stuck, and I feel like I'm going to roll off your lap."

With his gaze focused straight ahead, he brought one hand off the wheel and curved it around her waist as he slowed the boat. He radioed their coordinates to the Coast Guard and explained the situation. "Yeah, well, it would've been nice if they let someone know. Thanks," he said, then contacted the other charters.

Apparently a couple of kids had taken the fishing boat for a joyride, and the rudder had gotten stuck. They'd jumped off and swum to shore but failed to alert anyone to the runaway boat.

Once Luke had made sure that the passengers on board the *Captain Joe* were fine and the fishing boat had passed without incident, he increased speed, but he hadn't relaxed. Lila could feel the tension in his body.

"What's wrong?"

"You could've fallen and lost the baby. I shouldn't have let you come out on the boat. I shouldn't have let you up here."

His reaction didn't make sense to her. She sat up, freeing the back of the jacket from under herself, and removed her hands from the pockets. She placed one on his chest. She could feel his heart pounding beneath her palm. "Luke, I'm fine, but you're not. What is it?"

"Nothing." A muscle flexed in his jaw.

She reached up to smooth it away. "Please tell me. You listen to me talk about my family and David ad nauseam. You've always been there for me. Let me be there for you."

He blew out a breath and glanced at her. "Three years ago, my fiancée came out with me on the *Captain Joe*. She didn't like being on the water, but I thought if she was with me, I could ease her fears and change her mind. She slipped and fell. She was six months pregnant and lost the baby."

"Oh, Luke, I'm so sorry." Without thinking, only wanting to comfort him, she pressed a kiss to his hard, firm mouth. She froze, looking into his eyes. They'd darkened, the gray iris barely visible.

He made a sound low in his throat, and his arm went around her. Bringing her tight against his hard body, he kissed her back. She placed her hands on his chest, but instead of pushing him away, as she knew she should, her fingers curled into his T-shirt, and her lips softened under his, deepening the kiss with a man she shouldn't be kissing.

He wrenched his mouth from hers and shook his head. "No, I won't do this. I can't." He lifted her from his lap, setting her on her feet beside him.

"I'm sorry. It was my fault. I just felt so bad for you. I wanted to comfort you. We didn't do anything wrong."

"I think your fiancé would disagree with you. You need to go, Lila."

"Luke, please—"

He shook his head. "We've been walking a fine line between a business relationship and something a whole hell of a lot more. You know it and I know it, and we both should've put a stop to it before now. You have cold feet, and I won't be that guy. I can't be. I won't do that to someone else." He stared straight ahead. "It's better if we don't work together."

"Are you firing me?"

He nodded without looking at her. "It's for the best. I appreciate everything you've done for me, and I'll give you a glowing recommendation. You deserve it, and you deserve to be happy, Lila. There's nothing more that I want for you than for you to be happy."

Everything he said was true. She'd been looking for excuses to spend time with him. She liked him, she liked spending time with him, she liked talking to him, and she liked his dog and his house and...She bowed her head. She was half in love with him. She hadn't even known it herself until this very second. Until she was faced with not seeing him anymore, not spending time with him anymore.

He was right. They couldn't do this. It wasn't fair to David, and it certainly wasn't fair to the child she carried.

"Thank you. I want that for you too, Luke. I hope you find someone who loves you as much as you deserve." She blinked back tears. She wouldn't cry. "You're a great guy, and I loved working with you. I don't doubt SUP Sunshine will be a huge success."

But she wouldn't be a part of it, not anymore. She carefully made her way to the deck, taking a minute to get herself together before facing her parents.

Luke's deep voice came over the speakers as she walked to where her parents were standing at the bow of the boat. He'd spotted a pod of endangered right whales on the port side and slowed the boat. She couldn't have asked for a better distraction. Her parents would be as mesmerized by the sight as everyone else. It didn't matter how many times you'd gone out whale watching, it was always magical.

She glanced up at the bridge as she walked to the right of the boat. Luke was watching her and pointed to the left. She always got port and starboard mixed up. He knew that, just as he knew her favorite color and her favorite ice cream.

Rhonda took over for Luke. He'd finally given in to Lila's pleading to hire her a few days before. As her father had told her and she had told Luke, you have to spend money to make money. He'd also bought the smaller boat Lila had recommended for fishing charters. He'd been missing out on lucrative business. And as busy as he'd be this year, she'd predicted that next year, with the added revenue stream, he'd be able to afford to hire two more captains and free up more time for SUP Sunshine.

The whales stayed with them for almost twenty minutes. People didn't move from the rails, hoping for another sighting. They weren't disappointed. Less than ten minutes later, a humpback whale breached fifty feet out of the water.

Lila knew Luke would do his best to stay at least a hundred yards away, but sometimes the whales got a lot closer than that. Like this one.

The whale breached again, closer this time, close enough that, when his tail slapped the water, the passengers, including her parents, got wet, and Lila got it on video. She replayed it, shaking her head at her parents, who looked gorgeous and sickeningly in love. But besides that, the footage was incredible. She went to post to Luke's Instagram account and hesitated, wondering if he'd mind. She posted it anyway. She'd do the same for any business in town.

A wet nose nudged her hand. "Hey, you." She leaned down to hug Admiral. He put his big paws on her shoulders and hugged her back. Tears welled in her eyes, spilling over at the thought that she wouldn't get to see him anymore. Admiral licked her tears away. "Good boy," she whispered at the sound of her parents' approach.

"Was that not the most incredible sight?" her father asked, rubbing Admiral behind the ears.

"It was, and I got it on video. I'll send you a copy." She avoided looking at her mother, who was frowning at her.

A squeal went up from the bow. "Dolphins!"

Sure enough, a pod of dolphins entertained them for most of the ride back to the pier.

As Luke expertly docked the boat and the deckhands tied it off, Lila joined the crowd to disembark. "Aren't you going to wait for Luke?" her father asked. "I thought you guys had a few more hours to put in. I was going to see if he wanted to join us for dinner."

"I think he has plans for tonight, Dad. And I've pretty

much finished up my contract with him. I'm actually going to see David. Now that my workload is lightened, I should be able to fit Windemere in." She glanced at her mother, praying she didn't question her. "You, Nonna, and Zia are okay with that, aren't you?"

"Now that David and Jennifer will be running Windemere, of course we are."

"Nothing's been finalized yet, Mom. It's still early days." Gavin had gone from groveling to threatening, and poor David was caught squarely in the middle. No surprise that his brother was firmly on Team Gavin.

"Yes, but your cousin is Jennifer's lawyer."

"She is, and Gavin should be shaking in his Dockers," she said, making her parents smile. "But I need you to be okay with me helping out David, even if Gavin's around for a while."

"Sure," her mother said.

"Great. I'll check in with you guys later."

"I'm going to stick around and talk to Luke. I'm thinking of getting my captain's license." Her father grinned as they both stared at him. Her mother was clearly as shocked as Lila.

"Dad, it takes a lot of time. There are classes and—"

"I know. I've checked into it."

"But James, you don't live here. You're going back to London after Lila's wedding," her mother said.

Lila didn't think her dad heard the panic in her mother's voice—he was too excited about his new venture—but Lila did.

"I'm thinking of staying. I found a great place not far from the beach house, and with the baby on the way, I want to be close by. And this really interests me," he said, gesturing to the boat. He looked from Lila to her mother and put his hands in his pockets. "I thought you guys would be happy about it."

"Of course we are, darling," her mother said, attempting a happy smile that Lila could see through.

As much as she knew that her mother loved James, she also knew she wouldn't be able to commit to a long-term relationship. And if Lila's father was willing to pack up his life and move here, she knew that was exactly what he wanted.

Lila pressed a hand to her stomach, feeling sick for both of them. They were going to break each other's hearts, and she had to do something. She wouldn't say anything to her mother. Not after the last time. Lila had hurt her, and she wouldn't do it again. Her mother meant too much to her.

"Mom's right. There's nothing I want more than to have you here. But what about Sheena and Faith? London? The estate? You love it there."

"There's a lot to love about Sunshine Bay too," he said, and smiled at her mother. His smile faltered a little, and her mother shored hers up. Lila knew how difficult this was for her mother and appreciated her trying to hide her true feelings. "Your sisters can come whenever they want, and I can go back whenever they need me. I didn't get a chance to spend as much time with you as I did with them growing up, sweetheart. They'll understand."

Faith would, but Lila wasn't so sure about Sheena, and that was when she realized exactly what she had to do. She had to get her father to go back to London. He needed some distance from her mother. He wasn't thinking straight. He had to see what he was giving up.

Lila kissed his cheek and gave him a hug to make up for her less-than-enthusiastic reaction. "I'll see you later."

"I should go relieve Gia. I promised I'd work the dinner service," her mother said, which clearly wasn't what her parents had planned given her father's obvious disappointment. She leaned in and kissed his cheek. "I'll try and get away early."

"Are you okay, Mom?" Lila asked as they walked along the pier.

"Of course I am. Why wouldn't I be?"

"I just...Nothing." She smiled, even though it hurt a little that her mother wouldn't confide in her. But why would she after what Lila had said to her that morning after the shower?

"What about you? Are you okay? You're a little pale and subdued."

"I got queasy. I guess I haven't gotten my sea legs back." Unlike Luke's former fiancée, Lila loved being on the water.

"Or maybe it's the baby. You should go back to the beach house and lie down, or come to the restaurant and I'll make you something to eat."

"I'll come after I finish up with David."

"Okay, good." She patted Lila's cheek before heading off. Eva talked to a couple of people she knew before stepping off the pier and slipping off her shoes. Lila watched as she walked along the shoreline, looking as if she carried the weight of the world on her shoulders.

Lila brought her phone to her ear. Her sister picked up

on the second ring. By the time Lila walked through the doors of Windemere, she'd convinced Sheena to call their father and tell him she needed him to come home.

Lila looked around for David. He wasn't in the dining room or out on the patio, so she headed for the office. She knocked. "Coast clear?" she asked, poking her head inside.

He looked up from where he sat behind the desk and gave her a tired smile, sitting back in his chair to run his hand through his hair. "If you mean is my father here, you're safe. He has an appointment with his lawyer."

"We missed you whale watching."

"I'm sorry I couldn't make it. I'm under the gun. My father didn't approve any of the ideas I came up with for July Fourth weekend. According to him, they're not big enough," he said, his brow furrowing as he glanced at her. "Did you have a good time?"

She followed his gaze. She'd forgotten to return Luke's jacket. "We did, but it would've been more fun if you'd been there. I think you would've enjoyed it." He needed to get away from Windemere, or, more to the point, his father. "So what is it Gavin wants you—"

A woman walked in without knocking. It was Sam. "Chef made your favorite," she said, depositing a tray holding what looked like a club sandwich, a leaf salad, and a glass of iced tea in front of David. "And don't tell me you're not hungry. You need to eat. You're fading away." She reached over and brushed his hair from his eyes.

David flushed, clearing his throat with a pointed glance in Lila's direction. "Thanks, Sam."

She whirled around, and the soft smile that had been on

her face disappeared. "Oh, hi, Lila. I didn't see you there. Can I get you something to eat or something to drink?"

"No, I'm fine. Thanks for asking, though."

"No problem." She nodded at David. "Make sure he eats. He hasn't eaten since yesterday afternoon," Sam said, seeming to imply that Lila wasn't doing a very good job taking care of her man.

"Good thing he has you to look after him, Sam."

Sam blushed, and she gave Lila a strained smile before hurrying from David's office.

"Lila, it's not what it looked like."

"Really? Because it looked and sounded to me..." She inhaled a deep breath. After what had taken place on the bridge with Luke, she had a lot of nerve acting like the jealous fiancée. "I'm sorry. I guess I'm overly sensitive. But in my defense, you've made it pretty clear you didn't want me here."

"It's not that I don't want you here. It's that I didn't want you to have to put up with my father and his snide remarks."

As she looked closer at David, she saw what Sam did. He was pale, and he had lost weight. "It hasn't gotten any better?"

"No. If anything, it's gotten worse." He gave her a weak smile. "I have a better insight into what it must've been like for you growing up."

She didn't think he did, not really. He was an adult, and she'd been just a kid. But she could sympathize. It wasn't fun to be caught between your feuding parents, no matter how old you were. "What can I do to help? Do you need a hand with your plans for the Fourth?"

"No, I should be okay. And I don't want you to take time from your other clients for me."

She shrugged, a little hurt he'd so easily brushed off her offer. "I've wrapped up my contract with Luke, and I've already got Heather's business plan and website done." The week before, she'd convinced Heather to start thinking of her photography as a business and not a hobby. "Willow's business is just at the planning stages, so I can't do much for her yet. But if you don't want my help, that's fine."

"I didn't want you overdoing it. But if you've got the time, there's nothing I want more than to work with you on this." He smiled. "It'll be just like old times, the two of us working together. I think I've missed that the most these past couple of weeks. We always made a great team."

She relaxed. "We did."

Chapter Twenty-Four

They were streaming the Fourth of July live episode at the beach house, and it wasn't going well. Eva sensed Lila trying to get her attention from behind the camera and was afraid to look, wondering what she could've done wrong this time.

At a subtle throat clearing, she glanced to where her daughter stood, giving Eva an exaggerated smile. She wanted her to smile? Eva thought she had been. She smiled, and Lila's eyes went wide. It seemed Eva couldn't do anything right today. She'd given the viewers the recipe for grilled eggplant and tomatoes with parmesan basil bread crumbs, only to realize halfway through that she was making summer farro—a nutty Italian grain salad.

She blamed James, not to the viewers, of course. At least she hoped she hadn't. She missed him, and it was making her crazy. Because she didn't want to miss him. She'd been relieved when he'd left for London the day after he'd announced his intention to stay in Sunshine Bay. The thought of his moving here had been terrifying, just as terrifying as seeing him only when he visited Lila, a few times a year.

She never should've started back up with him. She

should've put a stop to it after their second night together. But she couldn't bring herself to. She enjoyed being with him, cooking with him, taking long walks with him, sitting curled up beside him and binge-watching Netflix, simply being with him. She'd convinced herself it was just a summer fling, but somewhere along the line, it had turned into something more. She was in love with him, the head-over-heels kind of love, the can't-think-straight kind of love. Which she'd certainly proved today.

Her sister stepped on her toes. "Eva?"

"What?" She heard Lila groan from behind the camera. Eva reached for the bottle of wine and laughed. "Sorry, I may have had one glass too many of this gorgeous albariño from California." She hadn't had any. "With its crisp notes of melon and lime, it's the perfect accompaniment to our Italian-sausage burgers with garlicky spinach, our summer farro salad, and our farfalle noodles with zucchini and parsley-almond pesto." She poured herself a glass and started to lift it.

"Aren't you forgetting something?" her sister asked.

"Sorry." Eva covered her groan with a laugh and poured Gia a glass.

Her sister sighed. "Thank you, and I'm sure the albariño will also pair beautifully with our simple but delicious wildflower honey–sweetened mascarpone topped with berries and pistachios to enjoy at your Fourth of July celebrations."

Unable to resist, Eva leaned over to take a spoonful. "*Madonna santo*, this is divine." She helped herself to another spoonful, moaning. "You outdid yourself, G."

"You made it," her sister said dryly, trying not to laugh.

"Really?" Eva choked on a berry and reached for her glass of wine.

"Say goodbye and sing," Lila hissed from behind the camera.

Eva and her sister raised their glasses. As soon as their eyes met, they started to giggle. "To the good life. Happy Fourth!" they gurgled, trying to keep it together. "Come join us at La Dolce Vita if you're in Sunshine Bay. We're featuring all of today's recipes on this month's menu."

They not only sang Katrina and the Waves' "Walking on Sunshine," they danced to it too.

"I thought that was never going to end," Lila said, lowering her camera. "Mom, what was up with you today?"

Eva shrugged. "It threw me off not having Ma with us, I guess." It didn't have anything to do with Carmen. Then again, maybe it did. They'd barely spoken since the day she'd found out her mother had accepted Bruno's resignation. Eva was still furious with her, but she hated being on the outs with her mother. They always had fun together, but there was a distinct chill in the air in the restaurant's kitchen these days.

Eva's phone vibrated on the counter. She walked over and picked it up, smiling as soon as she saw James's name.

"I know exactly what's wrong with her. She's missing your father. She's been walking around like she's lost her best friend," Gia said.

Eva glanced at her daughter. Lila hadn't said anything to her the day James had announced his attention to move to Sunshine Bay, but she had a feeling Lila had noticed Eva's panicked reaction on the boat. Just as Eva had noticed her daughter's. As much as Eva didn't want to admit it,

Lila knew her as well as she knew her father. She'd known all along that it would come to this. The hurt from Lila's accusations the morning after the shower had lessened, but Eva needed to forgive her fully. Because she was right.

Lila gave her a sympathetic smile, no judgment in her eyes.

Eva returned her smile as she connected the call. "James," she said on a sigh, sounding as if they hadn't talked at least once a day since he'd been away.

"You have to make that dessert when I get back, just so I can hear you moan." His deep voice made her shiver, and she walked out of the kitchen to the patio doors.

"You don't need the dessert for me to do that—all you have to do is touch me," she whispered, closing the patio doors behind her.

"Let me guess, our daughter is listening in."

"She was, but I'm on the deck now. She wasn't happy with my performance today."

"She should be thrilled with your performance today. Yours and Gia's. You rocked the song, the food looked fantastic, and better yet, you two looked like you were having fun."

"How can you say that? I was talking about the wrong recipe, and I stood there eating the dessert I thought my sister made."

He laughed. "I know. It was hilarious."

She sighed. "James."

"Eva." He sighed her name like she'd just sighed his. "That video is going to keep me entertained the entire flight back to you. I've missed you."

"I've missed you too."

"Then you'll be glad to know I'm not going away without you again."

Her legs went weak, and she slowly lowered herself onto the lounge chair. Three days earlier, he'd sounded as if he was having second thoughts because of Faith and Sheena. Eva didn't know what had changed his mind. She knew only that she'd been as devastated then as she was now.

"You're moving here. To Sunshine Bay?" She forced herself to sound over the moon with joy. Part of her was, part of her wanted this with all her heart. But the other part, the older and wiser part, the Rosetti part of her, didn't want this at all. She was terrified by what would come next. She knew what he'd want, what he'd expect from her, and she didn't blame him.

"I am. It took some convincing to get Sheena on board, but in the end, she just wants me to be happy, and she knows you make me happy. You do, you know."

"I know." How had she let this happen? How could she have been so foolish? "You make me happy too." It would be so much easier if it were a lie.

"I was hoping to spend tonight with you, but my flight's been delayed. I thought we could have a picnic under the stars at Paradise Cove. It'll have to wait until tomorrow, I guess."

Her heart seized. He'd asked her to marry him under the olive tree in Tuscany on the Fourth of July. "That sounds lovely," she said, past the ball of emotion stuck in her throat. "Gia's waving at me. I have to go. I'll see you soon, darling. Safe travels." She disconnected before he could say, "I love you."

She wiped her eyes and went inside, forcing a smile for

her daughter and her sister. "We should go, G. I'm sure Ma could use our help."

"Mom, what's wrong?"

"Nothing, darling. Your father was just sharing his happy news. He's moving to Sunshine Bay after all."

"That's wonderful news," her daughter said, but Eva knew Lila as well as she knew James. Her daughter was torn, happy that she'd have her father close by but afraid that Eva was going to break his heart.

She gave Lila a hug. "I'll see you later."

"You guys are coming tonight, right?" she called as Eva and her sister walked to the door.

It was Lila's bachelorette party. They were doing a pub crawl on bikes. "I don't know if we can get away from the restaurant," Eva said at the same time her sister said, "Of course we are. We wouldn't miss it."

"We're starting out from La Dolce Vita, so you can decide then."

Eva nodded. "We'll have the sex on the beach Jell-O shots and woo woo cocktails ready. Virgin ones for you, of course."

"Great. I'll be the only sober one," Lila said, then shrugged. "It's probably for the best. Someone has to look after Sage and Willow."

"Don't worry. We'll make sure they eat lots so they're not drinking on empty stomachs," Gia said.

"Don't ask," Eva said to her sister as she closed the door behind them, hurrying to their mother's car sitting in the driveway. Tim had done a wonderful job on the bodywork. He'd even gotten the back doors to open. He'd tried telling them their mother had paid for the repairs, but Eva knew James had.

"I won't, but Eva, I know you love him as much as he loves you."

"It doesn't matter, G. You out of anyone know it doesn't. There's only one way this ends," she said, and got into the car.

Her sister leaned in and hugged her. "You know I'm here for you."

She nodded, unable to speak as the tears rolled down her cheeks. As soon as she parked the car in the back of the restaurant's lot, she jumped out, wiped her eyes, and ran inside.

At the hostess stand, Bruno looked up. "Eva, *cara*, what's wrong?"

"I'm okay. I just need to talk to Ma." Fast-walking to the kitchen, she ignored the curious glances from the waitstaff and the three customers who sat at the bar.

Her mother looked up from kneading bread dough and searched her face. She held out her flour-covered hands, and Eva walked into her open arms, sobbing, "I'm sorry, Ma. I'm so sorry. I understand now. I understand why you can't do it."

"I know, *cara*. I know," Carmen murmured, patting her back. When Eva's tears subsided, her mother stepped back, putting her hands on Eva's shoulders. "You go fix your face and your hair and put on a pretty dress. And then you go to the bar and sing and dance and flirt with handsome young men, party with your sister like old times. You show our Lila that she doesn't need a man in her life to be happy. She has us. She has her family and her friends."

Eva nodded. She didn't tell her mother that, as much as she worried for Lila, she wouldn't try to change her daughter's mind. Even as a little girl, Lila had stayed true to whatever course she had set for herself. There would be no changing her mind, and Eva wouldn't damage their relationship any more than she already had by trying.

And Eva wouldn't tell her mother that she didn't want to party the way she used to. It no longer held any appeal. She'd realized these last few weeks with James that it hadn't for a long time. But her mother didn't want to hear that. She wanted Eva to be happy with her life, their life, just the way it had always been. For her mother's sake and for her own, she'd try.

She helped out in the kitchen for several hours and then went up to her apartment to get ready. She had a shower, did her hair and makeup, and then pulled out a sexy siren-red dress that screamed *I'm up for a good time, not a long time*, hoping it would get her in the mood. It didn't.

She was almost tempted to fake sick when her mother and sister walked into her apartment. Her sister grinned and hit Play on her phone, and Eva laughed as the Black Eyed Peas' "I Gotta Feeling" filled her apartment. It was the song she and her sister always played to get in the mood to go out. The three of them were dancing and singing when Lila, Sage, and Willow, with their pink sashes and sparkling tiaras and cocktails, walked into Eva's apartment.

Lila smiled and lifted her phone to film them as they kept dancing and singing.

"Woo-hoo," Willow cheered. "It's just like old times." She took the drink from her sister and the phone from Lila and put them down on the coffee table, and then the three of them joined in. When the song ended, they fell together, laughing and hugging. Eva's mother looked at her and smiled. "It's a very good life indeed."

The six of them trooped out of Eva's apartment singing Beyoncé's "Single Ladies (Put a Ring on It)"—another of their going-out-on-the-town favorites—then filed into the restaurant to the delight of their customers and the rest of the bachelorette party. Eva worked the bar with her mother and sister, tossing back Jell-O shots as fast as they were handed out.

Lila put her fingers between her lips and whistled. "Let's get this party started before all of you are too drunk to ride your bikes."

"Okay, you girls call me if you need me. And remember to watch your drinks," Bruno said, lecturing them as he always did when they went out. Eva's heart twisted as she thought about how much she'd miss him, how much they'd all miss him, and she walked over and gave him a hug. "I love you." Her sister, Lila, Willow, and Sage did the same.

Carmen looked away, but not before Eva saw her eyes glistening with tears under the lights from the bar.

Jennifer threw her arms around Bruno. "I love you too."

Bruno blushed, and they all laughed when Eva said, "Lightweight alert."

Jennifer laughed too and then threw her arms around Eva. "I don't know when I've ever had so much fun."

"Okay, that's just sad," Eva said, "Come on, girls. Let's show Jennifer how we party in Sunshine Bay."

Jennifer crashed her bike into a parked car at the third stop on their pub crawl. "No more biking for you," Eva said.

"But I'm having so much fun. I don't want to stop now."

"We're not. You're just banned from riding your bike. We'll go to Last Call. It's down on the beach."

Her sister hesitated. "Eva, I don't know if that's a good idea."

"It's not. It's a great idea." Last Call was another of Eva's favorite bars. It was a popular hangout with the locals and tended to get rowdy. They parked their bikes at the back of Surfside. Johnny would make sure they weren't stolen, and she'd pick them up in the morning. Lila and Sage looked a little nervous when Eva told them where they were going, but Willow pumped her fist and said, "We'll join up with you after here."

Gia reluctantly tagged along as Eva took Jennifer through a shortcut down to the beach. Decorated with Christmas lights, Last Call sat back from the shore, the music so loud its wooden walls were practically pulsating to the beat. The place was packed to the rafters, but Matt, a giant of a man behind the bar, stopped pulling beers to yell, "Heartbreakers are in the house!"

People started cheering, and Eva laughed, waggling her eyebrows at her sister when Jennifer said, "I love this place!" Eva introduced her to several of the people she knew as they made their way to the bar.

"I hear Lila's going to be the one to break the Rosetti curse," a man at a table near the bar yelled. "We've all got a chance now, lads."

"Get in line, old man," said a familiar voice at the bar, and Ryan swiveled on his barstool to smile at Eva. The young woman sitting on a stool beside him, a pretty blonde, didn't look impressed.

"Hey there, handsome." Eva patted his chest and smiled at the young woman. "Aren't you going to introduce me to your girlfriend?"

"Eva, Pam. Pam, Eva. We just met. Pam's in town to celebrate her parents' anniversary." Ryan smiled. "What can I get you ladies to drink?"

"No way. They don't get their drinks until Eva sings. Who thinks Eva should sing for their drinks?" Matt yelled at his customers, then began chanting, "Eva, Eva" as he thumped a beer bottle on the bar. The crowd soon picked up his chant.

"Fine," Eva said. "The three of us will sing."

But her sister and Jennifer shook their heads. "We'll watch."

"That's no fun. Come on, you can be my backup dancers." She couldn't change their minds, and a couple of guys at the bar gave them their stools. Eva shrugged and walked to the small stage with a karaoke machine to the right of the bar.

"What do you want me to sing?" She already knew what one of the songs would be. She'd been singing the Sister Sledge song here for years. "'We Are Family,'" half the bar yelled. She brought up the music and lifted the mic. It felt like old times as she sang and danced on the stage. Good times and great memories. She smiled at her sister and Jennifer, who clapped and cheered louder than nearly anyone in the bar.

She didn't ask what they wanted to hear next. She already knew what it would be. People laughed and cheered when they heard the music for Helen Reddy's "I Am Woman." She put on a show she knew they soon wouldn't forget. At least thirty people crowded around the stage, Gia, Jennifer, and Ryan included, singing the lyrics with her. She could barely hear herself singing and leaned over to pull her sister and Jennifer up on the stage, the three of them dancing together. When the music ended and she put down the mic, Ryan jumped onstage and lifted her up, twirling her around as he kissed her.

"Eva!"

Laughing, she broke the kiss and looked to where her sister was pointing. James stood with his hands in his pockets watching her, and then he turned and walked away.

"Ryan, put me down," Eva cried, feeling as if she was going to throw up.

"What's wrong?" he asked as he set her on her feet.

Desperate to get to James, she didn't answer him. Her heart was racing as she pushed her way through the crowd. James was halfway down the beach when she finally managed to make it outside.

Fireworks exploded in the night sky above him, and she started to run after him, and then she stopped. She just froze right there in the sand beneath a shower of twinkling starbursts. She wasn't meant for the life he wanted. She wasn't made for commitment and long-term relationships. She was a Heartbreaker. It was better this way. Better for all of them.

Chapter Twenty-Five

Stop worrying about it. Your parents are fine," Sage shouted in Lila's ear.

Lila glanced at her phone on the table. Her father had called fifteen minutes ago. He'd touched down in Boston at ten and then hired a helicopter to fly him to Sunshine Bay. "You didn't see my mom this afternoon. I should've warned her that I told my dad they were at Last Call," Lila yelled above the noise in Surfside. The crowd had grown steadily since they'd arrived.

Sage scrolled through her phone and then grinned. Turning the screen to Lila, she pressed Play and turned up the volume. Lila's mother was on the stage at Last Call, looking stunning in her red dress, surrounded by cheering fans as she sang Helen Reddy's "I Am Woman."

Willow grabbed her sister's phone. "Zia's singing the Rosettis' theme song!" she squealed, wobbling when she got up onto her chair. "Watch your drinks!" she shouted as she started to stand up in the middle of the table, singing along with Lila's mother.

"Willow Rosetti, get down from there right now," Johnny, the bar's owner, yelled.

Her cousin just laughed, motioning for all of them to join in as she started the video over. All the women at their table stood, linked their arms, and sang at the top of their lungs. It wasn't long before the rest of the women in the bar joined in.

"I love Zia so hard," Willow said as she climbed off the table. "I want to be her when I grow up."

Johnny walked over with a tray of drinks and set them on the table. "Courtesy of the guys at the bar." He shook his head at Willow. "Never a dull moment when the Heartbreakers are in the house." Then he winked at Lila. "Now that you're gonna break the Rosetti curse, I expect you to put in a good word for me with your mother."

Lila groaned. She'd heard the same thing at every bar they'd visited. Johnny eyed Megan and Willow as they got up to go to the restroom. "You two are cut off. Leave your bikes at the back."

"Johnny's right," Lila said when her cousin and Megan returned to the table. "We should probably call it a night."

"We can't. I told Mom, Zia, and Jennifer we'd join them at Last Call," Willow said, gathering up her things. "We'll just leave the bikes here and walk to the beach."

Lila was more than ready to call it a night, but she wouldn't mind checking on her parents. They went to settle the tab, but it had already been taken care of.

When they walked onto the sidewalk, they were swallowed by a crowd of people. Main Street was packed, parties from the bars spilling onto the sidewalk, people blasting their horns, waving and yelling as they drove slowly down the road. There was a loud boom, and then red-white-and-blue fireworks exploded over the bay. Tourists and locals alike cheered, lifting their faces to watch the show.

She smiled, thinking of the view the guests from Windemere were getting out on the bay on the *Captain Joe*. David had seemed a little squeamish about her suggestion that they charter Luke's boat for a late-night cruise, but like Lila, Jennifer had thought it was exactly the event to leave an impression on their guests. They'd eventually won David over. Gavin had, of course, been a harder sell. Lila had been a little uncomfortable reaching out to Luke, but even he couldn't turn down the amount of money Windemere was offering to charter a two-hour cruise.

The chef had supplied a picnic basket for each of the guests and was offering a fabulous brunch the next day for the person who took the night's best photo from the cruise. Lila had come up with designated hashtags for Windemere's guests to use on their social media posts to promote Windemere and Captain Joe's, hoping to generate buzz for both businesses.

"Hurry, we can watch from the beach," Willow said as she danced across the road, stopping traffic. People called out to her, asking about Super Duck and the weather.

They eventually made it to the beach, flopping onto their backs in the cool sand to catch the end of the fireworks. Lila was lying between her two cousins. They glanced at each other and smiled, remembering, she imagined, as she was, all the July Fourths they'd spent together doing exactly this. "Thanks for this," she said. "It was a great night."

"Even though you couldn't party?" Willow asked.

Lila laughed. "I did. I was just sober doing it."

"What was your favorite part?" Sage asked.

"There were so many, it's hard to pick. But I think it was when we were singing and dancing to 'I Gotta Feeling' in

Mom's apartment." She'd gotten a little teary eyed watching her family dance and sing together. Some of her best memories were of moments just like that. She'd wanted to freeze the moment in time, and in a way she had. She scrolled through her videos, held up the screen between them, and pressed Play.

They laughed, pointing out their grandmother's signature move. They called it the Carmen Twerk.

"It was the best," Willow said, then pulled them in for a group hug. "We're so lucky."

Lila and Sage agreed that they were, and then Sage said, "You should totally post that on La Dolce Vita's Instagram account."

"I already did." Lila went to the account and saw the numbers of comments, likes, and shares. "Wow, it looks like it's going viral."

"We're Insta celebs." Willow cheered as she stood up, brushing herself off. "Time to head to Last Call before it really is last call."

Lila laughed. "I don't know how you're still standing. I'll catch up with you in a minute," she said, and opened Windemere's account.

She scrolled through the photos attached to the hashtags, surprised and relieved to see the incentive of a fabulous brunch had worked. Or maybe it was the handsome captain and his faithful dog who had incentivized the guests to take photos, Lila thought as she scrolled through all the shots of Luke and Admiral. She hadn't seen them in over a week, and she couldn't deny she missed spending time with Luke. Admiral too. There was still a dull ache in her chest whenever she thought about them. Although working with David on Windemere's account had helped.

"Lila!" Willow and Megan yelled from down the beach.

"Coming!" she called back, but as she was about to close the Instagram app, a photo caught her attention. She zoomed in. It was David, and he was kissing Sam, and it wasn't just a friendly peck on the cheek.

"Where are you going?" her cousin yelled as Lila ran past the bar and down the beach with her cell phone fisted in her hand.

"To the pier." She pointed at the lights from the *Captain Joe* as it docked alongside the wharf. By the time Lila reached the pier, passengers were disembarking. She recognized a few of the guests from all the time she'd been spending at Windemere, and they stopped to tell her what a wonderful time they'd had.

"I'm so glad you did. Don't forget to post your photos before seven tomorrow." Lila's cheeks ached from forcing a smile. Her fake smile faded when she spotted David and Sam holding court, shaking hands with several guests.

Lila held back, waiting near the ticket booth.

David and Sam startled when she walked from the shadows. "Lila," David said, pressing a hand over his heart. "I didn't expect to see you tonight. How was your pub crawl?"

"I'm sure you didn't," Lila said as she removed her sash and tiara, offering them to Sam. "You should probably be wearing these, not me."

Sam glanced from her to David. "I . . . I don't know what you mean."

Lila held up her phone, showing the photo of them, zooming in so they could see what she had.

David shook his head, stepping toward her. "Lila, no, it's not what it looks like."

"Really?" she said, turning the screen toward herself. "Because it looks to me like you and Sam were making out."

"I didn't mean for it to happen, Lila. It was just...I'm sorry. I'm really sorry," Sam said, and hurried down the wharf.

David's gaze followed her, and then he pushed his glasses up his nose with his forefinger. "Don't blame Sam. It was my fault."

"Please don't try and tell me you have cold feet because I won't believe you. All you've ever wanted is for us to get married. At least you did before we moved here."

"This has nothing to do with us getting married. I want to marry you. There's nothing I want more. We're having a baby together." He put his hands on her shoulders. "I'm afraid of being on a boat in deep water. Sam was just trying to distract me."

"Looks like she did a good job of it."

"Lila, please, don't be like that."

She lifted a shoulder. "You've never once mentioned you're afraid of being on the water to me, David. Not once in all the time I've known you."

"It's embarrassing. It's why I didn't come whale watching with you and your parents. It's also why I wasn't a fan of your idea to charter the *Captain Joe*." He gave her a tentative smile. "But it was a great idea, honey. Everyone loved it."

"So I've heard, and I'm glad they did. I'm just not sure I believe you. How long have you been afraid of deep water?" she asked as she searched her memories for signs that he was telling the truth.

He shoved his hands in the pockets of his chinos and looked out onto the bay. "My dad always had a speedboat.

He used to take us on it when we were young. He'd tease me when I asked him to slow down."

That she believed. David was cautious, always thinking two steps ahead to what the consequences of any move would be.

"My brother was like my dad, the faster the better. He was also more athletic than me and was the first to suggest waterskiing and wakeboarding. I got out of it for a while, pretending I preferred driving the boat. Which I did, because I could control the speed. But that ended when we got stopped and my dad was fined. I didn't have my license. Anyway, long story short, I ended up having to wakeboard. My brother was the spotter, and when I fell off, he didn't tell my dad. Maybe he didn't see me, but I was out there for more than fifteen minutes, bobbing in the ocean. Even with my life jacket on, the waves were so high from the other boats, I thought I'd drown. Either that or get eaten by a shark. I swear I saw a whale breach fifty feet from me." He shuddered, the fear of that day written on his face.

Lila hugged him. "I'm sorry. I never liked your brother, but I think I hate him now."

His arms tightened around her, and he smiled into her neck before pulling back. "I'm really sorry you saw that photo. The last thing I ever want is to hurt you."

"I know."

He searched her face. "So we're okay? You're not going to cancel the wedding."

"No, I'm not canceling the wedding. But David, you need to let Sam go."

He frowned. "You mean fire her?"

Lila nodded.

"But I just told you—"

"I know what you just told me, David, but I'm pretty sure Sam has feelings for you. It's not fair to keep her on. Not only for her sake, but for ours."

"But—" His cell rang. "Sorry, I have to take this." He answered, made a face, and then said, "Okay, I'll be right there." He disconnected and raised an eyebrow. "So it sounds like my mom had a really good time at the pub crawl."

She winced. "Is she sick?"

"Actually, no. She's playing the piano and singing really loudly, and they can't get her to stop."

"I didn't know she played the piano."

"She doesn't." His lips twitched, and then he leaned in and kissed her cheek. "I really am sorry about tonight."

"I know. I am too. Go save your guests."

"Thanks." He smiled and jogged down the pier.

She watched him go, a little surprised that he hadn't asked her to come with him or asked if she needed a ride home. She glanced at Last Call, the music carrying over the water, the party still going strong. Rejoining her cousins and friends held little appeal, and she sat on the pier, dangling her legs over the edge the way she used to. She gazed up at the star-littered sky, listening to the waves lap against the pilings, the briny smell of the ocean filling her nose.

"Admiral, careful."

Lila turned to see Admiral loping toward her with Luke jogging to catch up. Admiral plunked himself down beside her, giving her a goofy doggy grin. He licked her face. "Hey, you. I've missed you."

"He's missed you too," Luke said, lowering himself onto the wharf beside Admiral. "Are you okay?"

By the tone of his voice, she was pretty sure he'd seen what she had. "You saw David kissing Sam, didn't you?"

He nodded. "I did."

She explained what had led up to the kiss.

"And you believed him?"

"Don't you?"

He lifted a broad shoulder. "It doesn't matter what I think. I'm not the one marrying him." He glanced at her. "Are you still marrying him?"

She nodded. "It would be a little hypocritical of me to hold it against him."

"What do you mean?"

"Last week on the bridge, when you said my feelings for you had crossed the line?" She looked out over the bay instead of meeting his gaze. "You were right. I really liked spending time with you. You and Admiral. I think it's probably the same for David and Sam. They've spent a lot of time together too. But we have a baby to think about." She glanced at him, and a muscle flexed in his clenched jaw. She'd probably embarrassed him by talking about her feelings. "What happened to you and your fiancée?"

"She dumped me a few weeks before the wedding and married her best friend six months later."

"I'm so sorry, Luke."

He shrugged. "They're happy. They're expecting a baby any day now. She wouldn't have been happy here anyway. She wasn't a fan of small beach towns, my house, or my dog." He rubbed Admiral's head.

"It sounds like you're better off without her." She hugged Admiral. "I bet you think so too, don't you, boy?"

He woofed. Luke smiled and then started to stand up.

"I've got an early morning tomorrow. Do you need a ride somewhere?"

"If you don't mind, I'd appreciate a lift to the beach house," she said, taking the hand he offered. As his warm, callus-roughened hand closed around hers, she felt a moment of longing, of wishing things were different. She brushed the thought away. Luke was right: life turned out the way it was meant to.

"How was the charter? Do you hate me for twisting your arm to take it on?" she asked as they walked down the pier.

"You didn't have to twist too hard. The money's fantastic. And in case you haven't checked, our Instagram account is blowing up."

She high-fived him. "Awesome."

"Yeah, it worked out better than I'd expected. I had some trouble getting people to work. The Fourth is a big draw in Sunshine Bay for the twentysomething crowd, which is the age of most of my deckhands."

"You're right. I completely forgot about that. But you managed okay?"

"I had to twist some arms of my own, but I eventually got Grams and the aunts on board. Now I'm kind of regretting it. They had a little too much fun, and they're already asking me when's the next sunset cruise."

Lila laughed. "I bet the passengers loved them."

"They did," he said as they reached his truck. He held the door open for her and Admiral. "But I spent half my time trying to keep an eye on them, especially after I caught Grams sharing shots with one of the guests."

Lila brought Captain Joe's account up on Instagram,

laughing as she scrolled through the photos of Ruth and her sisters and sisters-in-law and the comments. "They're calling them the Golden Girls. You know, you could totally capitalize on this, Luke. They could be a big draw."

"Lila," he said in a tone she was familiar with. The one he used every time she had another idea.

"Just hear me out," she said, and told him what she was thinking.

He sighed as he pulled into the driveway of the beach house. "You know, if I implemented all of your suggestions, I'd never have time to work on my boards."

"It may sound like that now, but you have seven months a year to work on inventory and custom orders for SUP Sunshine. We just have to figure out a way to get people to order within that time frame. But remember, our long-term goal is for you to be able to hire more people to free up your time."

"I'll think about it."

She nodded, even as she realized she'd slipped back into forbidden territory. They weren't supposed to be working together anymore. But she loved what she did, and she really wanted to help him. She'd just have to figure out a way to keep her distance. She leaned over the console to give Admiral a hug. "Thanks for driving me home, Luke," she said, and got out of the truck.

"Lila," he called to her as she walked across the lawn.

She stopped midstride and turned.

"It wasn't one-sided, you know. I felt the same way about you."

She pressed her lips together and nodded. Then she stood hugging herself, watching until his taillights faded from view.

Chapter Twenty-Six

The week had passed in a blur. In less than forty-eight hours, Lila would be married. She pressed a hand to her stomach, and her mother walked over and handed her a breadstick.

"Thanks, Mom."

Eva patted her cheek and walked away, calling to David's mother, who was trying to get Carmen to part with the Venus fountain at the front of the restaurant.

Eva thought Lila's nausea was because of the baby—everyone did. Everyone except Lila. They'd been working late into the night to have the restaurant ready for the next day's rehearsal dinner without disrupting business at La Dolce Vita. But that had nothing to do with her nervous stomach. Except that it sort of did because her dad was helping out, and Lila had to watch her parents' painfully polite interactions while also catching each of them glancing longingly at the other when the other wasn't looking.

Her father hadn't told Lila what had happened on the Fourth of July. All he'd said was that he'd had a change of heart and thought it was better if he didn't uproot his life at his age. But Lila knew better. She'd watched the video of her mother at Last Call again, only this time she'd watched it all the way to the end. She saw Ryan jump onstage and kiss her mother, heard the panic in her aunt's voice when she called Eva's name, and knew her father must've been standing out of the camera's range.

She hadn't meant for this to happen when she'd told her father Eva was at Last Call. Unlike when she'd called Sheena and asked her to call their dad and guilt him into coming home. Lila had honestly thought she was doing it to protect her parents from heartbreak, but that had happened anyway. In the end, maybe it didn't matter. They seemed destined to hurt each other.

But that didn't alleviate Lila's guilt. She wanted to shake them both. She wanted to shake her grandmother too. It was so hard standing around watching four people she loved pretending that their hearts weren't broken.

"You feeling okay, sweetheart?" her father asked as he came over to join her. She was polishing the family table to a glossy shine.

"I'm good, Dad." She straightened. "The restaurant looks great, doesn't it?" They'd pulled up the worn carpets to reveal honey wood flooring and peeled off the crimson wallpaper that Lila swore was coated in decades of dust and grime, then painted the walls sunshine yellow and the trim a glossy white. The restaurant looked updated and classy, but still retained its warm, old-world charm.

He nodded. "It does, and we'll actually be done in time for the rehearsal dinner. How's David feeling?"

And that was probably another reason her stomach was acting up. "He's upset his father and brother won't be coming to the rehearsal dinner, or, from what Jennifer told us just before you got here, the wedding." Which explained why thirty people from Gavin's side of the family had canceled the previous afternoon. "But as much as he's hurt by it, I think he's relieved. He'll be able to relax and enjoy the rehearsal party and wedding without worrying he'll have to mediate between his parents."

Her father smiled, probably at the idea of David relaxing. It wasn't as if Lila could say anything; she was just as bad.

"At least he knows his job is safe at Windemere, and he and his mother work well together."

Jennifer had offered Gavin her family's estate in Hyannis Port, the condo in Boston, and all Gavin's toys, including the speedboat, in exchange for Windemere. Sage had been beside herself, but in the end, she'd had no choice but to accede to Jennifer's wishes. Jennifer had also bought out the other shareholders, so she owned Windemere free and clear. Something they all planned to celebrate tonight.

"They work great together, and even better, I've got several ideas for joint promotions with La Dolce Vita, and Nonna is as excited about them as Mom, Zia, and Jennifer."

At a spate of rapid-fire Italian, her father winced. "Your grandmother isn't exactly thrilled with Jennifer right now."

When Lila and her father reached the front of the restaurant, she had to slap a hand over her mouth to keep from laughing. Her grandmother was kneeling *in* the fountain with her arms around Venus, yelling in Italian at Jennifer and Lila's mother and aunt.

"What did she say?" Lila whispered to her father.

"She said, 'You'll have to take her out of my cold, dead arms.'"

"Of course she did. Is it any wonder Mom is dramatic?"

Her father smiled and glanced at her mother, the smile fading from his face. He was just so damn sad, and Lila hated it. Her father walked over and crouched by the statue, speaking softly in Italian to her grandmother. Carmen shrugged, then said, "*Sì,*" and let Lila's father help her out of the fountain. Lila glanced at her mother. She had her fingers pressed to her lips, looking away as she blinked, and Lila thought she might cry too. This was worse than when her parents had fought over her.

James said, "Carmen has agreed to let me have someone come and clean the statue on-site with the caveat that none of the coins are removed."

"Okay," Jennifer said. "I'm sorry I upset you, Carmen. And I hate to do it again, but I think the walls need something."

Lila's mother nodded. "Yes, they..." A smile spread across her face. "I know exactly what they need. Come with me," her mother said, grabbing Jennifer's hand.

"Eva, no!" her aunt cried. "Don't you dare." She ran after her sister and Jennifer, who'd escaped through the doors off the deck.

Lila's cousins walked into the restaurant. "Wow! It looks amazing," Willow said, coming to join them.

"Are you happy with it, Nonna?" Sage asked.

Her grandmother shrugged. "*Sì*, it's all right."

"Translated from Nonna-speak, that means she's over the moon," Sage said dryly.

"Bah, over the moon." Their grandmother waved her hand, but Lila caught the flicker of a grin before it disappeared.

"Where's Mom, Zia, and Jennifer?" Willow asked.

"I think Mom and Jennifer have gone to raid Zia's studio, and she's trying to stop them."

Sage snorted. "No one can stop Zia Eva."

Sage was right. The women returned ten minutes later with stacks of canvases, some framed, some not. Lila had known her aunt was talented, but as her mother and Jennifer began placing the canvases on the tables, she was stunned.

"Zia, these are amazing."

"They're okay." Her aunt shrugged, her face flushed.

Lila's father stood over one of the paintings, seemingly mesmerized. His hand hovered over the canvas as though he longed to touch it. Lila walked over to see what had captured his attention. It was a painting of her mother standing up to her hips in the ocean, draped in a diaphanous white sleeveless gown that teased the viewer with a hint of her voluptuous curves. Her arms were out, her head tipped back, her long, black hair swirling around her as storm clouds gathered above her and lightning crackled in the magenta sky, mirrored in the turbulent ocean waves. The painting was bold, alive with energy, just like Lila's mother. Her aunt had painted Eva as Venus.

Her father noticed Lila standing beside him and lowered his hand self-consciously, moving to the next painting. He smiled. It was Lila and her cousins, playing in the sand when they were little, her mother, grandmother, and aunt watching from the window by the family table.

"Gia, how much for this one? I want it," her father said.

Tears burned the backs of Lila's eyes. He wanted to take a piece of them home with him. She glanced at her mother and caught her eye, silently begging her to put her father, and herself, out of their misery. Her mother gave a helpless shrug and then turned back to the canvases on the table.

Lila couldn't take it anymore. "I'm going to get some air."

"We'll join you," Sage said, nudging her sister and nodding at Lila.

The three of them were quiet as they walked down the stairs to the beach. There was a full moon laying a shimmering golden path out to sea and lighting up the night sky.

Lila sat in the cool sand, wrapping her arms around her knees. "I hate this," she whispered. "I hate seeing them like this and not being able to do something."

"You are doing something. You're going to break the Rosetti curse," Sage said.

Lila scoffed. "You don't believe in the curse any more than I do. If anything, it's a self-fulfilling prophecy."

"Maybe," Sage acknowledged. "Or maybe they've just seen too many women hurt."

"Did you see my parents? Have you seen Bruno and Nonna? How is what they're going through now any better than what they think might happen? Why can't they see that the risk is worth it? We all take risks every day."

"They can't help that they're scared, Lila," Willow said. "They've grown up living under the shadow of the Rosetti curse."

"So did we," Lila said. "And I'm willing to take the risk."

"Are you, though?" Sage asked.

"What do you mean? I'm getting married."

"I'm not trying to sabotage your wedding or disparage David," Sage said. "But would you be marrying him if you weren't having his baby? You don't even have to answer me. I just want you to think about it."

"It's a moot point," Lila said, unable to keep the defensive note from her voice.

"So, reading between the lines, you wouldn't."

Lila buried her face in her knees.

Sage rubbed her back. "I'm sorry. But as much as you're worried about your parents and Bruno and Nonna, we're worried about you."

"Sage is right, babe. You look like you haven't slept in a week, and you're losing weight. I know weddings can be stressful, especially in our family, but to be honest, Jennifer and your mom and dad have basically taken care of everything, so I wonder why—"

"I didn't want a big wedding. It's not important to me. I just want to give my baby, our baby, a happy life."

"But you're not happy, Lila," Sage said. "How can your baby be happy if you're not?"

"I'm not happy because I've spent the last week watching my parents..." She trailed off and bowed her head. She'd just made Sage's point. And in that moment, Lila knew that it wasn't just her parents, her grandmother and Bruno, or even David's issues with his father and brother that were responsible for her queasy stomach, for her not being able to sleep or for her not feeling like eating. It had been the same when David had asked her to set a wedding date—she knew she was making a mistake.

"Look, we know now how hard it was for you growing up and trying to keep the peace between your parents," Sage said, "but it doesn't mean that you and David would do the same to your child. I can almost guarantee that you wouldn't, given your experience. Besides, David lives in Sunshine Bay. It's completely different than if he lived in London like Zio James."

"It doesn't matter. It's too late. I'm getting married in less than forty-eight hours. I couldn't do that to David."

Her cousins shared a glance, and then Willow put an arm around her. "You're going to be an amazing mom, whether you're married or not. And you have us. We'll always have your back."

"What are you three plotting out here?" her mother asked as she came to join them.

Lila froze, terrified that her cousins would tell her mother that she was having doubts. She should've known better.

"We were just telling Lila what a wonderful mother she'll be," Willow said.

Eva smiled. "Of course she will. She's a Rosetti. We do mothering really well."

They did. It was just too bad they weren't as good at facing their fears and taking risks. Lila briefly closed her eyes. She had no business criticizing them when she was exactly the same way.

Her aunt and grandmother joined them, carrying glasses, a bottle of wine, and a bottle of water. Carmen nudged Willow aside to take her place beside Lila, handing her the bottle of water while her aunt poured everyone else a glass of wine.

Her grandmother raised her glass. "A toast to La Dolce Vita. It has given us a good life, and may it continue to do so."

They all turned to look back at the restaurant that had been in their family for generations, standing solid and proud behind them despite the many storms it had weathered, and clinked glasses. "La Dolce Vita!"

Her grandmother lifted her glass again. "To you, to all of

you. You are the biggest blessings, the greatest joys of my life. You are my heart."

Lila's mother and her aunt wiped their eyes, lifting their glasses to Carmen. "You're the heart of this family, Ma."

Lila and her cousins agreed, leaning in to hug their grandmother and tell her how much they loved her.

But Carmen wasn't finished with her toasts. "And to David, the poor, brave boy. May God rest his soul."

"Nonna!" "Ma!"

"What? My Romeo died two days before the wedding, and your great-aunt Sophia's fiancé dropped dead at the altar."

"That's one way your problem gets solved," Sage murmured behind Lila.

"Really, Sage?" Lila muttered at her cousin.

Willow stood up. "Okay, we're a couple weeks late, but it's time to welcome summer to Sunshine Bay the Rosetti way," she said, and then ran to the deck. "I'll get the towels."

It was skinny-dipping time. A summer family tradition, and one Lila hadn't taken part in, in several years. She stripped off her clothes, laughing with her family when Carmen fell in the sand trying to take off her pants, and their shrieks filled the warm, salt-kissed air when they waded into the chilly water of the bay together, and a thousand memories washed over her. All the joy, the laughter and tears, and the frustrations and fights that came with being a family of six strong women filled her up, banishing the fears. She knew what she had to do.

"Lila, where are you going?" her family called as she ran out of the water, toweling herself dry.

"To see David," she said as she pulled on her clothes. "There's something I have to do."

The man at the front desk at Windemere, whom Lila thankfully knew from previous visits, handed her a key card to the manager's suite. She got turned around several times before she found herself standing outside David's room. Heart racing, nerves jumping, she turned away from the door. She couldn't do this to him. But as she started to walk away, she thought about what had brought her here in the first place and lightly knocked on the door, sliding in the room key and opening the door. David was in bed, but he was a light sleeper, and his head lifted off the pillow as he patted for his glasses on the nightstand.

"It's me," she said, walking over to the bed. She slipped off her shoes and lay down beside him.

He put on his glasses, reaching over to turn on the bedside lamp. "What's wrong? Are you all right? Is the baby—"

"I'm okay and so is the baby." She linked her fingers with his and briefly closed her eyes before turning her head to look at him. "I can't marry you."

"What? Why? This isn't because of Sam, is it? Because Lila, I'd never—"

She gently squeezed his fingers. "No, it's...I guess in a way it is, but not for the reason you think." She let go of his hand, rolling onto her side to face him. "When I walked into Surfside that day the staff threw you the shower, you looked happy, happier than I've seen you in a long time, and you laughed, really laughed. We—"

"It wasn't easy working with my father, but—"

"Let me finish, okay?"

He nodded. "Okay."

"We haven't spent any time together other than when we're working on plans for Windemere. Anytime I've asked you to do something with me, you've said you were too busy. But you went to the bar with Sam, and you went on the Fourth of July cruise with her, and you're afraid of the ocean."

"It's not just me, Lila. You were busy too. Busy with your consulting business, busy with Luke."

"I know, and I'm not casting blame or saying any of this to hurt you. I'm just trying to explain why it would be a mistake for us to get married."

"Is this because of Luke?"

"No, not in the way you think, but maybe, like Sam, he's a catalyst. I do love you, David. I'm just not *in* love with you, and I don't think you're *in* love with me." She rested her hand on the side of his face. "We haven't made love since we found out I was pregnant. You don't kiss me anymore. You haven't told me you loved me in weeks. We've grown apart."

"But what about the baby? You went through it, Lila. Surely you don't want our child to grow up like you did."

"Of course I don't. But we're not my parents. I think part of their problem was that they were still in love with each other, and obviously my dad living in London made an already difficult situation worse. But that's not something we have to worry about. We're both living here, and we work well together."

He gave her a sad smile. "You're right, we've always made a great team. You're right about everything else too. I just hate the thought of telling my mom. She'll be devastated. She loves you. She loves your family too."

"And I love her. But we're still a family, David. You, me, the baby, and your mom. Nothing can change that. And my family has kind of adopted her."

His eyes glistened behind his glasses, and she hugged him. "I do love you, you know. I just think two parents who are happy and fulfilled is the best gift we can give our child."

They talked for another twenty minutes, and then David glanced at his phone. "It's getting late, and you're tired. I'll take you home."

"Do you mind if I just sleep here?"

"Not at all," he said, then grinned. "As long as you don't hog the covers."

She smiled, slipping off her engagement ring and putting it on the nightstand. They were going to be all right.

Lila woke up to the alarm on David's phone going off at six a.m. "Why don't you just stay here and sleep," he said as he shut off the alarm and got out of bed.

"Can't." She leaped out of bed, making it to the bathroom before him. She used the toilet and then called through the closed door as she washed her hands. "Do you have an extra toothbrush?"

"In my shaving kit."

She brushed her teeth, ran her fingers through her hair, and then ran out of the bathroom to the door. "Don't cancel the wedding."

"But I thought we weren't getting married."

She almost laughed at the disappointed look on his face. "We're not, but I have a plan. I'll fill you in later. Can you and your mom meet me at La Dolce Vita at ten? If my plan doesn't work, we'll figure out how we're going to deal with everything then."

"Yeah, sure. We'll be there."

She opened the door. "And David, you should rehire Sam."

He pushed his glasses up the bridge of his nose with his forefinger and gave her a self-conscious smile. "I, uh, didn't fire her."

She smiled. "I'll see you later."

"Lila."

She stuck her head back inside the room. "Yeah?"

"I like Luke. He seems like a great guy."

"He is, but that's not why—"

He shrugged. "I know."

Lila was heading past the dining room when she spotted Sam setting out water glasses on a table. Sam noticed her at the same time and gave her a weak smile, looking as disappointed as David had a few minutes before.

Lila ran over. "We canceled the wedding."

Sam looked stricken. "Lila, I promise, we didn't do anything. I wouldn't do that to you."

"Trust me, it didn't have anything to do with you." She hugged her. "I've gotta go. And Sam," she said as she ran for the door, "be good to him or I'll kick your *culo*."

Lila smiled as Sam's laughter followed her out the door. She ran down to the beach. As she was running past the pier, a familiar deep voice yelled, "Admiral!"

Lila turned in time to brace herself before Admiral jumped up and put his paws on her shoulders.

Luke jogged over. "I don't know what it is with you and my dog." He fit his fingers under Admiral's collar and dragged him off her. "Are you okay?"

"I'm great. David and I canceled our wedding."

His gray gaze roamed her face. "It didn't have anything to do with what I said to you when I dropped you off at the beach house that night, did it? I wouldn't want—"

She felt a small twinge of disappointment at his reaction but ignored it and shook her head. "No. We realized we were getting married for the wrong reason. It's a lot of pressure to put on a baby to keep their parents' marriage together, don't you think?"

"I do." He gave her a smile that she'd been waiting a long time to see. "So, any chance you want to take a walk with me on the beach tonight?"

"I'd love to."

He stepped closer. "How about a bike ride to the dunes on Sunday?"

She smiled and nodded. "It's a date."

"Yeah, it is. One of many, I hope," he said, sliding his hands down her arms to her waist.

"Me too." She rose up on her toes to kiss him. She'd meant for it to be only a quick kiss, but Luke had other ideas, and then she did too. She'd always wondered what it would be like to kiss Luke Hollingsworth—a real kiss, not like the one they'd shared on the bridge—and he blew her expectations out of the water. She might've kept kissing him if Admiral hadn't stuck his nose between them and given them his goofy dog grin.

"I'd better go," Luke said, gently shoving Admiral off them. "I've got a fishing charter at seven."

"Yeah, and I have a wedding to arrange." She told him about her plan.

"Good luck," he said, and leaned in to give her a quick kiss. Which ended up with the same result as when she'd tried giving him one. This time it wasn't Admiral who ended their kiss, it was a woman yelling, "Bear!"

Luke grinned. "Sounds like my passengers have arrived."

Lila laughed and patted his chest. "Have fun."

"You too." He lifted her hand to his mouth and brushed her knuckles across his lips. His eyes met hers. "Go now before I kiss you again."

"I could be convinced to give you one more kiss, you know."

"Lila," he growled.

"Luke," she mimicked him, and then took off with a wave, happier than she'd been in a very long time.

Chapter Twenty-Seven

Eva opened the door to her daughter. "Lila, what's wrong?" It was seven in the morning. "Come in." She ushered her inside.

Lila looked around her apartment. "What's going on? Why are you taking down your wallpaper? And when did you start taking down your wallpaper? It didn't look like this the other night I was here."

"I'm not sleeping. The menopause, you know. So I decided I might as well do something productive with my time."

"Like redecorating your apartment in the middle of the night?"

"My wallpaper's as old as what was up in the restaurant. And after seeing the state it was in..." She shuddered. "But surely you didn't come to talk about my redecorating plans. Is everything all right? David's okay?"

"He didn't die, if that's what you mean." Lila smiled and walked back into Eva's bedroom. "Is there a reason all your bedding is on the floor?"

She sighed. "Night sweats."

Lila sat down on the mattress, patting the spot beside her. "I know Zia wants you to go the natural route, but maybe you should talk to Dr. Alva about starting the hormone replacement therapy now."

"You sound like your father," she said, ignoring the quick stab of pain at the mention of James. "Are you going to tell me what's wrong, or would you like a tour of the apartment?"

"David and I canceled the wedding. I mean, we're canceling the wedding."

"Oh darling, don't listen to your grandmother. David's not going to die…I mean, I'm almost positive he won't."

"Uh, that's not what you said at the family tea. I think you said he had a thirty percent chance of dying."

"Is that why you're not going to marry him? It's my fault, isn't it?"

"No, I was just teasing you. We were getting married because of the baby. But we don't love each other, not the way we should. It's not fair to any of us, the baby, David, or me."

"And you're not worried anymore about you and David sharing the baby? You're not scared you're going to scar the baby like me and your father did with our fighting over you?"

She shook her head, linking her fingers with Eva's. "I was. But I realized, with some help from my cousins, that marrying someone because you're afraid of something that might never happen isn't a good enough reason to get married. And I know from watching you and Dad this week that it would be harder on our baby if David and I were unhappy." She gave Eva's fingers a gentle squeeze. "I hate seeing you and Dad like this, Mom. You're both so unhappy, and you don't need to be. I'm so sorry I said what

I did to you the morning after the shower. I was being overprotective of Dad."

"I know you were. And it was hard to hear, but in the end, you were right, weren't you?"

"It's my fault. All of it. I got Sheena to call Dad and ask him to come home. I thought, if he was back in London, it would remind him of what he was giving up. I saw your face that day on the *Captain Joe* when he told us his plans. You were panicked, you were scared, and I was scared for both of you. You as much as Dad. I wanted to protect you both. Because I know you love him as much as he loves you, and I know it would break your heart to hurt him.

"And then when Dad called on the Fourth, I told him you were at Last Call. But Mom, I didn't do it to hurt you or Dad. I honestly didn't."

Eva wrapped her arms around her daughter. "All I ever do is hurt you and your father. Please don't cry, darling."

Lila pulled away from her. "No, don't say that. Don't ever say that. You were and are the best mother any daughter could ask for. Never once did I doubt how much you loved me. I knew I could come to you anytime about anything, and you would support me. And Mom, the only reason you hurt Dad is because he loves you and wants to be with you, and you—"

"He wants to marry me, Lila."

Her daughter's eyes went wide. "He proposed?"

"No, but I knew he was going to." She told her what he'd said after the live streaming on the Fourth and why the date was special to them.

"When you saw him at Last Call, you didn't go to him, did you?"

"No." She swiped at her eyes. "And letting him walk away was the hardest thing I've ever done."

"Why did you?"

"Because he wants to marry me, and I can't marry him. I know you girls don't believe in the Rosetti curse. At least you and Sage. But when I was a little girl, I'd hear your nonna and your bisnonna and the aunties talking. I'd hear them cry. I'd hear how much they suffered. And then I went through it with my own sister when her husband ran off with—" She caught herself before she shared their family secret, the one that had the potential to tear their family apart.

"But Mom, even if you married Dad and you couldn't make it work, I don't think you'd be suffering any more than you are now. At least you would've given it a chance. Isn't that what life's about? Taking chances? And for what it's worth, I believe you and Dad would make your marriage work." She stood up. "Would you at least think about it, for me?"

"Yes." Eva nodded.

"Cross your heart and hope to die?" Lila said, daring her with her eyes.

She knew Eva was too superstitious not to keep her promise. "Cross my heart and hope to die," she said, making the sign of the cross over her heart.

"Thank you, and now I have to tell Dad the wedding's off," she said, walking from Eva's bedroom. "David and Jennifer are coming at ten. I thought we'd tell everyone else at the same time."

"Poor Jennifer, she'll be so disappointed. But at least she'll be living here, and she can visit with you and the baby."

"And that's another reason you need to marry Dad. If you're not living together, the two of you will be fighting over who gets to spend time with the baby." Lila grinned. "I'm teasing. Sort of."

Eva angled her head to study her daughter. "I didn't notice until now. But you look better. You look happy."

"I am, and you could be too. All you have to do is get past your fears and take a leap of faith. But, Mom, whatever you decide, I love and support you."

"Thank you, darling. I love you too."

Four hours later, Eva carried another pot of coffee to the family table. Everyone who mattered to her was there: her nieces, her mother and sister, Bruno, Jennifer and David—whom she now considered part of their family—and the two people she loved the most in the world, her daughter and James. Eva avoided Lila's gaze. She saw the hope in her daughter's eyes, eyes just like her father's, every time Eva came close to James, every time she looked at him, and then the disappointment that quickly followed. But as much as Lila wanted them together, Eva knew she wouldn't hold it against her if she couldn't bring herself to face her fears and take a leap of faith.

Willow said something, and everyone laughed. But it was James who drew Eva's gaze, every time he laughed, every time he smiled, every time he spoke. She couldn't stop looking at him. He was beautiful, and she'd loved him for what felt like a lifetime, and still, whenever their eyes met, she'd open her mouth, and no words would come out.

He pushed back his chair and stood up, bending down to hug Lila and kiss her goodbye. Eva knew he was talking, but she couldn't make out what he was saying, the buzzing in her head was too loud. He shook David's hand and then moved to say goodbye to Jennifer.

He was leaving now. She couldn't let him go. If she did, she knew he would be lost to her for good.

She squeezed the words past the lump of emotion stuck in her throat and blurted, "Marry me."

Everyone turned to look at her. Jennifer touched her chest. "You want me to marry you?"

She shook her head, pointing the coffeepot at James.

"You want me to marry you?" he asked as he straightened, his gaze intent and unwavering.

She shook her head, then nodded. "Yes."

"Are you asking me to marry you because you don't want me to leave?" he asked as he walked around the table, coming toward her.

She nodded and then shook her head. "No. I'm asking you to marry me because I love you, and I don't want to live without you anymore."

He took the coffeepot from her, handing it to her sister. Then he framed Eva's face with his hands. "Yes. I'll marry you because I adore you, and I don't want to go another hour, another minute, without you in my life."

Their daughter cheered, jumping to her feet and running around the table to throw her arms around them. "I'm so proud of you, Mom. I knew you could—"

Lila broke off at Carmen crying, "Call Father Patrick. It's my heart. I'm dying."

Eva sighed. "I should've known this would happen," she said, and began to go to her mother.

"Let me," James said, and walked to Carmen. He crouched by her chair, speaking softly to her in Italian. Her mother nodded. "*Sì. Sì,*" she said, and nodded again. She took James's hand and pressed it to her cheek, and then she got up from her chair, walked to Eva, kissed her, and said, "Don't let him out of your sight. Lock him in your room if you have to. I'm going to church to pray. I'll light candles. Bruno, you come too. We'll pick up Ruth and her sisters along the way."

Eva stared after her mother and then turned to James. "What did you say to her?"

"I promised I'd never abandon you, I'd never betray you, and I'd cherish and love you for as long as I lived." He smiled. "I think I got her blessing."

Her eyes filled, and she nodded.

Gia, her nieces, David, and Jennifer came over to congratulate them.

Her sister kissed her. "I'm happy for you, for both of you, but could you hurry up and set a wedding date? I have a feeling Ma won't be leaving the church until James is safely married to you."

"They already have a date," Lila said.

Eva said at the same time as James, "We do?"

"You do. Tomorrow, and everything's arranged so you don't have to do a single thing."

Eva's knees went weak, and James wrapped an arm around her. "Are you okay with that?"

"Of course she is," Lila answered for her. "Now, Dad, you have to leave. You can't see the bride until the wedding."

"Carmen said your mother wasn't supposed to let me out of her sight and to lock me in her room. I like her plan better than yours."

"Me too," Eva agreed with James.

"But Sheena and Faith's plane lands at Logan International in about ten minutes, and then they're taking the helicopter you booked for them." Lila gave her father a *checkmate* smile.

"She's right. I forgot to call them and tell them the wedding was off." He raised an eyebrow at Lila. "Can I at least have an hour alone with your mother?"

"How about twenty minutes?" Jennifer said. "We have to go to Wedding Bells and find Eva a dress."

"Do you still have that dress?" James pointed at the portrait her sister had painted of her that now hung behind the family table.

"I do, but what—"

"Great. Eva doesn't need a dress, and Gia, that painting is sold. To me."

Her sister didn't argue. No doubt because Gia had tried gifting the painting of the girls playing in the sand to James and knew it was a waste of breath to argue with him when his mind was made up.

James led Eva out onto the deck, and she sagged against him. "We're getting married tomorrow."

"Look at me and tell me the truth. Are you really okay to do this?"

She was about to shake her head, and then she looked into his eyes. "Yes."

He patted his jacket and slipped his hand inside the right-hand pocket. "I had this jacket on when I flew back on the Fourth." He held up a ring box. "I guess there was a reason I didn't take it out."

"Oh, James. I'm so sorry about that night. That you saw me kissing Ryan. I started to go after you, but then

I froze. Letting you walk away was the hardest thing I've ever done."

"Sweetheart, I didn't walk away because that boy kissed you. I walked away because I saw the panic on your face when you saw me there and it had nothing to do with me witnessing that kiss. I'd heard it in your voice when you disconnected before I said, 'I love you,' and I'd convinced myself you were just in a hurry to get to the restaurant. But I knew, no matter how much you loved me, you'd say no when I proposed to you that night." He smiled and opened the ring box. "Look familiar?"

It was a white-gold engagement ring with an heirloom-cut emerald between two princess-cut diamonds. "Was it Grace's?" She wouldn't mind if it had been.

He angled his head to look at her. "It was yours. I gave it to you the first time I proposed to you, and you looked at it like it was a snake."

"I didn't see it. I was blinded by my tears and panic." She held up her left hand, and he slid it onto her finger. "It's beautiful. I love it, and I love you."

"I love you too," he said, and lowered his head to kiss her.

The door opened, and their daughter stuck her head out. "Sorry. Faith and Sheena are at the beach house. They got an earlier flight. Oh, and Jennifer thinks she might be able to make a last-minute change to the bouquet and table arrangements. She wants to know your favorite color and favorite flower, Mom."

"Red and roses," Eva and James said at the same time.

Lila grinned. "I'll give you five minutes, and then I'm coming to get you, Dad."

"She's bossy just like you," Eva said at the same time James said, "She's bossy just like you."

They laughed, and then James said, "She's happy."

"Of course she is. This is what she wanted."

"You didn't ask me to marry you because of Lila, did you?"

"No. I love our daughter, and I'd do just about anything for her, but not this. I asked you to marry me because it's what I want. More than anything. Although in a way, it's because of Lila that I confronted my fears, facing what was keeping me from making a commitment to you. I'm proud of her. She's strong and brave."

"Of course she is. She's your daughter." He glanced at the door. "We need to stop talking and start kissing before she comes and drags me away."

Three minutes later, Lila was back. "Promise me you won't change your mind and leave me standing at the altar," James said.

"I'll be there," Eva said, unable to contain the tremor of nerves in her voice.

"Cross your heart and hope to die," their daughter said.

Eva repeated the words and made the sign of the cross over her heart.

Eva had been determined to keep her promise the day before. She loved James and saw no reason why she wouldn't be at the altar on time. But she froze at the top of the stairs that would take her to the beach where James waited for her. He stood under a driftwood arch draped in flowers with white voile sheers blowing in the ocean breeze. Her heart was racing, and the lush bouquet of red roses clutched in her hands was shaking.

"Mom, are you okay?" Lila whispered.

She shook her head. Her family closed around her. "You've got this, Zia," her nieces said.

"Sing, *cara*. Sing the song you picked for James," her mother said, and then she began humming Christina Perri's "A Thousand Years." It had taken Eva hours to find a song that captured what she was feeling and how she felt about James.

Bruno, her sister, her nieces, and Lila joined in with her mother, and then Eva began singing the lyrics, quietly at first, in barely a whisper. Her mother nudged her, and as Eva began the walk down the stairs in her bare feet, her dress fluttering in the breeze, she caught James's eyes. He wore a white shirt and black suit, no tie, the sun shining down on him, casting him in a golden light. His eyes held hers, a soft smile on his handsome, familiar face, a face she had loved for what felt like a thousand years. Her heartbeat slowed, the bouquet steadied in her hands, and her voice soared.

The chairs on either side of the red petal-strewn aisle in the sand were filled with family and friends. It looked as if half of Sunshine Bay had come to their wedding. James and Grace's daughters sat in the front row. Sheena looked like her mother, and Faith looked like her father.

Everyone stood, turning, as she walked to James, standing in front of the arch, his feet bare in the sand. She held his gaze, focusing on him and not the flutter of nerves as the song ended.

"And who gives this woman to this man?" Father Patrick asked, directing his question to Eva's family, standing behind her.

"I do. I give myself to him," Eva said. Her mother,

Bruno, her sister, and her nieces kissed her and took their places in the first two rows with David and Jennifer. Lila kissed her and then went to kiss her father before taking her seat with Sheena and Faith.

James reached for Eva's hands, turning her to face him. "And I give all of me to her."

Father Patrick asked if anyone objected or had a reason why they shouldn't marry. Eva sighed when Johnny, the owner of Surfside; Tim, the owner of the garage; and Ryan held up their hands. The pretty blond girl she'd met at Last Call gave Ryan a look, and he lowered his hand with a grin.

James glanced at Father Patrick and shrugged. "This is what happens when you marry one of the Heartbreakers of Sunshine Bay."

"I'm officially out of the heartbreaking business," Eva whispered to James.

He grinned. "Yeah, and I think that's what they're objecting to."

When her family turned in their chairs to give the men the Rosetti stare, Johnny and Tim lowered their hands.

James, holding both of Eva's hands, repeated their vows. Sheena and Faith gave their father Eva's wedding band, and he slipped it onto her finger.

Eva repeated her vows to James, and Lila gave her James's wedding band, which she slipped onto his finger.

Father Patrick smiled. "I now pronounce you partners for life. You may kiss."

James gave her a quick kiss, took her by the hand, said, "Excuse me, Father," and ducked through the arch, pulling Eva along with him.

"James!" "Dad!" "Where are you going?"

"To make out with my wife! We'll see you at Windemere in an hour," he yelled over his shoulder.

"Make that two hours!" Eva lifted her dress as she ran along the shore with her husband.

Epilogue

It was a cold, blustery day in December, a north wind tapping on the frosted windowpane and dancing on the silver-gray bay. But inside La Dolce Vita, it was warm and cozy. The restaurant was filled with the sounds of laughter and cutlery clinking, and colorful lights were strung behind the bar, twinkling on the Christmas tree and smiling faces at the surrounding tables.

Lila sat tucked in the corner of the family table while the rest of the Rosettis served the staff and their families at the annual Christmas party. Lila hadn't been home during the holiday season in years, and she'd been making up for it this past couple of weeks. But as her due date went by and the snow began to fly, her family, David, Jennifer, and Luke had insisted she stay close to home, which meant she'd missed the Holly Jolly Shop and Stroll on Main Street.

She didn't complain, though. She was happy just to hang out with her family and friends, and at least she'd gotten to watch the Jingle Bell Run from the deck at La Dolce Vita. Besides, she was beyond uncomfortable at this stage of her pregnancy.

The door off the deck opened, bringing with it a gust of unwelcome frigid air, along with a welcome sight. It didn't matter that she'd seen Luke mere hours earlier; her heart pitter-pattered against her ribs. If the baby hadn't started kicking at that exact moment, Lila had no doubt the pitter-patter would have been joined by the same fluttery feeling in her stomach that she always got when the man she loved walked into a room or gave her a slow smile that was meant only for her. The same smile that crinkled the corners of his gorgeous gray eyes when he turned to see her sitting there.

He walked over, bending down to kiss her. His lips were cold, but his kiss was warm and sweet.

She smacked her lips together as he took the seat beside her. "Chocolate fudge?" Whenever Luke went out on a delivery, he came back with a care package of Christmas baked goods.

He smiled as he removed his Santa hat and jacket. "Yep. I saved the vanilla for you."

She looked down at her stomach. "Thanks. So how did the deliveries go?" He'd been working flat out since October, trying to fulfill orders for paddleboards before Christmas.

"Great. Last delivery of the year. I'm all yours until after the holidays."

"Mm, I like the sound of that."

"Me too," he said, blowing on his hands. Once he'd warmed them, he placed his palm on her stomach, grinning when the baby kicked. "What do you think? Is today the day?"

"She seems happy to stay right where she is. If she's anything like my mother, she'll want to make a grand entrance. She'll probably wait until Christmas Eve." She sighed and rested her head on his shoulder.

"You're tired. You wanna head upstairs? I left Admiral at your place."

Lila had insisted that her father keep the beach house for himself and her mother, and Lila was living in the apartment she'd grown up in. She'd baby- and dog-proofed the apartment a couple of months earlier, even though she spent the majority of her time at Luke's. They'd agreed to take their relationship slowly. Lila had a baby on the way and was working hard to make a success of her business. Between his businesses and taking care of the women in his family, Luke was busy too.

Surprisingly, Lila's mother hadn't made any changes at the beach house. Then again, her parents had been making up for lost time. Lila glanced to where they stood kissing under the sprig of mistletoe her father held over her mother's head. Lila didn't see the honeymoon phase ending anytime soon for those two.

She snuggled into Luke. "Maybe I'll take a quick nap on you. I want to hang around until Santa makes his appearance and get some pictures and video."

Luke wrapped his arms around her. "I'm happy to be your pillow, but just so you know, it might be a while before Santa makes his appearance. I heard suspicious noises coming from your grandmother's apartment when I walked by."

Bruno was playing Santa. He'd gone to put on his costume close to an hour ago. Of course, her grandmother had gone with him. The two had been inseparable since Bruno had made a surprise appearance—without Ana or a ring on his finger—at Carmen's birthday two weeks before.

They'd learned that he hadn't been able to go through

with the wedding. It was the happiest Lila had seen her grandmother since Bruno had left in September. Those months without him in Sunshine Bay had been tough on everyone.

"Captain Luke! Captain Luke! Did you see Santa? He's late, and we think he's lost," one of Heather's twins said, running over to grab Luke by the hand. "Come on, let's go look for him."

His brother joined him, tugging on Luke's other hand. "Yeah, Captain Luke, come on. You can find him."

"Yeah. If anyone can find him, you can, Captain Luke," Lila teased.

"Thanks a lot." He leaned in and kissed her.

The twins made gagging noises.

"Talk to me when you're sixteen," Luke said, and stood up. As he walked off with the boys, Lila called her grandmother. The call went to voice mail. She tried Bruno next and got the same result. She spotted Sage texting on her phone near the bar and called her.

Her cousin frowned and brought her phone to her ear. "Why are you calling me? You're like twenty feet away."

"Your mother and mine ordered me to stay put with my feet up, and I don't feel like walking to Nonna's apartment." She explained the situation with Santa and his little helper.

Sage sighed so loudly that Lila didn't need the phone to hear her. "Fine," her cousin said, disconnecting and pocketing her phone and heading for the door. As she opened it, she told Lila to order her a glass of wine. "On second thought, make it a bottle."

Lila texted Willow, who was manning the bar. With a red-sequined Santa hat on her head, Willow arrived with a glass, a bottle of red wine, and a cup of hot chocolate on her tray. "Hot chocolate is courtesy of your hot boyfriend." After depositing the contents of her tray on the table, she gently tapped Lila's stomach. "Anytime now, baby. We're all waiting to meet you."

⌣

Lila's water broke during Christmas Eve dinner at the beach house. Sage looked at her and said, "Did you wet your pants?"

For some reason the question sent Lila's mother, her aunt, and her grandmother into peals of laughter, which quickly morphed into panic when Lila scowled at her cousin and said, "My water broke."

Even Lila's father, who was calm and collected in any situation, was as panicked as the rest of her family. Thankfully, Luke stepped in and took control. He called Dr. Alva and handed Lila the phone while he timed her contractions. Lila hadn't realized she was in labor. The discomfort she'd been feeling for most of the afternoon had been in her back, not her stomach. She wanted to wait until the contractions were closer together, but Luke reminded her that they had at least an hour's drive to the hospital in Hyannis Port.

It took them almost three hours. Luke blamed the weather. It started snowing the moment he backed her father's Range Rover out of the driveway. Lila blamed her parents, who yelled at Luke anytime the speedometer veered close to forty miles an hour. Lila suggested he drop them off at the nearest gas station, but Luke merely smiled. Her parents were lucky she had such an easygoing boyfriend.

She was lucky too. She didn't how she would've gotten through her six-hour labor without his calming presence. He'd calmed David down too. She'd realized just how much David had appreciated Luke being there when their daughter had arrived an hour earlier. David had hugged Luke before he'd hugged her. She smiled at the memory as her family, including Jennifer and Sam, cooed over the baby. Despite it being three in the morning on Christmas Day, they'd all stayed at the hospital.

"Keep it down or the nurse will kick us out," Sage warned, standing guard by the door.

Everyone was arguing about whom the baby looked like. All Lila cared about was that she'd arrived safely and she was healthy. But with her perfect little face, thick head of dark hair, and powerful set of lungs, Lila had a feeling she might turn out to be Eva's mini-me.

"Um, hello, would you mind if I hold my baby now?" Lila asked, waving to get their attention.

They ignored her as each of the women assured the others that she could make the baby stop crying. "Sorry, ladies. Mommy wants her daughter," Luke said, deftly scooping the baby out of Carmen's arms and into his. He cradled her close, lowering his mouth to whisper in her ear. She immediately stopped crying.

"What did you say to her?" Lila asked as he laid her daughter in her arms.

He sat on the chair beside the bed and smiled. "I'll tell you later."

Dr. Alva poked her head into the room. "Everyone out, except Mommy, Daddy, and their partners."

There were more laughter and happy tears as everyone

kissed Lila and the baby goodbye. David and Sam stood to leave twenty minutes later. They were hosting Sam's family for brunch at Windemere. David kissed Lila's cheek and the baby's. "Get some rest. I'll be back later this afternoon." Then he turned to hug Luke. "Thanks for everything, man. We couldn't have done it without you."

"I'm pretty sure Lila could have," Luke said.

David laughed. "Of course she could have. She's a Rosetti."

Sam hugged Lila. "I'll see you and the baby when you get home. Let me know if you need anything."

"Thanks. I will."

As the door closed behind them, Lila patted the bed. "There's room if you want to join us."

Luke carefully stretched out beside her, putting an arm around her and the baby and drawing her close. "You should get some rest."

"I will. I just want to spend some quiet time with you and the baby, and I want to know what you said to get her to stop crying."

He stroked the baby's cheek. "I told her I loved her mommy." He lifted his gaze to Lila's. "And that when her mommy was ready, I was going to ask her to marry me, and if she said yes, I would be the best stepfather a little girl could ask for, and I'd love her like she was my own."

Lila smiled at him through her tears. "Yes."

"Yes, you'll marry me?"

"Yes to all of it. To marrying you, to you being the best stepfather she could ask for, and to you loving her as your own. I love you, Luke Hollingsworth."

About the Author

USA Today bestselling author **Debbie Mason** writes romantic fiction with humor and heart. The first book in her Christmas, Colorado series, *The Trouble with Christmas*, was the inspiration for the Hallmark movie *Welcome to Christmas*. When Debbie isn't writing or reading, she enjoys cooking for her family, cuddling with her granddaughters and granddog, and walking in the woods with her husband.

How to Use This Book

These symbols will help you find the listings you want:

- ◉ Sights
- 🐠 Beaches
- 🔱 Activities
- ⊖ Courses
- 📷 Tours
- 🎪 Festivals & Events
- 🛏 Sleeping
- 🍴 Eating
- 🍷 Drinking
- ⭐ Entertainment
- 🔒 Shopping
- ℹ Information/Transport

These symbols give you the vital information for each listing:

- ☎ Telephone Numbers
- ☺ Opening Hours
- Ⓟ Parking
- ☺ Nonsmoking
- ✱ Air-Conditioning
- @ Internet Access
- 📶 Wi-Fi Access
- ☒ Swimming Pool
- 🥗 Vegetarian Selection
- 📋 English-Language Menu
- 🧑 Family-Friendly
- 🐾 Pet-Friendly
- 🚌 Bus
- ⛴ Ferry
- Ⓜ Metro
- Ⓢ Subway
- ⊖ London Tube
- 🚊 Tram
- 🚉 Train

Reviews are organised by author preference.

Look out for these icons:

FREE   No payment required

🌱   A green or sustainable option

Our authors have nominated these places as demonstrating a strong commitment to sustainability – for example by supporting local communities and producers, operating in an environmentally friendly way, or supporting conservation projects.

Map Legend

Sights
- 🐠 Beach
- 🛕 Buddhist
- 🏰 Castle
- ✝ Christian
- 🕉 Hindu
- ☪ Islamic
- ✡ Jewish
- ❶ Monument
- 🏛 Museum/Gallery
- 🏚 Ruin
- 🍇 Winery/Vineyard
- 🐘 Zoo
- ◉ Other Sight

Activities, Courses & Tours
- 🤿 Diving/Snorkelling
- 🛶 Canoeing/Kayaking
- 🎿 Skiing
- 🏄 Surfing
- 🏊 Swimming/Pool
- 🚶 Walking
- 🏄 Windsurfing
- 🔱 Other Activity/Course/Tour

Sleeping
- 🛏 Sleeping
- ⛺ Camping

Eating
- 🍴 Eating

Drinking
- 🍷 Drinking
- ☕ Cafe

Entertainment
- 🎭 Entertainment

Shopping
- 🛍 Shopping

Information
- 📮 Post Office
- ℹ Tourist Information

Transport
- ✈ Airport
- 🛂 Border Crossing
- 🚌 Bus
- 🚠 Cable Car/Funicular
- 🚲 Cycling
- ⛴ Ferry
- 🚝 Monorail
- Ⓟ Parking
- Ⓢ S-Bahn
- 🚕 Taxi
- 🚉 Train/Railway
- 🚊 Tram
- Ⓣ Tube Station
- Ⓤ U-Bahn
- Ⓜ Underground Train Station
- • Other Transport

Routes
- Tollway
- Freeway
- Primary
- Secondary
- Tertiary
- Lane
- Unsealed Road
- Plaza/Mall
- Steps
-)=(Tunnel
- Pedestrian Overpass
- Walking Tour
- Walking Tour Detour
- Path

Boundaries
- International
- State/Province
- Disputed
- Regional/Suburb
- Marine Park
- Cliff
- Wall

Population
- ❸ Capital (National)
- ◎ Capital (State/Province)
- ● City/Large Town
- ● Town/Village

Geographic
- 🛖 Hut/Shelter
- 🔦 Lighthouse
- 👁 Lookout
- ▲ Mountain/Volcano
- 🌴 Oasis
- 🌳 Park
-)(Pass
- 🧺 Picnic Area
- 💧 Waterfall

Hydrography
- River/Creek
- Intermittent River
- Swamp/Mangrove
- Reef
- Canal
- Water
- Dry/Salt/Intermittent Lake
- Glacier

Areas
- Beach/Desert
- Cemetery (Christian)
- Cemetery (Other)
- Park/Forest
- Sportsground
- Sight (Building)
- Top Sight (Building)

Our Story

A beat-up old car, a few dollars in the pocket and a sense of adventure. In 1972 that's all Tony and Maureen Wheeler needed for the trip of a lifetime – across Europe and Asia overland to Australia. It took several months, and at the end – broke but inspired – they sat at their kitchen table writing and stapling together their first travel guide, *Across Asia on the Cheap*. Within a week they'd sold 1500 copies. Lonely Planet was born.

Today, Lonely Planet has offices in Melbourne, London and Oakland, with more than 600 staff and writers. We share Tony's belief that 'a great guidebook should do three things: inform, educate and amuse'.

Our Writers

NEIL WILSON

Coordinating Author; Edinburgh, Stirling & Northeast Scotland, Skye & the Islands, Inverness & the Highlands Neil was born in Scotland and, save for a few years spent abroad, has lived here most of his life. A lifelong enthusiasm for the great outdoors has inspired hiking, biking and sailing expeditions to every corner of the country. On his latest research trip he mountain-biked at Laggan Wolftrax, went canoeing on Loch Lomond, hiked up Eaval on Uist and Carnan Eoin on Colonsay, and drank too many BrewDog beers. Neil has been a full-time author since 1988 and has written about 60 guidebooks for various publishers, including Lonely Planet's guide to his home town of Edinburgh. Neil also wrote the Loch Lomond section of the Glasgow & Loch Lomond chapter.

Read more about Neil at:
lonelyplanet.com/members/neilwilson

ANDY SYMINGTON

Glasgow & Loch Lomond, Stirling & Northeast Scotland, Skye & the Islands, Inverness & the Highlands Andy's Scottish forebears make their presence felt in a love of malt, a debatable ginger colour to his facial hair and a love of wild places. From childhood slogs up the M1 he graduated to making dubious road trips around the firths in a disintegrating Mini Metro and thence to peddling whisky in darkest Leith. While living there, he travelled widely around the country in search of the perfect dram, and, now resident in Spain, continues to visit regularly. Andy also wrote the Survival Guide and the History, Wild Scotland and Golf chapters.

Read more about Andy at:
lonelyplanet.com/members/andy_symington

Published by Lonely Planet Publications Pty Ltd
ABN 36 005 607 983
2nd edition – April 2013
ISBN 978 1 74220 572 4
© Lonely Planet 2013   Photographs © as indicated 2013
10 9 8 7 6 5 4 3 2
Printed in China